March 12 1993

HEARTS OF FLAME

KATHERINE GOVIER

It was a pleasure meeting you—

Katherine

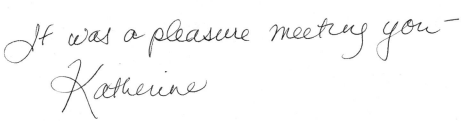

VIKING

VIKING
Published by the Penguin Group
Penguin Books Canada Ltd, 10 Alcorn Avenue, Toronto, Ontario, Canada
M4V 3B2
Penguin Books Ltd, 27 Wrights Lane, London W8 5TZ, England
Viking Penguin, a division of Penguin Books USA Inc., 375 Hudson Street,
New York, New York 10014, USA
Penguin Books Australia Ltd, Ringwood, Victoria, Australia
Penguin Books (NZ) Ltd, 182-190 Wairau Road, Auckland 10, New Zealand

Penguin Books Ltd, Registered Offices: Harmondsworth, Middlesex, England

First published 1991

10 9 8 7 6 5 4 3 2 1

*Publisher's note: This book is a work of fiction. Names, characters, places and incidents
either are the product of the author's imagination or are used fictitiously, and any
resemblance to actual persons living or dead, events or locales is entirely coincidental.*

Printed and bound in Canada on acid free paper ♾

Canadian Cataloguing in Publication Data
Govier, Katherine, 1948-
   Hearts of flame

ISBN 0-670-84191-9

1. Title.

PS8563.085H4 1991   C813'.54   C91-094180-7
PR9199.3.G6H4 1991

For my mother
Doris Govier,
with love and admiration

Acknowledgements

The author would like to thank David Livingstone for sharing his insights into the fashion world, and also Philip Ng, Dean and Dan, and Emily Zarb. Special thanks go to Jane Corkin for her help and to Sheila Metzner for taking the beautiful photograph on the cover.

KG

Contents

HEARTS OF FLAME

1

Your Body Dies But Your Spirit Goes On

It was too beautiful to stay indoors.

On September 4, 1989, before noon, a woman threw open her front door to the molten gold of the fall day.

She walked past the close-packed, uneven housefronts of MacPherson Avenue, waving to the aged Mr. Boswell, who was bent over in his peaked cap, raking orange leaves into a clear plastic sack. She turned up Poplar Plains, crossed it and carried on up to Clarendon, where she took the path to the ravine. Reaching the open space, she angled down the grass slope to her favourite picnic table and sat on the bench.

In warier moments she had taken careful stock of the table, eyeing the distance it stood from the edge of the woods. Could she be dragged that far? Not if she positioned herself with her back against the woods, so she had a view up and down the clearing. No one could approach unseen, except through the underbrush—and a premeditated attack launched from under a bush seemed far-fetched even to Blair.

Blair Bowker. So carefully placed in the familiar but not entirely trusted landscape, her face upturned to catch the sun, she was forty years old, the daughter of a teacher and a scientist from Medicine Hat, Alberta, the mother of one. After an intoxicating year of fame as a singer twenty years ago, she had gracefully declined to semi-obscurity. She had moved east four years before. It was a desire for excitement, and perhaps for privacy that brought her; she still remembered what she had believed twenty years ago, that Toronto was the centre, *where it all happened.* You could lose yourself in Toronto.

Today her chosen city was at its most beautiful; the sky an effortless blue, the trees rusted but still full, like plump chrysanthemums, yellow, electric orange, red. The air was not sweet, not like the air in Alberta, but for once it was fresh. Squirrels played tag in the branches, leaping through clouds of dried leaves that burst with their passage like soft, silent fireworks. The reservoir to the north-east rose in three flat planes above a little stone house with a greened copper roof. A crest over the door bore the initials W. T. W.— Toronto Water Works—and Roman numerals MCM XXX. It was neoclassical, symmetrical and solid, impersonal—the creator forgoing individual glory, assigning his works to the greater whole of the city.

Steps descended from the door of the stone house to an archway with its own miniature copper roof. It looked for all the world like the gatekeeper's cottage attached to a mansion that had been scraped off the top of the hill. That severe flatness, the *man-made*ness of the surface hinted of something buried underneath: a bunker, the tomb of a forgotten, new world Pharoah?

Let's say the Nile then, and pyramids. There were planes along it, levels; the path below, the intermediate rim, the razed top. Joggers inched along the edge, meeting and passing. A bicycle wheel spun slowly, generating sunlight. A man with his suit jacket slung on a crooked finger over his shoulder walked down the diagonal. His profile, made flat, became that of an Egyptian slave on a vase.

Now, out of a third dimension, a springer spaniel bounded

down from the top, straight toward Blair. He passed her and skidded to a stop, pointing into the bushes behind. The leaves rustled. The dog trembled but did not bark. Blair held herself absolutely still. She knew there were animals in these ravines. She had had a naturalist on her show not long ago discussing the wild population of Toronto: porcupines, raccoons, foxes, skunks, rabbits. Nothing dangerous, though a skunk would be inconvenient. She had to go in to work at three.

Animals did not frighten Blair. People did. But wasn't that normal for a woman, "a hick from the sticks," as she called herself, living alone in Toronto? Surely only large white males felt secure here. Blair had had one on air the other night. "Rosedale is the last safe place in the world," he'd said. His proof? That Graham Silkin, reputedly the eighth-richest man alive, walked his dog on Chestnut Park alone and unprotected every day at exactly the same time. That revelation brought in the joke calls.

"Don't spread that around," said one. "But is it true?"

"Where and when did you say?"

"I consider jokes about hold-ups in very bad taste," said another, sniffily.

"Oh, Toronto the Good *speaks*," said Blair into her mike. It was a slip, the kind that got her into trouble with the fat producers.

The dog crashed into the leaf-fest. Two bluejays rose up, then settled again on the brush top. The dog circled impotently. *Get 'em, dog!* Bluejays were bad birds; they ate the eggs and young of other birds. Only Toronto would name a baseball team after them. Once again, the Jays were choking on the way to the playoffs; served people right. Blair had said that on the air, too, and got her second warning from one of the fat producers, who seemed to be twins, at least she never knew one from the other.

"You can't make those smart cracks! You gotta realize,

you're not on some little fringe outfit, sniping from the side-lines. This is a *major Toronto station*! People love their Jays." He filled the doorway, his regular scowl stretching sideways and downward in a boiled-cabbage face. At this rate Blair was unlikely to pass probation on this job, either.

The dog bounded away up the slope. Temporarily the walkers were out of sight. A plane moved in the sky directly overhead, its outline glazed by the invisible poisons that coat the distance. The crack of a helicopter was there, and then not there, disappearing southward toward the city. A dragon-fly whirred over her shoulder and turned sharply left, a miniature replica of the helicopter. Under Blair's feet was the sound of water running past a metal grate, overhead the periodic surge of traffic on the Spadina overpass. In between was silence.

Silence, and Blair's own breath going in and out. To her surprise, peacefully, even happily. She was on her own, and if she lost this job she didn't know where she'd get another one. Her daughter was a little strange. Company would be nice, and there were no men on the horizon. *But what the hell.* It was September. The day was incomparable. Her daughter had started grade one. Blair had nursed, coddled and cajoled that warm dumpling into a walking, talking, cognizant being who was now joining society, or at least the society of twenty-two other six-year-olds. Congratulations were due. When you're alone, you learn to award these to yourself. *Congratulations, Blair. You had a tough time, but you've done it. So far, so good.*

She felt connected to everyone—the joggers, the drivers, the mothers pushing prams, her friends, seen and unseen around the city. There was just enough warmth in the air, and a dusty smell of fall coming on. There was forgiveness in the air, in the decline of summer. This futile, fruiting season would pass, and she too could get on to some non-biological project.

Berenice ducked out of the house and took the untidy clutch of letters from the mailbox. The porch floor was ankle-deep in leaves, red and yellow and green and orange, weightless, ancient. A gust of wind rattled down. Berenice was uneasy about all those leaves coming down. "The wind *hastens* the leaves to fall," she said, using her new word from yesterday.

Blair had been sitting at the window looking out into the dark as Bernie came in.

"'Like as the waves make toward the pebbled shore, so do our minutes hasten to their end.'"

She'd said that in the voice that Berenice had come to recognize as her poetry voice.

"Who said that?"

"Shakespeare. A sonnet."

"What's that word, *hazen*?"

Every day Berenice took one of the words Blair used and asked her how to spell it, found the meaning and then practised using it.

"Hasten," Blair said. "H-a-s-t-e-n."

Bernie went upstairs and looked it up. All the words together, one after the other, explained themselves.

"**hasten,** 1. v. **trans.** To cause to make haste, to urge on, to accelerate, expedite, hurry.

2. v. **intrans.** To make haste, to come, go, or act quickly, to be quick, to hurry."

Most of the words she knew separately; she could puzzle it out. "To make haste" was to go quickly. "To urge on"—well, "urge" reminded her of "urgent," which people always said on the phone when they wanted Blair. It meant right away, or else there will be trouble. "Accelerate" had to do with cars, which Bernie knew because she had taken her learner's permit and then the driver's lessons, and got her licence.

So "hasten" meant to go fast, like in a car, because it was an emergency. It was what they did, what they all did, all the time. Berenice, whose name had been hastened to Bernie, had wondered about all the hurry when she'd arrived in Toronto, but she did not wonder now. She could manage acceleration in all activities.

She picked out two air-mail envelopes from the pile, the pale-blue, lightweight paper ones with the red and blue notches around the edges of the envelope. Both were addressed to Miss Berenice Serapion. Both were from the Philippines. One was from Dugale, and the other was from her sister Philomena.

Putting the other letters in a careful pile on the pine hutch in the entranceway, she picked up hers and set off up the two flights of stairs to her room, carrying her paper towel and her Windex with her. On the last flight she swung around the banister on the landing and turned off into her bedroom. She had the attic floor, two rooms and a bath, rent-free, plus $200 a week, for doing the housework, picking up Sissy after school and looking after her for the evening, while Blair was at work. It was a good deal. She could keep her other jobs, which were many: on her key-ring she had keys to twelve houses and she cleaned at least two of them a day.

Shutting her door behind her, she sat on the edge of the bed. She turned the letter over in her hands several times before tearing the seal. It was a satisfying thickness, several sheets of the fine paper were obviously folded inside. She hadn't heard from Dugale in three months.

At first he had been so angry that she left that he had not written. After one year, a letter came to say that he was engaged to marry someone else. After all, what did she expect, leaving a man such as himself, good-looking, healthy, young? But he did not mean it. Bernie continued to send the money every month, and Christmas and Valentine's cards. Last spring he'd started to write her love letters again.

She unfolded the rustling blue sheets with their small, Greek-styled letters in black ink. She bent her head over the letter. The clock ticked.

On the walls of her room were two posters. One was of

herself, at the Ex, in a very short red miniskirt and black halter-top with a chunky metal belt and net stockings. In this photograph Bernie stared into the camera in a glow of what might be anger or injuredness. (Whatever it was, it was understood by the furnace man who entered her room to check the radiators to be smouldering sexual energy. He gaped and whistled.) The second poster was a blown-up colour portrait of Jesus Christ. Bernie didn't go to mass much in Toronto, but she liked him as decor because it made her feel at home. He was like a father but he stayed in the frame. Her own father was a fisherman. He was a kind man but he had too many children, thirteen in all, whom he could not feed, which was why they had to go away.

Bernie's shiny black head remained bent over the pages of onion skin.

dearest beloved, he wrote. *i am missing you every day and more every day. we are made by God to be together and how is it you are over there so far from where i sit? my mother is ill once more and we are taking her to the doctor but she screaming all the time. they say she is crazy and give her some medicine which makes her quiet.*

She read on and was transported to the village, where he lived with his mother and his father and his brothers and sisters and their children. It was only a stone's throw from her parents' nipa hut. She saw the corners she had swept and the walls she had wiped, and the light falling in squares through the small windows.

i do read the books you send and one week work with my sister's husband to build a wall against the sea. So now no more is fishing hut swept away in rainy season, sometimes the fishermen with it. i sit beside the door of the house and watch the children, all the children of my sisters and brothers who are away like you, and i wonder if i am left behind all my days. Do you still remember our love Berenice? the fifty dollars you send each month does not buy so much food now I think you must send more. My mother must have medicine . . .

She put the letter down, to finish later. She could not untangle the complicated knot of questions it raised. Money, love, love, money; it was up to Bernie to give, and give more. She had not understood when she came to Canada to work that she would become a figure of authority to the entire clan of twenty or more, the one who said who got what and how much.

She heard the clock tick. It was time to tidy the house. In two hours she must get Simplicity at school. She folded her hands and said a prayer for Dugale and her relatives at home. She said a prayer for herself—the same one she said automatically, every day—that she should one day marry Dugale. She picked up her spray bottle of Windex and her roll of paper towel with something like nostalgia and hurried downstairs.

The Windex bottle was nearly empty, and she would not get another. Blair had cut an article out of the newspaper that said you could do all your household jobs with baking soda, vinegar and ammonia, and that these cleaners were safer for the environment. Environment had been her new word several months ago. Because Windex was bad and paper towels a waste, Blair wanted Bernie to use vinegar and old newspapers to clean the windows. They tried vinegar and old newspapers together on the mirror in the bathroom.

"It's very effective," Blair said. "I don't even mind the smell. What do you think, Bernie?"

Bernie said that it was okay and she would do it, although in fact she did not like it as well. All the other housekeepers at the Loblaws at St. Clair and Spadina bought buggyloads of Pledge and Fantastik and Wisk and Sparkle and Vim, of Easy-Off. ("That's the worst!" said Blair.) It gave greater value to their work to know that the household was putting out this money for materials. Reducing to vinegar would lower Bernie's status, and, by extension, Blair's.

Balanced against that was the fact that Bernie loved saving money and was good at it. She knew Blair, being alone, was not so rich as other people here. Bernie brought coupons home from Canadian Tire and Loblaws; she saved the folders offering 25 percent off that came in the mail. She'd gone to St. Clair West and come back with a new backpack for Simplicity that had been on sale for $9.99, the very same one she had seen for $25 in the Kitchen Bazaar.

At first Blair didn't notice Bernie's thrift. It took Bernie's friend Conchita to explain why. It was because Bernie went quietly around the house doing the very best job she could, and not drawing attention to herself.

"It's different here. Not like at home where girls are meant to be soft and make work seem easy. Here you are in the business world, even though your business is a house. You must describe in all the details how you did your job. Make it sound very very difficult."

So Bernie stood firm on the diamond-shaped tiles that she had washed so many times they were like her own feet, and said, "We saved fifteen dollars today. I looked at the Kitchen Bazaar and Grand and Toy and those places in Forest Hill Village but I knew I could get it cheaper. So I went down to Bargain Jimmy's and there were some. It even matches the colour of her jacket, see?"

And Blair smiled absently and said, "That's great, Bernie. You're wonderful. Thank you for going to so much trouble."

The door slammed. Blair came into the house. She stood at the foot of the stairs holding something brown and shrivelled in her hands. Bernie looked down at her.

"I bought some ginger root because it looked so fresh. Would you like some ginger tea?" she said.

Bernie smiled brightly, although she did not feel bright. She felt confused, by questions about love, questions about money. "No, I have to do work now," she said, and ran into the bathroom, shutting the door behind her. She took the toilet brush and pumped it up and down, making a sucking whirlpool in the bowl. Sometimes Bernie's aunt asked her, did she not get bored of doing housework and looking after a child? She should go to school and take a course, because soon she would be a citizen.

"You're landed now," her aunt said. "Down from the clouds. No air under your feet." Working in other people's houses wasn't a proper job at all but something to be ashamed of, her aunt implied. Bernie didn't agree. It felt good to scrub a toilet. Besides, she learned from Blair; she drove a car now and she could shop. She could clean twelve houses in a week. She was not shy like she used to be. When she first met Blair she called her "Madam." Blair laughed.

"Oh heavens, don't say that here. My name is Blair. You mustn't call people sir and madam here."

She finished the bathroom and walked out into the hall. The telephone rang. Berenice answered. "For you! It's Ruby." As she handed the receiver to Blair, she remembered. "She called already. She wanted you to call back."

Blair lifted the receiver to her ear. "Hi Ruby," she said, warily.

Philip sat in the open window of the Future Bakery on Bloor. He raised a mug of café au lait to his lips. It was a warm day, like summer again. The steam from the coffee made drops on his already damp forehead. It was nearly eleven now, and everything was opening; across the street the Lick'n Chicken, which had had nothing to do with chicken for a decade, and the Vinyl Museum. Two doors down, a black man on a step-ladder was roller-painting the ceiling of a store that sold Latin-American crafts.

A low, red car pulled up and parked. A dark-haired, steroid-stuffed muscleman withdrew from the driver's seat. Out from the passenger side climbed a woman with a tiny waist and a short, incredibly tight black skirt. He stepped into the lanes of traffic. She stopped on the curb. Checking out the oncoming traffic, he then strolled across the street, thighs rolling and buttocks tight as an apple. On the opposite curb he rotated to face her, as she fretted on the opposite sidewalk. He jerked his hand. Fast, fast, very delicately placing one high-heeled shoe directly in front of the other, she crossed the street like a trapeze artist. Reunited after the tension of the crossing, they clasped hands and went into the Lick'n Chicken.

At the table next to Philip three women were talking politics. The Rosedale candidate, they said, made his EA pregnant, got her an abortion, left and then returned to his wife, and still beat out the feminist.

"When I win the Nobel peace prize," said one, "I'm going to wear a shocking-pink strapless dress. Just to show, to show you can do it and still be *feminine*."

Philip thought that, these days, there were too many women in restaurants. "What do you object to?" Blair had said to him, when he expressed his view to her. "The fact they're not with men or the fact that they're not home cooking?"

"They're flushed out of their natural habitat. Too *visible*," he insisted. "It's not a good sign. It's like animals when they're going extinct." Blair just laughed at him. He was an old shoe to her, he thought. Philip with his storefront smile, his sheared-off black trousers, the genial, faded blue eyes. He looked like an overweight, balding ex-hippie, but he had looked like that at twenty, too. The diffident rancher's son from Cereal, Saskatchewan, by way of Los Angeles. He had walked out of Hearts of Flame in a rage, tried law school and hated it, and ended up in California making masks for the movies. After two decades, he had come to Toronto. It wasn't really clear why, except he'd never made a home down there. Like Blair, like Ruby, like Oswald too, probably, he had made no permanent connections anywhere. It was the curse of

Hearts of Flame, they joked.

Los Angeles had not affected him. Philip was as solid, as *there* as a horse in the barn, the very opposite of Californians, indeed of Torontonians, most of whom still seemed like flashy, insubstantial people. Another hick from the sticks, Philip had become the essence of the city, the artist underclass. He'd proven his worth a hundred times over, and had nothing to show for it.

The coffee was finished. Breakfast was over and it was almost lunchtime. He signalled the waitress and ordered a beer.

Philip did special effects for films and stage productions. When the film and television contracts didn't come in, he paid his bills by working as a make-up artist. The night before he had made up the girls for the Miss Canada pageant. They were all so obsessed with their appearance they screamed bloody murder over a pimple. One today was bitching about couldn't he do something to cover up this one zit. So he gave her a dab of plastic wood. All he really wanted to do was spend all his time making chandeliers fall and eyeballs pop out.

The beer came. Philip drank deeply from his glass. He'd had a call from Ruby on his machine that morning. He thought she was in some kind of trouble. Philip's eyes opened wide, watered, and then narrowed down on their privacy again. Even as he thought about her, his great relaxed body expressed resistance. He pushed her away, pushed what she had to say away, pushed all difficult and unhappy things away.

He hadn't seen her in ages. Didn't know what she was up to. Married man, he'd heard from Blair. That was inevitable, he'd also heard. The men all were, apparently. He wouldn't know. Philip was apart from all that. He didn't enter the fray. He never had. It added to the security of his presence, his utter faithfulness, his crotchety, stubborn, principled views, his having no entanglements, no *side* as they said in the west.

He put his hands flat on the table and looked at them. His

hands were beautiful, large, with long-boned fingers. They were darker in colour than his pale face, reflecting childhood days in sunny fields, perhaps, or even this past summer's rides around the city on his bicycle. His fingers had calluses on their tips from the strings of his bass, still, after all this time. The skin furrowed between Philip's eyes. He pushed his rimless glasses back up his nose.

He remembered that night in Banff when he was with Ruby. Blair said he should have stayed with her, kept her out of trouble. Not Ruby: she didn't want the likes of him.

Philip leaned back in his chair and looked out the window. A tall woman with a long French braid, like an exposed spine down her head and back, was locking her bike to the Toronto *Sun* box. She stood up and looked straight at him, blankly, and looked away. No curiosity.

He wondered if anyone wanted to know him, to know what his life was like. He spent Saturday sleeping till three. Then he went to Bay-Bloor Radio and looked at systems he couldn't afford and got depressed. He had no money. He'd gone out and done exactly what he loved. The income was a bit unsteady, but it was worth it. And he had some great jobs coming up . . . that horror film . . .

Philip kept on looking out the window. Knots of people stood on corners and in front of stores. Another cheerful thing was that his uncle was dying of cancer of the esophagus. It was Sam. Sam was the musician in the family. When Philip dropped law for show business, Sam had calmed his father's apoplexy. His dad had come to town, and they all got together on Sunday for dinner. And Sam was there, looking all tanned and brown and slim, as if he'd spent two years at tennis camp instead of the Princess Margaret Hospital for people with terminal cancer. And he was super cranky. All he did was demand special food and drink. He wanted caviar and then he wanted marinated lamb kebabs from this fancy butcher—and his wife ran around and got all this—and then he threw a fit because there wasn't any chestnut purée in between the layers of the cake. He hadn't always been a fussy eater. He'd started out eating meat loaf thirty years ago and graduated to peanut butter sandwiches and macaroni. No money.

So then Sam took Philip by the elbow and led him out through the sliding glass doors onto the balcony of this hotel, and gave him some advice. He said, "I wanted to play music so much and I spent years teaching here and there and barely making it, and now I'm going to die and I have nothing. Don't make the same mistake I did. Give up this special effects bit, this clowning around, and go out and go back to law school."

Philip shook his head and directed a snuffly laugh down into the bottom of his beer glass. That was not how it was supposed to go. When people were dying they were supposed to come on to you and tell you to do exactly what matters most to you, not to worry about money. He always had this argument with Blair.

"You don't need a lot of money," she said. "You don't have a kid. You don't rent a house that eats your money. You might as well do what you want. Life is short."

"Life is not short. Life is long," said Philip.

"Short," said Blair.

"Long," said Philip.

He stood up, put five dollars on the bill, then pushed his hands into his pockets for a two. He wondered if they should do anything about Ruby. He took off his glasses and rubbed his large, soft, red-rimmed eyes. He could do something. Stage a mishap. A special effects mishap. Get this married guy off her case. But it was probably the last thing she wanted. If they were talking mishaps, it's the wife he had to do. And he didn't do wives. Get Oswald on the case, thought Philip. Isn't that his specialty? Changing fate?

There was a girl standing on the corner with a tame rat on

a leash sitting on her shoulder. Two drunks came and leaned against the door frame.

"Your body dies but your spirit goes on," said one drunk in a confiding tone to the other, as if he were explaining a fact unaccountably left out of the operating instructions.

"That's what I'm worried about, where does it go on to?" said his friend.

"Me too," said Philip, passing through the doorway.

The man, who looked as if his nose had been bloodied some hours ago, looked puzzled.

"Not anywhere around here, that's for sure."

"Maybe Varsity Stadium. The bleachers on the west side," said Philip. He bent to unlock his bike. The drunk looked surprised and elbowed his friend. They moved off.

Max Ostriker strode out of the house on Castle Frank into the noon sun. He'd been in there all morning, attending to the will of an aged descendant of some branch of the Family Compact. Mr. K. New would have burnt his money if law allowed, rather than let anyone else get hold of it. "Are you telling me I hafta . . ." said the testy old guy.

"You don't have to do *anything*," Max had said, sitting at the old mahogany table beside Mr. New's wheelchair. "Well, let me say that again. The only thing you have to do is die, some day." The old man had actually liked that remark; he'd chortled and gripped his arm rests, pulling himself half out of his seat. But it had not made him any easier to deal with.

In the park, a group of boys was playing ball. Max jogged toward second base and scooped up the ball as it rolled near an inattentive shortstop, legs scabby with insect bites.

"Can I play?" Max shouted, tossing the ball back to the pitcher, a serious blond boy with an oversized cap on his head and a rat-tail hanging down his back.

"Sure!"

He chucked the shortstop under the chin and told him to look sharp and then trotted out to field. The batter fielded the ball and took off around the bases. Max ran up to intersect his path between second and third, and, waving his arms, prevented the kid from reaching the base until the other fielder threw the ball to second.

The kids were screaming at him, and each other. While the frustrated batter kicked at his legs, Max held his head, laughing out loud. Then he let the kid go and slapped his shoulder to let him know it was a joke.

The kid's face puffed up red and tears burst from his squeezed-up eyes.

"He *cheats*, it's not fair. Get him outta here."

The batting team cheered Max.

"It's a game, it's a joke," protested Max.

The serious pitcher glared at him from waist height. "I know kids who play like that, but not grown-ups," he said.

Max's long, lean jaw jutted forward. He was dashed. He was just trying to have fun. Kids weren't like they used to be, couldn't take a little teasing.

"Okay," said Max. "You got it!" He picked up the ball again and threw it way, way up. They all stared blindly after it. It came down in its own split-sun halo and landed smack in Max's hand.

"Hey, give it, give it!" They were around his legs.

He let the ball drop into the pitcher's hand and walked away, rousing a rough chorus of protest behind him. Halfway across the park he stopped. The boys were still watching. He saw something glint in the grass. He bent to pick it up. It was a loonie, gold in the sun.

"Look what I found!" he called back at them. "My reward."

"Ah, no fair! The guy *cheats* and then he *finds* money!"

"Just luck, kids. My luck!"

"In your *dreams*, bub!"

He waved his arm and swung off the grass onto the sidewalk. Luck was Max's today, and all life, too, to toy with. And about time. He didn't mind lording it over the kids: people had lorded it over him long enough.

He was a tall man, indifferent to his height, broad-shouldered enough to be taken for a football player. He was strong, but his strength had been usurped by others; he had carried their burdens without complaint. His father had bullied him. His mother had depended on him; he was her daily visitor until she died. He offered a brass shoulder to suffering women friends. Still single, he styled himself as a rake. Though he had little justification, it was the best protection. Fake it 'til you make it, they said, and that's what Max had done.

He'd been faking it, basically, since elementary school, when he was gawky, timid and friendless. He grew tall and strong without noticing, developed his profession. Then, when he was thirty-five, his mother died. He suddenly realized he was an eligible man, and free to find a life. These were facts she had kept obscured from him, or perhaps he had kept obscured from her, and hence from himself.

At one point he'd longed to be a musician, but he played an indifferent guitar, and besides, it was an unreliable line of work. He went to Woodstock a year after everyone else and took a photo of himself, with his guitar. He had it framed. "This is me, playing at Woodstock," he said when he showed people. During law school he tried to manage musical groups, but that was a dirty business. When he got out in 1971, he formed his own firm, with Andy Mugwell, and began to write wills—a quieter life.

Ostriker, Mugwell: it was an unusual firm. Clients were struck by Max's nonconformity, by the relaxed way he leaned behind his desk, jacket off and tie loose, by the rumpled hair and the fact that every time he stood up he had to hitch up his pants. Secretaries were struck by his courtesy, by the way he accorded them dignity, asking them serious questions about their views: "Are you in favour of pay equity?" "Do you feel safe in your apartment?" They were struck, as they were meant to be, by his openness, but they never really got to know him.

Andy and Max fit nicely together, trading on each other's strengths. Max had steady, reliable clients who paid good money. Andy had inherited money, and could do the kind of law he wanted. His flamboyant civil rights cases attracted attention and gave credibility where they wanted it. (Anyone who went to law school in the late '60s wanted that.) Meanwhile, the reassuring social history of the Mugwells, being descended from the Colonel and all, helped bring in the trust business for Max. Andy amused himself with his defence of the bizarre, the friendless, the forgotten. Yet the minute that he took such a case, it revealed itself to be irresistible to the media. They called it the Mugwell touch: whatever he put his hands on turned to ink.

At Bloor and Sherbourne Max glanced at the *Star* in its blue dispenser. Speak of the devil. Blurred by the glass, grinning above the fold line, was Andy himself. Max did not put in his thirty-five cents; he got all he wanted by looking. Andy had been photographed going into the courtroom, holding hands with the young lady whose boyfriend had wanted to stop her abortion. In the photograph, Andy's balding pate, his avuncular smile, his firm, strong arm showed up to advantage, with the young blond girl looking appropriately grateful as he protected her from the outflung arms and waving placards of pro-life fanatics.

Moving off, Max groaned audibly. Some admired Andy greatly for defending the downtrodden, the unclean, the powerless. It was indeed noble, because these rights cases were never perfect. Each victim of the system was himself (or herself) a victimizer. To the extent that he has been victimized, he is damaged, and damaged people tend to bring a lot of trouble upon themselves. To Andy this was not a problem;

indeed, it made his work more interesting. But it gave Max headaches. The likes of Mr. New did not appreciate meeting an exotic dancer and her leather-clad keeper in the waiting room, much less a tattooed ex-con.

Take this woman: three previous abortions, a job at the Zanzibar Tavern, and she was a "slow learner." Okay, you don't expect them to be paragons of virtue. But Andy seemed to prefer those he championed to be as suspect as possible, the rape of a drug-addicted prostitute posing much more of a challenge than that of a Branksome schoolgirl, or the defence of *High Times* from charges of promoting drug use a sexier case for freedom of speech than, say, *The Merchant of Venice* banned. He loved a case to rub Torontonians' noses in their own doodoo, their own tight, tense and unreasonable set of rules.

Andy continued to be on Max's mind as he sped along Bloor Street toward his lunch date with Ruby Mason. Max was not among those lawyers who said Mugwell was only out for himself, that he never acted without first calculating the amount of ink that would flow, and then the amount of money. He knew for a fact they were wrong about the money. It was merely a by-product. But then Andy was born to it. It comes more easily to people like that: money goes to money. He didn't include himself in that. His father made money but he didn't come from it. A big difference.

Max was good at placing other people, even if he couldn't place himself. Successful, self-made, a free agent, that was his vanity. He was well liked without having close friends; he kept himself apart, even from his old classmates; his family, too, had been singular and outside society. About his clients Max felt an endless, almost prurient interest; and for the rest of Toronto, *out there*, a general—probably defensive—disinterest, though he must confess, he would have loved to see his picture in the newspaper. Always, when he thought he was on top, there was Andy to remind him: some lived in another realm.

The sun went in again, and rain began to splatter. It was just about noon. He was meeting Ruby Mason at Enoteca. She said she had a problem to discuss. He never thought of Ruby as a fashion designer, as everyone else did: he remembered her as that shimmering, radiant singer he'd seen perform at Mount Norquay. It was a memory at once erotic and touched with shame: the spotlights and the sweat, the bare brown arms, the press of swaying bodies up against the stage, voices that could break down all the chambers of the heart. Hearts of Flame: they could have been great. Too bad they split up. He'd had a hand in it, too, to his regret. That night was buried in him, under a stone marked "Failures: don't look too closely." He never heard from the others, though he knew Oswald was in town—who didn't—and Blair, too. Only Ruby called, from time to time. He didn't know if she wanted free legal advice or to pick up old ties. Either was okay with him.

He dodged down the subway at Castle Frank and went over to the westbound platform. Behind him a black woman in a brown velvet jacket and miniskirt with very high heels walked briskly down the escalator on the right side and turned toward the track. The train entered the station, its central light diffusing in the lit and white-tiled platform area. The crowds were no more than one-deep at the platform. The woman elbowed, nonetheless, to the very edge of the platform with a look of great concentration.

Max watched her; something about her face and her posture drew him; she was so determined. Her hair blew back as the train approached. She narrowed her eyes; everyone did, in the intense headlight, the gritty wind. When the train was ten feet away she dropped her purse on the edge of the platform. Calling out over her shoulder, "Excuse me!" she leapt off the platform.

Max lunged forward to grab her arm but she was gone. She

fell onto one knee but righted herself when the train was still a few feet away. Looking down, Max saw that there was room under the lip of the platform; she could have drawn back in there. But instead she pushed off the wall and dove forward again into the path of the train. The driver's face distorted, he shouted behind the windshield. She was three feet above the track, flying horizontally when she met the train.

Max was in a direct line to see the body smash against the metal catcher and fall under the rails of the train. He felt the blow as in his own guts. Then all hell broke loose. The driver pounded the window. Brakes squealed; people on the platform screamed. The lights went out. The train pushed past in the dark before finally, somewhere down the platform, brakes grabbing, the engine sobbed to a stop.

Bent over, Max tried to vomit, but his throat only clutched dryly and let go. As he stood up he retrieved the woman's purse. The station seemed to go mad. Someone behind him toppled over. There was an eerie silence in the darkness, then voices yelling for calm and to let them through. A yellow light came on the sides of the tunnel, and two guys in transit uniforms appeared telling people to keep back. Passengers inside the train pressed their faces to the window.

Max moved back. The crowd was crazy with people crossing themselves, shaking their heads and covering their faces. He didn't know the tears were running down his own face until a woman offered him a kleenex. Some saffron-robed character was chanting and would not be moved, and a guy beside him who looked like a stockbroker swore repeatedly, "I shoulda walked, goddamn it I shoulda walked, I'm gonna be late."

Meanwhile, it got more and more crowded on the platform. No trains left, but one arrived on the other side. More people came down the stairs. The passengers were let off the train. The platform was jammed, a solid mass of people. It was hot, and there was no air. He wanted to get out, but he knew better than to start pushing. Max kept thinking she was under there, under the train.

Finally a voice came over the loudspeaker saying "*Please leave the station, please leave the station. Eastbound travel will be interrupted for some time.*" A way opened up on the staircase. He made for it.

Then he realized he still had the purse in his hand. The handle, which was plastic made to look like horn, was still warm. Max found the police and offered them the purse, which they took. He said he was a witness but they had plenty already. Some uniformed medical workers rushed down the stairs with boxes of tools and plastic bags and shovels. The driver, with his head down, was led away by an ambulance worker.

At last he found his way back upstairs to the outside. He was wondering why the woman said, "Excuse me." It wasn't for pushing people aside, or for dropping the purse, or even for inconveniencing them. It must have been for making them witness to this death she had designed. "No, I don't excuse you, lady," he cursed as he hailed a cab. He was going to the office to hide; he didn't trust himself in public. He'd have to call Ruby and cancel lunch.

Ruby Mason was not having her best day.

At ten o'clock that morning, when she was still in her spaghetti-strap satin nightgown, sitting with a huge mug of coffee in front of her on the turquoise arborite table, the phone had rung. It was Marvin.

"Trouble," he said. "The wife figured out where I was last night."

"She did?" Ruby said evenly. "Oh no. How?" She looked down at her acrylic fingernails. She turned the radio lower. This was the news she had been waiting for. Still, it could go either way. Marvin's wife had been a stumbling-block for a year; Marvin said he didn't love her, but he never complained about her. She remained entirely unknown to Ruby, a kind of headless monster.

Marvin was a producer at City-TV, a day-and-night operation. It was easy most of the time to say he was working. This time, however, the wife had phoned the office and got no answer, so she drove over and found it was all closed up.

"When I got home she was sitting up waiting for me."

A Cheshire cat smile on her face, Ruby began rubbing her satin thigh. She was proud of her thighs, long-muscled and hard. They were the products of diligent exercise, a skimpy diet and the nearly constant state of nervous excitement in which she existed. She was pleased, yes, about the wife; curious, too. That was normal. It was the pity that took her by surprise.

"So how's she taking it?"

"Bad bad bad," he said. "It's a gruesome scene. I had to promise her just about everything to keep her from completely falling apart."

"Poor you," said Ruby.

"For instance, I had to promise I'd stop seeing you," he said. "Oh-oh, there's my other line. I'll call you. Lunch tomorrow, okay? You'll have my undevoted attention."

"Undivided, you mean," said Ruby to dead air. He always got his clichés wrong. She put some kisses onto the receiver, and then she thought about what he'd said. Promises not to see Ruby, was it now? Marvin could never keep a promise like that. Again, she felt for his wife. The poor woman would find she was bargaining with the devil.

Slowly she got dressed and, without hurry, went in to work. She'd only been there long enough to sift through her messages and decide there wasn't anyone she wanted to talk to, or even any single piece of business she could handle, when Max Ostriker called.

"I can't make lunch," he said. His voice was shaking. "I was on the subway and some damn woman committed suicide right in front of me."

"Oh shit. Poor you," said Ruby, for the second time that day.

"We'll do it another time," he said, and hung up abruptly.

Instantly, before the bad feeling could hit, Ruby phoned Blair. When she didn't get her, she waited fifteen minutes and tried again.

"Hi, what're you doing?" she said, through her teeth. She'd spied a hangnail on her left pointer finger and was trying to bite it off.

"I went and sat in the ravine. Now I'm going to sit on the porch in the sun, drink ginger tea and read a novel," said Blair. She gave the impression she did not want to be dislodged from this position.

"What's it called?" Not that Ruby knew the names of novels; she just wanted to talk herself past this little bit of aggravation with Marvin.

"*Fly Away Home.*"

Ruby waited. "As in Ladybug, Ladybug?" Her voice had a familiar needy quaver.

"As in." Blair relented. "Why, what about you?"

"Max Ostriker cancelled lunch because somebody jumped in front of a subway train, right in front of him."

"Max Ostriker? You still see Max Ostriker?" Blair remembered him as a supercilious, smug kid out to make millions off the backs of poor folk singers. Of course, they were all kids back then.

"I see lots of people you don't know I see," said Ruby. "Come down, can you? Half an hour? I'll get take-out."

"No don't, I hate that miso soup. We'll go out," said Blair reluctantly. She didn't feel like going downtown. But Ruby sounded bad. Old ties pulled Blair. She wondered what it was this time. She put down the telephone and gazed out the window. It was still too beautiful to stay indoors.

2

Banff
1969

The Trans-Canada Highway out of Calgary exploded west-ward across the broad sweep of foothills, heading upward into the Rocky Mountains. On either side the grasslands unrolled, tacked at corners with cabins, banded with narrower, criss-crossing tracks. Ahead the peaks were still topped white, though it was July, and the air buzzed with heat. Green, gold and blue clapped hands in the huge summer sky; light broke out each unit onto its own plane—hill, horse, field.

On this day, July 10, 1969, in the early afternoon, a black Ford Econoline van hugged the pavement, beetle-sized in the open space. Its panelled side bore a plump burgundy heart engulfed in orange flame. Under it, in florid script, were the words "Hearts of Flame."

An eastbound Volkswagen with a loose tarp flapping on its roof tooted its horn; its occupants waved and shouted and hung their long hair out the window. The black van honked back and cheered; its wheels spun onward. It was filled with the sound of singing; two voices carolling in jest, half-shout-ing a song in which the words "travelling on" were repeated. The song, the roar of the pavement, the éclat of the light and

the colour and the air: it was too strong, too alive, too penetrating to be borne by anything but the blindness of youth.

The sun struck the windshield and fractured into beams so
bright they nearly washed out the face of the driver. He was
Philip Mark, bass player and unappointed group leader. He
had pale, wispy hair tied in a ponytail, an untrimmed beard,
watery blue eyes and rimless spectacles, which were trained
ahead on the dotted line even as his voice warbled over the
wheel. Having grown up on a ranch outside Cereal,
Saskatchewan, he was currently (and perhaps permanently) in
revolt against everything middle-class, set off against the
world by his father's alcoholic rages.

Beside Philip in the front seat sat Blair Bowker, her legs
drawn up to her chest, cowboy boots kicked off on the floor.
She too was blond, but vibrantly coloured, with fierce, dark
brows, deep brown eyes outlined in black, and russet cheeks.
She had a classical, judging look. Her lipstick, freshly applied,
was white. A trained singer unlike the others, Blair had been
practising in a music studio at the University of Alberta when
Philip turned up outside the door.

"You've got a great voice, but if you're going to sing folk
we've gotta loosen you up." He recommended cigarettes and
booze to get authentic. They got together to sing and discovered Blair's voice was perfect as it was, a contrast to his rasp-
ing but rich tones. People said she and Philip sounded like
brother and sister. She could go alto, under him, or up above
him; she liked to do both, winding in and out of the melody
like a skater outstroking the throng.

"— for I'm bound to be tra-aa-aa-velling on." Head back
against the seat and eyes closed, Blair sang secure in her place
in the world, her special talents, her gift for friendship and
for happiness; none of these were things she could name, but
she knew them to be hers, nonetheless.

In the back seat Ruby Mason and Oswald Yakibuchi were
silent. Ruby was half asleep: through the fog, she heard what

she was missing, but she didn't like to sing much anyway. Ruby could sleep anywhere, especially after a party like last night's. She was small, rounded and brown-skinned; her hair, almost black, thick and curly, fell around her face and down her back. Her bow-lips were open as she slept, her face was smooth and untroubled. She slept like she lived, full tilt, without restraint, taking what she needed. Her legs were curled up beside her, feet in holey socks extending across to the other seat and pressing against Oswald's hip.

Up against the door, Oswald sat erect and gazed out the window. If there had been telephone poles, he'd have been counting them. His eyes took in the logging road up the east side of the Kananaskis, swept down to the scattering of homes in the reserve, rested on the group of horses that grazed behind the wire fence. He was as contained as he looked, measuring, calculating, *preparing*, it seemed, for some moment when all his resources would be required. His family had relocated in Calgary after their release from the camp in the Slocan. The Yakibuchis had been fishermen in Vancouver, before the war. Although he had known it all his life, he hated this range of mountains, which divided him, he felt, from some natural home, some other world, some Eden where he belonged.

Behind the second seat, in the open back, were the instruments: Philip's stand-up bass and Blair's guitar, Oswald's portable keyboard, and all the amplifiers, wires and microphones, cleverly and safely packed in by Oswald. Against the rear door was the huge cut-out burgundy heart bathed in orange flames with the lettering beneath it—Hearts of Flame—that went up on stage with them. And suitcases, big ones, four of them, because they were off on a long tour this time, their longest so far: six weeks, starting in Banff and going to Vancouver, Edmonton, Calgary, Medicine Hat (Blair and Ruby's home town), Regina, Winnipeg and finally Toronto.

The song died for a moment. The sound of the highway,

pressed and blown back by the hot rubber tires, entered the van.

"Reason to Believe," announced Blair. She hummed the key. "If I listened long enough to you —"

"I'd find a way to believe that it's all true," Philip joined in, caressing the words with his rich, low voice.

"Knowing that you lied straight-faced while I cried . . ." They camped it up, shouting to the tin roof and out the open hatch into the dry summer air, forcing their music out into the world.

"Aw shut up," growled Ruby, thrusting her legs away from Oswald, up to the ceiling, and lying down on her back. "I gotta get some sleep."

Oswald seized the moment of her moving to try to reclaim a foot of space. He stared down at her, his face still but not disguising his feelings—perhaps desire, perhaps distaste.

"Ruby, look at you," he complained. "You are one-half of the people in the back seat, you ought to take up one-half of the space."

"She doesn't think she is," Blair tossed over her shoulder. "She thinks she's all of the people in the back seat. She thinks she's all of the people in this van."

"Aw shut up," said Ruby. "Just because you guys went to bed early."

"Just push her aside," said Philip. "She won't mind." He hummed the note again. "Take it again."

"Someone like you makes it hard to live without somebody else —"

"Someone like you makes it easy to give, never thinking of oneself —"

"Yourself. Ramblin' Jack Elliot would never say *one*self."

"Yourself!" sang Blair, and slapped Philip's thigh.

"I think they're in love," said Ruby, her voice rising from the seat where she had laid her head. "Why don't you just do it and get it over with."

"Fuck off, Ruby," said Philip.

"Give it up, okay Ruby?"

"You two," she muttered pleasantly, "don't know nothin' about nothin'." She went back to sleep. Oswald, still cramped by the window, moved his lips silently; whether he was writing another of his strange songs, or praying (Oswald was a devout Christian) was impossible to know.

"So what are we going to do tonight?"

Blair looked at Philip for the answer. He made the musical decisions. The others went along. The group was Philip's property, in a way. He had been singing on his own, and then he brought in Blair. They did all the folk clubs in Edmonton—Giuseppi's Pizza, Room at the Top, Zorba's. Just two guitars, two voices, a folk sound. They met Oswald when he was working backstage in the SUB theatre, moving props, setting lights. He was an electrical wizard as well as a keyboard genius. He was quiet offstage. "Oswald is so quantitative he can't even masturbate," Philip said once. But he played passionately, his long black hair tucked behind one ear, draped like one wing over his forehead as he swept from side to side.

"We'll do the same first set we did in Calgary." They'd played Mount Royal College; after a rocky start with the sound system—something to do with Oswald's cables—the concert was a smash hit.

"Not *again*," said Ruby, her eyes still closed.

Ruby may have been a mistake. After Oswald joined, Philip decided they needed to balance him with another girl. They couldn't be two guys and a blonde, like Peter, Paul and Mary. Blair said offhand that her friend Ruby from high school was kicking around town, and that she could put on a good show, though she wasn't much of a singer. But she was comic relief. With Ruby in front, swaying and crooning and making faces and being outrageous, the group took fire. It was Ruby who named them: four chambers of the heart, one flame.

Success came so fast, so easily, they were still trying to believe it. They were booked all over Edmonton. Last summer, an outdoor concert on campus with Great North turned out fifteen thousand fans. They travelled east. They travelled west. They cut two singles, one of which was number one for two months. They made money. They got used to seeing their faces on posters stuck on telephone poles, hearing their voices on radio. They were booked to open for the Byrds. An L.A. studio was interested in doing an album.

Classes for Philip and Oswald went down the drain, but Blair managed somehow to hang on to her credits and get a degree, writing papers in the small hours of the morning, sleeping three hours, going to class, rehearsing and performing night after night. Ruby hadn't been in school to begin with.

"And what for the second set?"

"I wish we had more of our own songs."

The weakness, if there was a weakness, of Hearts of Flame was their sound. They had a look, a personality, no one could touch. But a sound that was only their sound, a sound that, heard only for a few bars, spoke the name Hearts of Flame, that was still to come. Philip had a sense of what it was to be—something to do with the silken, classical quality of Blair's voice, the raw edge on his own, and Oswald's contrapuntal keyboard antics might add up. But they had to write or find the songs to show it off.

Philip began to go down the list. A Beatles song, some Crosby, Stills and Nash, one Joni Mitchell, a little Band, their own four, from the two singles, a Lightfoot, some Ian and Sylvia, the new one Oswald had written that they'd just practised —

"I don't think it's ready," said Blair.

"It'll never get ready till we start singing it."

"Never mind, never mind, it's not important," said Oswald. "It's not important that we sing my song. Leave it, leave it for a while. I can improve it."

"And we've got to do at least a couple of political songs."

"Like what?"

"Country Joe? One, two, three, what are we fighting for?"

"That's a musical lump of shit," said Oswald. "I don't see why we should be political. It's an American movement. It's an American war. It's not for us to comment. We should steer clear."

"Steer clear and we're a laughing-stock."

"People don't notice if you've taken a stand. They're so busy taking their own."

"Like hell they don't!"

"Canada's in the war too. Supplying. Just because I'm not American doesn't mean I have to keep my mouth shut about it," said Blair.

"Is that the Park gates? You gotta pull over," demanded Ruby. "I wanna pee."

The van rolled up to the window of the stone gatehouse. A cheerful face protruded. "Hey, how're ya doing? I hear you're playing Norquay tonight."

Ruby sat up. The whole world knew them. They all beamed at the gatekeeper. Fame was having friends every-where. There was no threat to it.

"Ya gotta buy a licence, unfortunately," said the gatekeeper.

Philip turned to Oswald. "Money, sir," he said. Oswald kept track of their expenses. He pulled his wallet out of the pocket of his jeans and peeled off a twenty-dollar bill. "Get a receipt."

Philip rolled his eyes. Ruby laughed.

"Reality, huh? Don't like keeping track of the bills?" she said. "Go on Philip, get organized. You can do it."

"Go fuck yourself, Ruby," said Philip again, steadily, grimly.

Blair and Ruby spilled out the side door of the van and headed for the little stone house where the washroom was.

"You gotta let up on Philip, you know that? You're always riding him," said Blair.

"He's such a prig," mumbled Ruby, her wallet in her mouth. She needed both hands to get the snap on her jeans undone. "Spoiled rich kid. Just like a preacher, that's what he reminds me of. Doesn't like to worry about money. Wants to do all this dreary old anti-war stuff. Who needs it? We gotta have *fun*. Show these guys a good time, eh? That's what they pay their money for. Not to be—harangued."

Blair leaned against the cool stone wall and looked at Ruby's feet under the cubicle. Her frayed jeans ended just where the platform heel protruded. She wouldn't be going hiking, that was for sure.

"Harangued? That's a big word for you, dear," she said.

"Took it out of your book," said Ruby. The tinkle began.

Blair turned to look in the mirror and smiled, revealing white, even teeth. She was pleased with her face. Aside from being pretty, it was right for 1969. It was one of the faces of the times. (The other was still in the cubicle.) Clear-eyed, with a look of health and wholesomeness, and something higher, a touch of the angels, too. Only its high colour offended her; she wore makeup to flatten her features. She touched the mole to the side of and below her left nostril, and the other beside it, on her cheek. These blemishes she deplored; if she wasn't careful, they were all she saw in the mirror. She pulled out her white lipstick and did her lips again.

Ruby emerged, squeezing her jeans together again at the waist. As she bent over her hair fell forward over her face—so much of it, a brambly thicket. When she got the snap she sighed and pushed forward to the mirror, using her forearm to sweep her hair off her face.

"Sex," she said, peering at a blackhead one inch away in the mirror, "that's what he needs. To get laid. On a regular basis."

Sex was Ruby's message at the moment. It was her calling card. Other people might be uptight about it, but she was here to demonstrate their absurdity, showing off how relaxed she was with her bold, loose breasts, her pinched-in waist and blooming hips. She presented herself as one who loved sex unquestioningly, was generous, without hang-ups, and scorned the self-protective bargaining of other females.

She rubbed some blush-on into her cheeks, eyeing herself critically, and then rummaged in her bag to find her lipliner brush. Blair watched, her forehead furrowed. Ruby might be the expert on make-up, but she was wrong about sex. Without being able to put it into words, Blair knew Ruby's message was a lie. That Ruby was smart, she was ambitious, she used this ruse to get to the inside of men, to find out what she needed to find out, for whatever her purposes. She didn't know what those purposes were. But Ruby was on her way to somewhere. And she would take Blair with her if she wanted to go.

"You think sex is what everyone needs," said Blair. "I'm not so sure."

"Look who he goes for," said Ruby, ignoring the larger question. "That last one, the figure-skater from Glenora? Millie Shamrock? Classic Philip. Talk about hopeless."

Philip did have a habit of falling for beautiful, sought-after women, preferably from wealthy families, girls who wouldn't have been caught dead with him if he wasn't a singer. In the clubs, they'd sit at the band's table because of the cachet it afforded, looking at Philip with pity. Then he'd dream of grand romance for weeks.

"He likes that type," said Blair, scuffing the floor. She thought to herself, secretly, that Philip was in love with *her*, and that in order not to offend the taboo that the band had set up—Hearts of Flame was a family, no sex allowed—sought her stand-ins everywhere. "But why not? I mean, what man doesn't? It's hard to say to a guy, you're weird-looking so better find a weird-looking chick."

Ruby examined herself, not touching the make-up that

covered acne scars on both cheeks. Her look of scorn was nearly as thick.

"Bet you think it's because he's in love with you," she said. "Well if he is, why doesn't he do something about it? All this repression gives me pimples." She tossed her hair back over her shoulder with a keen look at her profile in the mirror, picked up her saggy suede bag, which held cigarettes, wallet, notebooks, scarf and mosquito repellent, because someone had told her the bugs would be horrible up the mountain at night, and pulled out a joint. She lit it and held it out to Blair.

"Don't," said Blair. "There's Mounties all over the place."

Ruby rolled her eyes, took a drag and went out the bathroom door.

Blair pushed herself off the wall with her high-heeled cowboy boot and clomped after her. The heels dug into the loose gravel on the walk, then snapped on the road surface. Following Ruby: she did that a lot. And the brat couldn't even sing!

Oswald and Philip were leaning on the rail over by the van, also smoking a joint.

"You're in full view of the gatehouse," she said as she drew the van door aside. "If that's what you want."

Philip made a noise with his lips pressed shut, his nostrils tight against escaping smoke. Oswald just beamed at her, beamed his beatific smile, his round face glowing between the curtains of black hair. When not judging, watching, calculating, Oswald radiated such simple happiness it was difficult not to ask him his secret. Particularly when he smoked. He played well stoned, too, unlike Blair, who couldn't do anything except wail and shake and cry, as demons she hadn't even known she owned came out to dance.

Ruby pulled a football out of the back of the van and they kicked it around on the flat grass. Blair outran everyone, even Philip. Ruby specialized in body tackles. Oswald crouched low over the ground and rammed himself, making noises like a siren, into people's legs. They ended by lying in a tangle on the grass, laughing, panting.

"We better get going."

"Where are we staying?"

"The Rundle."

"That dump? Why not the Banff Springs?"

"Next tour. When we're rich. Right now we've got to be careful," said Oswald, the accountant. "If we're in the studio after this tour it might be a while before we make money again."

"Not if we sign. If we sign we'll be loaded."

"We've got to get the contract first," said Oswald.

Ruby extricated herself first. "I figure we should live it up," she said. "Who knows how long it's going to last?"

The others said nothing. Fat lot Ruby cared what happened to Hearts of Flame. She was on her way somewhere else, she made that clear. Too bad for them; now they couldn't do it without her. She was too strong a presence. Blair and Philip pulled themselves upright and tucked their shirts in, wiped the dirt off their pants and headed back to the van. Oswald followed.

"You haven't forgotten this lawyer from Toronto's coming tonight? The guy who's going to manage us?"

"We haven't." Nobody looked at Oswald.

"You wanna make money, he's the guy to help us."

The others were silent. It was Oswald's idea, to hire a professional manager to do their contracts and sell the album when it was done, to organize the tours. So they'd have more time to write and rehearse, he said. They were suspicious, righteously counter culture. It sounded too much like business.

By habit, Philip took the wheel. Oswald jumped in the other front seat to escape Ruby. Blair sat in the middle of the back and dared Ruby to push her aside, but Ruby didn't notice, she was swaying, dreaming with her eyes open, making owl eyes and fish mouths at Philip.

They rolled the windows down. The early mountain twilight was approaching.

"Take the Tunnel Mountain cut-off," said Blair suddenly. "Saves about five miles." The van lurched to a sharp left, crossed the railroad tracks and headed up the undivided highway, up the back of Tunnel Mountain, which would lead them around the slope and down into Banff Village. They slowed. The trees were closer now, thick and fragrant. The hills rose steeply; there was the sound of water somewhere. A great black crow flapped off a branch in their path. They began to climb, into the green and sky. And all at once, Blair knew she would remember this forever.

There are moments like this in a life, when the air is thinner, cooler, like pure energy; when you move with the easy grace of simple creatures, on a piece of earth that you claim, that claims you. Maybe, if you are lucky, this moment of unity comes, this life beyond life comes, at the same time when you touch the *zeitgeist*, the spirit, of your fellows. It happened that day. They belonged. It was the music they sang, the blue jeans they wore, their mood, which was taking over the continent, their time. They belonged to joy, to earth, to the moment.

The whole van hummed, and the earth hummed back.

At the Mount Rundle, the women showered and washed their hair. Philip wrote out the order of songs; Oswald limbered up his fingers. Each one was lost in a private fantasy of performing, joining voices, streaming into the live energy of the instruments, the heat of the lights. They'd be *on* tonight. There would be the thrum of Philip's electrified stand-up bass, the pluck and quaver of Blair's guitar, her neat fingers flying over and back, the trill and thump of the keyboard. Their voices, four of them. Separately raised, mutually engaged, the rough and the sweet, the indifferent and the rich.

Ruby, loosened up, would be banging that tambourine on her leg. No one could say she didn't try. She banged so hard that her right hip, the one she habitually hit, was two inches smaller than her left. Banging that tambourine, and singing in that unremarkable, barely trainable voice, and making faces and smooching with the mike, and sliding her miniskirt up and down her thighs.

Philip, with his steady, resonant strings, would be mooring Oswald's fantasies to the melody. Putting Ruby in her place, gently, for the audience to laugh. "That's enough out of you, shortstop." Ruby was a mascot, a sensuous doll, an actor. Oswald, so fierce over the keyboard, burning with a white inner heat, at once repellent and deadly attractive. And Blair, the calm centre, the musical touchstone, Blair, whose sheets of ironed blond hair swung beside her face like stretched white toffee, somehow untouchable.

It was time, nearly. Time to get up on stage and do all this, time to get back to it. It had already been too long since last night, since the great rush of sound, the faces out there, moving in and out of invisibility, of starbursts of light, the footlights blotting out their features, only the cheers, only the clapping, the flood of love.

It was five o'clock, and they played at ten. The dance was after, at midnight. They smoked another couple of joints and thought about eating. The Banff Café, they decided, was too busy, full of tourists. Better to try Phil's Pancake House, over the bridge and up the road to the hot springs, which served a more decorous crowd.

"Blueberry waffles with whipped cream, that's what I'm having." Ruby slid across the booth seat. Her skirt, the size of a bandana, rose even higher; black tights showed her muscular legs. The fringes on her shirt dangled over onto the table top.

At the table they were raucous. Philip was flipping peas off his fork at Blair. Oswald twitched with nerves. Ruby kept on needling, powdered sugar rimming her lips. Philip ordered his second beer.

"Be careful, that's enough," said Blair. There was an optimum level of inebriation for performing. A little booze and dope made his vocal chords loose and rich, and his body warm to the music. Too much was a disaster. He slurred, and his timing was off; worse, he tended to announce his own songs, songs the rest of them weren't ready to play.

Philip cancelled the beer. A big man, and weighty, he was mild and she could manage him, at least within their agreed-upon territory.

By six, the sun had impaled itself on the western peaks and its gold was seeping away. When they stepped into the parking lot the air was suddenly cool against bare arms. They drove back over the bridge, tooting the horn to waves and cheers from the sidewalk. The whole town was their friend. On Banff Avenue, crowds of hippies sat on the wooden fence that surrounded the museum; more long-haired, beaded and bearded people in moccasins collected in front of the café. A quiet, seemingly enraptured row of hippies sat on the curb all along the block by the public washrooms, watching traffic.

Oswald asked Philip to stop at the Rundle to see if the lawyer had called. Blair went into her room too, to find a pair of earrings that didn't bob so much. When she came back to the car, Ruby had moved to the front seat beside Philip. Her head was on his lap and her feet were pressed against the ceiling of the van. Philip looked over at Blair helplessly.

"I guess you'll have to sit in the back."

Blair slammed the door on Ruby's round hips. In the back, she rolled down the window and stuck her head out so as not to have to listen to Ruby's crooning. Something was up. Ruby was either trying to seduce him or trying to make him fear she was trying to seduce him. Either way it was bad news. When Oswald opened the back door his eyes met Blair's in silent alarm.

"He left a message at the desk. He's gonna meet us up there."

Nobody was as interested in this lawyer as Oswald was. The other three resisted the idea of being "managed" by anyone. One of their favourite mocking words was "organized." Anyone who looked too organized was a joke.

"I don't know why we're heading up there so *early*," said Ruby. "There's no place to go."

"It's crazy to drive that road in the dark. And we've got to set up. There's some rooms. The dormitories for the staff in winter. It's all empty now. They said we could get ready there."

Philip took the back route, crossing the tracks in the flat area by the river's marshy widening and missing the traffic circle. They wheeled onto the Trans-Canada, heading east this time, and took the turn up the steep hill to Norquay. The road wound around the rocky outcrops into the thick trees at the bottom of the mountain.

The first hairpin turn took them out of sight of the highway, the town, the hotel, and into the towering black-green firs. Philip's heavily muscled arms hauled the steering wheel first this way and then that. He geared down, as the van toiled angrily. It was a long way up. They passed the Timberline Hotel, where two mountain sheep stood, or maybe it was one, reflected in the plate glass window.

"*You* guys have to set up, but we don't have anything to do," continued Ruby, whining.

"You'd be smart to take a nap."

"Oh shut up, little mother." Still lying on her back, Ruby slid one leg up and down the other, like a fly, making the black tights hiss.

"When's he coming?" Blair said to Oswald, not because she was keen to meet this man from Toronto, but because she wanted not to see Ruby. She had begun to think they *would* need something to keep the group together.

It was chilly at six-thirty at the Mount Norquay Lodge. The top of the downhill ski run, another few thousand feet above, was rock and grass; about halfway down was the tree line, and the little spiky firs began. Blair walked out onto the lower slope. The ground was spongy moss. From her height, the moss looked smooth, like a carpet, but when she bent over she could see it was made of tiny blue-and-white stars on top of bristled stems. The smell of pine and cedar was so rich, she wandered, breathing deeply, trying to forget Ruby's weird behaviour. She had gone to lie down now. Maybe she'd be over it when she woke up.

She turned and looked back at the lodge. Made of narrow, varnished logs, it ran long and low across the bottom of the slope. Most often it sat on snow, covered with snow; now, with the green everywhere, it seemed to have come alive and to be growing out of the ground itself. A car pulled into the parking lot beside, spitting gravel. Soon the early ones would begin to arrive, as darkness fell.

From this car a man, tall, with very wide shoulders, emerged. He looked first up the slope and then back at the trees, as if he had never been here before. His eyes stopped at Blair. When she did not move or signal, he turned away and strode toward the clubhouse, strode deliberately, but halted once, as if he would rather have turned around and come out to her. Then he kept on.

This was the lawyer, she decided.

She turned and walked farther, to where the first rocks began.

In the dormitory, there were six beds, with space between them for cheap, narrow bureaus. Cotton curtains were pulled against the twilight, which was now a powerful blue-grey, the colour of stormy lake water. This colour absorbed the pines that stood at intervals, like symmetrical ink spots, on the open slopes from which Blair had just come. She touched the curtains: a puff of dust rose around her hand. She threw down her garment bag and her purse; she flipped on the bathroom light and realized that it was too weak to allow her to properly put on make-up. She flipped it off again and, enjoying the sinking day and the rising bird noises from the forest, dropped down on the nearest bed, stretched out, and put her arm over her eyes.

Her heart was beating fast. It was a matter of hours until they played. They'd warm up soon, in an hour at most, change, and that would be it. She tried to find again the joy, the sense of rightness in time and place that had visited her that afternoon on Tunnel Mountain. She breathed in and out, calming herself, claiming her happiness as one does before it ends. As she lay, she became aware of noise nearby—whispered voices, the creaking of a floor or bed, muffled giggles. Philip's rumble of resistance.

So Ruby was making good her promise to seduce him. That was Blair's first thought. But the sounds were not those of contented congress. If she tried, she had failed: what seemed to be going on instead was a lot of whispering, and horseplay with anger mixed in.

Again the anxiety, even fear, rose in her chest. It was against their code. It could ruin everything. The family that was Hearts of Flame was for her a perfect haven, a safe house. Outside lovers were the rule, and even they were barely tolerated. There wasn't time. That did not trouble Blair: the men could avail themselves of stage-door groupies in one place or another. Encounters with fans were encouraged, especially when the group moved on the next day.

But not this.

She blamed Ruby. Ruby being trouble. Ruby wanting possession, wanting *in* from the outside. Forcing herself on people the way she felt entitled to. She *deserved* Philip, she believed, because of some deprivation, because she'd had to fight for everything else; she would be *good* for Philip, she thought.

And—Blair forced herself to know this, though the idea had lain dormant in her memory for a year at least, and she had not let it grow—besides all of that, Ruby was in love with Philip. She covered her face more tightly with her arm, as if the idea had a physical presence, as if it stood there in front of her. How dare she! Philip was *hers* (though not in that way); he was *theirs* (the group's); he was *nobody's* (a father, a leader). He was not for Ruby. Not for the adoration of one round and pleasing and easy little body, Ruby Mason.

But she loved him. Adored him. Gazed at him with lust and greed. Criticized him and mocked him savagely. Saw her longings spurned and, worse, ignored. It was, Blair dimly recognized, for all the things Ruby pretended to despise in him that she wanted him: his comfortable upbringing, his familiarity with powerful people, his assumption of position, his high mindedness, his held-back passions.

Even as these thoughts, like words buried in cloud, floated half-articulated across her mind, the noise changed. The voices stilled. There was a rhythmic squeak of bedsprings. Moaning, a half-laugh, and more animal noises.

Blair lifted her arm off her eyes and stared straight up at the ceiling. A flush began between her collarbones and moved slowly up to her face. Was it what it sounded like? Were they truly, honestly doing it?

Blair was innocent, by precise definition a virgin, though not entirely untried. But these botched, interrupted and ultimately unsuccessful acts of love, like eruptions from some interior well guarded and armoured, had been rapidly suppressed. It was a standing joke, Blair's propriety. The others asked her what she was waiting for. Saving yourself for marriage? A great insult that was, and not even true. She did not feel she was saving herself for anything except for that time when she was ready. She believed that making love would move her into a new country. And for now, she liked being where she was.

The noises in the next room accelerated. The walls were only made of struts with pine across; there were cracks below and above the door. Blair might as well be in the same room as the lovers. Sound was all around her, filling her with shame, with revulsion, with embarrassment. She bit her arm, stopping the words with her flesh. *Ruby! Ruby! You slut! I hate you! Stop it!* She could not move. There seemed no way to stop them. She remembered the dogs, in the wide streets at home. They used to pour buckets of cold water over their backs to separate them. She could not get up and get out, either; something held her. His voice, letting out sounds without control. Her coos and murmurs, the shifting of weight on ancient, creaky bedsprings. Blair began to try to picture how they lay, in what position, what she was *doing* to him, and he to her.

Ruby must be on top. Philip she imagined helpless, on his back, called by biological imperative rather than will, or even desire, bemused. *He*, the Philip who was Blair's property, the kindly leader, the enabler, the warbler, with his hollow, pear-shaped bass before him.

Blair began to cry. The noises of congress continued. Was this how long it took? She had no idea. It seemed it was an hour since she'd lain down here. At least her own crying blocked her ears a little. But the noises became more intrusive to make up for it, building. They were off the bed now, and somewhere else—up against the wall, perhaps—and they were making little cries of pain, grunting disgustingly. At last Blair rolled away, blocking her ears and screaming.

"Stop it! Stop it!"

But she was not loud enough to disturb them. They were fighting like dogs. An end was coming, and the noise was dreadful. She leapt off the bed as Philip's siren-like shriek came. Ruby, the noisier one until now, seemed suddenly to have been swallowed. Philip growled. He began, it seemed, to cry. The sound pursuing her, Blair ran the length of the dormitory and threw open the door.

There on the step, hand out to the doorknob, were Oswald and the tall, curly-haired man, who must be the lawyer. She raised the back of her hand to wipe her smeared face, then wiped it on the side of her blue jeans. Oswald, filled with the energy of his plans, took a moment to assess Blair's state. But the tall man instantly reached an arm to steady her.

"What's the matter? A bear chasing you?"

"This is Max Ostriker from Toronto," said Oswald, too correctly.

Blair tore her arm away from the man. His kindness she could not tolerate. It was likely to set off torrents of she knew not what kind of grief. They all stared at each other, held motionless by a sense of happening. The air was expectant. The silence could not hold any longer.

It was nearly dark, seven o'clock. Across the gravel parking area, where the road emerged from trees, car headlights swept, set after set of them, as the audience began to arrive. They would sit out and drink, and then go inside to get a good seat. For once, Blair wished she were one of them.

"We've gotta talk," said Oswald. "Let us in."

Blair blocked the doorway. "Somewhere else," she said.

"There *is* a bear," said the affable Max. Oswald pushed her arm off the door frame.

Max now faced her. He was as shocked as she was, but by her nearness, and her fright. Until now he'd seen only the publicity shots, in black-and-white, where she looked cold, an ice queen. But here she was in colour, brown and pink, russet in her eyes and skin, all of her face much darker than that white-blond hair, which seemed to take on a night light, though there was no moon. Something happened, in the pit of his stomach: thud, a space opened. Visceral knowledge: I recognize you. You are in my future. Then nothing. It was forgotten.

"Don't," Blair's voice scratched, imperative. Behind her from the other room now the men could hear sounds of reorganization.

"Who's in there?"

"*They* are."

Oswald and Blair locked eyes. He was shorter than she was, and guarded. He did not show his fear, or his love, if he felt such things. Oswald and Blair were not friends. They were too severe, each of them needing the others as buffer to share a laugh, to make music. Force them too close together and they would repel each other. But they were both aware, they knew. Now this thing had happened. It would change everything.

Max watched as Oswald and Blair held looks of blank acknowledgement. He did not understand. That was all right with him. He fell back a few steps, put his hands in his pockets and gazed upward. The patches of snow at the top of the rocky summits had turned a ghostly blue in the twilight. At this time of year, the nights should be long, but these mountains swallowed the sun, letting it travel only halfway across the sky.

Oswald had Blair by the arms. She was crying. Max squinted at the ground: "*Heavy,*" he whispered. "*Heavy.*" He did not want to witness this, but he felt a tug. To be in this foursome, so bound by feeling.

Behind Blair in the now dark dormitory a door opened. Ruby and Philip emerged, Ruby swaggering, flushed and rosy. Philip looked sideways, he did not meet eyes, he slouched. Ruby came to the doorway, her face catching the last remaining outdoor light. She too touched Blair's arm, but Blair jerked it away.

"What the fuck—" said Ruby, grabbing her friend's purse. "You got my cigarettes in there? I know you took them off me."

"Get out of my bag!"

Blair stepped off the porch at last, breaking the bottleneck there, and walked away into the gloom.

Ruby got a cigarette from Oswald and lit it, leaning on the door frame. The red end glowed, sullen. Philip pushed past them both and sat down on the step.

"Max is here. We've gotta talk business," said Oswald. "He's got news."

"Not good news, I take it," said Philip.

"I think we should talk after the concert," said Max quickly. "Hey! You guys have gotta get up there and make music. You probably need to break or something now, don't you?"

"This *was* a break," said Philip. His voice carried in the darkness. Thirty feet away and almost invisible, Blair heard it. She picked up the tone, and it pleased her. Philip bitter, feeling used. Philip disclaiming responsibility. Philip sorry. It wasn't his fault. For a moment her heart lifted.

"We gotta get out there and warm up."

"There's a couple of songs to go over."

"I'll just sit in the back and listen, you do your thing," said Max happily.

The others were assembled, testing their levels, tuning their instruments, when Blair walked in, her face suffused with the darkness she'd come from. Without a word she found her guitar and began to play chords, one after another, while walking in a circle. She spoke to nobody. Everyone knew she had been injured in some way: no one quite understood how. Philip called the songs and they set the first few chords together. All but Ruby were stiff-faced; Ruby, her bow-lips turned down, danced and shimmered in her own orgy of sadness.

"That was the shortest warm-up on record."

"Who cares?" Blair stepped loudly off the stage, walking

the length of the aisle, past Max and out the door. Oswald quickly went to Max's side. Head to head the two sat talking, Oswald nodding eagerly every few seconds. Philip became highly engrossed in a faulty string on his bass, ignoring Ruby. She sat down abruptly on the edge of the stage, like a marionette whose strings had been dropped.

"It was good," she whispered to Philip.

He acted as if he didn't hear.

Ruby parted her legs and began to examine the beginnings of a run coming in the crotch-piece of her tights.

"Really good. You're good, Philip. I never thought you had it in you."

His head jerked around furiously, causing his glasses to slide down his nose.

"Shut up, Ruby."

She turned her leg inward, then outward, admiring its black shape. His tone was rough, she was tempting fate. Anger would mean, perhaps, he loved her. She stood up and walked over to stand directly in front of him.

"I've wanted to do that for a long time," she said, her eyes moist.

He bent over the bridge of his bass, hiding from her.

"You want to all the time. With anyone. It's nothing special."

Ruby tried to keep smiling. She licked her lips. A muscle in her neck twitched.

"It is," she said, stepping forward. She touched his neck. The wooden swells of the bass were between them. She stroked its curved edge. "I love you."

Behind her, Oswald approached the stage. "Guys," he said, "we've gotta talk." He wanted to end the trouble, separate them.

"After. We're talking after," said Philip, motionless, his face close to the strings.

"Yeah, we're talking after, but Max has some news about

Toronto."

Ruby turned slowly to Oswald. Her face was wild and still, a knot coming undone. He backed off. She turned to Philip again, determined. If she couldn't make him kind, she would make him cruel.

"I said I love you."

He slammed the neck of his bass against his palm. The slap of wood on flesh was like an assault, it was as if he'd struck her face. Then deliberately, moving surely, he set the instrument on its stand, kicked a wire out of his way, grabbed Ruby by the upper arm with hard, tense fingers and yanked her back into the wings.

"You slut!" he shouted. "Don't talk that shit to me. I'm sorry that I did it. I never meant to. It was only because you teased me."

Ruby began to laugh, wildly, though water streamed from her eyes.

"Let me go!"

And when he didn't she went cold and still. "I never meant it either. I wanted to see if you were human," she said. "Or if there was something wrong with you."

The lodge was absolutely silent. Their voices, at least the rage in them, could be heard at the back of the hall, where Oswald and Max now stood, nervous, pretending to talk. Oswald was furious. It seemed to him they were doing this deliberately to foil his plan to get the group good management. He had just told Max how solid they were, like brothers and sisters.

"A family squabble?" said the smiling Max. "Happens all the time in the business, right? You stay in close quarters. On top of each other, right? And a show practically every night. You'd be better to allow yourself a little time . . ." He held himself back, a big, dominant man being careful. His gentleness was practised, as was his air of knowingness. In fact, he strained with a well-trained ear to catch the meaning of the passionate exchange backstage.

"*You're* the one who's not human," said Philip to Ruby, back on intellectual grounds, where he knew he could beat her. He dropped her arm and blew a long, escaped hair from his ponytail away from his mouth. Sweat stood out on his forehead, already too high and getting higher. "You're not like a woman, anyway. You're like a—like an animal in heat."

She took his stated hatred; it splashed over the acted love, burning. She pulled her hands inside the cuffs of her shirt and stood that way, helpless, like a child waiting for more punishment; it was the attention she needed.

"Always bugging me. Always telling me what to do." He was expert with his damage, his cruelty. Ruby felt the full force of it. It ran over her like scalding water. She almost smiled, but the pain stopped her.

"I love you, I love you," she repeated idiotically, until he reached out and cuffed the side of her face, as a bear would a cub, solidly, less with malice than brute force.

"There," he said. "I told you. Don't say that. You *don't* love anyone. You're not that kind of woman. You're not the kind of woman any man loves. You're like—someone to have as a mistress. That's you, Ruby. Get used to it."

Philip was gone. Ruby lay on the wooden floor backstage, her hands between her legs, crooning. It was completely dark outside and the crowds were gathering. Oswald and Max had given up, they were out somewhere drinking. Blair returned, her hair damp where she'd splashed her face. She stood above Ruby and prodded her with her toe.

"Get up. You've gotta be in shape to go on." Her voice was calm now.

"I'm okay, I'm all right," Ruby whispered. "Are they out there, are they all out there yet?"

The four ran to their instruments in semi-darkness.

Oswald hit a chord on the keyboard; instantly his fingers began their spidery dance. The lights burst on, the song exploded into life. Cheering rose up over the lights, the gulf between stage and seats. Each one alone felt the light hit his face, and lifted to it his best self. Blair took the microphone from the stand. She heard Philip's soft growl begin behind her and threw her voice over it gladly; she turned him a radiant face and blew a kiss.

The clapping began, rhythmic, warming. People stood in their seats, not to sit down again for the duration. Ruby began to shimmy and glow and bang that tambourine. It was beginning. They could do it. Once more from the top.

After the crowd pressed out into the night, lighting up, finding their bottles, waiting for the midnight dance. Some took off dangerously down the mountain road, unmuffled engines banging into the sweet, silent forest. The techies came onstage to set up amplifiers for the disc jockey. Oswald and a helper had barely disconnected their own. Philip moved the black van up to the end door of the hall, for loading. They were alone now. They'd delivered, and were cast off. The euphoria out there, caught from the music, seemed to exclude them.

It was cold, and there were mosquitoes. Someone stumbled along the road ahead of the van's lights, then went off into a ditch.

"Better watch out, there's bears," muttered Philip. It was the first thing anyone had said. He was driving, as always, but recklessly. Max followed in his car. No one said anything.

At the Rundle, Blair and Ruby sat on one bed, leaning back on the pillows. Oswald sat on the floor cross-legged, blocking the door, and Philip stood, a darkness, a shadow in which he moved heavily, making them all give way. Max sat on the little linoleum table set out with the motel's tin coffee pot.

Everyone but Blair was smoking and drinking. It was one-thirty in the morning.

"So the Toronto concert isn't going to go—it's off," Max began.

"What do you mean, it's off?"

"Not enough advance sales. The backers pulled out. We can't keep Varsity Stadium without them."

"You came all the way out here to tell us this?"

"That was your job, selling tickets. That's what Oswald said."

"It's easier said than done. You're not so well known down there."

"Look at tonight. They love us."

"They've gotta know that first, before they buy."

"We sing. We travel. *You* get the concerts going," said Philip.

"It's the numbers. If we haven't got the numbers, we can't do it. You gotta understand something that simple."

Oswald watched as his fellow singers attacked Max. He drummed his fingertips on the floor. It wasn't working. They had been drawn together by the show but now they were falling apart again. It was like looking at a vandalized painting, slashed in the middle. The edges curled; the figures in it rolled in on themselves, away from each other.

Ruby was the first person to move.

"If Toronto's off," she said, kicking one leg out to lift her torso from its reclining position, "what else is? Winnipeg? Niagara Falls?"

"Winnipeg should be all right."

"L.A.? The album?"

She stood beside the bed yanking her tights.

"Don't fidget," Blair snapped. "We *see* your legs, okay? This is serious, Ruby. You're just, you're just—"

"Just not good enough for all this, am I? Just not one of you? Is that what you were going to say?"

"I don't know why we need some guy from Toronto to take this on and then come out and tell us we've got no fans down there," said Philip slowly. "This was a dumb idea, Oswald. This guy's no good."

Blair reached out and punched Ruby in the shoulder. Then she put her hands over her face again and started to cry.

"If you hadn't of done that with Philip none of this would be happening. It's wrecked everything," she sobbed.

Ruby threw her hands up in the air and groaned. "Can you believe this? The woman thinks a little sex is the cause of all evil. You're as bad as my mother."

Philip stepped forward out of the darkness and put his hand on Blair's shoulder. She went quiet. Oswald looked through them all, out the back window, into the scrubby black pines behind the motel.

"Hold everything," said Max, still agreeable, still even. "If I've stepped into some family business here I'll get right out. But if you want, I could help you. I can see what you guys need is a little proper management."

Three of them groaned in unison.

"You've got a terrific sound. You look super on stage. Nothin's gonna hold you back, once we get these pieces in place."

They looked at him as if he were speaking Chinese. Oswald was grim and fierce; he cared little for Ruby's tricks but he took it personally: they were doing this to stop his plan. His plan, which would make the band big, lead to a breakthrough. The others only wanted to play and play and have everybody hear them. Only Oswald knew what dull work had to be done first.

Ruby kicked the bed and began to laugh.

"So it's all my fault, is it? The whole damn thing's gonna fall apart, and it'll be my fault—"

"Shut up, Ruby! This isn't about you. You're nothing!"

"You can't speak to me like that. You can't." She looked defiant, and full of power. Everyone was afraid of her. She felt it.

"You can't even sing," said Philip. "We don't need you."

But they all knew they did.

"She'll quit, that's what she'll do," said Oswald.

"We don't need her. She never could sing," repeated Philip.

"You do," said Max. "You need what she adds."

"The expert?" said Blair, not daring to go further and tell Max to get out of there.

Ruby began to shake, so hard it was like vibrating. She closed her eyes. Blair was worried, despite herself. "You look like those people you see in revival halls, possessed by devils," she said quietly to her friend.

Philip laughed.

"Lay off her," said Blair.

"Lay off is right," said Max, getting up off his chair. "I move we put this all off till tomorrow morning. Afternoon, even. Talk some more. Maybe we can work something out."

"She'll quit," Philip repeated, staring at Ruby as if he could make her just by saying it.

Ruby turned her hands inside her cuffs. Her head dropped. "Shut up, Philip."

"No, I won't shut up. Ruby's out. She broke the rules. She's trouble anyway and she can't sing."

"You broke the rules too," said Blair to Philip.

"We need Ruby—"

Max was at the door. "Goodbye, Hearts of Flame," he said. "See you tomorrow."

"If there still *is* a Hearts of Flame tomorrow," said Blair, bitterly, to him. Max shut the door behind him. Ruby jumped up and ran after him. Blair could see out the window. Max put his large, protecting arm around Ruby and they walked away.

Philip stepped out of his own shadow. "I've got a feeling," he said. "This was it. Our last concert."

Everyone sat, stunned. Philip had made them; Philip could unmake them. Everyone was too angry to argue.

3

Whatever Ruby Wants

At the Coffee Express the walls were deep grey, and the tables black triangles up around the level of armpits. You perched on the edge of high stools and leaned your elbows on the table. Glass canisters named after impoverished Caribbean regions—Black Mountain, Jamaican Dark—or methods of extraction—Swiss Water Decaffeinated—were stacked against the wall.

"Herman, Christ," said a woman in a black pillbox hat, banging the receiver of the pay telephone back onto its hook. "Christ, Herman. I'm trying to get through." She put her finger into the worn metal cup and dragged out her quarter. She gave the machine a good shove before she plugged it again. She pulled a veil over her eyes, twisted the tight, short skirt of her suit and pressed the numbers again. She dropped her jaw, listening, and dangled the receiver from two fingers. Still busy.

Her frustration matched the obsessive rap song that bounced off the hard walls into the empty air. Ruby was jittery too. The crusts of toasted European sandwiches lay on her plate. Ruby sipped her coffee and crossed her right leg over her left.

You never knew what Ruby would look like on a given day. Today she was elfin, in an antique jacket made of a fine and elderly silk velvet, fitted at the waist and flared over black leggings. It looked vaguely like the skating dresses kids wore in 1955. She was rounded, buxom, and tapered down to delicate ankles and wrists. Despite the hot wall of sun that fell in the plate glass window from the Queen Street pavement, she looked cool, inhumanly so. Across from her, in jeans and tweed hacking jacket over an Oxford cloth shirt, Blair steamed. The peace and satisfaction she'd felt in the ravine was gone. She did not want to be here. Ruby had summoned her. Now her whole day felt disrupted.

"It was Simplicity's first day of school. She clung to the side of the car when I dropped her off. And here's all these decked-out mums in their baby jeeps. How they get their make-up on before eight-thirty in the morning is beyond me. All their kids trotting along looking so sweet and happy, and Simplicity sets up this roar, hangs off the doorhandle, it's like I'm trying to have her killed! Why didn't God give me a normal child?"

"There are no normal children."

"Sure there are. What about those other little things in their brand new Roots sweats tumbling around in the schoolyard? They're not clinging to their mother's car."

"Everyone knows any little kid who's well-adjusted in grade one is going to grow up to be a bore! It's only the weird ones who are worth keeping alive. Remember me when I was a kid? Bottom of the pecking order."

They both remembered. Ruby coming in to the flat-roofed suburban school in her country clothes, Ruby fighting off bullies with her dirty fists. Ruby, who peed her pants because she was afraid to put up her hand. "There's a background," the mothers used to cluck, though no one ever defined the background in words.

"The absolute bottom," said Blair cheerily. She didn't mince words; it was a point of pride with Ruby now. "You look great," she said, taking in Ruby's pale chic. "Is that new? I haven't bought a thing to wear this year."

"What's the matter? Punishing yourself?"

"Would that I had something to punish myself for."

Their laughter whooped up over the table. The waitress, with a dark red ponytail on top of her head and a black T-shirt painfully spattered with neon, looked up from her book and raised an eyebrow. The music, and the café's clatter and squawk, seemed designed to block out the sound of a human voice, but then Ruby's had always been peculiarly penetrating. The waitress raised her eyebrows at Blair.

"An affair would do you good."

"What would Sissy say if she came into my room in the morning and a man was there?"

"I dunno. Hello?"

Blair frowned. Ruby put on this insensitivity to irritate her. "Anyway, I don't want to get *involved*."

"You don't have to get *involved* to have an affair, God knows. Try an m-squared."

"That's not for me," said Blair. She had to be careful what she said. Ruby proselytized for the married man solution. "For a big city, this place is awful small. People find out. People talk."

Here was a point of agreement. "It's not just that they talk," said Ruby, dramatically shifting her legs to the other plane of her triangular seat. "They actually *mind*."

"They do. They're not just gossips. They're *moral*. I think they disapprove of sex, actually," said Blair.

"Don't want to think anyone's having any fun they haven't paid for!"

"No sir," said Blair. They whooped again. Toronto-bashing united them in a rude salute to the place to which they were irresistibly drawn. First Ruby, then Blair had made her way here from the coulees of Southern Alberta, where they used to lie against the banks and dream big city dreams.

But Ruby's laughter caught. Her eyes took on a glint. She was in one of her dangerous moods. She got like this, prodding, poking at sore places and soft spots, looking for mischief, like a vicious gremlin, when something was wrong.

"Still, you can't let a little gossip stop you from getting what you need."

Blair resolved to steer away from difficulty. She looked out the window onto Queen Street. That day, all over the city, people had appeared selling peacock feathers for one dollar each. She wondered if the feathers were real, and where they had come from. She wondered where all the plundered peacocks were, these legions of tailless male birds. In front of her a shopper had tied his sweater around his waist and was perusing the stall in his "Guardian of the Rainforest" T-shirt.

"I'm not buying a single thing this fall," said Blair again. "No money. I'm sick of being a consumer, anyway."

"How am I supposed to stay in business when everyone talks like you? Everyone is exhausted by their own extravagance. *Spent.* Literally and figuratively." She drummed her nails on the black triangle table. "I can feel it, you know? Something's coming. Some . . . downturn."

Again Blair veered, afraid of tapping Ruby's pool of misery, her millennial superstitions. Her unhappiness, when it came, shaped itself around a belief that the world would end in greed, corruption and violence. Maybe it was guilt, coming from her upbringing at the hands of a raging fundamentalist, her subsequent rejection of rules. Ruby's unhappiness: not many people saw it, but it was there, built up, fuelling every move she made. One day the pain in Ruby would erupt, scalding everyone in range.

"It sure is warm! Just like summer."

Not fooled, Ruby gave Blair a withering look.

"Oh yeah, it's warm, but don't you think it's a strange,

unnerving kind of warmth? Greenhouse. It's not like warm weather, it's like *heating*. Artificial."

When Ruby got going, she was deadly. She could do just about any subject. Or more like any opinion: facts were not something she collected. She was what they called on radio "a good talker." Blair had promised to have her on the show, but somehow she'd never got around to inviting her.

"We don't actually have weather in Toronto. You know, sunrise is over there at the Scarborough Centre. Sunsets, well that happens in those red brick walk-ups out Bloor Street. The only wind we get comes from the highrises and—"

"You need a break. Go to Tuscany for a couple of weeks."

Ruby came to a dead halt. "With who?" she said gloomily. "Travel takes time and money. People who have one don't have the other. Besides, this is my absolute busiest time."

"You see? You're your own worst enemy. Work, work."

Ruby stuck her legs out in front of the booth and examined pointed ankle-boots with a malevolent eye.

"Should I have another capuccino?"

"If that's what you need."

"What do I need, what do I need, what do I need?" chanted Ruby.

"I hear what you need for the '90s is three things: a baby, a jeep and grey hair."

"Not me," said Ruby. "What I need is a new face, thinner thighs and somebody else's husband."

"Your thighs are perfect."

"Are they?" said Ruby, with a great wide grin, thrusting one leg forward, picking up Blair's hand and putting it on top of the muscle. "Squeeze."

Blair squeezed. "Perfect."

The grin, startling and game, faded instantly.

"You know you can buy the thighs now," said Blair. "There's a figure salon in Yorkville where you can exercise electrically and get nine hours' worth in one hour."

"Great concept. I'd like to get nine hours' worth of anything in one hour." Ruby waved at the waitress, who remained engrossed in her book, the tail on the top of her head vibrating in the breeze from the fan.

"You want to get back to work?"

"Not right away."

"You wanna walk a bit?"

"Sure."

They stood up and rattled their purses until the waitress finally bestirred herself. Ruby took a toothpick from beside the cash register and began to chew on it.

"Did I tell you why Max cancelled? He was standing on the platform at Bloor and Yonge when a woman jumped." Ruby had gone even paler. "I'd love to know what was on her mind when she did it." She stabbed out her cigarette in the metal dish. "I'd like to know how she geared herself up."

"Gives me the creeps," said Blair, stepping from the chill doorway into the sunlight. They began to walk south.

"I didn't know you still saw him. Max."

"Not much," said Ruby. "Not my type, nice guy though."

"I just remember he had a lot to do with our tour falling apart. I blamed him. You know, 'If it weren't for Max Ostriker, Hearts of Flame would still be alive and we'd be rich and famous.' That kind of thing." Now Blair remembered disquiet. Max had been Ruby's defender, hadn't he? *And I blamed you*, she thought. *You were so determined to get what you wanted.*

"He was a green kid. We all were," said Ruby.

They walked a little in silence, dodging the green kids of today, in leather and chains.

"So how is your m-squared?" said Blair cautiously.

"Oh he's fine."

"It seems weird you've been seeing him so long now, what, a year? And I've never met him."

"You saw him."

"I did?"

"In my office. When you brought the lunch the other day."

Blair remembered an elegantly dressed man with a long nose, large, sensuous, slightly crooked lips, a chalky white face, huge hands and a jangling, jumpy manner. "God, I didn't realize that was him."

"Yeah."

"No wonder he was so nervous. Thinks I disapprove."

"No, he's always like that," said Ruby.

They were nearly at King.

"The thing is, his wife found out."

"Oh no. When?"

Ruby's eyes were bright now, focussing on Blair, the air of preoccupation gone. "Last night. At last."

The sun was hot on their heads. Blair lifted her sunglasses and looked around. There was a bench set back from the street, beneath a skimpy, new-planted tree. "Come and sit," she said, taking charge. "Tell me about this."

Ruby followed.

"There's not much to tell. He fell asleep at my place and went home at four o'clock. When he came in she was sitting there waiting for him. Apparently she'd called the office and found out he wasn't there, and she just put it all together."

Sitting side by side with their feet stretched out, they both gazed across the street. Just down the block, past the construction site, an orange flashing light signalled the place where the city was digging up the sidewalk yet again. A sign over the streets read, "What's going on between Peter and John?" When Blair turned to Ruby she saw dark-green rectangles of her sunglasses. Reflected in them was the parking lot across the street, and the crane that was backing out of it.

"Now the shit has hit the fan." Ruby's tone combined satisfaction and fear. "She went berserk, I guess. Causing this most terrific scene. You can imagine. How he felt. He's really a very elegant person. Gentlemanly." She looked up.

"Anyway, she doesn't know my name."

Blair scowled down at the sidewalk. She imagined Marvin's too-white face, his impassivity even while twisting his wife's wrists.

"He's really such a gentleman," Ruby said, again. "He promised her not to see me while they're trying to work it out."

Blair shook her head. "But he will. You're going to see each other soon. Tomorrow, I bet."

"Right."

"So he's a double liar, now." Blair's casual tone was strained.

"Well, she asks for it. What a dumb thing to do, make him promise."

"Don't you see what he's doing, Ruby? He's trying to draw you into this drama. And moreover, he's shaming his wife."

Ruby spoke in a flat voice. "You see, you *are* a moralist."

Now Blair had to defend herself. "I'm not. I just—hate to see him doing this to both of you. Imagine. He's been married to this woman for how many years? He's supposed to love her."

"Well he doesn't. What can you do? He fell in love. He fell in love with me."

Blair groaned.

"Come on, Ruby, we're all grown-ups. I remember when he came to your booth at the festival. He followed you out. He kept coming in to the showroom. He set out deliberately to involve you in an affair. It's not as if Cupid came down from heaven and shot him with an arrow."

Ruby sighed. "I don't understand marriage. Imagine promising you'll never get the hots for anyone for your whole lifetime. It's obscene."

"What he's doing to his wife is obscene."

"He's very loyal to his wife. Until she found out about us I never heard a thing about her."

"He's deceiving her and she knows it. I'm in total sympathy

with her," said Blair hotly. She knew this amounted to betrayal of Ruby, but she didn't care, not at the moment.

"You don't know him. He's really very fond of her. He doesn't want to hurt her."

"He has hurt her. And now he's humiliating her on top of it. Why doesn't he just leave her?"

Ruby struck the bench with her hand. "He's tried! She says she'll kill herself! He can't bring himself!"

"Oh balls," said Blair. "Don't you believe it. If he's staying with her he's doing it for himself, not for her. He wants it both ways."

Ruby drew her feet up under the bench as if to stand.

"Well, who wouldn't?" she said. "I'd want it both ways, too, if I could have it."

They both stood up, half-turned toward each other, as if they were going to reach and touch, take away the anger. Blair wanted to rant. *Ruby, what are you doing? You're selling out women! You know better! You made your choice long ago not to have a husband. Now don't think you can just reach out now that it suits your fancy and grab someone else's. You've been so selfish all your life, you don't deserve a man.* But she said nothing.

"I know what you're going to say. I can't believe I'm arguing for the man," said Ruby, finally.

Blair looked at her friend. The corners of Ruby's once-celebrated bow-lips pulled this way and that, the worn lipstick line at the top and bottom wobbling. She tried to laugh. "I guess you're just—what's that expression people use—'in love with him'?"

"You didn't like him," said Ruby, still looking away. "You don't like love."

"I don't even know him. I don't like how he's behaving, is the point. It offends me." She left the second charge unanswered.

Ruby grew taller. "Good behaviour is very hard to define these days. I don't feel I should judge a fellow human being. I know he's in pain."

"I have no doubt he's in pain. He is, and so are two women, because of him."

They began to walk west on King, in the direction of Ruby's studio. Their two shadows ahead of them on the pavement jerked from side to side, merged with each other and the crowd.

"The problem is," said Ruby, coming around slightly, "that he wants someone else to make the decision."

"Of course."

"And then his wife is hanging on. But I refuse to ask him to leave her. I would never do that," she said.

Blair rolled her eyes. *Oh, virtue. She's rehearsed her position, checked it out with herself, found a way to make it okay. 'If I don't ever actually ask him to leave his wife, then I'm innocent.'* How painful it was, she thought, to listen to an intelligent woman deceive herself.

"It's not in my interest to ask him to leave. Then I'd be responsible. I'd have to be there for him if he leaves her. We're talking about a man I've never even been out to dinner with. I've never been on a date with him. I've never been on a holiday with him. All I've done is fuck the guy. It'd be practically like an arranged marriage."

Blair laughed. "He wants a sure thing. That's what these guys look for. That's how they do it. If they had any balls they'd decide whether their marriage was on or off before they went out and got involved with another woman."

Ruby said nothing.

"He's not the first guy to use an affair to keep his marriage together. There's a lot of them out there."

They were in front of Ruby's building now. Ruby's shoulders were high, tensed against attack. Blair followed her up the steps.

"You act as if I'm nothing. You act as if there's nothing going on between us." Ruby was rigid.

"Look, I know there's something going on," she said. She put her hand on Ruby's arm. It was hard, like rope. "I know he's in love with you and you with him." But she felt false when she said it. "In love." What was that supposed to mean?

"But he's married, he's been married to this woman for ten years. What that means is that everything they do relates to each other—even so-called falling in love with someone else. You're part of their marriage now. You're something he's doing to her, whether you like it or not. When he starts telling you what she's done to him, he's just trying to draw you in farther. People like this are dangerous."

"You know so much about marriage? After your big sixteen-month run?" Ruby was up one stair, above Blair. Her mascara was smeared. Her lips were trembling. She stopped herself.

"I can't go in like this," she said. She opened her handbag and took out another cigarette. She backed up and sat on the edge of a wide concrete planter. She lit her cigarette, drawing composure as she exhaled out of the side of her mouth.

"He told me we'd go to Africa. He said we'd have to buy a house, my place was too small. I love him. I understand him. His wife doesn't understand him at all." Suddenly she began to cry.

Blair scrabbled in her purse for a kleenex. The tears, more than anything, shocked her. Never in their thirty years of friendship had she seen Ruby cry. Not when the kids threw mudballs at her at recess. Not when Philip rejected her love that long-ago night in Banff. Not when Hearts of Flame broke up. Not when, in the intervening lifetime, she teetered on the edge of bankruptcy, or a new design line failed, or even when she was "discovered," and praise rained down on her. Now she was crying about this Marvin, or she appeared to be. For months she'd been flippant, mocking him—his complexion, his chin, the way he mixed up expressions. Saying she didn't care how many wives he had, as long as she got him in bed twice a week. This man, *this*, made her cry.

After all these years—Ruby was nearly forty though she looked twenty-six—all these years of flaunted independence, it turned out she wanted a man. Of course he happened to be someone else's. He was no prince, either, but then *who* he was seemed almost irrelevant. It wasn't the man himself but what the man could offer: an excuse to let down, a safe harbour. Respite Blair steadfastly refused herself.

The other thing Ruby wanted, Blair thought, as she found a kleenex in relatively good condition and handed it over, was to *beat* this other woman. Why should she bother? Ruby, after all, was Ruby Mason. Why did she have to prove she was better than some nameless, no doubt downtrodden wife? Some freight train of anger was coming in to the station, overburdened with reapings of the years of Ruby the strong, Ruby the free, Ruby the lone.

"If it's winning you want," she said, as Ruby blew her nose, "this isn't even the way to do it. You're just asking to get stuck in a threesome. Refuse to see him, until he's left her. That's your only power."

"I did that once," Ruby said. "For a whole week. He said it was terribly painful for him. Then I felt sorry for him, so I said I'd meet him for lunch."

"Sure it was terribly painful. But the next week would have been less. And a few weeks later the whole thing would have been over."

"Discipline," sniffed Ruby. "Control. Management of emotions. Those are all your virtues. Not mine." She wiped her eyes. "Not mine."

They rode up in the padded elevator with a rack of sequined tops from Hong Kong. The sequins got off at the second floor, and their bearer, a short, bearded man sweating profusely in a khaki shirt, pushed them off down the hallway. At the third floor Ruby strode off the elevator and opened the door with "deBoltz Designs" on it, pushing it behind her so Blair caught it with her shoulder. She swung past the desk where Audrey sat, her hand automatically grabbing a sheaf of pink telephone message slips, carelessly, the way you might, walking down a path, pull off the top fronds of a fern.

Blair trailed behind. *She doesn't care about her business any more. Her famous bloody business which she burnt up the last fifteen years of her life to build. She absolutely doesn't give a hoot about it any more. She has become someone else while I've not noticed.*

Ruby dropped into the chair behind her desk.

"I'm not interested in getting over him. I don't want to behave well. I'm not thinking about the wife. I'm not thinking about anyone else. I'm thinking about me," said Ruby tiredly.

"That's nothing new."

Ruby smiled. Her chin went forward, and her face changed. It became concave, like the mocking face drawn in a crescent moon. She had always done that, as if she enjoyed being insulted.

"Who else should I think about? His wife? You think his wife is sacrosanct. Because she's a sacrificer. She's not, okay? She got something out of it all this time. She looked after herself. This idea that everyone should stay away from wives' turf is crap. If people are miserable in their marriages they should get out. Maybe they don't behave perfectly while they're trying to do it, but who cares?"

"Say that again," said Blair.

"If this woman was fool enough to stay with him ten years there's nothing I can do."

As always, Blair could not stand up to her.

"I don't know why we're having this fight," she said, moving away from the front of the desk. "Whatever you do, I'm on your side."

Ruby stared for a minute, as if she were going to argue. Then she blew out her cheeks. "The Blair cop-out. How well I know it," she said. She went to open the door onto the roof. "It's so hot in here. Let's get some air."

"You need air-conditioning."

"Have it. Hate it," she said. "Destroys your skin. Do you want some water before you go?"

Blair said yes.

Ruby walked to the little fridge in the corner and pulled out two bottles of Evian. She twisted off the tops and stuck a straw in each one. She walked back across the office. Her walk was self-conscious, sinuous, dangerous.

"I have to go," said Blair. "Give me that water."

"The thing you're forgetting," Ruby said to Blair, handing her the bottle, "is that he doesn't love her."

"Don't tell me we're back on love."

"I helped him find his spiritual side. Another dimension. He said I changed his life. His whole way of looking at life. He said he couldn't live without me."

Blair had a flash of sympathy for this man, about whom she knew so little. "You do take hold and tell people what they ought to do," she said, half in fear.

"It's all I ever had," she said. "The power in myself."

Blair was silent. For a moment, she could see Ruby's little house by the highway outside Medicine Hat. Blair used to drive up outside in her Volkswagen and wait until Ruby came out. She never did talk to her mother. She was afraid to, this wide, ferocious woman in her strange, flowered wrap with the billowing sleeves. Arthur, her tall, angry brother with his narrow eyes, looking as if he wanted to stop his sister from going out into the world. But Ruby came to high school in a different outfit every day: she must have spent every penny she could get her hands on on clothes. Blair put down the water. Her hands were clenched, her nails biting her palms. Ruby had the power to create, but also to destroy. Ruby didn't always get what she wanted. But if she wanted something, and she couldn't get it, by the time she was through, it wasn't worth wanting any more. Look at Philip.

"Poor Marvin. He probably doesn't know what hit him."

Ruby laughed, without mirth.

Blair went for the door.

"You know, the other night I was so worked up I actually called my mum," said Ruby. Blair shot her a glance. "She'd been calling me, asking me if I had some kind of trouble or something. So I got on the long-distance phone and I told her. And do you know what my mother said? She said, 'Oh Ruby, where is God in your life?'"

She waited. "Can you imagine that? What a cruel thing to say to your daughter."

Blair stood for a second by the door. But she didn't leave.

"I mean, talk about vicious," Ruby prodded. She raised her voice, imitating a gospel preacher. "Oh Ruby, where is God in your life?"

"Why is that so cruel?"

"Oh, it's just putting me off. Refusing to accept my world." Ruby had her baleful look on.

"I guess it's—what works for her," said Blair. She couldn't defend Ruby's mother now.

"What are you talking about? You don't even know her."

"What does Oswald say?" said Blair, as a last resort. "Is he still advising you?"

Ruby glared. "Oswald," she said. "What do you care?" Her mouth was hard, her nostrils flared in a face Blair knew only too well. It was the Ruby of Hearts of Flame, the face in the spotlight. Taunting, direct, with a grin that split open a face all pleasure, all innocence. But there was something else, a gleam you could just catch before it disappeared. Trouble, Philip used to say. "Ruby's face says trouble." It said more to Blair. Ruthless defiance. All Ruby for Ruby's sake. A will to be, past reason.

As Blair went out the door she looked back and saw that her friend was smiling, that there were tears in her eyes and she was not angry, not angry with Blair at least, not any more.

4

Not Available to Answer Your Call

Morning, but so dark it might be dusk. Simplicity slid out of bed and went into her mum's bedroom. It was seven-thirty. Blair was asleep.

"Can I come under?"

Her mum grunted, okay.

It was hard to lift the duvet while she was sitting on it, but she managed, sliding down inside the warm. She put her arm over her mother's chest. It went up and down with her breath.

Blair rolled toward her and put her arms around her. "Morning, darling."

She put her arms around her mum's neck. They hugged. Then her mum got heavy again. A long time passed.

"You're lying on my hand," whispered Sissy.

Blair moved.

"Can I play with your machine?" Sissy whispered.

"Mmmm."

She extricated herself from the duvet, slid down the side of the bed and stood by the bedside table. On it was the machine. It was like a box, with a black top. There was a row of silver buttons like licorice lozenges. Small round lights went on and off when you pressed the buttons. Right now, one green light and one red light were on. If she pushed the last button, the last red light went on. If she pushed the next button, the red light would flash, and it would begin.

She reached out a finger and touched the third silver lozenge. There was a whirly, buzzing noise, and then it stopped.

"I can't do it!" she cried.

Blair leaned over with her eyes mostly shut. "There," she said. "Push the one that says Announce Only, and then the one that says Play."

Sissy looked for the long word that started with A and pushed the button above it. Then she pushed the one marked Play. The light flashed. The soft, whirly sound began. Then came the magic. Her mother's voice.

"Hello. This is 235-8875. I'm not available to answer your call right now. Please leave a message stating your name, number and the time you called. Here's the Beep!" Beep! Then there was a crackling, rolling sound that went on for a long time and then a long Beeeep. The flashing light stopped and the red one went off.

Sissy leaned forward. Biting her lip to be sure she remembered it right, she pressed the button. Announce Only. Play.

"Hello! This is 235-8875. I'm not available to answer your call right now . . ."

She moved her lips with the words. After this many times it turned into a song. The words fell in line. Sissy liked their lift and fall and the way they rhymed—5, and then 5 again—the gentle stroke of "please" and even the wait through the crackling silence, and especially the little beep, the soft swirling and then the big long beep. When it finished she started it again. Her mum lay like a dead person.

She moved her body to the rhythm of the words. In the part that was nearly quiet except for the turning sound she turned around in a circle. To the big beep she bent way down to the ground and threw her hands out to the side. End! She jumped up and got it going again.

"Hello! This is 235-8875. I'm not . . ." She swayed to the voice-print, twirled to the silence. At the end she fell on the rug.

Blair opened her eyes. She squinted at the clock. Sissy was dancing to the message. At the part about leaving your name she scooped something up, and on "Here's the Beep!" she dropped it. As the tape ran, she ran around the end of the bed and out the door. She was gone for a few seconds and then reappeared, her eyes rolled to the ceiling. She cast herself down on the floor, playing dead.

The room looked empty. Blair heard her own voice echo— "not available, not available." She felt Sissy's love like a burden, a burden and a tribute.

"That's a nice dance."

She heard the child scramble clumsily to her feet.

"Mummy?" she said warily, "Are you awake?"

Blair let go of Simplicity's hand in the schoolyard and blew a kiss. The little girl watched her mother turn away. On her face was not rage, for this happened every day and she expected it. Not panic, because it was manageable. ("Can you manage?" That was what the teachers at the school said to the children.) A manageable despair: desolation. Her thin, fair ponytail went straight down the back of her navy sweat top, and fine wisps blew from her hairline onto the clear porcelain face.

Blair was gone. The other children were clustered at the foot of the slide and by the bike rack. They were calling and pushing and giggling and showing each other treasures. The babel of voices would swallow Sissy if she didn't stay on the edge. She began to move sideways towards the door where, before too long, a teacher would come out. If it was Mrs. Kleinfeldt, she would hold her hand. The other one wouldn't. Simplicity would stand there alone until the whistle blew and they lined up to go in. She saw herself as if from a long way away: Sissy, alone by the school door holding her lunchbox.

Up on the fire escape at the side of the building were Jessica, Alex and Emma. Emma looked at Sissy dubiously, about to say hello, but Sissy turned her head and Emma changed her mind.

"I'll be King Counter!" shouted one girl.

"No I will!"

They stood in a circle and each one put a foot in, touching, on a central point.

"Eeeny meeny miney mo, catch a tiger by the toe, if he hollers let him go, eeny meeny miney mo . . . Not because you're dirty, not because you're clean, just because you kissed a girl behind the magazines!"

Sissy knew all the rhymes by heart though she never sang them. Standing with her back against the brick wall of the school and her two hands clutching her lunchbox, she made the noises of the children go away and began to count the square stones leading to the door. *One, two, three four five—* no, start over, I counted that one twice. *One, two, three four five, once I caught a fish alive. Six, seven, eight nine ten, then I let it go again. Why did you let it go? 'Cause it bit my finger so.*

"Hi Sissy."

Rachel appeared, poof, like the genie in the bottle that they read about in story time, in front of Simplicity. Her shiny black hair matched the black stripes in her sweatshirt and leggings. The other stripes were yellow. Her shoes were yellow-and-black and matched too. Simplicity looked at Rachel. Next to Bernie and her mum she liked Rachel best; they used to be best friends. But this year it was different.

"Rachel, look, I've got my watch on," said Simplicity and

put out her wrist. But Rachel danced away backward and joined a circle of girls who were holding hands and jumping. Sissy covered up her watch with the sleeve of her jacket and let her hand drop. She started to sing her song again, and this time her lips moved and the words came out in a whisper. *One, two, three four five* . . .

When the whistle blew they all ran into line. Sissy hung back until the pushing ones had filled up all the front places. Then she went around them. She stood near the end. She spoke to no one. No one spoke to her. The whistle blew again and the line began to advance through the door.

Sissy knew every step of the way—down three steps, around the corner, across a landing, down three more steps, then a sharp left turn into the narrow corridor. Halfway along, she came to her cubby and stopped, putting her lunch-box down. The hubbub swelled around her. She pulled at the zipper of her coat. It stuck, but then it came undone. The lining of her coat was plaid: red and green and yellow. There were very small green leaves in the red squares. She thought maybe the green leaves were new; she hadn't seen them before. She looked at them very carefully; she began to count them. The noise around her was less now. Everyone was running down to the gym.

Simplicity couldn't run as fast as other children. She couldn't do anything as fast as they could. And what were they saying all the time in their squeaky voices? Kids were not like grown-ups, who at least stood in one place and spoke clearly to her face. You could tell when a grown-up was going to be mean, because their faces got hard and changed shape. But you couldn't tell with a kid; they looked exactly the same whether they were being nice or mean.

When she first came to this school, when she was little, maybe three or four, she used to go right into the middle of a bunch of kids. In the sandbox or by the climbing ropes. She tried to go up the twelve steps of the ladder with them and down the slide on her stomach. Once she fell and broke her arm and had to have a cast on it. Other times she only bumped her head and got a bruise, or a cut on her knee.

The other girls used to come up and say "Hi Sissy!" when she came to school. They used to hold her hand and take her with them to jump on the tire. But then they'd all start to talk in their squeaky voices, or run up fast and push her out of the circle. She used to cry. Now she didn't cry. She knew she was not like other kids. Maybe she wasn't a kid at all.

But she was little. And she needed help. Her mother and Bernie usually helped her, but lately they didn't want to any more. Her mother said she was old enough to dress herself. "But, Mummy," Sissy said this morning, "children need help!" But Blair wouldn't. She even got Bernie to stop helping too. Now even Bernie would sigh sometimes and say, "Sissy, I'm *working*."

She wasn't a kid or a grown-up, so maybe she came from somewhere else. There were places you could not see, places you didn't even know were there. Like the places in books.

Mrs. Kleinfeldt and the other teacher herded the children into a circle in the gym and told them to sit on the floor. The floor was cold, but Sissy sat down obediently, because she could see the book in Mrs. Kleinfeldt's hand. Usually someone read them a story first thing in the morning. To make the kids be quiet. They had a special way of holding the pages between two fingers like a fan and turning it to face the kids, to show the picture.

The teacher put her finger between the pages of the book and waved it over the kids' heads.

"What if the scaredy-cat lost the mother's letter? That wouldn't be very good, would it?"

"Yes, that would be good," sniggered one.

"Yeah, good good!"

"If he lost it he could go home and get another one." Ben was flailing his arms and hitting the pillow.

"Yeah, yeah. Another one."

The teacher frowned. "You can't just get another of everything when you lose it, you know," and opened the book again. Her voice was louder now.

"The scaredy-cats continued on down the road . . ."

Simplicity thought it was a silly story. The scaredy-cat should just hold on tight to the letter and make sure he didn't lose it. She made the gym and the kids and the teacher go away and she made up her own story. It was about where she came from, a place where there were no kids and no grown-ups, but in-between people who had no wrinkles and soft voices. They would always help each other, and their hands were very gentle. Simplicity was blowing bubbles with some other in-betweens. It smelled like perfume in the room where they were. Some music came on and they all began to dance. It was floaty, bubble music. Simplicity yawned and closed her eyes.

"Sissy!"

The story was over. Sissy didn't know what the teacher had told them to do. She began to walk between the tables and chairs looking for her name card. Everyone else was sitting down already. She found her name card at the easel, beside Matthew. She tried to get a brush but he pushed her hand away. The blue paint tipped over and splashed onto her leg and her shoe. She stared at it while it ran. She could feel it soaking into her leg. She could see it sliding across the floor like a flat bubble.

"Simplicity! Get a rag and wipe it!"

The paint bubble stretched farther along the floor.

"Quick, Simplicity, move!"

Simplicity moved.

With the paintbrush in her hand, Simplicity made a sky. She dipped it in the puddle on the floor and painted the sky, and under it a road. She is walking along the road with her mother. There is a beach by the road and that's where they are going. They are carrying their bathing suits and they are going to swim. Blair is ahead of Simplicity.

"Hurry up, darling," she says, and sighs, that mother-sigh. "You're so slow."

"You don't need to tell me, Mummy, I already know," Simplicity says.

The painting had bright blue and bright red and black in it. Simplicity is flying away while her mother's feet are firmly on the road. The road is long and goes right off the paper.

Simplicity stood by the chain fence in the playground at the end of school. Some of the mothers had already come and the children were gone. Usually Berenice was the first one there. Today Berenice was late. Simplicity stood beside Katie and Rachel and Jessica, who were in a circle with their sticker books.

Simplicity watched the other girls. They especially liked shiny stickers. There were fuzzy ones, too, which were special, but the shiny ones were best.

Rachel had her book open. She had a new sticker. It was a big circle and had pink and silver on it with a pair of pink ballet slippers with pink ribbons curling around them.

"Ooooh," said the little girls. "That's *beautiful*."

Rachel did not look down at the sticker as her friends did. She looked over the top of the book with pride and modesty on her face. *Look at me, how nice I am sharing my new sticker with my friends, and how they admire it!* said Rachel's face.

"It's such a good sticker, isn't it?" said the girls.

Simplicity studied Rachel's face. She tried to make her own face look like that. She lifted her chin and gazed off toward the slide. She raised her eyebrows, made her lips turn up slightly at the edges and drew her neck back, like the turtle in the terrarium. By the time Sissy had accomplished this, Rachel had changed her face. Now she closed the book with a snap, and her black eyes were like stones.

"I'll give you my jungle adventure sticker for it."

"I don't want to trade that one! I'm keeping it!"

Rachel came up to Simplicity, a solid presence, the dark shag of bangs over her eyes and her firm shoulders, stocky body. She had a way of narrowing and widening her eyes, to make them small and then big again, so they sent out beads of power. She also spread her lips wide, showing her teeth. She did not really seem to be laughing, but it was a laughing face.

"Simplicity! Will you show me your sticker book?"

"I left it inside. In my cubby."

"We can go and get it."

"No Rachel, we can't. We're not allowed to go inside after we've come out."

"We can ask Pamela."

Pamela had hair that was very short and clung to her head at the sides but rose up over her head in a flattened crest, like a woodpecker's. Pamela had brown skin and brown eyes, and she spoke slowly so Simplicity always knew what she was saying. They found Pamela at the corner of the chain fence watching some boys who were kicking up a huge pile of leaves. She had very dignified posture; she talked to them without bending down.

"Hello girls, what do you want?"

"Simplicity wants to go in to get her sticker book to show me. She left it in her cubby."

Pamela looked at Rachel. Then she looked at Simplicity and smiled. "Is that what you want, Simplicity?"

Simplicity made her face eager, as she had seen the other girls do. She made her head go up and down. "Yes it is."

Pamela looked dubious. But then someone came to talk to her. "All right, if you don't make any noise you can go in the side door down the hall to the cubbies and get it. And then come right out!"

Just to be running behind Rachel across the schoolyard

with a plan in mind made Simplicity feel happy. She could see herself, in her mind's eye, a running little girl in a fenced yard full of noisy children, and she felt for a moment as if she were one of them.

Inside was weirdly quiet. All the cubbies, with their hanging knapsacks and untidy stacks of books, their white plastic bags with boots stuffed in them, gaped unprotected. Rachel and Simplicity skidded to a stop in front of the one with the name card Simplicity Bowker.

"There's your lunchbox," said Rachel.

Simplicity lifted the blue plastic square and unsnapped the buckles. Inside was the sticker book her mother had bought her. "Miss Rushton said that the other girls trade stickers at recess and that you might like to have a book so you could trade with them," Blair had said. "We can go and choose some stickers for you too."

"The kids at my school like the shiny ones," Simplicity had reported as they stood in front of the stand where rolls and rolls of stickers hung, going right up over Simplicity's head. "And they like fuzzy ones too, but shiny ones more, I think."

"Which ones do you like?"

Simplicity liked pencils and paper and clipboards and workbooks, but she knew that she wasn't supposed to work all the time. She was supposed to play like other kids.

"Shiny ones," she said. And they chose yellow ducks, a green camel, some fuzzy bats, because Hallowe'en was coming, and two spotted black-and-white cows, which were neither shiny nor fuzzy but Blair liked them. Simplicity went home and put them in the sticker book, under the plastic pages, carefully, in rows, like the other girls did. Her mother gave her a special one, which was an old-fashioned girl wearing a hat and holding a kitten. She had bought it at the same store, but after, so that Simplicity didn't see. It was a surprise.

"I really want to keep the girl with the kitten," she said, after she stuck it in the book. "I really want to keep that one.

That's my favourite."

Slowly Simplicity drew the sticker book out of her lunchbox. She turned to Rachel. "Will you do up the catch? Because I'm holding this," she said. Rachel snapped one of the buckles on the box and pulled on Simplicity's arm.

"Come on! Hurry!"

They ran down the hall and out the door to the schoolyard.

And then Simplicity was standing in the circle with the other girls, holding her sticker book open, and they were leaning their heads over and saying Oh and I've got that one and I like that and That's an old one about her stickers. And their little hands went in and lifted up the plastic and they started taking out the stickers to look at them.

"Can I have one of the ducks, Simplicity? I'll trade you for a dog. It's at home but I'll bring it tomorrow."

"Okay," said Simplicity, in her high, "good girl" voice. "That's fine. You can have it." And she watched the plastic as it was lifted, and the hand remove the duck from her page. She turned the page to cover the hole that was left.

"Look, she's got some black bats."

"They're fuzzy," said Simplicity proudly.

"Let's feel them." The hands reached over again and lifted up the plastic. Simplicity's own hands were occupied, holding up the book, which was heavy.

"Can I have one? I'll give you one of my ladybugs."

The ladybugs were old. Everyone had ladybugs. Even Simplicity had ladybugs. Rachel had given them to her for free a long time ago.

"Okay. That's fine," said Simplicity. "I only have one I don't want to trade."

"Can you give me one of your bats free?"

"Yes, Rachel," said Simplicity. "Yes. Because you gave me one, Rachel. I'll give you one."

Rachel took a bat. There used to be four. Now there were

only two. Before Simplicity realized it, the cows were gone and the bats were gone. Simplicity felt a little bit sad. She wanted at least one bat to keep.

"Show us the one you don't want to trade," whispered Rachel.

"I don't remember what page it's on."

"I'll help you find it."

"Okay," said Sissy.

The girls all got down on their knees and put Simplicity's sticker book on the paving stones. Rachel's eager fingers turned the pages. Simplicity was ashamed because there were a lot of empty ones. She didn't have many stickers to begin with. And now she'd traded a lot of them away. On the second page from the last, they found the old-fashioned girl with the kitten.

"Ahh!" said Rachel. "That's a good one!"

"I'll give you two ladybugs for it," said Kate.

"She doesn't want to trade it," said Rachel.

"But if I give her two stickers for one, she'll trade."

"I can give her two camels. They're bigger than the ladybugs and they're shiny," said Rachel. She didn't want Simplicity to give her girl-and-kitten sticker to Kate.

Simplicity looked over the heads of the girls and saw Berenice at the gate.

"My nanny's here," she said.

"Let me take the kitten sticker out."

"Berenice! I'm right here!" said Simplicity. Berenice did not hear.

Rachel lifted the plastic and began to peel the sticker off the page. Simplicity saw it going. She did not say anything.

"I'll need a backing to put it on," said Rachel briskly.

"I have some backings," said Simplicity, in her pretend-happy voice. They kept the old backings tucked in a little pouch at the end of their books. Rachel held the circle on the ends of her two fingers while Simplicity turned the last page and found the backing. They tried to put the sticker on it, but it was too big, and they got a little fold in the middle so it was a little messed up.

"Oh," said Rachel. "It's kind of ruined."

Simplicity felt like she was going to cry. The other girls had run away.

"Don't you want it any more, Rachel?"

Rachel looked at it carefully. "Oh I guess so. Yes, sure, I'll take it. But I think 'cause it's wrecked maybe I'll only give you one camel for it."

"Okay," said Simplicity.

Rachel put the sticker on its backing in her coat pocket. Then she ran away too.

Berenice opened the car door for Simplicity. Simplicity was tired and pale. Her sticker book was so heavy she dropped it on the street. Berenice picked it up and put it on the car seat.

"Seat belt!" she said, and shut the door.

Simplicity pulled the seat belt around her. She liked it because it held her tight.

Berenice got into the car. She arranged the pillow she sat on in the driver's seat. Berenice was so small she almost wasn't like a grown-up. She had to move the driver's seat way forward and sit on that pillow. Whenever Blair got in the car after Berenice had been driving it, she picked up the pillow and tossed it over the seat back into the rear. Then she got in, sent the driver's seat zooming back and said, "Midgets have been in here!"

Berenice slowly guided the car out into the choked lane of traffic, which was filled with mums and nannies driving Jeeps and Wagoneers back to Rosedale and Forest Hill.

"Did you have a dream?" said Sissy. Berenice had a lot of dreams. And her dreams always meant something was going to happen. She always told Simplicity about them.

Berenice looked surprised. "I did have a dream. I dreamt that you had diarrhea. It's a warning."

Simplicity knew what warnings were. You got warnings at school before you were asked to leave the class. She never got warnings, because she was very quiet. She didn't think Berenice needed a warning either, because Berenice was very good.

"There's nothing wrong with me," she said.

Berenice changed lanes. Her face became more pointed when she was thinking, and her eyes focused sharply on the road. She was a little bit afraid of driving, Sissy thought.

"Did something bad happen?"

"Something bad is going to happen," said Berenice. "But not to me."

"To Mummy?" said Simplicity.

"No, no. To someone you know. Your mummy's friend."

"A girl or a boy?"

"A girl, I think."

"Oh," said Sissy, "that's bad."

"Very bad."

"Is that all?"

"I'm not sure," said Bernie.

The car continued in a smooth, flowing river of cars that gradually slowed and came to a halt at a red light. Simplicity could just see over the edge of the door to the sidewalk. There were kids on bikes out there, big kids. They were pushing each other at the stoplight.

"How do you know?"

Berenice patted Sissy on the leg. The light changed. The kids began to walk their bikes across the intersection.

"In my dream a wild pig got loose in the house. It came to life, or grew, suddenly, and leapt out of my arms. Then it was running through the rooms, growing larger. That must mean something very bad coming, a dream like that. And it was from your mummy, someone she knew."

"A very bad pig?" said Sissy.

"When I get home I'll look up black boar, or pig, in my book of dream interpretations," said Bernie. She hoped she was right about this bad thing—that it would strike someone else. She hoped the bad news coming would not be immigration, telling her to go back to the Philippines. It would be wasted—all her waiting, and her hard work. All the *dues* she paid. I do not have money to pay the dues, Berenice said once to Blair. Blair laughed and said you couldn't pay dues with money. You paid with blood and sweat and tears. "They think it's a fair system," she said, "because everybody's got some of those."

"Can I have some juice?" said Simplicity as they both mounted the front steps of the house. She knew her mum would not be home. Her mum had a new job, so she was never home until after bedtime. "Then I am going up to my room to do my work. And I don't want anyone to bother me."

Blair went to her fitness class. She always went before work. At her locker she pulled off her clothes and untangled her gym clothes. As she bent over her Nikes, she noticed the letter. It was still there, tucked into the sole of the shoe, where the ball of her foot hit on each aerobic bounce.

The letter came to her door months ago, with a long, white florist's box holding thirteen white roses. It was a love letter, anonymous, written in turquoise ink, an elaborate hand. In a state of shock she read it, devoured it even. Then she folded it into her purse. She walked immediately out of the house without even opening the long, narrow box with the ribbon around it. She walked down the street with the letter, not wanting to keep it, not being able to destroy it.

She felt guilty, but why? She was single; there was no reason she shouldn't get a love letter. But she had no idea who it came from. To receive such a document implicated her in unknown actions. And to possess, to *keep* the letter was to enter into a relationship with its author. She stopped at a garbage can. But to throw it away implied she had an emotional reaction. She would not admit to that. She put the letter back into her purse, and walked straight here, where she transferred it to the sole of her left Nike high-top sneaker.

The letter lived a cramped and damp life after that. Three times a week she untied the laces, put her foot in and danced on it. Each time her sock-clad left foot encountered it, she curled her toes and wriggled the ball of her foot up and over it. In class she bounced up and down, the foot heating up, for an hour at a time. She was comfortable with the letter's thickness, the slight ridge of its corners, under the ball of her foot. Each time she drew her foot out, the letter looked molded, papier-mâché by a new method. She had become familiar with the language, with the unknown author even, by osmosis; the letter had become what was missing, something she could not quite throw away, although it had no place in her life.

Today she retrieved the letter from the sole of her Nike. The cheap white envelope with its design of grey spirals on the inside had become oddly transparent during its ordeal. It had been folded twice, into four sections: these sections now were welded together by time, weight and sweat. Some of the peacock-coloured ink had run, smearing the letters on the page. The paper itself, she was interested to note, had acquired a distinct odour of sweaty feet.

Fingers delicate, like an archaeologist on a dig, she peeled the leaves of paper apart.

My dearest B—it began, as it had begun then, splitting her heart's slow logic into rapid stutters.

I love you so much. I am utterly distracted by the fact of your existence. Without you, the beauties even of my roses, their profligate, flaunting "volupté," is as nothing. If we could share life even for a day, three days, if I could only just see and touch you—

No longer did the sentiments hold her captive. Those she had memorized long ago. Now, months later, it was the physical destruction of the billet-doux that moved her: passion under duress. So far it seemed the ink itself was holding firm to the shape of the letters in the spidery hand in which it was written. But the paper was dissolving. Where it had been folded twice, first side to side, then lengthwise, it had worn through, so that there were two intersecting lines where the paper nearly came apart. She observed this with scientific curiosity; it was why she had put the note there in the first place, other than that she could think of no other safe place to hide it, to see what happened, how it died.

—being unable to mention your name has made it impossible for me to communicate with another human being. I am sinking into a torpor of longing, a pit of my own desire. I rise infrequently in fear to wonder—what should happen to me if you die? I should have to become a Trappist lay brother. After all, what have I to renounce, for without you my life has a net value and meaning of less than zero . . .

The locker room door burst open and an army of leotard-clad bodies marched in, fanning out down the rows of lockers. Blair looked up from her reading. The twelve o'clock class must just have got out. She ducked her head further into her locker, pretending she was searching for that elusive lost shoe or elastic hairband, and continued reading.

—you have become a kind of sex goddess. I fall at your feet in my mind a hundred times a day—

The letter had arrived apropos of nothing and had been followed by utter silence, unless you could count a number of grunts and inarticulate sighs on her answering machine. But who would believe that? Who would believe, if the letter was found, that she had no knowledge of its author? What did it matter? She was free, she was unattached. The letter writer might easily have come forth to claim his prize, if he wanted. And he hadn't.

It was this recalcitrance she had come to love about him. That, and the way he began in the middle of things, as if this particular communication followed uncountable numbers of passionate conversations. For his desperate edge, touching, flattering, finding, by its sheer candour, his nakedness, his lack of irony.

—whatever you do, don't die. I couldn't survive that. I have always believed that I would go first. If only we could share life even a bit, the lights would go on for me.

Let's try each of us to endure without seeing, without touching, for at least this summer, and then embark, while we can, on something audacious—

Head out to some isolated farmhouse in Quebec for incalculable bliss.

"Hi Blair, is that you?"

Blair folded the letter and withdrew her head.

"Recognized the dimples on your ass."

Carol marched up to her locker, three inches away from Blair's, grabbed the lock like a cop grabbing someone by the scuff of the neck and began to twirl the dial. Carol was a teacher who'd gone through a bad divorce last year. Blair knew no more about her, not even her last name, though they saw each other here every week and were well acquainted in a certain way.

"Don't remind me. I haven't been here all week."

"What you got there?" said Carol. "A love letter?"

Blair laughed. "I should be so lucky." She flapped the letter in front of Carol and then refolded it into the palm of her hand. "Old shopping list, found it in my locker, I was just curious." *You're explaining too much*, Blair said to herself. She picked up her purse with the letter still in her hand and went off to the washroom.

"That bra's no good. You need more support than that," said Carol to her back.

It's time to get this letter out of my shoe, Blair told herself in the washroom cubicle. It's going to get ruined for one thing. And for another, what would happen if I get hit by a streetcar on the way home and die? Someone would come and clear this stuff out and they'd find it. Or let's say the place burned down—it's got my name on it—it'd probably be found in the rubble, just my luck . . .

She must protect the author. If *she* had nothing to lose, he might be attached. *Must* be attached, or he would have appeared by now. And Blair had been so self-righteous about Ruby's married man! She considered throwing the letter down the toilet, but it was too beautiful for that. Also, in her present state, it seemed necessary to keep the evidence that someone, somewhere, loved her. She supposed she could get a safety deposit at the bank, but that would only emphasize its significance if she were to die. Then she'd look a fool. Reminding herself that she must find a better place to dispose of it, she put the letter back in her Nike and headed up to class.

Harold was inclined to slide around behind Blair when she was doing side stretches, to poke her buttocks with his finger and say, "You must keep them down, down, do you see? While lifting up in front . . . Do you mind if I touch you?"

She minded rather seriously when he touched her, partly because of the ingratiating way in which he asked. He was like one of those creepy boys who asked if he could kiss you at the end of a date, everything about his attitude letting you know that he expected you to refuse, and that you must refuse, or be creepier even than him. But she never told Harold he couldn't.

As Blair warmed up she asked herself why. *Why* was she never able to tell a man she minded? Along came Harold and attempted to place her shoulders and back in the right alignment. "Just here," he said, poking her breastbone. She glared. *Don't think you can get me with that concerned jock look*, she said to herself. Not that any sane man would be secretly harbouring flames of passion for her, the way she was aging. There was a roll developing above her waist and saddlebags on the sides of her thighs. The mirrors all around the room let no sin go unseen.

For an awful moment she wondered if Harold had written the letter. If, ironically, it had gravitated back to its author at the fitness club. What a cruel trick that would be. But he couldn't have. He had no poetry in him, he didn't know the word *volupté*, and he certainly had no idea of her address. At least she hoped he didn't.

Blair's failure to reprimand Harold was partly responsible for her bad humour as she walked up Yonge Street to work. The day was another float in the parade of perfect fall days they'd had. She passed the little area of green in front of the Rosedale subway and the park benches across the street; office workers had spread their jackets to lunch on the grass.

Back there in Ramsden Park was the playground she frequented when she first came to Toronto with Simplicity as a toddler. Sitting by the sandpile had reduced Blair to blubbery tears of boredom and frustration, but it did not seem so bad now she looked back. Then Sissy had been a force to resist, representing not who she would become, or even who she was, but the past—with its wasted womanhood, oppressed mothers, silenced females. Now that melting lump of soft flesh that had longed for nothing but Mummy Mummy Mummy had become angular, secretive, solemn.

Past the park, the street began to climb through the perennial congestion of the Rosedale stores. The women who shopped here had blond ponytails, tight jeans and leather jackets open over silk blouses. They evidently arose each morning in full make-up and earrings; they were on chatty, even intimate terms with the butcher and baker. They double-parked along the curb to run in and buy their New York strips and six-grain bread. The clock face on the old train station tower, hands ripped off and without numerals, gave the same wordless message as always. On the wall by the beer store was the old CPR beaver, carved in stone, like some modern hieroglyph.

Where Yonge Street took a dip under the railway track the sidewalk stank of piss and homeless drunks. Here lived the little man with his Lear-like great head and silver locks and beard. Another man was with him there today, younger, darker skinned, with a much-battered face and a hopeful expression as he approached her.

"Spare change for a coffee?" he said. Blair dug into her coat pocket. She handed over some change, knowing that it wasn't doing him any good, but unable to pass him by.

Above the railroad tracks, the street ran to fancy condos and Italian restaurants with yawning interiors paved in white tablecloths. Halfway up the hill were the CLIK offices, where, for a three-month trial period, Blair was host of the driving home show—on air from four to eight o'clock. The music came chiefly from "stress-buster" tapes, the chat from local celebrities, lobbyists for obscure causes and devotees of passing fads.

"The trouble with those fanatics is they won't leave the rest of us alone," was what Blair's dad used to say, back in Medicine Hat. He was a patient, gentle scientist who worked all his life on the life cycle of the aphid at the experimental farm. He died before he was fifty, of cancer, maybe something he caught from all those sprays. He used to sit in the backyard after barbeques, and the mosquitoes would line up on his bald pate. "Daddy, Daddy, you're getting bitten!" she'd cry. And he would smile, and lift her hand away from where she was aiming to swat.

"I've eaten my fill, let them eat theirs," he'd say.

One of the things that was missing in her life now was people like her father. People who understood life cycles, who weren't frantic about the unfair auto insurance industry rebellion or even Meech Lake, who were not working themselves to death to pay for a new sunroom and a "Caledon Cadillac," a jeep for getaways to the hills north of Toronto. Who were not working themselves to death at all, but working themselves to life. Dying for a living: she once had a guy on who wrote a book about that, too. It was about people who worked in jobs that produced toxic substances and finally killed you. It could have been about any of them.

Today she had planned to play Country Joe and the Fish to amuse the commuters; she might even sing along. When she got really brave she'd play Hearts of Flame.

She breezed through the reception area with a word to the secretaries, and found her desktop covered with notes. The line-up for today was on top: nothing to do but read the background material. Settling into the recording booth and talking through headphones to the lone, bored technician, Blair thought how she *could* have liked this job. She *could* have made them sit up and grip those steering wheels, if only the fat boys would let her. "Fat boys" was her generic term for everyone else in the station. They rarely spoke to her, but slouched past with their giant armpit-sweat stains. From time to time one of their fat memos would arrive—more and more frequently, as it happened. There were two there now, on pink slips. Today the messages said: "No more PMS guests. This is a family show!" and "Can the highbrow critics. Ninja Turtles was great. The wife thought so too."

"Give me a level," said the technician.

"And it's one, two, three, what are we fighting for? Don't ask me I don't give a damn—"

"Okay, okay. I didn't know you sang." And then the red light came on and she was away, her voice borne on the airwaves over greater Metro Toronto. "Hiya folks, it's Blair Bowker here, your drive home host. It's a hot day and I wonder how many of you have got those little air-conditioned wooden spoolie cushions . . ."

At ten o'clock Blair walked out the door of CLIK-FM, her shift finished, her green sheets ready for tomorrow. It hadn't been too bad a day. She had interviewed a sociologist about a type of person called "strivers." They were not "achievers," who had a lot to begin with and did well with it, but people who had little, and got some, and wanted more. They were still in the rigors of rising, apparently. They sounded very attractive. Her second guest was a feminist poet with a nasal whine, who identified her difficulties in accepting the orthodoxies of the left while rejecting hierarchy and authoritarianism. That was a bit dull, until the poet began to read autobiographical work that dealt with being raped, thirty years ago, by a neighbour, and read out his name and address. Luckily, as the saying went, it was in another country. Oh, the fat memos would fly tomorrow.

Heading home, Blair cut down Walker and through the shortcut behind the new condos, across the little park by Cottingham School and over to Avenue Road. The house was dark. Inside, the kitchen was tidy. Sissy was in bed. Blair stood in front of the window looking out. The lights in the Boswells' second floor made her lonely. Usually she had a hot bubble bath and read magazines. All winter she would do that. Tonight, she was not tired. She called up to the top floor.

"Berenice, are you in?"

Berenice was on the telephone. She had her own line, which made it possible for her to carry on the four or five hours of calls she made every night with her extensive network of friends and relations. They spoke for hours, she and her Filipino friends, whipping up their feelings in long, rhetorical bursts of Tagalog in which phrases of English could be heard—"in consideration of me" or "respect for me" were the most common. Pride was insistent where pride had so little footing. "I will only work the weekend if she promises never to be late home again." And "I told her"—as they were domestic workers, the authority figure was always "she"—"I told her, don't even speak of overtime." And you knew they'd told her no such thing.

"Yes, I'm in. I'm not going out," Bernie called down the stairs.

Blair went to the telephone, dialled a number, waited a moment or two and then began to speak, quickly, without pausing for a response, in the composed way of people talking to machines. Philip wasn't home. She put down the receiver and grabbed her jacket anyway.

At the end of MacPherson, she cut across the pumping station lawn and went uphill to Poplar Plains. Again she took the path into the ravine. High searchlights on top of the reservoir threw shallow white washes of light down the slope. On the western side was darkness; she ran lightly under the Spadina Road overpass and up the wooden steps built into the side of the hill.

Without slowing her stride, she headed straight south past the big brick and stone houses, where the new, ruched drapes resolutely closed off inner spaces no doubt richly lined with colour and brass. Casa Loma, that imported heap of pseudo-history, unaccountably made her smile, its outline in pale stone vibrant against the royal-blue sky. In the garden, klieg lights blazed. A lone model in ostrich-trimmed lounge pyjamas arranged her long body in a series of static grimaces for a photographer. By the Baldwin Steps, ornamental cabbages, purple and green, lolled their heavy heads amongst a litter of orange leaves.

Still walking south, she passed the construction site where "magnificent condo living" was rising from where the milk trucks used to load. On Dupont, a glass-lozenge roof disguised the subway entrance. A few blocks west was Brunswick, with modish metal awnings and sandblasted fronts, square jutting windows on the second floor where houses had been blown up from inside to be tight as balloons.

She followed it southward, passing the park with the statue of Jean Sibelius, a stone head brooding over an empty sandpit.

She crossed the park and continued up to the church, where she turned along Lowther. She was going to go through the darkest streets, just to prove she wasn't getting agoraphobia like all those poor stay-at-home mums. Back she walked, to her home and child. "I do not remember choosing all this," she said out loud. "I only remember wanting to have a little child walking along beside me." She was not made to be this—tamed and housed and maternal, reduced to nurturer and care-giver and playmate. Not Blair the singer, Blair who had an affair with a travelling Englishman and kept the kid. She was a free spirit, a daring extrovert.

She got to Dupont and walked east along the dipping line of the road. It must have been a wagon track to the small towns west of the Humber. It had that touch of human creation in it so unusual in Toronto: a curve. As in throw a curve. Weird she might be becoming, but not timid. She couldn't take timid. Had to keep forcing herself to do the things that were frightening or that disease would take her over, and she would pass it on to Simplicity.

Blair walked faster.

5

A Fashion Statement

Ruby emerged from the bathroom in her peach satin slip ('30s) with a towel around her head. She cast herself across the sofa ('20s), which was recovered in white brocade. But it was the sofa of a woman who valued style above comfort, and the position she was in, lying down with her head on the arm, didn't work. In another minute she pushed herself upright and dug her toes into the white shag carpet ('80s); clenching them, she tried to pull out strands of wool, childishly. Catching herself, she yanked off the towel, shook out her damp hair and went into the kitchen.

She came back a moment later with a bottle of Aqua Libra and pulled a chair up to her desk, a white lacquer deco-look number that had been a mistake: it didn't offer much surface to work on. She took her favourite Pilot Fineliner pen between manicured fingers, acrylic nails done apple-blossom pink. In front of her was an orange, hard-backed Grand & Toy record book, unlined.

She opened it. On the first blank page she'd written "Ruby's Fashion Diary." She flipped the pages. Inside were sketches, marginal comments, memos to herself and, increasingly, long patches of observation, in her bold, uneven script. She began to read at random.

————————

GOSSIP. People tell me everything. It must be that I know how to listen. Or that my peculiar sphinx-like face inspires confidence?

Right now, all over Toronto, private information is going public. Two people are having lunch and discussing shocking facts about an absent third. Saying, don't tell a soul, you didn't hear it from me. Replying, you know I wouldn't. Then they go back to their offices and pick up the telephone, and at the moment they pass it on, extract promises of perfect discretion.

Kinda purrient, isn't it? Like sex to teenagers—no I won't, I couldn't. Then—make me. Like an addiction; once in on it you can't get out. You take some, you owe some. You give what you can, and then you give more. Like some sort of religious observance, too: chanting, humming, walking in lines. Only you do it two by two, then split, and form another duo. Grapevine's the image, but grapevine doesn't suit. Grapevine means network, all points linked by a strong tendon; it means linear, purposeful. Gossip is more dangerous, more divisive, more like lightning. It sparks maliciously and then branches out; creates fear, makes people toe the line.

I don't gossip. But I hear things. When I can help it, I don't repeat what I heard. But sometimes it slips out. What can I do? Make it mine to receive but not to give? Allow the scuttlebut to stop at me? Pass it on. Pass the parcel. You don't want to get stuck holding it when the music stops.

The worst and fastest-growing kind of gossip is self-gossip.

In the locker room, a strange woman approaches me, towelling-down: "I've gained five pounds. I can't sleep at night and I roam the house eating. I'm not a bulimic, but after a few hours I do get sick and vomit it up."

Creaming her legs, she goes on to the problems she has with her husband over custody of the children, how he had bribed the nanny to turn against her. I tell her, "Hey, are we friends, do I know you, did I miss something here?"

It was funny, reading her own diary. Looking in on her life—even a week later—was a spectator sport. Last week—it could have happened to somebody else. Oh, she recognized it, it was familiar, but removed, like catching a glimpse of her own face in newsclips of a crowd at some big event. Hey, that's me. But I didn't know I was there that night. I didn't know I looked like that.

Her life. For what it was worth. Without the diary to bring it back it would have been gone, completely gone.

At first the diary had been for fashion impulses, sketches and ideas. But then she started putting in what she did, what she felt. She became fanatic about keeping it, the details. "God is in the details." One of her favourite sayings. She wished she'd made it up, but it came from a Russian ballerina.

She flipped backwards. Summer had been quiet. She'd been sketching cruise wear and a line for the following spring. Long, loose gowns with deep V-fronts made out of fine embroidered cotton she'd found in that collector's attic. Fabulous stuff, fabric you couldn't *get* anymore. She'd made up four of them. But the fall season was not going well. Only two of her black velvet suits went into stores. If it kept up like this, she'd end up spending the winter knee-deep in white lace and tulle, making wedding dresses. Again. Ruby Mason. Always the bride's dressmaker, never the bride.

Bridal trains, here I come, said Ruby to herself. No matter how far down the trade goes, people still get married, and they'll spend a couple of thousand dollars on a custom-designed white dress studded with pearls that they're going to wear once in their lives. To have to fall back on that was Ruby's punishment for her sins, she thought. But what sins?

She put the pen down. She shook out her hair. It was nearly dry, frizzy, the way she liked it. She glared in the general direction of the telephone. Marvin was supposed to call. Marvin, her married man, her m-squared. He hadn't. Maybe he was leading her down the golden path, as he would say. It was now—she checked the clock, an old Black Magic cat with the tail that went back and forth, which she had found in a gutted coffee shop in Uxbridge, where she'd gone to find old clothes—ten-thirty.

He'd left it too late. Well, too bad for him. She went to find her purse; there was an invitation in it. There was always an invitation; they fell through the office mailslot like autumn leaves. It used to be exciting, and flattering, but it wasn't any more. They weren't for anywhere you'd want to go. How many launches of a new perfume for men can any one woman take? And it wasn't really Ruby who was invited, but the *commodity* of Ruby. Ruby Mason, of deBoltz Designs. And even that commodity didn't have quite the currency it had. If you showed up too often you became banal. There was always someone newer, younger and higher in the firmament who attracted the attention.

On the other hand, when a woman was sitting at home waiting for her m-squared to call, these invitations had their uses. She knew there was one in her purse, tucked there by Audrey earlier in the day. She dug it out. It was to the opening of a restaurant called Ocean.

Ruby stepped out of her taxi in a black catsuit with her silk-tasselled Turkish vest over and a wide-brimmed red hat.

The bouncers outside were sweltering in big raccoon coats—Arnie and somebody. Funny they looked just like the guys who used to wear those coats to football games in Alberta in 1968, before pennant-waving went out. All these parties, and the same bouncers. Everybody knew them. They were the best guys to know; you could get in anywhere once you did.

Inside, the first thing that hit her was a feeling of wind-down. So few people were left you could actually see the decor. The walls were curved, the banquettes made like cresting waves. The paint slurped over the counter with froth on top like Japanese woodcut waves. And there was no food. As for fashion, it was the usual sea of black. Skinny pants and minis; smooth, straight hair or old '60s Sassoon-style snakes cut short and curling onto the cheeks; small black bowler hats. Ruby wore black to disappear, but what was their excuse, these perfect young whippets? They'd gone for the opaque black leg and they couldn't get out of it. Gone for the silhouette, for making their mark, a mark of themselves. Gone down a fashion rabbit-hole and couldn't get out.

The ever-present Hugh Mensa was there, his gleaming bald head up over the other heads in the crowd, always nodding. If it weren't for the fact that he knew everyone, he'd seem like an alien from outer space—genial, moving amongst us (ought we not to be honoured?) but not one of us, thought Ruby. Not to be trusted.

Ruby and Mensa used to be buddies. But he had ignored her now—at least in print—for a whole year. Because they were friends, he didn't write about her. His little blow against graft and corruption. His proof of virtue. Hah! Friends hold back, but enemies never stop themselves from rushing into print.

Recklessly, Ruby hailed Mensa. His shiny head sprouted like a pale shoot over the black hats, the carroty sprinkling of hair around his ears marking him as the only guy in the crowd over thirty. He had someone with him.

"We're leaving to find a restaurant," he said. "Place is so hip there's nothing to eat."

Ruby stood by the bar and ordered a draft. Mensa and his friend did not move.

"Bye, and good luck tonight," said a girl on the other side of Ruby to her friend.

"What's tonight?" said Ruby.

The girl was big, with long, black, curly hair and a fine, turned-up nose. Despite her evil-looking black leather jacket, she looked like your favourite babysitter.

"I have to write an essay."

"What's your essay on?"

"Infanticide."

Not what she expected. "Quite a topic," Ruby allowed.

"It was either that or cannibalism."

"Oh, I like infanticide better," said Mensa, horning in.

"Me too. I read four books."

"What are their names?" It was a slip-up. The girl looked at Ruby with a kind of pity: what was she? a librarian?

"I don't remember. But there's four of them."

She moved off. But she didn't leave either. Ruby stood at the bar and stared around the room, watching people. She saw the girl again and again. Moving off and not leaving. She drank her beer. (It was supper, after all.) The essay nagged at Ruby. Mensa was still beside her.

"Call me old-fashioned," said Ruby, "but she oughta get to work on that essay."

Mensa said, "I wonder what course it's in."

They both looked at the babysitter girl, admiring her chic. A choice between infanticide or cannibalism, these party dishes.

"Consuming topics," said Mensa.

Ruby laughed. Somehow the topics were exactly to the point: killing babies / eating humans. "I wonder why she preferred infanticide?"

"Maybe she's a feminist."

"More likely 'cause it's newer." Or is it? If Blair were here, she'd be able to give references to Greek tragedy and Shakespeare and God knows what all. Still, if infanticide wasn't brand new, it was up to date, at least. A more specialized, somewhat abstract version of cannibalism. Killing babies *is* the human race eating itself. "Canada is a country which eats its young." Who said that?

The girl (who was a woman, no doubt, but that didn't sound right to Ruby) had inherent taste. It showed in the bright way she insisted on books having no names. She probably didn't know what was in them, either. *Con*tent-free. That word—*con*tent. As opposed to con*tent*. To be *con*tent-free is to be con*tent*.

And that other stroke: "I read four books." Emphasis on quantity. How wrong it was of Ruby to let slip a little intellectual curiosity. The point was how much you could get, not how well you got it, how good it was, or even what it was. A book is a thing, a box, a container. It might as well have nothing inside.

And then the girl's voice, the sliding, half-ironic tone, with a buried question mark just nosing its way up to the surface. They all talked like that. But she put a different spin on it. Irony over irony, implying a deeper meaning, something profound, she's aware but not buying. Her tone said, I know I'm using the familiar tone they all do and isn't it funny, only you and I know it's all worth shit.

She turned back to the bar. Mensa was gone.

Ruby and the reluctant essayist ended up going out the door at the same time. They walked down King together, where they got a cab. The girl said she lived on Harbord. She was taking women's studies 'cause it was easy. Ruby was silent, secretly intimidated. She liked women's studies, the babysitter-girl went on, but also math, 'cause she wanted to go into business.

Why does this whole thing make me sad? Ruby asked herself. Then she realized: the girl reminded her of herself, twenty years ago. So cleverly of her time, and undamageable. Life could do her no harm. That was Ruby, in Hearts of Flame. Yet she had been done harm. It took this long to realize.

Ruby let her off in front of her house and went on home.

The light was flashing on the machine. Marvin had left one of his hot and humble messages. "I need you, I want you, I'm waiting for you."

"You're never waiting for me," she said crossly to the machine. She went to bed, half expecting him to let himself in the door, but he didn't, and she got right to sleep.

Ruby picked up a copy of *Metropolis* and saw that Mensa had written up the whole Splash show and never said one word about her dresses being in it. Just completely passed her by. It was the day after the Ocean party.

"He knew! Standing there at the bar, he knew! Why didn't he at least say he hated the stuff?" she shouted at Audrey. Audrey hunched farther over the desk, which was covered with order forms. Ruby had to answer herself.

"'Cause he's chicken, that's why. He knows he's got no good reason to hate it. He knows he can't muster the mental artillery to dismiss it. Oh, he knows how to get me." She paced across the little showroom, with its walls of mirrors, Victorian wicker chairs, Yucca palms, rolling clothes racks. She stopped in front of a mirror, and faced herself.

"What I hate the worst is to be ignored. As if I don't exist. If I were in Paris I'd be a legend by now. In Toronto there's no legends. After forty you're either an institution or a pathetic hack."

Audrey rolled her eyes. She had heard this before. She

moved the fabric orders around on her desk.

"Why? I keep going back in my mind over why he hates me. Years ago we used to talk. I can see us." She threw her head back, exposing her long, olive throat, down past the indentation at her collarbones. Three faint lines ran around her neck, her only sign of age. Her eyes were shut but not still, twitching.

"Me in my long skirts, floral print, him in his jeans. He actually had hair on the top of his head then. We had these cunning little Markham Street lunches, French crêpes, or escargot, which I thought was very chic at the time. Both of us just starting out. He wasn't such big stuff he couldn't ask me little favours like, "Tell your friend Bruce he should give me an interview before his show next time. If he's giving an exclusive not to waste it on the other paper." And like, when some new Italian line was opening up a shop in town, "Ruby, what do you think of it? I need an attitude.""

"That must have done it," said Audrey.

"I pride myself. I taught him, some. I gave him a few introductions. All right, he didn't need it long. He got bigger. The only thing I can figure is he didn't like to see me because it reminded him of back when. Not of anything particularly unpleasant, just that he wasn't always the big cheese on top."

"Old Toronto saying, 'No good deed goes unpunished.'"

Ruby stopped. "Yeah," she said. This was what she liked about Audrey. Sometimes, just sometimes, she could stop Ruby. Almost no one could.

"Yeah, I know it. Never heard it till I moved here." She walked away from the mirror, into the back workroom. She slapped the judy's seamed old hourglass form with the folded newspaper.

"It wasn't a good deed on purpose. I never expected anything from it. Well—not anything much. Just that he review my collections, the same way he would for anyone."

Audrey had nothing else to contribute.

Ruby circled back into the showroom. She flipped her hand over her dresses on the rack—velvet and sequins and silk and beaded fringes. They didn't show well on the hanger, which was why she had to keep Ramone, the house model. Ramone was a dinosaur. Five-foot-ten and size six, with a brain the size of a pea.

That was another reason she'd lost favour with the press. She couldn't afford to throw parties any more. A glass of wine in the showroom with Ramone doing runway didn't turn Mensa's crank, or anyone else's. The whole scene here was passé to them. Retro was passé. On that Ruby agreed. She was getting out of it herself. There was nothing more to flash back to. They'd done the '50s, the '60s, the '70s, the '80s. More cannibalism. Self-cannibalism.

"Anyway, Mensa's losing his credibility," she continued. "Look at what he writes. In practically every paragraph— 'Splash is the most brilliant Canadian designer.' Someone should put a stop to it! It's completely corrupt."

"Ruby, you're a big girl. You oughta be used to this by now," intoned Audrey.

"You know what he told me? He told me once I had 'an easy ride from the critics for too long.' What does he figure he is? An instrument of divine retribution? Did you see where he called the Design Group 'a bunch of nonentities'? If we're nonentities, what does that make him? He sucks our blood. I guess he's one of those parasite mushrooms that grows on shit."

Audrey finally looked up and laughed. "That's good," she said, the smile lingering on her plain, toothy face.

Ruby stopped. She was just hearing what Audrey said a minute ago, "You oughta be used to it by now."

"Thing is, I *was* used to it. I had my shots, you know. I'm supposed to be immune."

That was Monday. It was a panic week at work. Everybody

was on the phone, or waiting for her out front, and the creditors' demand notes kept coming in. Tuesday afternoon Audrey decided to come down with some female complaint and ended up in the hospital. A temp came in, but she kept giving Ruby the calls she didn't want and getting rid of the calls she did want. Wednesday, right at noon, Blair walked in, in her Rosedale running gear, the high-top runners and shiny leggings and a Vuarnet sweatshirt, with cold chicken salad. "I can't, I just can't have lunch," said Ruby. But she ended up taking half an hour.

Blair said she was on a day's escape from motherhood. That was how she portrayed herself, as a mother, beleaguered, home with the kid or out on an overdue break. Even though she had that job at the chat show. But for Blair, jobs never stuck. They weren't part of her, the way Ruby's were. Basically, what Blair needed was a husband, Ruby thought. But she had arranged her life not to have one. It was her only abnormality. Thank God for it, too. Otherwise she'd be unbearable.

She came in, sat down, started eating the salad and began to talk. Blair always was a good talker. She had that voice. Her voice had always been her best feature. There it was, a total, biological, physical fluke, to do with the structure of some cords and muscles in your neck. A gift from God, as Ruby's mother would say. It galled Ruby, in their younger days—the effortlessness of the voice and all the praise got for something that basically wasn't Blair's doing.

The voice went on, rich and sweet and perfectly modulated, about Sissy's school and Berenice, the nanny's hard life. Ruby grew bitter listening. Blair lavished love and attention on her chosen needy cases, while Ruby, her oldest friend, got nothing but low-cal lunch. Maybe Blair figured Ruby had no problems. They rarely discussed Marvin. She sat there, stiff as a post, saying nothing, listening to Blair making inane remarks, like, "You don't know how hard it is to wait for your immigration papers while your life runs through your fingers." At last she ran out of steam.

Ruby said nothing.

"Discuss," said Blair.

"Fuck it, Blair, you don't need my input," said Ruby.

Blair's eyes watered, she blinked.

Why does Blair irritate me so? thought Ruby. She's just talking, exercising her voice. I'm full of resentment, churning bellyful of anger. It's not Blair's fault she's pretty and has a sweet kid and an easy job and a monthly cheque from the guy she duped into getting her pregnant. It all seems so *effortless* to her. It always did. She doesn't seem to be hungry, doesn't *want*, in this gross, noisy way I do. Wears that fucking "you can't get me, I understand suffering and I'm above pain now" look on her mug.

Blair started up again, about being lonely and how maybe she wouldn't pass probation at her job.

"Why don't you go have another baby?" Ruby said. "You seem to be able to manage that."

Audrey came in and said someone was on the phone who Ruby had been trying to get, so Ruby took the call. Blair waited till she got off. Then she stood up to go. With her eyes lowered, she began to say that people don't know how to draw the line between work and personal life. They always let work seep in. They take business calls when friends are there.

"They do," said Ruby, coming around the desk. "And I do and I did, and I'm sorry. You are sweet to come. But I'll tell you, you're the one with the problem. There *is* no distinction between work and personal life. Hasn't been since roughly— oh, 1983."

Getting off the elevator at the end of the day, Ruby snapped the heel off her shoe. She took a cab to the shoemaker at Bathurst and Dupont. The shop smelled of shoe leather. He was working at his cross-cut, work-worn wooden counter. Behind him was a wall of cubbyholes. From each, the dry noses of old, battered shoes stuck out, like the snouts of doped animals. The floor was dark with piles of shoe-corpses—suede, patent, water-stained, foot-moulded, so mis-shapen it seemed as if no foot could ever have fit them.

He moved aside a pair of brogues to write her name on the claim tag. He said she couldn't get them back until next week. "Too much work," he said. "My son doesn't want to help." She sympathized. It felt oppressive, all that neediness stacked up. In his hands, her shoes looked as tragic and downbeat as the others. It was why, when she dealt in vintage clothing, she never did shoes. Shoes were not like shirts and jackets. They showed too much of a person's life. They were too expensive. They *marked*.

Standing there in her stocking feet, Ruby said, "I could come and help you, give up my job. I like the looks of yours."

"Look at my hands," he said. "Do something where you can have clean hands."

He gave her a brown cardboard ticket with a number on it, which she put in her purse. Then she walked the three blocks home in her stocking feet. She enjoyed the curious stares of two women standing waiting for the bus. It was nice to be without shoes. She could imagine being without a lot more—purse, clothing, the works.

At home she had a bath. Marvin hadn't called, again. In fact, she hadn't seen him since his wife found out. Only these phone calls. Maybe he was going to keep the promise he made not to see her. Ruby had planned on spending the night with him. She desperately needed to see him, to see anyone, to feel flesh against her flesh. But she wasn't going to sit around waiting. She put on a pair of black leggings and a red angora sweater with a low V-neck, found some shoes and de-cided to go back to work. She walked down to Bloor and flagged another cab. Sitting in the back, she had a feeling she was losing it. Losing it all. She rested her arm on the back of the seat and tried to *image* herself, as Oswald, her psychic consultant, directed.

She was Ruby Mason, fashion designer. Effervescent, powerful, self-possessed. Woman on the Move. Winner of the 1983 Designer of the Year Award. Businesswoman. Artist. Powerful—

It didn't work. No matter what she called herself, inside she felt like a freaked-out five-year-old. She often had hints of this—a great gap opening under her. But now it came on so strongly. She was standing on the edge of the Grand Canyon. All she was, and all she'd done, was ripping away from her as in a high wind. The dresses, the scarves, the wedding trains. She was powerless to stop their flight. She did not really even want to. She saw them go, one by one, out into the huge, empty space. They were of the moment—it had all been a game, to create them and see which ones survived. Some did last longer than others, but none of them really survived. Nothing would be remembered.

What a game it had been, the game of fashion. At first it seemed mysterious, but she had learned it. It was easy now to say which look was going to take. You float a lot of looks you know the world of women out there is going to resist. You float a brilliant one. The fashion writers hate it. It's either anti-woman or too feminine, it's a throwback or it's got no sense of history. If it's retro, it's too soon or too late. And so the really brilliant design, your first-born, gets destroyed. But the industry churns on, the pictures keep coming out, and while everyone's busy resisting, the look takes hold. Works its way down into the subconscious.

The second run at it is just about the same, only not so good. It does a little better. The screaming starts to die down. A few bold women are wearing it. That's nice for you, but it's not enough. You have to get the great mass of them out there. So it's the third take, some remnant of the original idea, some pale copy of it, that catches on. It takes because people are tired of fighting it. People are following those few bold ones. And it catches on because they're kidding themselves into believing *this is ours, we chose it*. And it's your baby, but battered down and compromised, so there's hardly any joy in it.

The cab jolted down St. George Street toward College. She cursed the Hugh Mensas of this world. Set up in their posts by accident, miracle or inertia. Dispensing favour and disfavour. The arbiter. The line judge. Now you're in, now you're out. They sucked you into a cycle of embracing and rejecting. Preyed on you with repeated acts of discovery and betrayal.

"You oughta be used to it by now," Audrey said.

Ruby *was* used to it. She played it that way. She used anyone or anything she could until she got to be the top. Then she wanted all the rules to change. Wanted it to be fair. Wanted to be there because she was good, and because she deserved it. No more of this chance or favour. Hey, guess what, a meritocracy! But there was no way. The same rules were in play. She'd been in long enough now, she was going out. She could feel it. Slipping out of style.

I've got to make it look like it's my idea. Ruby's heart was beating fast, and she was sweating. This had happened before. She'd been dumped before, a long time ago, by Blair and Oswald and Philip. And she'd made it look good, hadn't she? She could do it again. The cab was down at Queen, turning left.

"It's right," she said.

He grumbled under his breath.

Take control of this, Ruby said to herself.

But how could she? By going backward? "Thrift," the word she came in on, was out. Nobody wanted thrift now. Recycle, sure. But even if they did, it was a cheat. Thrift meant a basic respect for the materials, a philosophy of simplicity, love for the old. Thrift was a value; recycle was a strategy. People were just trying to capitalize now. Like Diana Louie. Not so long ago she was getting busted for coke. Now she's putting out T-shirts saying "Reduce, Reuse, Recycle." As a fashion statement, it stunk.

The problem for thrift all along had been that it was anti-fashion. Fashion *was* waste. The retread business, as Ruby knew only too well, had had a short popularity but never really paid off. People want to show that they've got so much money and such a wealth of ingenuity that they can afford to look great today and put yesterday in the shadow permanently. Eco-fashion wasn't thrifty, in fact, it was usually ugly, and an excuse to spend money. Here was the difference. Thrift was reincarnation. Recycling was death. Deconstruction.

While she went up in the elevator there popped into her head a clear vision for next fall. Decay. Decomposition. Shiny, draped fabric in putrid colours: chartreuse, pumpkin, brown, aubergine. Small bust and head, shoulders and waist gathered, like a bag clutched in a hand. Puffed-out hip, short skirts. How it should all come together. She tried to stay with her vision. Opening her office door, she felt a stab of the old fervour and rushed to her desk to get it all down.

But she couldn't concentrate enough to finish. Her thoughts ran ahead of the pen. Away from dresses to her life. Her badly designed, in fact, deconstructed life. She got up and walked through the showroom, snapping her fingers against her thighs.

Out of control, that's what her life was. Take Marvin. It was always his wife, his debts, his promises. Talk about immigrant workers. That was Ruby. Putting in all this effort for Marvin and taking her pittance of sex, but she was never going to get citizenship. Men insisted you act as if they were the centre of the universe. For a long time she hadn't had much to do with them. But then she got needy. For whatever odd reason, she had come to this time and place in her life:

she wanted a main squeeze. And if God had co-operated, like her mum always said he did, she'd have it by now.

But God wasn't co-operating, and neither was Marvin. If she was going to have to be dangling by strings, she might as well have a child. At least a child would love her. She hadn't used her diaphragm for a year. Part of her still hoped. So she would be sure, she only slept with Marvin. For that courtesy, he called her a ticking time-bomb. It was his affectionate little joke. That's what they called career women in their late thirties, desperate to have kids. Fidelity had not been wise: it gave Marvin a false sense of his own importance. Bad strategy, to be the mistress of an m-squared and not have another man on the side for yourself.

She stood in front of the big, metal-trimmed windows and looked into the night. The familiar, speeding panic began to build inside her. Her heart knocked against the inside of her ribs. She stepped back, as if the banging inside could break the pane of glass.

I've got to make it look like my idea. I can do it, too.

Ruby had always thought that getting pregnant was the easiest thing in the world to do. All the girls she grew up with had done it ages ago, girls who had nothing going for them. But Ruby Mason couldn't turn this simple trick. She'd been to talk to a load of doctors about why. They said she was older. They said maybe she wasn't relaxed. Too much coffee, too much coke. What bullshit. Blair drank coffee as much as she did and she had Simplicity. It wasn't fair. The last guy she went to said suppressed anger could stop couples from conceiving.

"Christ, you don't need to get personal," she said. "I didn't come here to be psychoanalysed."

"If you and your husband . . . ," he went on.

She didn't tell him she had no husband. She supposed she could be angry on her own, without a husband. Maybe not *as* angry, but angry. This guy described how some couples went into therapy and got big stuffed clubs and went around hitting things, and then after that they got pregnant.

Ruby considered getting a stuffed Fred Flintstone-style club right now. It would be fun to rampage around here, swiping the judies and clothes racks, swishing the pattern-maker's table clear. When they came in tomorrow morning they'd figure some junkie broke in and did it, when all it was was Ruby trying to get herself knocked up.

She laughed out loud. It made a hollow sound in her empty rooms. She went to the fridge, took out a bottle of Evian and poured herself a glass. She'd had no dinner; it was after ten o'clock. She went to the window again. She could see the scrawny little chained-up, city-planted trees getting ready to drop their leaves, dismembered bicycles locked to a rack, some without a wheel, some without seats, some without the whole front end. In this part of town you never left anything whole and complete out in full view.

There were trucks parked down the back alley and some guys standing around smoking behind the warehouses. There were new metal fire escapes, windows and shined-up hardware on some of the warehouses, and inside she could see lowered ceilings and long, white work surfaces. Designers and architects were moving in all around. Ruby'd been here ten years. Imitation might be flattery, but it was irritating.

She turned on the light to block out Toronto, to superimpose herself on the blackness. Now the room was shocking white, herself a figure in it, and you could not see out the windows: here instead she could be seen, from everywhere. She was alone. It was time for an invitation. What night was it? Wednesday. There was something tonight. Something she had intended to do. She went to her desk. On impulse, she picked up the phone and dialled Max Ostriker.

After one ring his voice came on saying hello.

"Hey what are you doing at work?" she said. "It's night. This is Ruby," she added.

"Working," he laughed. He had that good humour in his voice, always reassuringly *up*. "What can I do for you? You want to reschedule lunch?"

"Later," said Ruby. "I want you to tell me everything about the woman who jumped in front of the train. How she did it, how it looked, everything."

"Now?" said Max.

"I've kinda got it on my mind," said Ruby.

"Don't try it," he said. "It makes a mess."

"She must have meant to."

"Meant to make a public statement anyway," said Max. "At public expense."

"So what was the look on her face? Frantic?"

"No. Settled, I'd say. I was watching her 'cause she looked like someone who knew what they were doing. Strong walk. Not crazy."

"Maybe she had her reasons."

"No doubt she did," said Max. "But that's no reason I have to be her witness." Then, an edge of discomfort in his voice, he said, "Say, Ruby, how come you're so interested?"

"I was just thinking about her. What she looked like."

"Composed," Max gave her. "Determined."

"Oh." Ruby didn't say anything more. She had remembered what it was she was going to do tonight. Sam Chow's wake.

"You'll phone then, and make it another day?"

"Yeah, yeah, but I can't do it till morning."

"Okay," said Max. He sounded uncertain about letting her go.

"Oh and, Max, by the way, if I *don't* talk to you soon, I wanted to tell you something. Remember Blair, from Hearts of Flame? You know, the blonde. Well I've been thinking you should get together with her. She's around and she's single, with a kid, she's, well, I think you'd like her. I know you would. That's if you don't feel . . ."

Max laughed. "Insulted that you'd pass me on?"

"Something like that."

He laughed again. "Hey, we're friends, right?"

"She'll remember you. Blair Bowker. Here's her number—"

Somewhere it was written down. The wake. She remembered she'd been sitting at her desk turning the little roulette wheel when the call came. You put a coin in the slot and the wheel began to turn; it spun a couple of times and then stopped. You could bet against yourself, which was something Ruby did while she was negotiating on the phone. "Red they'll take it, black they won't," she'd whisper out the side of the receiver while some buyer harangued her in the right ear. "Even numbers say they'll offer high." "Black twenty-six says I'll do the festival this year again."

Private party, no press, the caller said, so keep this to yourself—and Ruby had taken some piece of paper that was lying on her desk and she'd written it down. Just his friends. She'd known Sam Chow for ten years, a designer. Died at Casey House, the AIDS hospice. Back in the recesses of memory she seemed to recall she'd slept with him. But it didn't matter. He had the fast kind, that you picked up recently, not the original, slow kind.

She looked at the clock. It was 10:29. It would be half over. She began to sift the scattered order sheets, the pink phone messages, the letters from creditors. No one was allowed to touch this stuff. Audrey was not allowed to tidy it. Stuff was either on her desk or it wasn't. She put it there when she was working and she threw it away or had Audrey file it when she was finished. Therefore she knew where everything was.

If she could only remember when the call came, and what she'd been doing at the time. She would have written it on something that had a link. That was her secret with notes to herself. If it was from her bank she'd write it on a cheque. If it was an invitation to a dinner party she'd write it on a restaurant receipt. Loosely, she tried to follow this plan. Where would she have written the details of the memorial?

Now she remembered. She'd been reading *Metropolis*. That was the exact moment, she was reading this ridiculous article about Faux Couture, their new spring line, and the phone rang and it was Guy, his lover, with the details, so she grabbed a pen and wrote it down in the margin of *Metropolis*. It was this week's.

She pushed through more piles. A hardcover book someone brought in on supermodel Monica Schnarre, a pair of earphones, an AGO bag with a bunch of postcards in it. She could never resist art gallery postcards. Aha! There was the slightly yellowing corner of *Metropolis*. Written in the top margin was—"Nickelodeon, Wed 9:30." In brackets, "King and Dovercourt."

Shit, shit, shit. She already had the jitters, and now she was going to be late. She dashed around getting her purse and taking some cash from Audrey's cash drawer, making sure she had cigarettes and kleenex. She felt like crying tonight. She was looking forward to it.

She didn't like what she had on, these leggings and the red sweater; the angora fluff that got up her nose. She felt like a cheap valentine, her shape hanging out for all to see. She had to go home and change into something more dignified. It was just possible, too, that if she dropped him a message at the office Marvin would show up outside. Marvin liked to go to these places, but he wouldn't go in, because he'd be seen, he thought. It occurred to her that Marvin exaggerated his own importance. Like all media people, he thought he could make or break you, when all he did was fill air time. The elevator was standing, door open, with a couple of cleaners in it. She jumped in, pressed G, and it didn't move. She put her thumb into the little recessed circle and jabbed it three times.

"Jammed?" The cleaners nodded mutely and shifted their feet. Portuguese, not much English. "Damn this thing," she cried. "Someone's put it on service." It seemed to Ruby outrageous that this should happen. Around the corner she saw a dolly being wheeled over, loaded with floor-sander, polishes, brushes, drop cloths. Behind it, the cleaners' boss. Ruby growled at them all, leapt out of the elevator and went for the stairs.

On the street, the light from the streetlight pooled beyond the doorway. She ran to it and stood a moment, as if she hoped it could hold her, one woman against a dark city street. But in a second she began to run again. Her eye expertly peeled for the lighted sign on the top of a taxi, she darted across the street, holding her bag into her side with her elbow to stop the clasp from springing open.

Kitty-corner across Queen, a cabbie was in the midst of doing a U-turn. Now he was on the far side, heading west. She jumped up and down and waved her hand over her head. He saw her now, she knew it, and lazily extended his U to come full circle and stop in front of her. The back door slid in front of her; she yanked on the handle and opened it, jettisoning herself across the plastic-coated back seat.

"Up to Bathurst and Dupont, then down to King and Dovercourt," she snapped. "We've gotta fly low." She was in a flat-out panic to get there, but she could not go in these clothes.

The driver was a tall, soft-looking black kid who gazed at her, over the glass barrier between the seats, with huge, frightened eyes. It calmed her.

"I'm late," she said, by way of explanation.

"By what street you want me to go up?" he said.

"I don't know. What's fastest?" she said.

"I think maybe Bathurst," he said.

Bathurst was fatal. Bathurst was always crammed with streetcars, trucks, people on bicycles and cars turning right against migrating tribes of pedestrians. But it was night. Maybe it wouldn't be bad. Ruby tried to keep herself from screaming. She lit a cigarette. The next best way to calm down was to ask people questions.

"So you had this bullet-proof glass put in," she said. "You get dangerous customers?"

"It's not my car," said the kid. "The owner, he did it. I just drive part-time."

"And the rest of the time?"

"I am a student. To George Brown College," he said.

"What are you studying?"

"To go to university," he said. "Queen's University."

"Where are you from?"

"An island," he said.

"Not the West Indies." His accent was different.

"From the African coast. Madagascar."

It was working, she was calming down, and he wasn't so scared. Ruby congratulated herself. "Jeez, Madagascar," she said. "You don't get too much news from there. There are lots of people from Madagascar in Toronto?" she said.

"I know one other guy in Canada," he said. "He lives in Calgary."

"Jeez," she said again. "You must be lonely. Better go out there and visit him."

In ten minutes they pulled up in front of Ruby's little semi-detached house, with its unrenovated angelstone front. She liked the awfulness of the front; the uglier it was on the out-side, the more perfect her little interior. She ran up the front walk, fished her keys out of her purse and let herself in. She sped across the white-carpeted, still front room, its mother-of-pearl surfaces and satin cushions gleaming secretly in their dark solitude. In her bedroom she threw open the closet doors and scanned the hangers as she peeled off her leggings. She found a good black suit, St. Laurent ('50s), with red but-tons, and got into it at the same time as digging her feet into a pair of jet-heeled suede pumps. She grabbed a red beret and, leaving everything where it lay, raced back out the door.

The kid in the cab waited patiently.

"South," she said.

Down Bathurst they went, past endless three-storey semis with storefronts. She looked across at the smooth, sinister Dome, which might have landed from space, to the glistening, blue glass towers flanking it. It was dark down here on the pavement, but overhead, lights fought each other for space—lines and circles and pictures in lights. Over the humpbacked railway pass, down into the ribbed and pillared tangle of expressways. There was a queasy feel to their movement, as if they couldn't adhere, as if they *slid* rather than drove. Ahead, the roads splayed out like frayed rope.

"Hey, you overshot. We missed the bridge."

The kid hunched, like he expected to be shouted at. "You want I go back?"

Ruby could have got mad, but she knew she wasn't going to. She'd lost her anger. It had gone out the cab window, as her dresses and her dreams had done earlier. The memorial would be nearly over. All those great-looking twenty-year-olds with their racehorse bodies, mourning the dead. She could do that without them.

It was a warm night. Ruby was sweating; the rayon showed big stains under the arms.

"Hey, wait up," she said. "I changed my mind. Not going to go after all. Take me back, turn around."

"I can't turn around," said the kid, looking scared again. "Not here."

"Well when you can," she grumbled, and sat back. She closed her eyes. She felt the car take a swerve like a figure-eight, first one way and then the other. Now they were at a stoplight somewhere. In a second she felt the car accelerate. She opened her eyes. The lake had gone; no, it was on the other side. They were heading east.

"Where you want me to take you, ma'am?" whispered the kid.

Ruby had begun to feel jolly. She rolled down her window, pulled off her beret and let the wind blow her hair. She rolled her neck to loosen the tension. "Oh I dunno," she said, mocking the rhythm of his speech. But then she saw the fear on his face again and regretted it. He didn't want to get caught up in any joy-ride with a crazy white lady.

"Just take me up York Street and drop me at the Royal York," she said. "You know where that is? Sure you do. Where the buses go to the airport. Just drop me right by that side door."

Marvin could wait for her, if he managed to get there at all, just like she had waited for him. Marvin and everyone else. Fashion victims farewell, thought Ruby. I'll catch you later.

And she let her head fall back on the seat, and felt the breeze, and decided not to worry at all about what she did next.

6

Sorry To Do This To You

Hugh Mensa circulated at the Nickelodeon wake with a glass of water laced with lemon. His bald pate with its glaze of sweat bounced just above the heads of the crowd like a helium balloon that was losing its loft. He tapped down lightly on this group, seemed to settle, then rose and drifted on. He had an idea he would see Ruby. She ought to have been there. Everyone was there. He looked forward to a confrontation in which she would call him the usual names and he would respond with his usual rapier wit.

At ten-thirty the event was well underway, the temperature in the room rising. Press had been banished, except for good friends. Mensa would have liked an opportunity to describe the scene. The fashion crowd parading by a microphone to grieve in public. Inept tribute following tearful praise. *Bartlett's Familiar Quotations* ransacked for references to scissors and fabric. But the larger world was not to be treated to his malice on the occasion of a death. He had *some* scruples.

Here was poor Sam Chow's lover now, quoting *Romeo and Juliet*.

"'And when [he] shall die, take [him] and cut [him] out in

little stars, and [he] will make the face of heaven so fine that all the world will be in love with night . . ."

"In love with night"? Yes, perhaps. Night was the time for gaiety and costume, for pretence, indulgence; the mood was very *fin de siècle*. But "in love with death"? No. Unless perhaps there was a trend to be spotted here. The new despair? He liked the sound of it. He headed for the men's room, stumbling into a couple of guys snorting coke behind the door, and made a note of it.

It was Ruby who insisted he was no critic (the title he assumed at *Metropolis*) but a lowly trend-spotter. He had an eye, but he also had a nose. An eye was for aesthetics, but a nose was lower down. If you had a nose you could smell out what was coming. One way he kept up was by reading the personal ads in *Now*. He knew, for instance, that a couple of years ago dads were in. Before that it had been slaves. Now it was transsexuals. Couture drag was in this year, which meant Ruby would be getting calls again at Hallowe'en from the drag queens who wanted to borrow her gowns.

Mensa did admire the way she'd stuck to her guns all these years. What she believed in—old-time, simple elegance and beautiful fabrics—wasn't an easy sell here. Feminism had hit glamour hard, then the schoolboy look came in. She had survived by being a good businesswoman, branching out and taking risks. And now her look was coming back in. He had a feeling she'd come back strong this year. He felt a little bad he hadn't mentioned her in his last piece. He'd make it up to her, maybe write about romance and use her new line.

Coming out of the can he bumped into Robina. Robina looked like a drag queen but she was actually a woman. In the '70s you'd have called her a fag-hag. In the '80s she'd have been romanticized, a muse for the cluster of effeminate men around her. Now she was a fashion accessory. The flamboyant ones took her everywhere: she looked great, her legs went on for miles, she never said anything.

At eleven o'clock the speeches were over. In the centre of the floor, a couple of queens were doing runway, backs on a tilt, faces slack-jawed and arch. A crew of black-legged, crop-haired androgynes danced in their heavy-soled shoes. Friends stood in circles affectedly wiping their eyes and talking about how Sam's death *was*, how he managed it, how he carried it off. Hugh moved from group to group like an elderly druid, his tall form curved over to hear, his ear always bending to allow the kiss. He never relaxed his removed, superior pose.

At eleven-thirty he looked at his watch. Ruby must not be coming. She had made herself scarce lately. He wondered if it was something to do with the man in the Italian suits with the deep-shadowed eyes he'd seen hanging around her place, this married man they'd all heard about. On a friendly impulse he called Ruby's home. No answer. No machine either. Weird. But the whole team from Splash was moving off to Zydeco, and he decided to follow them. He'd have forgotten about Ruby if it hadn't been that outside the door he saw someone standing, hunched, with his coat collar turned up. The Italian suit man. He looked so conspicuously inconspicuous that he had to be Ruby's married man, or an undercover cop. Mensa went up to him, extending a hand.

"You need help with the bouncer?"

The man's face was drawn down, indulged. He took the hand reluctantly, a man without trust recognizing one of his kind.

"I'm not going in. I'm waiting for someone," he said, un-willingly. He moved off.

But not before Mensa caught a glimpse of a visage he rec-ognized. A reflex expression of respect came over Mensa's face, a reflex that only occurred when he was in the presence of Someone Who Could Do Something for Him. But he said nothing, lit a cigarette and went off after the others.

At ten-thirty-five Thursday morning, Audrey looked up from her desk to see Ruby's ten-thirty appointment standing in front of her, a Mr. Walter from Harridge's. She replaced the large, encrusted clump of plaster that was her left earring, removed by necessity for answering the phone.

"Whoops!" she said. "I know she's expecting you!" She whirled on her chair and headed behind the screens to Ruby's office, which was, she knew, in a state of total chaos from some sort of tantrum she'd had the night before. She picked up Ruby's desk phone. Ruby wasn't at home.

"I can't believe it, she's slipped out! Maybe she had an earlier appointment," said Audrey, showing her large teeth in what was meant for a smile as she came back to face the buyer. "She must be delayed getting back. Can I get you a coffee?"

As the man sat stiffly in the Victorian wicker chair, sipping out of his turquoise Fiesta cup, she made conversation.

"Used to be you could get around town pretty quickly before noon. Now the rush hour starts at ten!"

By eleven o'clock, Audrey had tired of putting on this show. She went back into Ruby's office to phone again. Still no answer. Wondering what she was going to tell Mr. Walter, she called Blair.

"Do you happen to know what Ruby's up to?"

Blair said she had no idea. Maybe Audrey should call Marvin. You can't call Marvin, said Audrey. His instructions. Nobody ever calls him, not even Ruby.

Blair said maybe if she was sick she'd gone over to her brother and sister's. Audrey had that number. The first small wave of alarm overtook her. Just as she put the phone down it rang again: Mensa. She blurted out to him that she had some guy waiting and Ruby hadn't shown up and she couldn't find her anywhere.

To be told things was part of Mensa's talent, a singular talent and not necessarily a pleasant one. Mensa knew that people confide spontaneously and without consideration in loitering individuals with known malicious tendencies, perhaps for the simple fact that they seemed so ready to receive disturbing information. He had also perfected a means of seeming to confide, himself, while revealing nothing, and in fact pumping the other party for information.

Ruby hadn't shown up at Sam Chow's memorial either last night, which was peculiar, as she had once been his lover, had she not? he said. Audrey, without realizing that he was fishing, confided that Ruby claimed she couldn't remember. But then Hugh said he'd phoned her place last night and got no answer, which meant she hadn't been seen or heard from since yesterday afternoon. Hadn't Audrey better get on the phone to that married man they'd all heard about?

By the time Audrey got off the phone she had decided this was a crisis. Just naming it firmed her up. She pulled out Ruby's drawer mirror and applied fresh lipstick. Straightening her skirt, she went out to tell Mr. Walter that she had just received word Ruby had been in a car accident. She was not seriously hurt, but had gone to hospital to be looked at. Mr. Walter, who had several other appointments in the neighbourhood, left. Audrey sat down feeling much better. The phone rang. She took off her earring, lifted the receiver and repeated the story.

Mr. Walter went on to his next appointment at Ports International, where he mentioned, in passing, Ruby's car accident. By late afternoon, one hundred people had been told that Ruby Mason was in a car crash. Her injuries had gone from minor to major. Amnesia was a definite possibility.

Blair forgot about Audrey's call. Perhaps she was angry at Ruby, always making people worry. She went in to work as usual at three and did not give Ruby another thought.

Mary Mason, Ruby's sister-in-law, got the phone call from Audrey at eleven-thirty in the morning. Mary was small, round and maternal; having no children, she was Ruby's champion in the family, defending her from Arthur's wrath and her mother-in-law's fervour. She fretted at home until Arthur came in from his shift at four. Then, Mary bubbling with terror, they drove the short distance over to Ruby's house. Letting themselves in with the key she had given them, they found the place as always—perfect, dustless, styled like a shop window. Only the small puddle of clothes in front of the closet was evidence of anything strange.

"She could have been missing for weeks, we'd never know the difference," grumbled Arthur. "It always looks like nobody lives here." He was tall with a long, axe-handle head. He had never liked Medicine Hat; he'd been a loner. He joined the Mounties in Alberta; happily, they moved him here. He sat on the living-room couch thinking evil thoughts about Marvin, who he was certain was a bad influence and was married, anyway. But Mary went straight to the bedroom, opened the cupboards and drawers and tried to figure out what, if anything, Ruby had taken. The dazzle-painted duffle bag she carried on short trips was there, as well as her big nylon garment-bag. As for clothing, Ruby had so much of it Mary couldn't begin to figure out what was missing.

Marvin arrived in his office Thursday around noon, with his hair still wet from the shower and his ears burning from a fight he'd had with his wife. He'd taken a chance last night, telling her he was staying at work. Of course she'd phoned again. Result: full-scale battle. And all to stand outside Nickelodeon for an hour waiting for Ruby. The only good part was that, as she hadn't shown up, he was genuinely guiltless.

"A woman from deBoltz Designs has been trying to reach you," said his trusty assistant, whose antennae were excellent. Marvin believed, erroneously, that she was in the dark about his relations with Ruby. "She's calling back after noon."

He composed an enervated face. "I suppose they want to talk about coverage for the Fashion Festival," he said, "or maybe a little feature spot for their line." When you control an outlet like "City Time," everybody wants something. It was one of his cynical pleasures, to figure out what people wanted in advance and to decide, in most cases, that they weren't going to get it. He grinned amiably at his assistant, but when she turned away he scowled. He'd told Ruby never ever to call him here. Whatever stopped her from turning up last night, she was only going to make it worse. That woman has become a millstone around my neck, he said to himself. Or whatever the expression is.

No sooner did he get back to his desk than the call came. But it wasn't Ruby; it was Audrey.

"I don't suppose you have any idea where Ruby is," she began argumentatively.

"What's the matter, she gone off?"

"We can't find her."

"Well, I wouldn't be surprised if they found her in the bathtub with her wrists slashed," he said.

Audrey was so upset she said goodbye and hung up.

Marvin sat at his desk staring at the phone. He'd just said a very foolish thing. He couldn't imagine why. Ruby had been making trouble lately, but suicide had never entered his head. Of course he didn't want Ruby to be hurt. If something happened to her and people started looking for her, it would all become public. His wife, who already knew what he was up to, would know with whom, and where and when. Furthermore, he, Marvin, would be exposed to public ridicule.

Marvin sat at his desk and he fretted. He went out for a walk. He closed his eyes and saw Ruby. He opened them and she went away. It was a relief. The woman wanted too much. He missed her when she wasn't there but, compared to dealing with her demands, this was easy. Having made his decision, he rushed over to her house in a lather of premature mourning, opening the door with his key.

There, in the small satin-and-plush living room, leaning

forward with his elbow resting on the glass coffee table, sat Arthur. Marvin didn't like Arthur, because Arthur was a cop. Mary, who was right behind him, he didn't like either, because Mary was smart and gave him the impression she saw through him. They both returned the feeling, had done since they'd met him, a year ago. They all stopped short and glared at each other.

"You have a *key*?" said Mary.

Marvin was dishevelled in a way that suggested he thought dishevelled was the right look for the occasion. His tie was pulled half loose and hanging to one side of his chartreuse silk shirt; his jacket was flying sideways, his hair likewise, its gel having gone sticky in the humidity.

"Before you say anything, it's all my fault," he sobbed. "It's all my fault, I know it is."

"Marvin, you are mistaken," said Arthur in his low, slow voice. "This has got nothing to do with you. Wherever Ruby's gone, whatever happened, it's not for you to put yourself in the middle here. We are the family."

He stood directly in front of Marvin, legs apart. Marvin took this gesture as an invitation to cast himself sideways on the sofa, where he began to sob. "I knew it, I knew it," he said. "I was so bad for her."

Arthur stood with his hands in his pockets looking down in disgust and forming the word "worm" with his lips. Arthur was a kind person with an eye for the criminal type, both major and minor. He had spotted Marvin at the outset, suspicious because Ruby told him that one week after they met they'd gone to a beach in Jamaica, where they fell passionately in love.

"Everyone looks better on a beach," he said to his sister then.

"Not everyone," she answered. "Beautiful people do. He's not beautiful people. I met him at a reception held by the Mayor! He's a very important person in the media."

"I'm not happy about the kind of people you hang around with," he said to her. "You never could see beyond the bedposts."

His suspicions were confirmed when he saw the lapsed licence plates on Marvin's car. "Why would a television big shot have lapsed plates?" he said to Mary. Something was wrong. Probably he was a fraud with no job at all. It wouldn't be the first time Ruby was taken in.

Mary said nothing. She did not want to contradict her husband, but she was certain that if Ruby was missing, Marvin *did* have something to do with it. She thought Marvin was trouble. She didn't know why Ruby hung on. "It's just a lark, you know, I'd die if he ever left his wife, I wouldn't know how to get away fast enough," she had said. But why, but why, but why? Mary said. "He loves me, he needs me, and besides, it's hard to find men nowadays," Ruby answered.

It might be hard to find men, but it couldn't be *that* hard, thought Mary. "You think he needs you, to hell. He just needs a meal ticket," Mary said to Ruby. She and Arthur's mother, Martha, had often talked about it, how this guy came along and he wouldn't go away. He was a fake, with no job.

"He's got a good job, don't be ridiculous," said Ruby. That was the trouble with the family success story. They all thought Ruby was rich because her picture was in *Toronto Life* fashion magazine. They thought all men were after her money, while the truth was, if five Toronto ladies didn't decide to tie the knot this year, her business would go under.

Now Mary examined Marvin minutely, looking for the key to his hidden, villainous identity. He was, she had to admit, attractive in a sepulchral fashion. His lips were sensuous, he appeared explosively passionate, unlike Arthur. He looked like he had a lot of nervous energy, didn't fall asleep on the couch like Arthur, either. She was curious, she had to admit. Ruby's *lived*, she thought.

Without warning, the door opened again to a tall, thin,

bald man with red hair over his ears, introducing himself as Hugh Mensa, the fashion critic. Hugh wrung their hands.

"We don't need the press here, thank you," began Arthur, standing up to block his further penetration of the room.

"I'm not here as press. I'm a friend. I heard from Audrey . . . looked for her last night . . ." he said. "I didn't get your name." He extended his hand to Marvin, and this time recognized him: Marvin Arbat, producer of "City Time" on City-TV. Indeed, a man who could Do Something for You (if only in a small way), but most often didn't.

Marvin took the hand and mumbled something, not his name.

Mensa offered to go back into Ruby's bedroom with Mary because he knew Ruby's wardrobe well, and perhaps he could tell if she'd taken things to go on a trip. In the bedroom, he put his head close to Mary's.

"How do you feel about this man Marvin?" he said to Mary. "I sensed Ruby was unhappy . . ."

In the living room, Arthur and Marvin inspected each other in aggravated silence.

"Did you and Ruby have a *quarrel*, Marvin?" said Arthur. He said "quarrel" oh so carefully; it was a euphemism. What Arthur really implied was, Did you beat her up and throw her body under a bridge?

Marvin said Ruby worked too hard and she had a lot of stress.

"She's always happy, that girl," said Arthur indignantly. "And when she had stress, she talked to her family. She'd have no such problems if she listened to me."

Marvin nodded carefully. He'd already made that blooper about slitting her wrists. "I think maybe she was having trouble with her backers." It was a sore point; Ruby consistently refused to tell him who they were.

"Backers? What backers?" said Arthur. He rearranged his legs on the impossible chair. "We can argue all day but we aren't getting any smarter in the question of her whereabouts. We don't even know when she was last seen. She might just be gone to a *spa*." He said "spa" as if to spit on one.

"I think we should all go away and wait till tomorrow," said Marvin. "She'll turn up." He was twitching in his seat; he wanted to get out of there.

"Not even call the police?"

"What are the cops gonna do? She's nobody's little kid. She's not a wife or a mother. I suppose if she wants to go off truant for a while then it's her own business."

Marvin paced around the room for another minute. Then he said he had a meeting, and he went to the door and blew out, even more desperate-looking than when he came.

Mensa advised Arthur and Mary to report it to the police. "Likely it's nothing, but in case there was some foul play, every hour would count. Marvin doesn't want it, but Marvin may not be thinking only of Ruby," he said, with a smile on his transparent, freckled face. "Do you see what I mean?"

Friday morning Arthur talked it over with his buddies at work: should he call the city cops? The Mounties didn't like to give work away, not unless they had to. But so far it wasn't a case. He ended up dropping down and reporting her missing. He found himself talking to a regular beat cop. It was eerie. The guy said just what Marvin had predicted. Since Ruby was a grown-up woman and had no close family, she was perfectly free to take a powder for a few days or a week. When Arthur said she'd been expected at work, he acted like unreliability was part of her profession.

"You don't understand Ruby," Arthur said, a phrase he was going to repeat many times over. "She loved that business. She built it up. She wouldn't just not show up for work one day."

"We'll put a Missing Persons on the wire, but that's about it unless there's foul play suspected."

"But what about this Marvin Arbat? He told Audrey that he expected to find her in the bathtub with her wrists slashed."

"From City-TV? Oh yes. Mr. Arbat was the first to let us know. He thought you'd be filing a report. He did mention that remark," said the cop, rolling a finger over the pencil on his desk, up and down the blotter.

"What'd he say?" Arthur's suspicions rose even higher: a guilty man's move if there ever was one. Worse, Marvin had stolen a march on him.

"He allowed as how it was a pretty dumb thing to say. He explained to us that he was sick of having the screws put to him, first by his wife, then by Ruby." The cop grinned sympathetically.

Smeared by Ruby's conduct once more, Arthur got mad. He went home to Mary. Mary was on a crying jag, making no sense at all. He shouted at her a bit, told her to hold on to her hat, it was still only a day and a half. But Mary carried on until Arthur was forced to call his mother in Medicine Hat. She was bad, and then Mary got on the line, half weeping, and said that people were talking about suicide. Martha Mason began to hoot like a train whistle.

"No Mason would commit suicide. Ruby knew, when you have problems you take them to God! You hear me? Maybe things were not going well the last few weeks, but she was at peace with herself and with God . . ."

Arthur held the phone away from his ear until Martha stopped. "When did she go?"

"Wednesday night's the last anyone saw her."

"But I talked to her on the *phone* Wednesday night!" Martha howled. "She called me, she was fine! What are you talking about, she's gone and disappeared? Arthur Mason, she's there somewhere, you find her."

"It's a big city," said Mary, on the extension phone. "We don't even know where to start. And the police say they're just putting it on some kind of wire—"

"I'm getting on an airplane," said Martha Mason. "I'll phone right now and get myself a ticket, get that shiftless neighbour of mine to drive me in. You haven't seen nothin' until I get there. We're gonna find that girl if it's the last thing we do."

Mensa searched the files until he found a photograph of Ruby. It was a black-and-white shot taken as part of a portrait series on "Women on the Move." It was backlit, and her head was inclined slightly as if tuned to—yes, another world. She looked younger, more glamorous, and somehow dated, which she would hate. But it had the look, the right look for the occasion.

He'd done a little snooping, a bit of police-type work. Some people, like Mary Mason, hadn't known he was going to quote her, but that was a quibble. It turned out to be a long article, but he got it past the editor 'cause it was news. He was rather proud of his piece; once it was printed he collected a dozen copies of the paper to save. This was his story, he wasn't going to let it go. His eyes and his nose and all his reporter's instincts told him this was a big one.

Besides, Ruby was his friend. He remembered, doing all this thinking about her, how much he liked her.

WHERE IS RUBY MASON?

The fashion world is rife with rumour and innuendo since the disappearance Wednesday night, September 6, of fashion mogul (and favourite role model for upcoming female designers) Ruby Mason. More than twenty-four hours after she was last seen by a neighbour getting into a cab in front of her house, no clues have been found. Foul play has not been ruled out.

Miss Mason was expected that evening at a wake for

her former close associate, Sam Chow, who died at Casey House. When Ruby did not arrive, at least one friend became worried and called her home, to find no answer. Thursday morning she did not appear for work. Audrey Tippet, who manages the Mason design studio, deBoltz Designs, told a caller Mason had been in a car accident.

"Look, I just made up the story about the car accident to get this man off my case," said Tippet. "I can't believe how people talk. I got like a hundred phone calls this afternoon. Everybody wants to know. What happened, where is she? Is it amnesia? They don't want to be the last to hear."

Ruby's closest relatives in the city, her brother Arthur Mason and his wife Mary, were at her home later Thursday. In the absence of any explanation of her whereabouts, they were questioning their sister's life. The high-level success story did not come without troubles. The former singer with the folk band Hearts of Flame had many friends, but few intimates. Recently she had been seeing a man.

"He wasn't Ruby's type. You see, he latched on. He stuck, and told Ruby he needed her. I told Ruby he was bad news. Arthur said a while ago something serious is going to happen to Ruby," says sister-in-law Mary Mason.

Other questions involve the state of her business, and whether she could expect to enjoy the continued support of her backers.

In some quarters, speculations that Miss Mason had committed suicide were high. At least one person was quoted as saying he expected to find her in the bathtub with her wrists slit. Other friends point to Mason's long-term involvement with Oswald Yakibuchi, the former pollster who bills himself as "Consultant to the Stars."

Yakibuchi also sang with Hearts of Flame. Friends say that hypnotism and other unorthodox practices drew Ruby to him in times of trouble.

"Oswald knew her in a previous life, you know. They were King and Queen of Egypt or something," said Ramone, the house model at deBoltz Designs. "She listened to him more than anyone."

Mr. Yakibuchi could not be reached for comment.

Suicide seems unlikely to Mason's close associates. "If she did it, she'd do it properly, you know? If she was going to kill herself she'd have done it with drugs, like Marilyn Monroe, and she'd have dressed up for the occasion. She always wanted to look her best."

Ramone was one of many who heard the story that Mason had been in a car accident. To her mind that is still a likely explanation.

"You know she was in one before, and she walked away. How can you explain that? Except by saying that she's not from this world? Maybe she's gone on to another world again. You can't rule it out."

Police are not treating the case as a homicide.

In advance of any police investigation, *Metropolis* inquired of Ruby's next-door neighbour, Mr. O. Pike. Mr. Pike said she went in and out again Monday night around ten o'clock, looking "possessed by demons—in a tearing hurry and with her eyes smeared with black." She kept a cab waiting. He said Ruby always had a smile and a few words for him, but that night she did not look his way.

A memo left on Ruby's desk, and overlooked by Tippet, implied Ruby might be intending to do something serious. The memo read: "Sorry to do this to you. Ramone needs more zip for green velvet, can't get it done before, trust you with it—R."

But does an apology a suicide note make? Certainly

Ruby's glamorous life, when examined closely, looked ripe for tragedy. But perhaps, in the aftermath of a disappearance, all our lives do.

Audrey Tippet, carrying on business at deBoltz Designs while waiting for a sign or a word from her employer, hopes Ruby has not met with violence. If she did, it would be an irony. She was ready for a change.

"She missed the simple things. She told me someday soon she was going to give this all up, have time for long walks and seeing friends.

"But it's only been one day. She could walk in here tomorrow. It could be a stunt. It could be a career move."

7

A Nice Girl
in a Trunk

Blair heard about the *Metropolis* story from Audrey. Ruby's assistant was calling every day, reporting on how the fashion community had erupted in a froth of fear and horror and glee. Some believed the amnesia story, while some thought the note on her desk—"Sorry to do this to you"—was a sure sign she'd killed herself. The idea of suicide had a currency, a shock value, precisely because it was so unlikely. Those who found Ruby heartless thought it was a prank.

Blair ran over to Dupont to find a copy of *Metropolis*. She sat with the newspaper in front of her, that awful picture of Ruby staring out. It had the jelled, tragic, unknowing look of graduation photos that end up in the daily press over notices that young women have been raped or murdered. When she finished reading she phoned Philip.

"Ruby's disappeared."

"What do you mean she's disappeared?"

"Didn't go in to work Thursday. Didn't answer her phone at home. Finally her secretary called me. She's not there. Not anywhere. Hasn't been seen since Wednesday night."

"What do you mean she's not there?"

"She's not there. She's gone somewhere. No sign of her. Nothing."

"Maybe she just met a guy and slept over."

"Mmmm."

"Went on a trip, spur of the moment."

"And didn't tell her shop?"

"Maybe she's mad at them. Or maybe it's this married man . . ."

Blair sighed. "Anyway, her family's moved in. Somebody called the cops. The whole bit."

"God, that's weird," said Philip. "Still, knowing Ruby . . ."

"You're not in on it? One of your stunts?"

"I take offence," said Philip, "easily in the morning."

"It's not morning!"

"Well I just woke up."

"You're hopeless," said Blair, and hung up the phone.

Marvin showed no signs of going into hiding, or of running away to join Ruby, as some predicted. Saturday he was at Ruby's shop ostentatiously taking care of business while Audrey fumed; that night he spent in the Squeeze Club, leaning over his scotch with bleary eyes and dejected countenance. He stopped strangers crossing the room and held them by both shoulders, talking about Ruby. She was a beauty, a talent; she would have given you her last nickel.

"I was married but it didn't matter. Didn't matter one bit," he said, over and over. "She loved me and I loved her and we were going to get married."

Saturday night Martha Mason arrived, by Air Canada, from Calgary. The first thing she did when her feet touched the floor of Pearson Airport was throw a tantrum.

"Find me that Marvin and I'll find you the answer to this puzzle! Where my daughter is!"

She commanded a large audience in the arrivals hall, standing as wide as she was tall in her turquoise pant suit with her bags around her feet. Arthur hunched his neck down into the collar of his jacket and disappeared into the crowd around the baggage retrieval. Mary patted her mother-in-law's hand.

"You say it was Wednesday night. I told you on the telephone, I spoke to Ruby Wednesday night. But I can't tell you on the phone what she said."

"What time?"

"I was watching 'Wheel of Fortune' and then the one after that, and she called in the commercial, I'd say nine o'clock? Nine o'clock, maybe ten o'clock. *My* time."

"So that it was midnight here."

"She called me and we talked. She said she paid her phone bill just so we could talk long-distance, you know. And she told me, Mother, things are not going my way these few weeks. And I told her what I always told her."

Martha looked out at the crowd of people straining with their luggage toward the door. Defiant, proud of her answer to life's questions, Martha was never shy about her relations with God.

"I told her to bring her troubles to Him."

Mary looked over her shoulder to see how Arthur was doing with the bags. He was lost in the crush. "Where was she calling from?" she whispered.

"Now that I think of it, it was somewhere strange. Somewhere public with a lot of noise. And she's telling me something about not wanting to marry him, I don't know what all, and then Marvin comes on the phone. He comes on the phone and he says to me, 'Martha, don't worry. I'm in charge here.'"

"Marvin?" Mary's voice was full of dread.

"Wait, Mary, you just listen to me. Let me finish what I have to say. I said to him, 'No, Marvin, you're not in charge, God's in charge.' *God's* in charge. 'Cause you know He is . . .'"

Mary was forced to nod before she heard the rest of

the story.

"And then he said to me he says, 'It's not Marvin.' And then he says something weird about prayers and afterlife and energy somethin' and destiny somethin'."

Martha Mason was shaking her large fist, the flesh under her arm filling the large sleeve to bursting and wobbling like a pudding. Mary gave one more beseeching look to Arthur. He was struggling through the crowd with a suitcase.

"And then Ruby came back on the line and she just said she had to go."

"So *was* it Marvin?" said Mary, who had got lost somewhere in that tale.

"I'm not sure," said Martha. "You see, Ruby wanted to get away from him, she had wanted to for a year. Twice she broke off with him but he got her back. You know that."

"She never told me! How did he do that?"

Martha made a face. "Pure man-ip-u-lation!"

"Here we go, Mother," said Arthur.

"You gotta hear this."

When they were settled in the car, Mary began to cry. To her, the whole issue stopped with Marvin. His face swam before her eyes, like the devil's. "I don't know what she sees in that man, I swear to you I don't," she insisted brokenly.

Arthur tried to figure out which lane he should be in for the 401 eastbound.

"I suppose she saw him as a cause, that she could put him right. She took in stray cats, too," Martha sniffed.

"So she was with a man! But why would Marvin, or somebody else, want to harm Ruby?" asked Arthur.

"I think she must have known something, and she had to be put out of the way," said Martha confidently. "A man like that has enemies. Maybe he cheated somebody, and they were trying to get at *him* by killing *her*. A warning for her."

"Hold your horses, Mother," said Arthur. He successfully negotiated the curve off the 409.

"You're not going to believe your eyes when we show you this article from the newspaper."

"Oh, she's been written up in the newspaper," said Martha, folding her large arms in a cross on her chest. "Oh Lord, oh Lord, oh Lord. Your ways do need explaining to your servants here below."

Later that night, while her husband and his mother sat watching the television, Mary Mason had an idea. It had to do with Ruby's facelift powder. She mixed it with water and smeared it on so that it made a stiff mask, did this religiously every three days. It was a joke between them; Mary hated to see Ruby with the ghoulish green face. But Ruby never missed her regular treatment. Mary knew exactly where it was in Ruby's bathroom cupboard. If she left the powder behind, she thought, then Ruby was forced. She would not willingly go anywhere for three days without it.

Telling Arthur she was going to Shoppers Drug Mart, she drove to Ruby's house. She was shaken to see lights on. She knocked, then put her key in the lock, thinking wildly that Ruby might be back. But when she opened the door there was Ramone, the house model, and Marvin. Ramone stood in the middle of the living-room floor stuffing a suitcase full of Ruby's clothes, her tapes and her jewellery.

As soon as she saw them, Mary began screaming.

"What the hell are you doing, stealing my sister's things? Don't you lay a hand on that stuff!"

Marvin stepped over the mess on the floor. He walked, hands out, toward Mary, his long, white face twisted at the mouth.

"Relax, relax," he said. "I can assure you, these are Ramone's things. Ruby borrowed them. I wouldn't lie. I came here to watch and make sure nothing important got taken."

Now Mary knew Marvin was the devil. They seemed like they were drunk, or high on something. They had some kind of music on really loud, blaring out from a radio Marvin wore somewhere on his person.

"It's indecent," she muttered, standing a brave sentry by the bathroom door. "If she is in the kind of trouble they're sayin' now, you're like grave-robbers, you are. *Ghouls.*"

They made ready to leave, a lot of high giggles coming out of their mouths. Marvin put his hand on Mary's shoulder.

"Don't you worry about Ruby," he said. "Even if she's in the worst trouble we can imagine, she's not lost to us. I can communicate with her from beyond the grave, did you know that?"

Mary just looked at him like he was a head-case, which was what she thought, and rattled the doorknob till they left. She was shaking all over. Alone, she made her way to the bathroom cupboard. The facelift powder was still there, exactly where it should be. Mary's heart thumped down hard and seemed to stop somewhere in the gully under her ribs. That was proof positive. Ruby had been abducted. And that Marvin! Talking about beyond the grave. She wanted to call a locksmith and change the lock on Ruby's house, but then if Ruby came back, she wouldn't be able to get in. More frightened than she'd been since the first day, Mary went back out to the car. As she opened the door, the next-door neighbour came out of his house.

"You Ruby's sister?" he called.

She nodded. The man came down his walk; he had a gimpy leg and he was old.

"I got a piece of paper here," he said softly. "Guy came in to talk."

It was getting dark. The old man's face was creased up with concern.

"I'm Mr. Pike," he said. "And I'm tellin' you first 'cause I don't know what the cops would do with him. You see," he said, fingering a small piece of paper with some writing on it, "he was nothin' but a scared kid."

"Who was?"

He proffered the piece of paper.

"The cabbie. He came back. I saw him outside, he was hanging around outside her door. I came out and talked to him. He said he drove her somewhere that night."

They got the driver in to the station that night. Arthur told the cops to go easy on him, he came to help. Even so, Muhammed Surwa Balim shook so badly when the officer asked him questions that his voice had a gurgle. His eyes were huge, brown and guileless. He was slim and painfully young, maybe seventeen, although no doubt there was a birth certificate somewhere making him older so he could drive the cab.

"She was a very nice lady," he said. "Otherwise I never remember. Never say nothin'. I got her from King Street. We drove up to her house where she went in, real fast, came out. She wanted go someplace near Bathurst but when we drove past it she say never mind turn back. Then we went for a long ride down the Lakeshore Boulevard. She opened the window and let her hair blow. Singing old songs. Finally she ask me to let her off, Royal York Hotel. That's all."

The cops tried to keep him. They said they were checking to see if he'd stolen something, if he delivered her somewhere for a fee. But if he had, why would he come forward? said Arthur.

"Something happen to the lady?" Muhammed said. Even in the depth of his fear he could ask.

"Nobody has seen her since."

His eyes opened wider and their dark depths swam.

"Did she talk about any trouble she was in? Did she seem unhappy?"

"No. She ask me if I have any friends in Toronto," he said.

"But that's Ruby," said Mary. "She does that. That's the kind of person she is. She comes on strong, tries to make you feel good. She didn't ever give signs, not to me." Mary started to cry. "If she had trouble, I wanted to help her! I wanted to know!"

"Family members always feel guilty," said the cop.

Arthur pulled the officer on the Missing Persons call aside. He could talk to him, professional to professional. The alert hadn't turned up anything. He told the cop about the strange goings-on Mary saw with Marvin and Ramone, stealing her things and claiming they could talk to her from beyond the grave.

"What are you suggesting?" said the cop, not taking it kindly. Mounties, he figured. Ceremonies in red coats, riding horses around in circles. What do they know?

"There oughta be more energy put into this."

"I'm doing all I can," he said. "I've got twenty-seven other cases to look into."

"Don't get your nose out of joint," said Arthur heatedly. "She's my sister. I want her found. I want this thing moved out to Homicide."

"I wish," said the constable. "But we gotta come up with something better than this." He jerked his head toward Muhammed. "We'll let him go."

Monday morning, the fifth day after Ruby had vanished, Max Ostriker sat at his desk, staring at the yellow telephone message Maureen had given him: "Call Mary Mason." He did not want to call Mary Mason. What could he say to Ruby's sister-in-law, for that's who it must be. He knew Ruby was gone; he'd seen the article in *Metropolis*. He'd heard a couple of radio interviews. So far he'd done nothing, spoken to no one. Something stopped him. He thought over and over of their last phone call. How she had asked about the woman who jumped in front of the train. Had he presented an option which, in a vacuum of other options that Monday night she took? He was morbidly convinced he had. What he couldn't figure out was that if she'd done this, how the TTC and everyone else had managed to miss it.

He would not say this to Mary Mason. What could he say? Why was she calling? But he could not avoid the call any longer. He dialled the number and was lucky. He didn't have to say anything: Mary knew what she wanted.

"You're Ruby's friend. I want you to do something," she said. "Call the cops and tell them you think it's suspicious. They're not doing anything. We tried to push them but they think we're over-reacting, 'cause we're family. You're a lawyer, you know how to talk to them. Tell them they should move it over to Homicide and give us an investigator."

Max said he would. It was remarkably easy. He just adopted the tone Andy took when *he* talked to the police.

On Tuesday, Dick Nolan was assigned to Ruby Mason.

He was slight and worried-looking, with hair neatly parted on one side and slicked across to the other ear. He looked like a Sunday school teacher with a few guilty secrets. His secrets, whatever they were, he kept in his room in the Cameron Hotel, where he'd lived for twelve years of the twenty he had been a detective on the force. He liked to save his money for lavish gambling trips to Las Vegas and Atlantic City. He got time off for overtime when he solved a case, which wasn't very often.

In the picture they gave him, Ruby, in a fluffy, red, V-neck sweater and tight black velvet pants, was sitting on a high stool, laughing into the camera, her hands clasped together in front of her. He looked at the picture for a long time. He liked the look of her. But a disappearance with a woman usually meant only one thing. She must have been mixed up in something ugly.

He had a pretty big load now, a dozen other homicides to

try to catch up with. Ruby, he promised to her face, you will get special treatment. She *spoke* to him. *I want*, said the face. *I get*. A knowing, been-around-the-track-a-few-times face, but still innocent, yearning, believing, a face that could still laugh like a child. "I like you, Ruby," he said. "Which is just as well. I don't look so hard for the ones I don't care about. Together we'll solve this case," he said to her picture. She was easy to talk to, he found.

He began his work by talking with her mother Martha, Martha having been the last to speak with her Wednesday night.

"Ruby's talking on the telephone, something about this person telling her about past life and whatnot. I told her, keep away from those people. The next thing I know I'm called to Toronto, my child is vanished. I tell you, if she disappeared she didn't go under her own steam. Somebody wanted to get rid of her, and made that happen. What about the man who was with her that night?"

"No traces," said Dick.

"Man on the phone said he wasn't Marvin, but I think he *was* Marvin."

"Why do you think it's Marvin?" Dick doubted it; Ruby's married boyfriend was too obvious a suspect.

"Evil. This man is *evil*." Martha rocked herself for a minute, and then her voice burst out afresh, filling the little house on Montrose Avenue as it must have done the churches in southern Alberta.

"If my child was killed, the guilty ones are going to pay, mister. Had it not been for my faith in God, Jesus Christ as my Saviour, I would not be alive today to talk to you, because that is my baby. I leave them to God. And if we don't get justice here we goin' to get it over there!"

What a long way Ruby had come from that mother. You and I both know, Ruby honey, he said to himself, that it wasn't easy. Was not easy. He felt a little closer to her, knowing the background.

When he spoke to Mary, he asked her if she ever thought Ruby would disappear.

"I don't believe people can disappear, not clear away, not like this. You know, somebody somewhere's gonna see you, gonna notice something funny," said Mary.

"Some people disappear forever," said Dick. "Bad debts. Insurance scam. Unhappy marriage. End up somewhere else living a whole new life. You know, change the name and all. But that takes careful planning. I don't get the impression she had a strategy." Usually the women don't, he might have added. You don't need a strategy to get murdered.

"Why would she want to go away?" said Mary darkly.

"Something will turn up," said Dick. He hoped it wasn't Ruby's dead body. Nine cases out of ten, it was. Especially if she was involved with dodgy guys. Those were the girls who got done in. Well, mostly. Not that he was blaming her. The cops had a saying: You never find a nice girl in a trunk. If she was a bad girl, she was likely dead.

It would have been awfully convenient if Marvin or his cronies had murdered Ruby—satisfied the family at least. Marvin had gone away to the country, "to mourn." It made him look guilty. But Dick had a feeling it wasn't that simple. Something about Ruby's face told him.

It was another week or so before Dick tracked him down. He drove up to the cottage in the Kawarthas. All the leaves were orange, from the cold air that swept down there. He had a romantic feeling, behind the wheel of his car, Ruby's picture propped up on the dash. Dick never noticed things like leaves in the city. It was a revelation to get out here and see the spaces that light made. He had her to thank for that.

The cottage was down a muddy slope, off the road. Dick's feet were thick with goo when he knocked on the door. Marvin was lying on a futon, smoking dope with earphones on. Someone was in the bathroom having a shower.

"Police detective," said Dick. "Looking for Ruby Mason."

Marvin got to his feet. He said of course, and come in, and a lot of other correct sorts of things. He did not look like the devil, as Mary Mason had said, but like a somewhat wasted, indulged and tired man.

"Whose place is this, anyway?" said Dick, strolling into the middle of the single large room. The rafters were pine, and open to the boards that held up the roof. It was pretty.

"Friend of mine, friend of Ruby's, too."

"What about your job?" said Dick Nolan. "Aren't you still employed at City-TV?"

"Of course I am," said Marvin, with the air of someone who had this job by birth rather than by contract. "I'm on compassionate leave now."

"You can get that for a mistress, not just a wife?"

Marvin said nothing.

"The wonders of modern unions," said Dick.

"I'm management," said Marvin.

Dick was trying to get a feel for him. He was cool, but not that tough; *vulnerable*, he thought the word was. What women liked in a man, he understood. Looked as if he had been ravaged by emotional storms but held on, somehow, *managed*. He tried prodding.

"Has your wife left you?"

"She's gone to Europe to see her mother."

The small talk dried up. Dick asked if he could have a cup of coffee. Marvin went to plug in the kettle. The sound of the shower ran on and on.

"So you're looking for Ruby . . . ?" said Marvin, handing over the coffee. "You know, people shouldn't worry about Ruby. I can tell you she's all right, because I've been speaking to her."

"You have?" said Dick, trying not to show surprise.

"From beyond the grave," Marvin continued. He laughed

suddenly, a glad, light laugh that turned into a sob.

Dick took a large, scalding gulp. "Are you telling me you think she's dead?"

"Not dead. That's too simple. Energy is never destroyed. She's travelled beyond, my beauty. Gone to a better place. She's at peace now," said Marvin.

Dick Nolan thought for a moment. Crazy murderers had a hundred ways to bypass the word "dead." But still, he didn't quite think that was where Marvin stood in relation to it all.

"You sound," he said, "as if you really believe it."

"Of course I believe it," said Marvin. "I've got to believe something." He went to the fridge and got out a beer. He offered Dick one but Dick couldn't take it. When he returned, he sat in an old wicker chair and crossed his legs high above the knee, his thin, strong legs.

"So what did she say, when you talked to her? Did she say how she got there?"

"No," said Marvin. He was expansive now, believing he was being taken seriously. "We don't talk details, you know? We communicate, okay? She's there in me, I'm in her, we move together, I'm filled with her spirit."

They sat for a while, companionably, while Marvin swigged and the shower ran in the bathroom. The September sun gleamed on the surface of the lake, making it hard as steel. Dick figured if he stayed long enough the person in the bathroom had to come out. For a minute he fancied it would be Ruby. Wrapped in a towel.

"If you want to do something useful, Mr. Nolan, tell the Masons to stop fretting about Ruby. Ruby's gone where she wanted to be. I have it on her authority. I talk to her, I told you. I'm the one she left behind," said Marvin. "She was my lover. Those people, Masons. They carry on like they're the victims of this. I love her," said Marvin, eyes bulging. "I loved her."

"Beyond the grave, eh? I wouldn't mind talking to her

myself," said Dick. "Or to my dad. He died last year. How do you do this stuff anyway? Is it tough to get the hang of?"

The bathroom door opened. A six-foot-tall woman with a tiny head strolled out, her hair soaking wet and a towel around her middle.

He stood up to be introduced.

"This is Ramone," said Marvin. Then to the woman he said, "I'm going to send him to see Oswald, Consultant to the Stars. What do you think?"

"That's a great idea." Ramone looked as if she had been asleep for a week. Anything would have been a great idea.

Dick Nolan had hoped to avoid Oswald. He did not like the psychic business: it wasn't his area. *Ruby*, he said to his favourite missing person as he headed back down the high-way, *Ruby, you are gonna take me places I never been before. And that's saying something.*

He went over Ruby's desk calendar with Audrey. Most of the appointments were with clients, or beauty-care providers —manicurist, hair-stylist, massage, exercise. There were blocks of time with "m^2" in them, which Audrey explained were visits with Marvin. There were a few lunches with friends—Blair, Max—but most of them were crossed out, as an "m^2" or business crisis overtook it. Then there were these once a week, two-hour bookings with "O" written on them.

"Is that him?"

"Oswald? Must have been."

"Did she tell you why she saw a psychic?"

"Everyone goes to him. Ramone, Marvin, all those guys."

"I heard he was an old lover, from when she sang in the band."

Audrey made her mouth purse out like the tied-off end of a balloon and shook her head. She was still angry with Ruby, and she was going to have to get a new job soon because she wasn't getting paid.

"Who knows?"

"What did he do for her?"

"Oh, energy transfer. Destiny reform."

"You sound like you know all about it," said Dick, smiling.

"No, I don't know. How should I know? She liked advice, Ruby did. Whether she followed it was something else."

He went home and built a shrine to Ruby. In it he put photographs he had been given, a sparkling hairclip he had lifted from her bathroom, a swatch of fabric he had found in her workroom. He collected the newspaper articles on her disappearance and propped them up behind. He fell asleep in front of it.

Oswald's shop was in an old piano factory on Berkeley Street. The lobby had marble floors and gold-flecked pillars; pink neon script on the walls spelled out admonitions. "Direct the Power," said one. "Move into Oneness," said the next. A glass box on the wall enumerated promises: "Destiny Reform." "Energy Transfer." "Meet Spirit Guides." Stepping into the elevator, Dick looked over his shoulder, back at the everyday street, as if to say goodbye.

Upstairs, he presented himself to the receptionist.

"Mr. Nolan!" she cried, as if she knew him. "Oswald is resting. He will be with you when he is recovered."

He figured out sitting there that Oswald was something between mind-reader and market analyst. Pamphlets on the table advertised him as a "professional psychic consultant," skilled in "clairvoyance, channelling, destiny reform and energy transfer." "Like all true visionaries I am still learning," Oswald declared under a haloed head-and-shoulders photograph. His background as a musician and a pollster "of national significance" was cited. According to Dick's sources, Oswald still promoted struggling rock bands with names like Brain Damage and Strangle Cat. Their publicity kits were scattered on the table. It was odd, thought Dick, that none of the media stars or politicians who apparently consulted him took these choices as evidence of a lack of prescience on his part. For a man who made a living divining the public psyche, the fact that he was unable to pick a winner would seem to be a rather serious flaw.

It became his opening joke as he was led into Oswald's office. It was a large, darkened room with a fireplace and a great deal of brass and mirrors. The man himself lay back in a dentist's chair with ice packs on his eyes. His feet did not reach the footrest.

"You really know how to pick 'em," said Dick, stabbing his finger at a poster. "Brain Damage?"

"That's show business," said Oswald. He lay for a moment longer and then slowly turned the crank that angled his body back to the vertical. He raised his small, elegant hands to take the pads off his eyes. "That's what keeps a guy like me fascinated. No matter how long you've been in the business, how well you study what's gone before, you cannot predict public taste. Just like you cannot second-guess psychotics." He had cranked himself upright now, and sat like a tiny emperor looking down. "It keeps me humble. It must be the same in your line of work."

Dick Nolan squinted and wrinkled his brow. "Unpredictable, yes," he said, charmed in spite of himself. And flattered. Oswald was rich and very chic; he went on television during elections.

"The human factor," said Oswald. "Madly inventive, we creatures are. You see the darker side. No two murders are alike, right?" Then, without stopping for an answer, he swung his legs over the side of the chair. "The Prime Minister calls me for advice, did you know that?"

Dick inclined his head. He didn't know. He didn't want to know. He'd voted for the man. "I'm interested in Ruby Mason," he said.

Oswald wore a mushroom-coloured designer suit; his shiny black hair was slicked back like a department store mannequin. The diamond stud in his earlobe seemed to be a signal that he was plugged in to a higher communication system.

"Of course you are. Lovely woman," he began. "I've known her for a long time. We were nearly stars together, but then you know that."

"What do you think has become of her?" said Dick.

Oswald sat at his desk. He made a teepee out of his two index fingers and let them swing down to point at Dick. "You know, I've been expecting you," he said.

"Oh," said Dick. Oswald made him feel he was slow off the mark. He recognized that he did it on purpose. But still, it worked.

"I've been in touch with Ruby," said Oswald gently. "She has landed safely on the other shore."

"Not you too?" said Dick.

Oswald inclined his head. "You've spoken to Marvin, then," he said. "Marvin is very impatient."

They sat together in silence. Oswald, with a beatific smile on his small, ivory-coloured face, his small, uncreased shoes swinging slightly above the floor; Dick with his creased forehead and greasy tie. There was a sound in the room, a hum. Perhaps it came from the air-treatment system, perhaps from Oswald himself. The hum began to fill the room.

"It's not like Ruby to disappear," said Dick.

"It's not like anybody, is it?"

Dick had to agree.

"I've known Ruby for many, many years, as I said. On the one hand, she's a very visible person, as you know. On the other . . ."

Oswald's hands were beautiful, they waved like fronds beside his head. "On the other hand, she always *was* invisible. We don't *see* Ruby. We've never really *seen* Ruby. Ruby has been hiding behind a façade. Her own very obvious presence."

Dick nodded. He watched the hands.

"It is difficult for all of us who remain behind to understand why someone, particularly someone like Ruby, with such a *lust* for life, would choose to depart in this way."

"Depart?" said Dick.

"She has been removed, or has removed herself. We are looking at her absence, asking questions of the space she left. If space could talk, we would be wiser," said Oswald. "And of course it can talk. It is only we who cannot listen."

"What would the space she left say, if I could listen?" said Dick, feeling he'd kept up cleverly.

But Oswald frowned. His eyebrows joined, his head jutted owlishly forward. "But I cannot manufacture the voices!" he cried. "You're asking me to be fraudulent. *You* must listen. When you hear, you will know. The voices will come."

Dick pulled out his notebook and wrote "listen to her absence—voices to come." It made sense to him. As he wrote he perceived that he had lost control of this interview. He had become a client, a patient.

"I never knew her," said Dick. As he admitted this, it seemed like the saddest thing in the world. All the photographs he'd examined, her calendar, her clothing, the shell-pink cushions on her living-room floor—they all spoke of this harlequinesque woman who would never, now, come into his ken. Even an hour ago he had dreamed of finding her alive.

"You must be content with your memories."

"I have no memories of Ruby," Dick insisted.

"Ah, of course not, I knew that," said Oswald. "But you *feel* as if you had. On the one hand, her photographs tell you so much. She spoke volumes in her look. On the other . . ."

Dick sank in his chair.

"You know," Oswald's voice went on; disembodied, it seemed to come from behind him now. "Nobody ever dies. Energy cannot be destroyed. When the physical body is destroyed, the energy goes on."

Dick Nolan struggled to sit upright. He told himself this was a load of bullshit and he had better not succumb.

"Just what was it Ruby came to see you for? Did she have a particular problem? Or just for old-times' sake?"

Oswald shrugged elaborately and spread his fingers, stretching a web between them. He seemed to glow, like those children's toys that absorb light, and give it back, slightly greenish. "Why does anyone? Seeking counsel. Seeking answers. Seeking fulfillment. She was a *seeker*." The fingers stretched and relaxed, came together. "You know," he said reflectively, "Ruby was my most interesting client. Together we made an astonishing discovery. She was a highly spiritual being. Shall I tell you? I wonder. I think so. I think I trust you, Dick Nolan. We were lovers in a previous life. We were King and Queen of an ancient Egyptian kingdom."

Never mind that it had already been in the newspaper. Dick wrote in his notebook, "King and Queen, prev. life."

"Ruby was not like other people. She was exceptional. She was from another dimension. I was able to channel voices to her that she needed to hear. Voices of other entities."

Dick wrote down "other dimension." He put a question mark beside it. Then he wrote down "entities." He wondered what entities they were. Ghosts? But his mind had become too foggy to cut through and get to a solid reality. It seemed to him, as he listened, that Oswald must be right. Ruby *was* exceptional. Dick already knew that.

"How would you, um, know about the previous life? Did she tell you? Remember?" Dick made a superhuman effort to sharpen his intellect. It had become impossible to tell this man he was full of it.

Oswald smiled, his teepeed fingers swinging out and down to point at Dick, and then up again, to tuck neatly under the small fold of skin at the end of his chin.

"It emerges," he said. "Emerges. You've seen my

program?"

Dick looked down to see the pamphlet that, without thinking, he had folded into his notebook. "I have, but I don't know, I don't know what exactly you do here."

Oswald grew delicately practical as he began his sales pitch.

"It is the client's choice. Clairvoyance, clairaudience, mediuming. Energy transfer. The other is destiny reform."

Those terms again. Their resonance grew with each repetition. Dick too had his psychic skills. He was getting a feeling these words meant disappearance, in the language of this country. He waited, but no more information was forthcoming.

"Did Ruby do those?"

"Oh yes." Oswald nodded and sat luminously in his chair. A smile was fleeting, then he was stern.

"Can you explain that to me?" said Dick. "For instance, destiny reform?"

"No, I cannot explain," said Oswald gently. "I can only show you, if you choose the treatment."

Dick's reaction was instant. "Not just at the moment, thank you," he said. The interview was over. He was beaten. He found himself consulting the pamphlet. Thin clouds seemed to be drifting through his brain, confusing his thoughts. He told Oswald that he was certain to be back in touch with him, and went on his way out the door, holding on to that term, destiny reform.

Dick Nolan didn't know if energy had been transferred in or out of him, or if his destiny had been reformed, but he felt light, transparent. He felt like he was made of gossamer and gleamed in the daylight, just as Oswald did. He was a butterfly. All the sleaze and tarnish of his profession had been burned off him by the lights of that room, and he had become spirit. He flitted across the marble lobby and out into the day. He was troubled no more by the petty practicalities of where Ruby might be found; now he was embued with the breath of her life. "I love her," he said to himself.

He rested, eyes closed, before his little shrine. He would go to see the family. He had little in the way of hard information to give them, but he felt his love would make up for it. They would see, and feel, how changed he was, that he adored her and would do anything for her. He would not tell them he thought Ruby had gone peacefully to the other shore, though he now believed it himself. He felt strong enough, after his rest, to write a report.

Martha Mason howled with rage. Her bosom, on top of short, shapely legs, wobbled and swayed; in the folds of her neck were drips of water, sweat or tears that burst from her shiny skin.

Dick Nolan stood in front of her with a single sheet of paper in his outstretched hand. His head hung down, humbly, as if he were facing a queen, the mother of a queen.

"You come to tell me you work seven days and come back here with a *poem*? Have you gone crazy or somethin'?"

"I'm not saying there's no story here. I'm not saying there's nothing suspicious. Marvin's drug connections are big. Kingpins, yeah. There were people around Ruby you wouldn't touch with a ten-foot pole. But I don't think that's got anything to do with what happened. The poem," he said, "is just for now. A token of my affection, if you like. If they keep me on the case, I can follow up some of these leads. I can ask for wiretaps on all her associates," he mumbled. His heart was in his hand, in the poem he had written for Ruby. His heart was not in wiretaps.

Martha raged to Mary as if he weren't there.

"We ask for a homicide investigation and this cop goes to see a psychic. Then he brings me a poem. This is Toronto! North America! Nineteen hundred and eighty-nine! You call the police and they go off to see a psychic." She ripped the poem from his hand and waved it at Mary. Mary seized it.

"Mum, Ruby went to see him too. It's Oswald, the one who used to sing with her. Ruby was into some pretty weird—"

"Such evil! In the Dark Ages, people like that, calling up spirits, spreading wickedness, against good God, fooling around with dead people and living people, crossing dimensions, I don't know what all. These people are practising witchcraft! They are in league with Satan! I know this evil. I have confronted this evil, long time ago. But now I come to Toronto, and these witches are a big-name consultant. And got an office and claim the Prime Minister calls 'em up for advice."

Mary read:

> Ruby jewel of the dark
> Flash your piercing blood-red light
> Take me to your hiding place.
> Take the night from in your hair,
> Let me find a rest place there.

She smiled at Dick, trying to appreciate the ideas.

"I wasn't happy with 'rest place,'" said Dick. "But 'resting' wouldn't fit with the meter."

"It's nice," she said. Mary felt it was best to humour him. She liked it when people fell in love with Ruby.

Her mother panted in extreme anger.

"And the cops write poetry," she finally got out, through whitened lips. She collapsed backward as she said this, hitting the arm of the sofa. Her face quivered once more, then settled, the lips in a heavy horizontal line, as if closed against all the wiles of wicked Toronto, her eyelids, too, resolutely settling down against the daylight. And Dick Nolan tiptoed away to search for Ruby, chiefly in his dreams.

8

A Trick With Mirrors

Philip heard the telephone from a long way off. It was pitch-dark where he was lying; he couldn't tell if it was morning or night. It rang and rang. He rolled out of the van. He had overslept, and the dummy was due this morning. As he picked up the receiver, he could tell that whoever was calling had done him a favour: it was nine-thirty. He had half an hour to get over to the set.

He barked his hello. Laughter came down the wire.

"I must have missed the joke," he grumbled.

"It's just so funny to hear you struggle to sound organized," said Blair. "Did you sleep on the floor of your van again?"

Philip made a face.

"Listen," said Blair, "I have something big to ask you."

Philip crooked the telephone under his chin and began to remove his pants. He had a clean pair somewhere. Blair always told him to stop sleeping in his clothes, but it seemed weird to bed down naked in his van. In case he found himself on the road when he woke up.

"Hold on," said Philip.

His workshop was in a converted garage behind a boarding house in Chinatown. The garage was brick—small and square. On top of the roof was a decorative box that might have been a weathervane, although it had no moving part. One entire wall was the garage door, convenient for moving props and materials in and out. Philip liked to open it and drive right in, in his white van with the California plates and the purple lettering and gold stars on the sides reading SPECIAL EFFECTS.

Last night he had done that, and shut the garage door behind him. He left the cab door of the van open and turned on his tape deck. He was going through his collection of old Broadway musicals. *How to Succeed in Business Without Really Trying* marked the end of the golden era, as far as he could judge. He had fallen asleep listening. Now it was morning, and he had Blair waiting on the phone.

"A Secretary is not a Toy, no my Boy, not a Toy, her pad is to write in, not spend the night in . . ." he sang to himself as he sped to the bathroom. When he moved his operations up here from L.A., he'd worried about getting enough work. It was a slow summer, but now he was busy. Before Hallowe'en, a special-effects artist was like Santa Claus before Christmas. People wanted giant stuffed pumpkins that yielded smoke and vapours, rubberized artificial limbs for costume parties, tombstones that creaked open. Philip was not busy enough or rich enough to turn down work. Probably he would never be. Sometimes he worked himself into a state of exhausted silliness. Yesterday, to try out his handcuffs, he went down to where a friend was getting a haircut. He walked up to the barber chair and, in front of the mirror with the barber looking on, said he was arresting James. James went along with it, and the barber didn't figure it out till after he'd waved his razor and insisted Philip couldn't do that. It got a big laugh in the shop, which Philip liked.

He peed, ran cold water on his hands, splashed his face and

made his way more slowly across the workshop floor. Downstairs was where the large construction took place, and where he stored his cans of paint and his bales of wire and buckets of plaster, his bolts of cloth. He welded metal there, and nailed and stapled boards together to make the backdrops. He also made trick chairs, collapsing crutches, and designed electric wiring to lay over skin, which, when plugged in, set off a lot of little explosions that looked like gunshot impact. Upstairs he did the fine work—moulding masks and painting faces; there were mirrors and an easel, an industrial sewing machine, pots of make-up, buckets of fine clay. This was where he kept himself organized, to the extent that he did at all. He had a desk and a couple of filing cabinets, and a telephone with an answering machine.

He picked up the phone again. "Okay, shoot."

"Good morning," said Blair. "You're up early."

"What is it you want from me?" he said, with mock-formality.

"Simplicity wants to be Humpty Dumpty for Hallowe'en."

"You gotta give the kid credit."

"I can't find a costume for her."

He heaved an enormous sigh and looked around for his watch. "Why don't people want costumes in February?"

She said nothing.

He located the watch right in front of him on the telephone table. "I've gotta get my dummy over to the set by ten-thirty anyway," said Philip. He had pulled his trousers down over his knees and was stamping on them to pull them off the rest of the way.

"I know you're busy. That's why I'm asking early."

"Early is June, not September."

"Okay," she said. She sounded sad. "It's okay. Don't worry about it."

"Any word on Ruby?" said Philip. "Are you all right?"

"Yeah," said Blair in a small, lying voice. "They're talking about drug kingpins now," she said gloomily. "People you wouldn't touch with a ten-foot pole. Whatever that means. They haven't got any evidence though."

"The cops couldn't find a cow in a pasture," he said. "I've gotta run." He slammed the receiver and skidded across the floor on one foot, the other dragging his pants.

"What's the matter with that woman? Why doesn't she get a husband?" he ranted out loud. "Give the kid a dad." He ripped off his sweatshirt (black) and found another black sweatshirt, this one with two silver elephants on the front and a written message saying "Elephant. The Last Decade." Normally Philip enjoyed the sense that he gave Blair something no one else did—handyman services, half hours spent on the phone listening to her worry about Simplicity, or how she was going to lose her job. But that was when he wasn't busy. "The woman has no sense of timing."

He grabbed a pair of pants off the hanger and got into them, swung down the stairs and into the bathroom, where he started water running to wash his face and shave. He calculated the length of the drive to the set at Ontario and King from where he was. Fifteen minutes, at least.

He looked into the corner and saw that the dummy was looking fine, very fine; it was a good likeness of the actor, and well packed with blood. He found its jacket—a copy of the one the actor was to wear during the scene—and gingerly slipped it over the padded and stuffed shoulders and back, pushing the arms down the sleeves the way you would with a reluctant baby. He'd been working all weekend on this one. And now this panic to make the deadline. Blair wanting things at the same time. Ruby. How long had she been gone? A week? What kind of people didn't you touch with ten-foot poles? He would think about it after.

"Come on now, down you come." He tried not to speak to his creations. That way lies madness, he told himself. But sometimes he couldn't help it. He had trouble enough with his landlady and the neighbours, what with all the monster heads and fake corpses going in and out. No need to start rumours that he talked to them. It was important, too, to keep his distance. Every one of his creations was sure to meet a dreadful end.

He put the stuffed man very carefully over his shoulder and, still crouching, made his way to the staircase. He had to be careful not to fall, or put undue pressure on any of his firm pouches: they contained theatrical blood the thick, opaque, non-staining variety. This particular fellow was to be stabbed repeatedly and had to bleed a great deal.

The back of the van was lined with carpet. He swung the dummy down into his arms so he was holding it face to face, climbed with effort up the two-foot step and laid the thing down on its back on the bench. There were ropes to strap it down, and pillows and blankets to protect it. At ten minutes past ten he pressed the button to open the garage door and gunned the van.

Down Spadina to the Lakeshore, and east: it seemed to take an hour but it was 10:27 when he drove up to the red-brick warehouse where the film was being shot. He could see the PA still running around with giant styrofoam cups of coffee so he figured he was okay.

"Somebody here who can give me a hand?" he said. She gave the coffee to a couple of guys and came after him.

"A lot easier if you've got two to do this," he said, picking up the dummy under the arms and guiding him around so his back was to the door. "If you hold his feet we'll avoid undue strain on the torso. That's what I'm worried about. He's well packed."

The actors ran through their lines, received their instructions, soberly nodding. The actor for whom the dummy was a stand-in grinned broadly. They propped him up where he was supposed to be, sitting at the table, his back to the camera, his head turned slightly so that the light from the window fell on his cheek. The murderer was instructed to go mad, to stab wildly and uncontrollably all over the body, to dig and to cut with the knife, make a real mess. He nodded and nodded. You only got one take, that was it; the dummy would be ruined.

Watching the scene was his professional satisfaction, not the cheque that came in the mail, or even the occasional grateful letter from a director that accompanied it: "Dear Special Effects, you're a genius, we couldn't have done it without you." No, results were what he lived on, and a good thing too, because the cheque was more often than not delayed, withheld or gone astray. If he didn't have his trusty lawyer to collect bills he'd have starved long ago. But he did love to see his tricks work: to grow cold and feel his heart clutch on fear; to forget that he himself had planted all those plastic bags full of blood under the Arrow shirt, inside the Harry Rosen tweed jacket (which, incidentally, would be his for the asking afterward, except that it would be utterly ruined from opaque, thick blood, which *did* stain).

Philip drained his coffee. The scene was underway. Man and woman seated at kitchen table in their loft. They have cut open a large green melon; the knife is on the table. The woman flings some angry words over her shoulder and leaves the kitchen table. She crosses the tiles and is heard to shut the outside door hard. The man taps his fingers; thinking, clock ticking. Cut. The actor goes out, the dummy goes in. This time they shoot from behind. The window opens. A crazy-with-rage man crawls in the window. The husband, his intended victim, is incomprehensibly still. Doesn't turn around. The intruder taunts him—still no movement. Obviously these two know each other. Suddenly the crazy one darts around in front of the dummy, seizes the knife on the table and begins stabbing, shouting, gouging. Blood spurts up from the chest and shoulder bags. He keeps stabbing. Blood runs and it flows and it gushes. The actor stabs and stabs until finally there is nowhere left to stab, just a sodden, deflated mess, the blood on the walls, the tables, the Harry Rosen jacket, the other actor, everywhere.

"Cut."

Congratulations all around. "Wonderful. It was wonderful."

"Didn't that work well!"

A general air of festivity took over. Philip, after receiving a nod from the director, who was busier with his actors than with the guy who produced this stuffed creature on whom the violence is wreaked, was edged away from the action. There was some delay and then the announcement: "It's a take!" The clean-up team swept in. Philip strolled over to the open window.

It was just like summer, this third week in September. So hot and so limpid, with the golden light everywhere over the lake and the city. Airless: without fragrance, the air seemed to be a quantity unconnected with nature, a filler, an effect itself, and special, today, in its gilt. Squinting at the glass towers of the downtown over to the west, he felt the rough, red brick under his hands on the window sill. The two textures of the city: sleek and cold above, rough and earthy at his fingertips; these low, hangar-like brick warehouses still holding sway apart from that salt garden, that crystalline growth in the centre. It was what he liked about Toronto. This was east: unlike Alberta, unlike Los Angeles. Erupting fictions amidst the clutter of last century. But not for long. They were taking the old away, bit by bit, all of it. Straight below the window was a giant metal garbage bin. When the film crew finished in here the place was going to be demolished.

"Say, Philip, that was superb. Just wild. Wait'll you see it on film. It worked just like you said it would." The director shook his hand and moved back again into the circle of technicians. Philip watched the gofers shift the dummy off the chair and look around, wondering where to put him down.

"What do we do with this?" said one of them.

"I don't know. Ask him."

"Pitch it," said Philip, with a sad smile. Embrace the inevitable, that was his motto. He had learned this over long experience. He'd have loved to hang on to all his creations, but he just had no space. Literally or figuratively. You had to chuck them or your creativity got blocked.

The two hesitated with their burden. The dummy was strained, sticky and still dripping.

"If we had a great big garbage bag . . ." said one.

"No plastic bag needed," said Philip. "Just pitch it," he repeated. "Down there." He pointed to the bin one storey down from the open window.

"You wouldn't mind?"

Philip shrugged.

"Who owns that thing?"

"I dunno, but when they start they're never gonna notice it down in the bottom. They're gonna be throwing in huge planks of wood and old radiators."

"Yeah, you're right."

The two took the dummy and put him up on the window ledge, buttocks first. Then they folded him neatly, chest toward knees, and pushed him out. The head was heavier, however, and as soon as the dummy cleared the frame it shot backward, so that the body opened dramatically, the head plunging downward, the shredded Arrow shirt flying upward, its red tatters like a Chinese kite in distress. The dummy did one complete ragdoll flip, head down and heels flying over the top, head flying over again and then leading the plunge downward. It struck the edge of the garbage bin; the head and torso draped down the inside, the legs down the outside.

"Sayonara," said Philip. On the way out the door he got stopped by a make-up woman he knew. It wasn't until he was shooting down Richmond Street, homeward, that he let himself think about Ruby again. If her disappearance was a trick too. A trick with mirrors. It was likely. Most things were. He didn't like to consider the possibility she'd been murdered. That only happened in movies. Knowing Ruby, she'd gone off with some guy. That was what she was best at. He never said that around Blair, because Blair defended her. "Don't be bitter," she said to Philip. As if he had feelings about Ruby. As if!

He stopped thinking about it and instead thought about the Humpty Dumpty costume. He could do an egg-head with hinges that opened up with jagged edges to show her face inside. It could rest on pads on her shoulders; the body stuffing could hang from there too. He could do it easily if he could just get some light plastic, the kind they make kewpie dolls with, and get it moulded. Somehow. Somewhere. He imagined Blair breaking into a smile when he showed her. And Sissy too. It gave you a hit to see them both, identical smiles set in small, heart-shaped faces.

The principal's office seemed smaller than similar rooms in Blair's memory, though perhaps they had always been small and only loomed large. Blair's schoolteacher mother had never given principals names, they were only "the office."

Miss Rushton's office had three leaded-glass windows with diamond panes looking narrowly down over stone balls set in enormous vases on the front steps. The walls were decorated with the usual drawings of lopsided houses with the usual many-pronged sun shining on them, and the usual renderings of dinosaurs. Considering they were extinct, dinosaurs had an incredible presence amongst kids. Blair wondered why. Was it identification in some macro sense: do kids know we are close to our end? Or was it more personal—they feel akin to creatures who are lumpy, misshapen and stupid.

Miss Rushton coughed. She had a little mahogany desk with slim, curving legs, as if to underplay her power. Untidy stacks of envelopes for a fund-raising effort escaped their piles on the side table. Blair squeezed in along one wall, and Simplicity's teacher, Miss Jasmine Boggs, filled the only other possible air space.

"Call me Jasmine," she said, extending a small, dimpled hand. She wore a handknit sweater with a Beatrix Potter rabbit nibbling a cabbage on the front. The rabbit's nose moved when she reached. Blair wondered if primary school teachers chose their clothes to entertain their students. Or if people who liked sweaters with bunnies on them just naturally became primary school teachers. She shuffled her chair so that she could at least see the open door.

"Got to see out, avoid claustrophobia," she said. "Being in radio, I work in small spaces. You learn from experience."

Miss Rushton looked fixedly at her and did not smile.

"As you know, we asked you to come because we're worried about Simplicity," she said.

"Yes," said Blair. This was very official; she attempted to rise to the occasion. "Maybe it would be useful if you could repeat the kinds of things you mentioned to me over the phone. I was taken aback and didn't understand."

The long neck turned and twisted; opaque, teal-blue eyes took her in.

"Simplicity is very keen on *work*. We've noticed," she said, "that given a choice, she will always pick up a pencil and paper."

Blair crinkled her nose and began to nod.

"Yes," she said.

"She goes into her workbooks, and won't play in spare time."

"Oh."

"Furthermore, in regular class all she wants to do is read."

"*Oh*," said Blair, beginning to understand this was a problem. She wrinkled up her brow. "That's bad?" she said, interrogatively.

"She's hiding from other children. She's using books as a retreat."

"She does *like* books."

Miss Rushton looked crossly out of her too-blue eyes. Tinted contact lenses were the only possible explanation. "We do ask parents to curtail their impatience over children's reading. It will come later."

"But if she wants to do it now—"

"Work, work, work," said Miss Boggs, bursting forth. "She's not like the others. She doesn't laugh and giggle. She doesn't push and shout."

"She's got her mind set on reading and it's all she wants to do," said Miss Rushton, with feeling.

Blair could see this frustrated them. Her voice began to rise. "Perhaps it's because she's ready?"

Miss Rushton carried on in her modulated tones. "I might as well be perfectly straight. To add to the problem, we've also noticed that she *can* read." She paused for the effect of this scandal to be felt.

There were kids in Simplicity's classroom who couldn't sit still to listen to a story, who rolled on their backs and howled. Vangie sobbed herself sick because some raindrops fell on her new suede shoes. Alexandra cheated at Snakes and Ladders. This was accepted, "normal" behaviour. Being quiet and wanting to read a book wasn't, apparently.

Blair leaned slightly forward in her chair.

"You know we haven't taught her. You know the philosophy in this school. At present she is being encouraged to play. To socialize with the other children. That is the most important thing she can learn right now."

"I certainly haven't taught her," said Blair. "She gets out her songbooks and follows the words along. She likes that Muppet dictionary, you know, the one where there's a picture with each word . . ." Her voice trailed off. Miss Rushton remained unmoved.

"We think that she's just decided she wants to read, and she's going to do it, and she doesn't care if she does anything else right now."

There was a silence in the room.

"I'm afraid I don't see the problem," said Blair, firmly.

Miss Rushton's eyes widened in exasperation. "You know the principles of the Simcoe School. All the parents do. *Learning through play*. Yet every year the question of reading raises its ugly head. You're a reader yourself, I gather, Miss Bowker," she said, trying a different tack. "You have books around the house? You sit down with them and spend an hour or so?"

"You see *you* like books a lot as well, don't you? It must be very gratifying to you to have a child who also likes them," Jasmine said, accusingly.

Blair began to feel heated. "I think we have to give Simplicity credit for her own obsessions," she said.

"Perhaps you sit in the house with papers and pen, writing letters?"

Blair interrupted. "When you called and said she always chose a pencil I thought at least you were going to tell me she used it as a weapon."

This attempt at levity went unnoticed.

"Just what is wrong with what she is doing?"

"I'm afraid she's become a little isolated, socially."

"You don't want the other children to think she's kind of— quaint . . ." said Miss Jasmine Boggs.

A gust of kids' voices went by out in the hall. It was recess time. Through the window, Blair could see small bodies burst out from under the ledge and begin to run hither and yon, kicking balls, swinging arms, clawing their way up the chain-link fence, throwing themselves into piles of leaves. It had not occurred to her before to wonder what her daughter did at recess. How she spent her time, and with whom. Now it seemed to her mad that she had not considered this problem:

the child had six complete hours a day at school, and came home to tell her mother nothing.

"The problem is that she is concentrating on work to the exclusion of play," said Miss Rushton.

"Maybe she doesn't see it as work. I think she enjoys—"

"She never likes to join a group of girls who are playing jacks or skipping. It's almost as if," said Jasmine Boggs wonderingly, "as if she doesn't *like* them."

"You don't want the other children to give up on her."

"Maybe *she's* given up on *them*," Blair retorted. But the image of a sad girl standing by the wall when her mother left her in the schoolyard seized Blair and quashed her defences. "Why would the other girls give up on her?"

"Well, she is rather unpredictable, Ms. Bowker."

"Unpredictable? What does that mean?"

"She bites."

"Bites? Who did she bite?"

"Rachel." Gloom in the room, now that Simplicity's culpability was so firmly established. "Rachel's mother complained."

"Oh dear," said Blair. For the first time since Simplicity was born, Blair longed for her father. That half-crazed poet she'd married for all of sixteen months before he went back to Weddleston-on-Water, or whatever it was called, in his mildewed tweed coat with his foul tobacco. He would have been very good in here. He would pull his long jaw down and sideways to crack it, one of his unnerving habits, or rather habits to un-nerve.

"Excuse me, are you telling me she's weird because she prefers books to these little cretins? On the contrary, I should think it shows very good sense," he would say, and puff his healthy disdain out of the side of his mouth. "Bites, does she? Just make sure the kids get their rabies shots." He had his moments, he did.

"That's not acceptable," said Blair. "The biting has to stop.

But what—what makes her bite?"

Miss Rushton spoke obliquely. "You're not doing your child any favours when you encourage her to become a world unto herself. She has to live with her peer group, ultimately, doesn't she? Simcoe School children are all lively and out-going."

"I don't know about Simcoe School children," said Blair, "if she has to live with them. I do agree she has to live in the world. But books are in the world, books teach you about the world. Frankly, I'd be a lot more worried if you came to tell me she wouldn't read at all."

Miss Jasmine Boggs said nothing, only moved her lips a trifle primly. *All you egg-heads stick together.*

Blair asked herself what Sissy was doing in this school. She had signed her up at the age of two, when she first moved to Toronto. What had she been thinking? When she visited, the children were doing English folk dances on the flat roof of the school annex. Remembering the hours spent squirming on a shallow pine bench in South 'Hat Primary, Blair made up her mind: Sissy would have this. It was single mother's guilt. Although she wouldn't be able to offer a real family, at least she could provide a famous "free" private school, for which she paid $6,000 a year. (For the same reason, she paid too much rent on the house, on the edge of a good area.) So Simplicity went off to the Simcoe School looking like all the other girls and boys: Blair hadn't known who they were. It turned out that Toronto was a city where corporate lawyers and petty mobsters wanted their darlings educated in a non-competitive atmosphere. Non-carnivorous too, apparently.

But who was Sissy Bowker? When Blair started out, she had no notions. She would have been content to bring forth one of those mouthy, fearless girls you saw on soccer pitches. A Rachel or an Emma. But what she'd got was a child who wanted to sit at a desk, danced to telephone messages and fell off slides and swings.

"I'm not sure she feels at home in this environment. When she's upset she says 'nobody likes me,'" said Blair, deciding it was time for a counter-attack.

Jasmine Boggs smiled ever so slightly. "All children say that at times," she said, "and to a certain extent that's normal. But with Simplicity there are additional reasons."

"If you're saying the kid's off-track because she prefers books to kids I can't agree. It shows perfectly good sense if you ask me. You say she's stubborn. I'm delighted. She'll need to be stubborn. If she doesn't fit in, she'll need to know how to be alone. Simplicity is different," offered Blair finally. It seemed the truest thing she could say.

It was a word Miss Rushton couldn't resist. "That's what we're here to foster . . . the individuality in a child . . ."

As long as it's the type of individuality you have in mind, Blair thought. As she left, she caught Miss Rushton and the teacher looking at each other: unco-operative mother. She knew what she was being accused of. She was accused of that awful crime: trying to bring up her child *in her own image*. Trying to force her own values on a kid. Never mind that this was the history of civilization. It was not done in 1989. And besides, it seemed she had signed this right over to Miss Rushton. "You can't help her," were the principal's final words. "You love her too much."

Leaving the school, Blair felt sunshine on her face, painting her, masking her with its warm colour. She walked south of St. Clair on Spadina Road.

Blair walked everywhere now, searching for Ruby. As she walked she scanned the cars, the faces in the restaurant windows, the crowds at crosswalks. She was certain that Ruby's face was somewhere, suspended in the city, that she still moved and walked among them, unaccountably distracted from her own life, her own name even, but still going about the business of living.

She sat on the curved bench that protruded from the Baldwin steps halfway down the steep hill. The grind and roar of distant earth-moving equipment came from below, the high whine of a tamping machine. The Sealtest factory had gone, and with it the streets of shabby houses owned by the city and rented to students. New mandarins and the masters of the universe were soaking up the soil, turning it and paving it and making it into their territory. The less rich had now moved off, farther downhill, past downtown. Where to? To Parkdale, perhaps, where people crowded row after row on top of the last cliff before the lake.

She thought about Sissy. "She doesn't protect herself," said Berenice. This to explain the lumps on her forehead from when she fell. "She never puts her hands out to stop the fall." Berenice was sweeping the porch as she said this, sweeping the beautiful leaves up and putting them in Loblaws bags, which Blair didn't want her to do but didn't have the heart to tell her not to. She doesn't protect herself.

It was one of Berenice's profound utterances. But why didn't Simplicity protect herself? Berenice didn't know. Blair didn't know. Nobody knew. Her reflexes had been tested; they were all right. Perhaps she had been too protected? Had Blair, with her single-minded, single mother attention, made her this way? When she was small she was bruised from her forehead to her knees, purple and black, she looked as if she had been beaten. Now at six she still fell, over and over, a dozen times a day.

Simplicity was different. Her fingers had the touch of corn silk; her nose was so sensitive she could identify the callers at the door by smell. But she sometimes could not seem to hear, or to see; sometimes she grew dizzy easily; sometimes she had so little energy she just lay on her bed and stared at the ceiling. She was so pale. A fairy child, a mushroom child. In her mind's eye, Blair saw her fall on the sidewalk and slowly, awkwardly, place her feet back flat on the pavement, push herself back up on her spindly, long, weak legs, and teeter before she began to walk again, more carefully this time.

She doesn't misbehave. Wasn't that what Miss Rushton was saying? You couldn't make her. She would not find it interesting. What if Simplicity had been an eighteenth-century royal child, destined to be Queen at the age of nine? She would be perfect, except for the fact that her enemies would do her in, in the time it took to do a minuet. She had no aggression. None. She did not cheat, push or shout. She didn't protect herself.

Three Japanese tourists with a disposable camera climbed to the bench. "I-take-picture-you-sit-there?" She nodded agreement. Blair, a picturesque Toronto person. One of the tourists, a woman, came to stand beside her. She put her arm over Blair's shoulder. *Here I am in Toronto with a picturesque Toronto person, and we are friendly.* Snap went the camera. Then the photographer gave more direction to the models— closer! Heads together! Really close friends now! The woman put her hand on Blair's shoulder this time. Snap! Thank you very much.

They went off, taking something of Blair, her image which, unknown to her, would establish itself on a dresser in Osaka, or in a paper wallet squeezed in a pocket on the Tokyo subway. Perhaps it was that easy to transfer her body, too. Maybe that's what Ruby did.

She stood, and continued walking. She was on her way to Max Ostriker's office. He had called her yesterday, ten days after Ruby had vanished, and said they should talk. Walking south, she passed Bloor, then College. The El Mocambo, where she used to drink with Ruby. There she was, outside— jeans and leather, her hair all gone—but—no, it was not. The streets in Chinatown were crowded, full of people with tight, calculating faces. Farther down the folks looked crazed and shambling, smelling of drink or piss and sweat. At Queen Street she turned straight east, crossing University Avenue and the corner of Osgoode Hall where Torontonians always pointed out the cow-gates. How far they'd come: from *that* to *this*. How urban and sophisticated they were. Growing up, Blair had seen cow-gates all the time, and they didn't prove anything. She didn't see Ruby again. The glass walls bounced the sun back down and made the people swim together. She wished she had her sunglasses. Max Ostriker. What would she say to him? He had been Ruby's friend, not hers, ever since that night in Banff.

She caught a small movement at foot level. She rubbed her eye. The speck moved again. She bent down. In a square of concrete bounded by a wrought-iron fence post and the red metal foot of a mailbox was a small, brown bird. The bird was tipped over on its side, struggling to get up on its feet.

People began to bump her from behind. "Watch out, will you?" said one. She looked back at the man and then down at the bird, which showed signs of tiring in its struggle. Its wings moved less quickly than before.

"I think it's dying," she said. The pedestrian moved on, saying nothing.

The bird was unspectacular, dun-coloured, a sparrow, probably. It continued to jerk desperately upwards without managing to get on its feet. It might have a wounded wing. It might just be disoriented down there with all the stone and concrete. Probably sound waves bouncing off all these glass walls multiplied into a roar. To the bird, this place must be like a war zone.

She wanted to pick it up. All the admonishing voices of childhood rose up in her head: Don't touch! It's dirty! It might be diseased! You might squeeze it where it's broken, and that would be the end!

She cupped her hands around it. The bird was so light, it felt hollow, but it was warm in her two hands. It fluttered twice and then lay still. She brought her hands up near to her face and opened them. The bird's small jet eye was shiny. It blinked. Blair rejoined the press on the sidewalk, moving quickly now, toward Max's office tower.

Coming out of the elevator on the twenty-ninth floor to face two oak doors, Blair willed some fast-moving lawyer to wheel through and open them. At exactly the right moment, one did come out, on exactly the angle Blair expected him to: feet to the side, head and torso leaning back, as if pushed by the sheer momentum of work behind him. He arrested himself for an extra second with an arm stretched, as Blair slipped under and in the doors.

"Thank you."

His staring eyes took in her walking shoes, her wind-blown hair, her dampish face.

"Beautiful day to be outside!" he said, down his nose, and went on.

That bad, was it? Opening her crumpled linen blazer, Blair cupped both her hands against her ribs on the left side and approached the receptionist's desk.

"To see?" said the woman, in Oxford–East Indian elegance.

"To see . . . Mr. Ostriker."

"He is expecting you, Miss . . . ?"

"Bowker."

The corridor was wide as a prairie street and empty, paved with beige broadloom. The paintings were ten feet across. They were mostly of steam-rollered and smashed-up objects, tables, flowers, women in gowns. The hall went on for ages before she arrived at more desks, a humming computer and a telephone, which jingled unattended, like some autonomous musical instrument.

No secretary presided. The place had been abandoned. A surprise fire drill? Everyone out for a conference in the Ladies? All those office doors and nothing so vulgar as a sign. How was she to know where Max was? The sparrow twitched at her rib. An office door was ajar. She walked quietly up and looked inside.

The rug was thick and he did not hear her. The man behind the desk spoke on the telephone, head down, doodling on his blotter. His teeth were bared in a smile or an attempt to dislodge something caught in a tooth. At once the conviction of his setting hit her: Max was a Bay Street lawyer. This was the fabled quantity. She'd never met one. Said to be greedy, unprincipled and exploitative. Ruby had all kinds of friends. "People you wouldn't touch with a ten-foot pole, the detective said." But Max wasn't what they meant.

Seeing him, it all came back from that one long day twenty years ago. His *bonhomie*, his bigness. His black, curly hair looked firm to the hairline and vibrant, full of energy, the face kindly and long-jawed (sheepishness outgrown). Different was his tie (now loosened) and his confidence. He looked comfortable within the enclosure of that desk, easy in his rumpled shirt, his jacket cast on the other chair in the corner. She looked for the traditional photograph of wife and children. There was none. Only a large eight-by-ten glossy of a rocky shore and a boat tied up to a dock.

She was nearly in front of his desk. He still hadn't heard her. Maybe he thought she was his secretary and was trying to indicate that he didn't want to be bothered. She reached out her hands and put the bird, struggling, warm, in the middle of his blotter.

"Look," she whispered.

Max saw the bird. His head jerked back. He saw Blair, her wind-blown hair, her flushed face. Then he looked down to the bird again.

"Jesus Christ," he yelped, and put the telephone down. "What the fuck is this?" He pushed back his swivel chair abruptly and stumbled to his feet, tucking his shirt back into the waist of his pants with a fast, automatic hand.

"A bird," she said. "I think it's still alive, I found it on the street. It must have flown into the glass walls."

Max was looking at the telephone. "Did I say goodbye?" he said. "Did I just hang up?"

"You hung up."

The bird, which was lying on its side, brought its wings out and flapped once more, valiantly. It almost regained its feet.

"Jesus Christ," said Max again.

"I'm Blair Bowker."

"You want me to do something about this bird? Well let's get it out of here. Get my secretary, get somebody," said Max. He had his hands over his head, he was ducking. "Jeez, what if it starts to fly around in here?"

"It's a sparrow. Not a bat. It won't hurt—"

He looked back at the telephone. "I can't believe I hung up the telephone. That was Mr. McNaughton. A very major client. Major."

Blair noted that he hadn't said hello. Still, she was mainly interested in the bird. "I guess we could call the Humane Society."

He pulled the telephone book from under his desk. "I hate birds in houses. They fly into the windows. He'll just end up dead, if he isn't already."

"I couldn't just walk by and leave him."

Max found the number. He got on the telephone. As he pressed the numbers he looked into her face.

"Of course you're Blair," he said. "I remember you. You couldn't leave it there? One hundred and ten thousand other people could, but not you." He shook his head and turned his mouth to the receiver.

"Hello, I'm calling from Ostriker, Mugwell," he said, "up on the twenty-ninth floor of Canada Place? We've got an injured little bird here. What would you like us to do with it?"

The voice on the other end of the line began to purr soothingly; Max listened a little, and concurred, and listened some more, and demurred. "Someone picked it up down on the street," he said. And then waited and said, "You don't say.

I'd never have thought. Thousands, eh?"

"What's she telling you?" said Blair. She picked up the bird and held it against her heart. The bird's heart was beating hard; her own, too. She wondered whether it saw her hands and Max's as death, and was only waiting to be crushed. Whether it felt hope, or anything near hope. Imagined itself restored to the air currents that swooped and coiled between the towers, to its life on the wing? Or feared forever now a collision into the cold, ice-blue, mirrored walls.

Max put down the phone.

"I said we'd courier it over," he said. He buzzed. The secretary came to the door. When she saw Blair, her mouth screwed itself downward. "Oh!" she said, clearly annoyed. "I had no idea anyone had got in here."

"Maureen, can you rig up some kind of packing for this? And then Expedite it to the Humane Society?" He gestured to Blair's bird.

"Oh my," said Maureen, shifting her feet. Her face puckered here and there, rhythmically, in distress.

"I'll pack him. I prefer to," said Blair.

They made a cage out of a box that had held computer ribbons, softened the interior with the clear plastic wrapping paper that is full of air bubbles and settled the bird inside. When Blair was taping up the sides of the box Maureen came closer and whispered.

"I gather you're a friend," she said. "Mr. Ostriker has been a little nervous"—she gulped—"since he saw that woman—um"—she searched for a delicate word—"take her life in the subway."

"Oh," said Blair.

"He's not normally . . . so aggressive. I expect you surprised him."

"Perhaps," said Blair.

Blair saw the box into the messenger's hands. She told him

to handle it gently and to get it immediately to the Humane Society, before any other deliveries.

"Apparently thousands of them fly into the glass every night. And they die on the street unnoticed. Either that or they lie there stunned for a while, and then eventually they hop up and get away," said Max, watching, his hands in his pockets.

"Amazing," said the messenger. It was not clear whether he meant about the toll on birds or about the assignment. "I'll rush it then," he said.

Max sighed loudly and turned to go back into his office. "Maureen, will you get me Mr. McNaughton on the phone please? I've got to apologize for hanging up on him. Geez, he's gonna think I'm a *maniac*."

Blair stood in the hallway.

"I guess I'll be going then," she said.

Max turned on his heel.

"Oh sorry, sorry," he said. "No, don't go. We haven't talked. You just got me rattled. I've got to finish this call first. We'll have coffee."

Blair inclined her head. "I'll wait here," she said. She refused Maureen's offer of coffee, and stood, rather than sat. Maureen bristled over her desk until Max came out.

Riding down in the elevator, he hummed and stared at the numbers above the door. They slid down like butter, without weight. In these elevators you could begin to believe you were an angel.

"Didn't want to say anything in there," he mumbled, when they stepped into the lobby. "You never know who's going to get in."

"Oh," said Blair. "*Intrigue*."

"Not necessarily." He laughed. The laugh came from a long time ago, unaffected. He was careful of the way he used his size, apologetic almost. His arm went out along the wide metal bar on the door, and the door flew open before Blair as if it were weightless.

They sat on the rim of a stone wall by a fountain in the midst of towers. Someone had placed life-size cow sculptures there. They looked stupidly around at their pasture of pavement, their high-walled enclosure.

"It was about Ruby, you know," he said. "I don't want to make a lot of this, but she called me that night. The night they're saying she was last seen. When she was meant to be at that memorial? She called me at the office about ten o'clock. And she gave me your phone number." Now that Max saw Blair's eyes, the translucent skin of her cheeks, he was hit by memory. How he first saw her, walking into the dark on the mountain meadow, her long hair like a stream of water down her back. He recalled exactly the thump in his belly when they came face to face as she fled from the dormitory. *I recognize you*, he knew then, *you come from my future.* How had he forgotten? Here it was the future, and here she was.

"What did she call you for?"

"I dunno what for. I'd cancelled our lunch. She more or less admitted she was having some sort of business problem she couldn't get out of. Did you know?"

"No," said Blair.

"She mentioned you," said Max, again.

"What for?"

Now Max looked at her carefully. She hadn't changed; she still looked innocent. She wore no make-up. She was flushed, as if she had just run a mile. Her hair, which had once been long and white, was now light brown, chin-length; it was pulled back and tucked behind her ears. "Why would she mention me?"

Max did not have an answer to that. After a minute, Blair stood up. "Nervous," she said. "Can't sit."

"Let me tell you my worst fear . . ." He told her Ruby wanted to know all about the woman he'd seen jump in front of the train.

"If she'd done that, they'd know," said Blair. "People don't jump in front of trains and nobody notices. Anyway, she didn't do anything like that. She wouldn't."

"I guess," said Max. "But where—"

"But probably you should tell the cops," said Blair.

Max thought for a moment. He didn't tell her he'd already spoken with them. For some reason, he wanted Blair to see him as independent of that search. "I don't really think this is a case for the cops," he said finally. "Come and get a yoghurt cone."

They walked together to the underground concourse. The lights were too bright, and the signs were all orange-and-black. In the lunch crowd, Blair moved closer to Max; otherwise they might lose each other. He felt like safety. Someone who knew her so long ago, but didn't know her—and who she didn't know—at all.

"I guess nobody's gone back to work yet," he said. "Shop, shop, shop. I eat at my desk most of the time."

"I don't have a desk," said Blair. "I start work at three. All morning I walked. I keep thinking I'll see her."

Max handed her a strawberry cone. They worked their way back up the stairs. "I don't really know why I called you," he said. "Except Ruby told me to."

"Oh."

"I'm glad, though," he said.

"Oh."

There was a pause.

"Well, I'm glad too."

"Good."

"What I think it was," said Max finally, as if he were answering a question asked an hour ago, "I think it was like she knew, but she didn't know, that she was going away. And she wanted me to kind of, befriend you or something. Which is fine with me. Look," he said, "my partner Andy's having a dinner party. Will you come with me?"

Blair smiled. She was thinking about the bird. If it ended up in the incinerator. She'd bet it lived.

When she came into the house from work it was dark, as always. She turned on the light and saw the letter on the radiator. She recognized his handwriting. 'Though she hadn't seen it for six months. Her secret lover. He was, after all this time, still loyal.

I wait until nine o'clock. Only then do I feel that you are free, to be on the same wavelength as me. You are alone, your child has gone to bed . . .

He knew about her job. He knew about Sissy. And he knew about much more.

. . . this is to say nothing, of course, of dreams. Where we are in the altogether and frolic in a season of gold. I must see you, must know what I feel I know already . . .

I am bothered by you, in short. And must obey—your voice is wonderful. Sometime I'll hear you speaking from an inch away through your hair and think God is smiling on us. But down the road is sterility and death. And on the way is a straitjacket. You can't make this omelette without breaking all the eggs.

He was mad. There seemed no other explanation. He had come out of nowhere to say all this, as if he were a figment of her imagination. But the letter was real. She turned it over in her hand. She was disturbed by it. This time she would keep it in a drawer; she wouldn't even play at secrecy with this man.

Blair lay awake at three o'clock in the morning.

A dream about Ruby woke her up. In the dream Ruby looked well; it was early morning, and they were talking. Ruby's face had a renewed look; her skin was radiant and clean, and that made Blair feel elated. But someone was coming to the door. Ruby asked for money. Blair knew it must be for drink, or drugs, and that she could not stop her buying it. Don't, she said, handing over the money. But when she woke up she felt glad. Ruby was alive.

Now she couldn't get back to sleep. It happened to her every night. Sometimes she would be awake for several hours. Her body lay exhausted but her mind walked over Toronto, turned corners, investigated avenues.

Wild stories had begun to circulate. Ruby had been murdered by the drug-dealing friends of Marvin. Suicided because she had AIDS. Gone berserk because of quack "psychic advisers." In the stories, Ruby was always the victim. That could not be right, Blair thought. If there was a victim, there must be a villain. Marvin's face—long-nosed, vain, unnaturally white-skinned—began to flower exotically as sleep leant over her. Then the image burst, warping at the sides, like a photograph with a rock thrown through it, curling around the wound. There was something missing, some factor no one had accounted for yet. Ruby's will. What Ruby wanted. Maybe she wanted to disappear.

Maybe she wanted to escape the weight of life. No ordinary burial hers, in a black suit with her make-up on, filed in a careful box in rows with other careful boxes. Or burnt, turned to ash so as to conserve space in crowded Mount Pleasant Cemetery. No, she would go in some natural catastrophe, like the one that overtook the Burgess Shale, where thousands of animals were stopped in their tracks, squashed and impressed with mud, preserved, for ages.

Not here and now, like Blair would be, caught between the third floor and the first floor of her house. The mudslide would come down and compress it all to one inch thick, and within that graphic sheet would be all Blair's things, along with her skeleton. She would be buried and identified by things in the Egyptian way, with a catalogue of things, things above her and directly beneath her that would all fold together, all be reduced to one dimension in this event.

Skis, below, and poles and boots, in the basement furnace room, as well as the Christmas-tree stand and the strings of lights. Then, on the main floor, the CD player and the stack of discs, a brass parrot from Mexico and an Irving Penn photograph of (how fitting) a woman lying in bed draped in white sheets. The photograph was flat already. Probably all that would remain would be the frame, but that, too, would provide interest. On this floor, her things. Her earrings and hairpins, her closet full of shoes and dresses, the creams and ointments in the bathroom cupboard. And up above: on the third floor, Bernie's beauty aids and momentos of home. All of these things would be buried with her, naming her, identifying her for all time. In fact, Blair's things were more durable than she was. She would biodegrade, and they wouldn't.

This was not for Ruby. Perhaps her friend had a warning, advance notice of this disaster coming. And she had chosen to get away from all this stuff, this material claptrap, these *goods*, by which she lived but by which she did not wish to die. She had chosen to get away and to find an empty space in which to impress herself upon time. She would prefer, since she had to become a fossil, to be pure form. A simple, clear-cut shape, a skeleton—woman, end twentieth century—and nothing else.

Eventually, imagining that Ruby had walked out of the house and had found, miraculously, in the street, a stretch of pampas grass that was very soft, and clean, and cool, like sweet-smelling sheets, Blair's heart slowed and her breathing lengthened out and she went to sleep, dreaming of a singular and intact fossil.

9

Dinner at the Colonel's,
and a Bicycle Courier Arrives.

It was Friday. Ruby had been gone for eleven days. All week Blair had carried on at work without much caring what she said. She spent her spare moments calling people who might know something. Writing letters. And walking. Along Queen and King. Up Spadina, down University, up Bathurst. Looking for Ruby. The days went by, one after another, but real time had stopped. Everyone around Ruby was frozen into one attitude or another. Her family blamed Marvin. Marvin wrapped himself in romantic loss. Audrey was angry. Max felt guilty. Blair was disbelieving; she was certain she was unharmed, present, *nearby*. Ruby could not vanish like that.

Blair adjusted her headset and looked idly at the large white second hand as it swung past six and began to climb. The technician had his hand in the air. When it reached the twelve she began to talk.

"I went to a dinner party last night. You know, 'cause I've said before, that I'm a hick from the sticks. I have to tell you, this was yours truly in a foreign country: deepest Toronto. How shall I describe it? Ever so politely, these were stalwarts of every convention you can name: marriage, hard work, good manners, morals, good everything." She talked to her audience as if they were old friends, as if, in fact, they were Ruby.

"Once I was the kind of woman these men might marry. But not now. I'm a single mother. I kept on with my so-called career, without enough success to justify it. Hey, if you're going to get up in front of people and make a fool of yourself, you might as well make it worthwhile by being a star!"

The technician was smiling, so she kept on talking.

"So anyway, at this dinner the men kind of squared off right away, talking money and muscles, the usual. What struck me was how the women behaved. Career or no career, they wouldn't talk business at a dinner party. At least not before they established where everyone stood. Have you ever noticed that? "Do you work?" is not a proper question. So women at gatherings feel each other out. They give little clues. 'My nanny is taking a typing course this evening, we had trouble getting a sitter.' Or 'When I was volunteering in the school library . . .' Then once it's clear who is in what camp they get right into talking about *life*.

The technician was laughing, thumbs up. Time for music. She hoped Max wasn't listening.

"Too personal," said the fat producer, poking his head in during the music break. "No more Toronto-bashing, okay?" He smiled, dropping his chin and closing it upward again, his lips working like a ventriloquist's dummy's. He pulled his head back and was gone.

Personal, it was, but wasn't Toronto a little thin-skinned? Walking home after work, Blair's thoughts returned to the dinner with Max at his partner's house.

He had picked her up after work, and they drove into Wychwood Park, past the scrubbed brick faces of semi-detached homes. There was no place to park. Great mounds of leaves rested at intervals along the gutter, waiting for the vacuum to suck them up.

"Those leaf vacuums amazed me when I came here—the idea that streets had to be hoovered, like hallways. Only in Toronto . . . " said Blair.

"Just because you have no trees out west to worry about."

"So who's going to be at this dinner? Your partner and who else?"

"Old friends we went to school with. Andy has a thing about keeping in touch. And whoever Andy has there with him."

"Whoever?"

"He always manages to produce a woman companion: whether under false pretenses or with full understanding I can't figure. Not only that, they usually cook. Sometimes they're divorced, sometimes single, always attractive and articulate. It blows my mind. Maybe you can explain this to me," said Max.

"I guess there's an endless supply of women like that, apparently eager to cook meals for men and their friends." Blair made it clear she was not one of them.

Andy was gay but in the closet. Or rather, he was gay but only in New York. After looking in on the civil rights struggle in the '60s, he decided he wanted to be an actor, and went to New York. Nobody knew what he did down there. "It must have been too much fun," said Max, "because after two years he came back. Blew his little Toronto brain." Now, by way of atonement, he donated time to causes and kept up old ties.

Max drew the car up alongside the curb in a pile of leaves. Blair threw her door open and slammed it into Max's side as he was dashing to open it. While apologizing, she trod on his foot. "My fault," he said, automatically. The last time she'd waited for a man to come around to open a door for her he'd set off down the block and never looked back. Max made her feel nostalgic for chivalry, which in itself made her nervous. Almost as nervous as it made her to be going to dinner with the scions of old Toronto.

It had been raining all day, and the air was cold, gloomy, smelling of plant death. The trees, robbed of their filigree, stood naked and arrogant, fingering the fog-heavy night sky. A voyeur moon was tacked up crookedly over the gap at the end of the street. Blair's high heel slid on a decomposed leaf and she nearly fell. Max caught her elbow as she skidded.

Andy's house was gabled, with a wide, covered veranda, older by seventy-five years than the solid Victorians that ran on either side down neighbouring streets. It was the original farmhouse of the area, "built by Andy's three-greats grandfather," said Max, acting as tour guide.

"You do find these farmhouses tucked here and there around the city," said Max, "but hardly any of them are lived in by the original family." The house was sewn into the straight fabric of lanes and streets and schoolyards; only its idiosyncratic placement—too far back on the lot—its large and well-spaced trees, its country porch gave it away. "See how thin Toronto's pretenses are? When this place was built it was all cabbage patch and pasture. Andy likes to boast about how carrots keep popping up in the flower beds because that used to be the kitchen garden. He claims that when he dug out the basement to put in the sauna, he found a horse's skull."

They walked up to the front step and rang the bell. Stone urns on either side of the door overflowed with past-prime impatiens and Boston fern.

"Everybody grows impatiens in Toronto," said Blair.

"Toronto's official flower. Well-named," said Max.

No one answered the door, so Max kept on talking. Andy's antecedent was one of those old British colonels who on occasion got up a regiment to fight for the imperial cause. "Make sure you get a look at him; he's in an oval frame over the fireplace. On second thought, maybe you won't like him. He helped put down the Riel rebellion. Later he accompanied General Gordon down the Nile. Andy'll give a lecture on him with the slightest encouragement."

"I don't like him already."

Blair shifted her feet, crammed into old high heels with pointed toes. The decision to come out for dinner with Max was perhaps a foolish one: she never dated any more. She was ready to drop the twenty-year grudge she'd held against this man she hardly knew, but it was only for Ruby's sake.

"You know these United Empire Loyalist types, don't you? They act as if they invented Canada. But they're pussycats underneath. The more gracious Andy's behaviour—Andy's always gracious—the more surly I am," he said. "And the more he admires me."

The door was finally opened by a gaunt, big-boned woman with the face and hair of Princess Diana and the jaw of Brian Mulroney.

"Hi!" she said, "I'm Belinda, Andy's friend. Do come in. Jocelyn here will take your coat." She spoke in an upper-class English drawl that was slightly off. She stepped back, eyebrows arching, eyes fixed on the flagstone where they stood.

"I see you've brought in a few leaves on your feet."

Max and Blair looked down, guilty.

"Don't apologize, it's not a problem, we'll just have to pluck them off, won't we?" Abruptly, she doubled over, exposing a bony back, bare to the deep V of her little black dress. She peeled a layer of leaves off Max's shoes. When she straightened, not a trace of colour had risen to her face.

"Sorry," said Max.

"Inevitable at this time of year, isn't it? I'm about to call City Hall. Monster piles all over the walks. It's a menace, don't you think?"

Blair gave her coat to the stringy-haired young girl and tried to analyse Belinda's accent. Where did she come from, and why were leaves a menace?

"You're wondering where Andy is? He's just settling my

daughter with some of her homework. Such a dear he is, I find the science so difficult."

She led them into the living room, where two other couples sat uncomfortably in little brocade chairs munching on cashews.

"I understand you all went to school together, so I needn't introduce you."

"I didn't," said Blair, as Max set off shaking hands.

Belinda smiled, revealing small, even, transparent teeth.

"I'm at a disadvantage myself," said Belinda. "I went to a boarding school outside London—one of the best, of course, my mother made sure of that—but I came out totally uneducated. Got no A levels and I never went to university."

In her speech there was a *th* that wounded like *f*, in the Cockney way, and a choppy woodenness of delivery, which could mean German was in there somewhere. But the school had done a near-perfect job of making an English lady out of her.

"Field hockey, a bit of ancient Greek, needlework, piano, Cordon Bleu, I'm a dab hand," she said. "But I've basically no education and I was never fit for employment." And with this alarming combination of hauteur and humble confession, she went out.

"Farley and Sal? Have you met Blair Bowker?"

Blair shook her head while Max kept up a running commentary.

Farley had been in Poli Sci and Ec at Trinity College, University of Toronto, with Max. An academic, he played at municipal politics. He was tight-lipped and sharp-eyed; he could have been forty, or eighty. He looked peeled, nearly bald, with pinkish, raw skin and eyes animated by a malicious intellect. Sal, at his side, was a dry, lean woman who seemed made of tendons; her mouth was set in a permanent half-smile, and her gaze established that she dwelt at some distance beyond, a pose perhaps necessary for survival.

John Symonds wore a silver-grey, perfectly tailored suit with silk socks and black slip-on suede shoes, a luminous tie with peacocks on it; Marsha Symonds, a turquoise silk tunic, and leggings in the Muslim style. A gold-threaded matching scarf encircled her thin neck. According to Max, she had been a hippy. "Major," he said. "Beads, acid, the works." John was a lawyer. He had been a card-carrying member of the NDP, a fact he hid from his recent employers, a big development company.

All four raked Blair swiftly with assessing eyes, and then smiled extravagantly. The men looked away first, to greet each other. They started by shaking hands, but quickly became more familiar, punching shoulders, pinching waistlines, growing slightly raucous, talking about how "soft" or how "hard" the muscles were.

"You running?"

"Squash three times a week."

"Three miles every morning."

"I run up the stairs to my office twice a day."

"What's your cholesterol count?"

They felt each other's stomachs for muscle and fat. Peered into each other's hairlines, lifting locks to see the amount of grey over the ears, the depth of facial lines. Max strutted, showing off his slim silhouette. He was cocky, counting on his long athletic legs and high energy level to keep him young.

"Hardy peasant constitution," he said. "Can't beat it. Now you effete bluebloods are going to be sorry."

"It'll catch up to you," said John Symonds dourly. "No one escapes age."

"Not true. Not true. Some people get more life than others. You get more from one or both of two things—luck and money. Take a group of seventy-year-olds. Some of them might as well be dead. Others are as good as they were at fifty. One thing I've learned doing wills and trusts. We don't all get the same deal out of life."

After only the briefest pause, the women turned to one another with birdlike cries of greeting. Belinda's silent and dangerous-looking daughter took drink orders, and then went away. They were relieved. Her presence inhibited them. Everyone wanted nothing more than to ask who Belinda was, and what she'd done with Andy.

"Well, she's certainly got things in hand, hasn't she?"

"Cordon Bleu, we're in luck."

"Trust Andy."

That was when somebody said she knew Blair had been in Hearts of Flame. They'd been reading about Ruby this week. Blair supposed their curiosity carried criticism of them both for providing this diversion. Ladies had their names in the paper when they were born, when they married and when they died. It was a rule they too would have loved to have broken, Blair thought, but as the opportunity had not presented itself, they had to be satisfied with disapproval, or better yet, envy. Envy, after all, is a sharp feeling, rewarding the bearer with a stab and twist.

"I remember Hearts of Flame from the '60s," said Marsha Symonds. "I'd forgotten all about you until you were in the news again this week." She had bright acquisitive eyes, quick gestures like a squirrel.

"Yes, because of Ruby."

"Suicide, wasn't it?"

Blair said she didn't think that was likely.

"I suppose it's all been downhill for her since her singing career ended? Just like all those '60s types? The rest was anticlimax?"

Blair told them she had a great business, and she was about to get married. She lied a little.

"That'll do it," said a woman.

"I remember her, she was one of those favourite media 'successful women' stories. What a blow to the credibility of the whole superwoman scene," said another.

"But it isn't," Blair said. "No reason why it should be. We don't understand yet. We just don't know what happened."

Max let it go on a while, but he watched Blair, to see if she was minding. When they got back to saying how all those '60s people went downhill and eventually self-destructed, he butted in. He took a handful of cashews and began to throw them into the back of his mouth.

"What do you mean, all those people from the '60s?" he said to Marsha. "I remember you when all you wore was sandals and gunny sacks. You were stoned from morning till night. You lived in that commune with about eight guys and hung out at the Riverboat. Maybe it's you who's self-destructing."

Marsha laughed delightedly, fingering the gold chain around her neck. Farley and John's conversation about the World Trade Fair proposed for Toronto drifted between them.

"They're talking about building a floating hotel."

"Where?"

"On the lake, of course. Where else can you float in this town?"

"No," said Marsha to Max, "I'm not like that. I might get like that, though, if life doesn't get a little more interesting." She slid her hand a little way inside her neckline and stroked herself absently.

Andy finally emerged with a tray of drinks, dressed in a white, full-length apron that tied around his waist and brown, unpressed pants.

"Hello one, hello all," he said. "Sorry for the delay."

He began to pass the drinks, making no explanation for the chatelaine in his house. He was grey-blond and slightly puffy, with a forehead that easily wrinkled up in concern.

"How do you like my house?" he asked Blair.

"I've never been in one like it," she said truthfully.

"You know I inherited it from my father, who I hated. But he had in turn inherited it from his mother, so that makes it okay. Her grandfather was that guy, the Colonel." He pointed. The original inhabitant scowled out of his gold-leaf frame, to which a chrysanthemum corsage was taped. "I dressed him up a bit."

"You live here alone?"

"I have done forever. Can't afford to renovate it, even if I were so inclined. Can barely afford to heat it."

He cast his eyes around fondly. The walls were old-fashioned hospital green; the room was full of antiques, plant stands with Boston ferns, antimacassars, uncomfortable stuffed sofas in burgundy velvet and sagging, floral, chintz drapes. Only the plants looked healthy, thriving amidst the decline and fall of all that upholstery. The corners were full of the standard rich man's bad art—prints of Renaissance madonnas that might have been cut out of a guidebook to Rome, an occluded Paris street scene, a streaky, black-and-white abstract. But they were put in the shadow by an enormous Christopher Pratt of a woman three-times life size in yellowed nylon bra and panties with a slipped elastic.

"Dreadful, isn't it?" said Belinda, following Blair's eye. Her bloodless hand clutched a circular silver plate laden with bacon-wrapped water chestnuts. "Angels on horseback," she said, offering them. She had further blunt admissions to make.

"I'm a divorced mother with one daughter," she announced. "How old are your children?"

Marsha duly began an update on her children's ages and stages.

"Tonight Chloe is going to a semi."

"What do you wear to a semi these days?" said Sal. Marsha went on to describe the strapless tulles and ruffled satin gowns the girls had on.

"What's a semi?" Blair said, lifting a paper napkin from

Belinda's tray. The angels on horseback were greasy.

"Semi-formal. What else would it be?"

"Where I come from a semi is a truck."

Max laughed louder than the others.

"I love it. A semi is a truck . . ."

"You're from, where is it, somewhere out west?"

"Fifteen-year-olds don't go to semi-formals in Alberta, if you really want to know. They go to the drive-in. We did."

"Oh, but the girls are so sweet. They have such a good time," Marsha said to Blair. "They were all in my kitchen the night before, doing facials of cucumber and oatmeal. In the blender, they made this stuff, and got it all over the tiles. It hardened like stone. I spent hours scraping it off. Still, they're more liberated than we were."

"How do you mean?"

"The girls all stick together. You know what they did? Colour-coded the boutonnières they gave their dates. White means he's mine, hands off; pink means he's my cousin, you're welcome to try; red means he's a dog and I had no choice, don't blame me for him." She smiled triumphantly. "Sexual liberation. It's what we fought for, isn't it? Now *that* must have been the same out in Alberta?" Marsha said, a facile smile below her dangerous green eyes.

"Talking about the drive-in," said John, quickly, "have you been to see *Aida* in the SkyDome? We were in a box. I sat there in this padded seat with the glass screen in front of me and looked across the vast expanse at the screen, half a mile away, and drank my drink and ate my crackers and caviar. And it reminded me of nothing so much as sitting with my girlfriend in a field watching *Gidget Goes Hawaiian* with a tray of french-fries at the window. Except it wasn't half so much fun."

"What do these kids do for fun?"

"Sex," said someone.

Andy passed the wine bottle. "So we think, but what I want

to know is *do* they do it, Marsha?"

Belinda circled the chairs, bearing her trays of hors d'oeuvres. Each time she bent down, the bones in her spine stood out from her nape down to the demure white bow at her waist.

"Do they do what?" said Marsha, knowing very well what, and retrieving an hors d'oeuvre with a quick hand; how quickly the subject *will* come up, said the expression on her face.

"*It*," said several people at once.

She held them captive while she chewed, her pointed chin moving deliberately up and down, her eyes reflecting the dazzle of her tunic. She wiped her fingers on the little paper napkin.

"I don't think so."

"Too busy doing their faces. Just like their mothers," said her husband, in a grim effort to regain the stage. Marsha ignored him. The prudish lines around his mouth tightened as he laughed to himself.

"They don't need to," she said. "Because they aren't sexually repressed, like we were."

Sal, John, Farley and Max roared with laughter. "Now that's revisionist."

"You never seemed exactly repressed," said Sal. "At Branksome we believed that you guys at that free school slept with your boyfriends."

"All you uptight North Toronto kids . . . ," said Marsha. It was one thing to be remembered as being ahead of your time; it was quite another to be said to have slept around. There was a pause in the conversation.

"Oh no, I thought when I asked about children I'd introduced a safe subject!" she said. "Andy warned me you'd fight."

"Promiscuous, that's what you were," said Farley.

"Oh God! Where did you dig up that old word?"

"Out of some old sexist primer," remarked Blair.

He trained his round, bright eyes on her. "It applies equally to both sexes, in my opinion."

Guffaws greeted his owlish face as he scanned the room for confirmation. "Well, it *does*, technically. I once looked it up. Nowhere it is written that 'promiscuous' applies only to the female. But if you want to discuss prejudicial language, how about this tag 'uptight North Toronto kid,'" said Farley. He braced his two feet apart, prepared for debate. "What exactly does it mean? Up what? Tight what?"

"Sphincter," said Max. "To both questions."

Andy peered over people's shoulders, smiling, priest-like. He strolled to lean against the fireplace where, on a warped pine mantel, a couple of whalebone carvings stood. He fingered a walrus tusk and signalled an offer of help to Belinda, who refused.

"Where do your kids go to school?" he asked Marsha and John, falsely innocent. As if dinner parties had not collapsed when couples betrayed partisanship to public French immersion or private St. Clement's, or promoted the polyglot, downtown Jarvis Collegiate.

"UCC," said Marsha promptly, naming the reigning establishment boys' school.

Everyone laughed. "Marsha! You of all people!"

"It's not like it used to be," she protested. "It's not nearly so competitive now. The boys become really good friends."

"She tells me it's all lovey-dovey now," said John, dubiously. "I find it hard to imagine. I went there."

"And the uniform really isn't too bad. All sorts of immigrants go there too now, from Hong Kong and Pakistan. It's really a microcosm," Marsha insisted.

Andy smiled and nodded.

"Where are yours?"

"Public schools," said Farley stalwartly. "We've got four of them. Can't afford anything else. I'm a mere academic, you know. Our salaries do not reflect the gains of this decade of greed."

"They're all in French immersion. We took them on a wine-tasting trip to the south of France," said Sal. "They did all the talking for us."

"I understand *you* have a child," said Marsha, turning on Blair.

"One. She goes to the Simcoe School."

"*Ooooh.*" Suddenly everyone looked at Blair.

"Artsy-fartsy."

Marsha hadn't got the information she wanted. "From a previous marriage?"

"It was previous," said Blair. "But it wasn't much of a marriage, actually." She could see Max beaming out of the corner of her eye. He did seem to enjoy seeing her alarm his old friends. She set her glass on the mantel. "I wonder, does Belinda need any help with the food?"

"Belinda needs no help," said Andy. He smiled benignly at her. "No help with anything."

As they moved toward the table, John Symonds touched Blair's elbow.

"I heard some news about your friend Ruby," he said quietly.

Blair drew back into the foyer. "How?" she said. "What?"

"The criminal lawyers are saying big drug interests are involved in this. They say they've stopped the cops in their tracks. Nobody's going to find out anything. It's just too big."

"I don't know whether to believe you," Blair said. "Who's going to find her then? It'll have to be me," she said, half joking.

"I guess you've got to look at who she hung out with," said Symonds. "But you'll only find out what they want you to. And be very, very careful."

Marsha's face turned back; she caught the brief tête-à-tête.

"Coming, dear?"

The table was elaborately laid with Andy's mother's Queen Anne silver in a wide array to either side of the plates. Belinda instructed Andy; Andy instructed the rest where to sit. The guests pulled linen napkins out of wine glasses and spread them on their laps. Like a choir at the raising of a conductor's baton, they began their well-practised dinner-table turns. Turn your head and speak to the neighbour on your left. If she is already engaged with the neighbour on *her* left, become absorbed in breaking a bun.

"Do you sail too?"

"The south of France is too hot in summer. I never want to be anywhere but Muskoka."

"It's so rare to sit down with old friends like this. Really, we're so *busy*, we never seem to have the time . . ."

Blair sat to the right of Belinda's chair at the end of the table. She looked around her at the gleaming faces, established faces, white-wax, with fine wrinkles, hovering on prime. They were set in expressions of superficial eagerness to please. It was important not to offend, not to reveal unseemly depth. Yet there was a hardness in them. These people had made up their minds about any subject you cared to introduce. Blair narrowed her eyes so that they all went fuzzy. It was a trick she had, changing the context. She made them all farm-hands, at a harvest table. Then she imagined they were in France, before the Revolution. She put them all in powder and wigs.

"What part of Toronto do you live in?"

She opened her eyes again. Sal was across from her. Her peaked, intelligent face promised good humour at least.

"I suppose it's called the Republic of Rathnelly," said Blair. "Right down at the bad end. Where the shops are. Across from the hydro station. Where they discovered the PCBs. The city owns the house. And I lucked into renting it."

"We live in Moore Park. I don't know why I don't like it, but I don't," said Sal. "It's full of articulate, interesting

women who are ex-lawyers, ex-stockbrokers, ex-CBC producers. And now they do little jobs for the schools or for
charities, or give shows in the libraries, for no money, of
course. Sort of mother-hobbyists. I think the reason I don't
like them is that they all remind me of me."

Belinda came back with the first plate of soup. Andy was
permitted to carry every other bowl. She took her place at the
head of the table.

"Cream of watercress," she announced.

"This is really terribly impressive, Belinda."

When everyone's mouths were full of soup and hence they
were silent, Belinda began her frightening confessions.

"I think boarding schools are terrible, but I must say I'd
never have lasted in this country if I hadn't gone to Miss
Moira's."

Spoons continued to clink on the side of the soup bowls.
The men returned to the subject of building in the downtown
core. It was left to Blair to respond.

"How is that?"

"I was nine years old when I went, and it was a good thing
too because I wasn't wanted at home. I lived in for nine years,
and the message was it was up to you to get along with the
teachers and get along with the other girls and manage with
the work, because if you couldn't there was no place to turn
to. I've got forty other girls spread all over the world who I
can call up and ask anything, they're all like sisters. I was let
loose in London at nineteen and completely uneducated. I
met a Canadian on a trip to the Bahamas and married him.
Two years later I had Jocelyn and we divorced. I had to make
do."

She spoke with the clumsy forwardness of the English who
have rejected their countrymen's reserve but have little talent
for openness. Having delivered herself of her story, she attacked her soup. The bony spine curled over; a series of white
knobs protruded into the lamplight. Blair wondered about

that accent, again—was it Polish? The men were talking about Meech Lake.

"*Eggs*ually," Farley said at the end of the table, "it's worst for us. Without Quebec, Toronto will rapidly lose its rationale. No need to be the mediator between east and west."

Belinda accepted compliments on the soup, collected the bowls and was back to the kitchen in seconds.

Now Andy began to take the silver warming trays out of the cupboards, all brilliantly polished.

"I remember you used to be so disgusted with your mother because she had her burglar alarm set around that cupboard. That was the symbol of everything decadent," said Max.

Andy lifted one of the silver trays and smiled at his face reflected in it. "I've come to love my chains," he said. "Belinda tells me the more you use them the less you need to polish them and the more beautiful they look."

"How did you two meet?"

"I'll let her decide whether or not to make that public."

They all turned their eyes to the swinging door. It opened, revealing Belinda, this time bearing an enormous roast of beef.

"I was raising funds for the ballet," she said. "His name was on my list. When I rang him he sounded promising, you know, as if he might make a more substantial donation. So I arranged to come here to meet him. After that call, I only went home once, for our suitcases."

The silence that greeted many of Belinda's remarks was greater this time.

Marsha spoke. "And did he?"

"Did he what?"

"Make a substantial donation?"

"We're still discussing it," she said, nimbly saving the gravy boat from overturning in front of Blair, and passing it in the other direction.

A new wine went around.

"All right, charity," said Andy. "That's a good subject. Tell me how you all handle that one. What do you give, and how?" He looked as if he would take notes, if he could.

They all started to talk. John and Marsha had a foster child but they thought it was corrupt, because the $279 a year they sent him was three and a half times the $56 an adult male in his country earns per annum. Farley and Sal, along with their neighbours, had brought over some boat people. But that too had been unsatisfactory.

"It was all very odd," said Sal. "We did all the paperwork, and we found them an apartment and paid the rent. We furnished it for them, and they came and moved in. It was a man and a woman, married, and an older woman, their aunt, and a couple of kids. We didn't want to condescend. We decided finally we wouldn't be social workers and we left them alone. They got jobs quickly and just sort of settled in. We never saw them." Her narrow lips twitched up at the ends, her bony shoulders under the tailored white silk blouse lifted as she tore a piece of bread in half.

"Then one night they had dinner for us. We all went, all their sponsors, about five couples. They had rearranged the whole apartment so the one large room had two tables put together in the centre. They sat us down, but they didn't sit with us. They cooked and waited on us. It was just like going to a Vietnamese restaurant, except that at one point they all rushed in with cameras and took our photographs."

Andy clapped his hands. "Did you like it?"

"Somehow I felt cheated."

"It was *precisely* the way I expected it to be," said Farley.

Sal persisted. "We said we were only trying to allow them the dignity of making their own way, you know, of not interfering with them. But somehow—"

"Maybe you just didn't want to bother with them until they were settled. Then if they could act just like you, you'd be friendly," said Blair.

"You end up strangers."

"That was your aim in the first place," insisted Farley. "Not to get to know them. To give them an opportunity, that was all."

"I return to the question. How do we help others? Assuming we all want to."

"Of course we all want to. It comes with the territory."

"But," said Andy, "these are not satisfactory ways of giving."

"Why not?"

"Ask the boat people. Were they satisfied?"

"I want to satisfy *myself* while I'm at it," said Sal.

"I know some people who took in a Cambodian refugee. Right into their house. They said they'd pay for his university education, but after one year he had to move out."

"How did it work out?"

"He was around, he got to know the family, he did okay in school."

"Did he babysit?" said someone.

"That's my link with the Third World. They babysit," said Marsha. "Remember the Hungarian revolution? The Czechs? Every time one of these upheavals happened in Europe we got a new boarder in our basement, and whoever it was babysat."

"We had a Chinese who got out in the fifties. He was studying dentistry. He told me he'd helped build the Great Wall of China and I believed him."

"What happened to the Cambodian?"

"They kept him. After exactly one year, to the week—they made him move out. It was supposed to be the best for him."

The conversation wandered over to cottages, where to buy, whether you needed a summer place more than a winter place, what one did on those miserable in-between weekends in the city with kids. Sal ventured that her boys went to Sunday school and sang in the choir.

Andy nearly spit out his prime rib. "You go to what?"

"Anglican?" asked Marsha.

"That's what I was when I was a kid—"

"You've returned to the Anglican church?" Andy's face was red. A gulp or two of wine did not help, and Belinda dashed out to the kitchen to get him some water.

"It's the *music*. I like the music and the literature," Sal said gamely, eyeing Andy's throat, which was still seizing up.

"I am deeply shocked," he said.

"It's no different than your silver dishes," she said.

"Oh yes it is," he said. "I am shocked. This is total convention. This is worse even than Upper Canada College. The ruling class has got you back," he said. He shook his head, his eyes ran, and Belinda arrived to stand protectively behind his back while he sipped from a tumbler of water.

"Music and books seem as good a reason as any to go to church," said Blair.

"Oh my, oh my oh my," Andy said.

There was a lull until he regained himself.

Belinda had made a Pavlova and a chocolate mousse for dessert, both of which were passed around the table on crystal plates with long silver knives. Farley was unhappy about Andy's defence of the woman whose boyfriend wanted to stop her abortion by court injunction.

"Oh Farley, not after a big dinner," said Sal.

He persisted.

"We have no law. We have in effect abortion on demand until another law is made," he said, dramatically.

"The only people who have a problem with that are these, these crackpots who want to control women," said Blair a little more strenuously.

Sal sat with her wine tucked close to her chest, the twisting smile playing on her lips.

They all began to argue. Farley seemed to believe that

women would stop having babies altogether, if given the chance.

"I don't know what your problem is—" said Max to Farley.

"His mother didn't love him," said Sal.

"You've got four kids—" Max continued.

"Four and three-quarters—" said Sal.

There was a sudden silence. Looks of incomprehension on faces: did she mean what they thought she meant?

"You're not!" squealed Marsha. "You look so thin!"

"Six and a half months," said Sal with modest pleasure. "Due at Christmas."

"I'd *never* have noticed."

"Nobody has. I kept it a secret. Even Farley only found out two weeks ago," Sal added, modestly.

Belinda stopped in her flight to the kitchen. Andy raised his head from a line he was drawing in the whipped cream on his plate. A general howl of laughter broke out amongst the men.

"Farley found out? You mean you didn't tell him?"

"He finally put his hand on my stomach and said, 'What's this? I said, 'What do you think it is?'" Sal was enjoying her moment of fame, while Farley's high-domed forehead wrinkled slightly; his air of academic detachment appeared to be straining.

"How did you ever manage to keep him in the dark for six months?" Marsha's tone betrayed admiration despite herself. This was deception of a very high order.

"I think *dark* is the operative word there, all right," said John.

Farley sat straight in his chair, his knife and fork set neatly side by side on an angle across his plate.

"Why didn't you tell him?" said Blair.

"I'm forty . . . and I wanted to be sure everything was going to be all right."

"I can see not telling everyone else, but didn't you feel

sick? Weren't you scared when you had the tests? Perhaps I'm naive, having so little experience of marriage, but isn't that what husbands are for?" Blair persisted: she had plenty of experience asking questions.

"I had terrible morning sickness, in fact. And the test was awful. Just awful."

"You didn't want his support during those times?"

Sal, small and wiry, was nearly as straight in her seat as Farley when she answered. "Let's just say I *know* who I'm dealing with."

"Oh dear," said Belinda. "Oh dear, oh dear."

John put his head in his hands, while Max watched, fascinated.

Farley downed his wine. He remained pale, but sweat had appeared on his bald forehead. What were his options? To express regret? To laugh at himself? He made his choice. He would *ignore* the announcement. "I might want an abortion if I were pregnant," said Farley, doggedly pursuing his original conversational goal, "or want my wife to have one, but I still feel it shouldn't be generally available on demand. People aren't responsible. Women will simply have one after another."

Sal waited, disbelief on her face. He did not rise to her bait. Slowly her expression of victory drained away. She looked around, as if she wanted more jokes. She wanted help in ridiculing her husband.

"So is it better these irresponsible women should have children?" said Blair.

"Society has to rule on this. It isn't an individual's choice," insisted Farley.

"But society has ruled in fact. Society wants abortion on demand. That's why no jury will find Morgentaler guilty."

"Society is in an uproar," said Farley, with dignity.

"Oh, *hardly*."

"Is society in an uproar, or is the medical establishment in an uproar because they see themselves losing control of this one aspect of women's health when they've set themselves up as gods?" Andy beamed with pleasure at the fight.

"Someone must keep control," said Farley.

"And clearly *you're* not doing it," said Blair suddenly, in spite of herself.

Sal smiled, a small, thin-lipped, barely allowed triumph. Farley's pale face began to colour. It turned pink, and then very red. His mouth remained shut. The table went silent. Belinda loudly inquired of Max whether he'd ever been to New Zealand. She and Andy had gone, taking Jocelyn. It had cost them $10,000 in airfares, and the first night they got into their camper van they ran out of gas.

"Nothing's open after five o'clock. It's so small. It just shuts down. Every town," she said, eyeing Farley and Blair out of the corner of her eye. Sal began to cut herself a large wedge of cheese, while Marsha asked her about the sex of her expected child. Blair sneaked a look at Max. He smiled back, affably.

"I seem to have got into a fight with your friend Farley." Blair was contrite, walking down the sidewalk. "I can't imagine why."

"It was obvious. Sal wanted you to. She set that whole thing up."

"Still, I don't know why I bothered. He's not my husband," she said with relief.

"It made the party! Andy loved it too!" Max raced around the car to open her door. After Blair got in she slid over to be near him.

"Do you think bringing me put your friends off?"

"That was the whole idea. They're far too sure they know who I am."

"So the ruling class didn't get you back too?"

"It never had me, so it couldn't."

That was what stayed in her mind. That and the old-fashioned way he kissed her at the door, the firm lips on hers, the brief heat of his breath against her cheek.

"I'm an egg, I can't have feet," said Simplicity.

The egg was almost always dressed the same, in a stiff, white collar and a blue waistcoat with gold buttons. Red shorts, usually red, white tights and black shoes.

"Eggs don't have feet," said Blair, "but Humpty Dumpty does. And so should you. Otherwise, how are you going to get from house to house with your candy bag?"

"Yes," said Simplicity, and began to run up and down the hall, opening and shutting her pretend bag. "Trick or tree—eat, trick or tree—eat."

"We used to say, 'Hallowe'en apples!'" Blair raised her voice to the carnival bray all kids knew. "Haa—lowe'en Ap—pulls!" We also said, 'Shell out, shell out the witches are out.'" They both shouted together for a few minutes. Simplicity grew tired of it first.

"I have to have a bald head." Simplicity looked at herself in the bathroom mirror. "An egg-head. Pointed on the end."

Philip had been curiously silent about the costume. It looked as if Blair would have to do it herself. She went through a mental list. What was bald? An eagle. A coot. An old man. A lady in a circus. Did any of these provide ready-made costumes? Clowns were bald. How did they do it? They tied back their hair and wore a skullcap of some sort.

"We used to make jokes about people with pointed heads. It was an insult. Pointy-heads were dumb or something."

Simplicity didn't seem to care. "Mum, you always talk about what you used to do."

Blair opened up her arms. Simplicity's round, open, pale face, framed by wisps of hair escaping from her ponytail, was there before her, like a full moon, still brand new. She put her arms around her mother's neck and hung there. The arms were lithe and light, the skin where it touched Blair's cheek was soft, moist. Nothing surpassed Simplicity's skin in tenderness; none of those similes about flowers and silk worked. The closest thing was a first-day mushroom, just poked up through the matted leaves on the forest floor, almost sinister in its newness, fragrant.

"I'm sorry I keep talking about what I used to do. I used to hate it when adults did it to me. They pretend to talk about the children but really they are talking about themselves. Oops, I'm doing it again."

"It's all right, Mum," said Simplicity.

"No, it's not. It's not fair."

Simplicity let her arms drop. "Can we get my costume now?"

"I'll tell you this. I never was a bald-headed egg for Hallowe'en. I think it's a very good idea," said Blair.

Simplicity began to run up and down the hall again calling out, "Trick or treat! Trick or treat."

"We still have ten days—"

The telephone rang. Blair retreated down the hall to the kitchen to answer it. It was one of the fat producers. When business calls came, it was inevitable that Simplicity was making noise; Blair never got a serious call when things were quiet. She put her head into the broom closet to block the noise. He wanted her to come in to see him. Something about how she was offending Canadian sensibilities and she was too one-sided.

"I'm Humpty Dumpty and I am an egg," Simplicity sang, racing up and down the hall beside Blair's closet. There was a crash. Blair looked out; Sissy had slipped on the hardwood and fallen. Lying on the floor, she wept softly. Blair signalled, waving her hand frantically. Simplicity stood up slowly, the tears drying on her face. Blair's head was tucked down under the closet shelf, the phone cord wrapped around her leg. He was setting a time.

"Can you give me that again?" Blair reached outside the broom closet, took the pen from the calendar and wrote down what he was saying. Mocking local standards of behaviour. Not presenting both sides of an . . . attempts to be inflammatory . . . not restful radio.

"I realize," said Blair at one point, "that I'm an acquired taste. I'm not twenty years old, I'm not thirty. I've got a history. I've got my quirks and my pricklish bits."

The fat producer exhaled, causing static on the line. "I know that," he said. "But it doesn't necessarily make you interesting. If you could just tell me one thing about yourself our listeners would find *interesting* . . ."

When she hung up, there was a whole lot of writing on the plywood under the broom hook. It was exactly the sort of thing she told Simplicity not to do.

"Are you okay?" she called to her daughter.

Simplicity had forgotten about her injury. She had pulled the nursery rhyme book off the shelf again, and was sitting on the tiles cradling it in her lap and mouthing the words that went along with the pictures.

.

The bicycle courier dismounted; languidly, like a threat, he approached the door. Species of tough: they were a breed unto themselves, these urban jockeys dodged traffic all day, breathing exhaust. He had long, filthy hair under an orange bandanna, and wore a black leather jacket over spandex shorts. He had neon straps on his ankles and pumped-up track shoes. He handed Blair a package.

"From who?" she said.

He shrugged, and held out a board for her to sign.

When he'd swung his leg over the bar and departed, with no backward glance, Blair tore off the staples on the padded envelope. Inside was a clutch of yellow papers, torn from a notebook. She recognized Ruby's writing. Flipped forward and back. There was no note, no explanation for what looked to be a portion of a diary she'd written.

————————

Wed

No Marvin. No man at all. I'm in withdrawal, wrapping myself around bedposts. Terrible lust. Fantasize Marvin's here, whisper to him take me, hurt me, harder. Think about drugs, other guys, anything to get me through it. But so far no indulgence. The pain itself is a kind of answer.

Tea-reading yesterday with Blair, at the old Red Shoes down in the east end, past Beaches.

"I remember this. I know when this was," said Blair. "About a month before she disappeared. Mid-August?" She was talking to herself; no one was home. She bent her head over the page again. Why had it come? Who had sent it? What was she meant to understand by it?

————————

Juke box selection at every booth. Brown, javex-smelling tabletop. Thick glass flutes with cubes of jello on display, orange, green, red. Clientele varied: pregnant woman in huge T-shirt, rough teenage boys, tired salesmen.

Jeannie read my leaves, nothing memorable except that she said I'll move across a border or sea soon, and will have success within two years. What would Oswald say about this little amateur? Still, it's fun. She says there are two people trying to do me harm—a dark-haired man and a fair woman. Who are they? Mensa was darker when he had hair. And—who—? Blair? I thought that once.

We talked about old times. We thought we were famous. But the stars of our youth—Blair, Philip—have set. The understudies are risen—Oswald, me. Blair goes on about who made it and how. I feel like she's keeping track of me. I don't like to be kept track of. The great thing about fashion is you can't. It's untraceable, non-linear. You spring up fully dressed from the brow of some smart young designer: wiped out is your background, wiped out your social class, wiped out your colour. Anyone can get it, so long as you've got purchase power.

"Isn't it interesting . . ." Blair always says. What is this "interesting"? Interesting you don't say, not when it's yourself. She's an observer. She sidelines herself that way, invests the major part in other people's lives. Like a proper woman, isn't it?

Not me. The only trajectory I care about is my own. Not a wife woman, but one for a mistress, like Philip told me, that night in Banff at our last concert. The story of my life, he laid on me. Oh well. There's worse life stories, I think. Worse would be to never have done what you wanted and to watch everyone else and to say "that's interesting."

Right on cue, my mother calls tonight. She tells me how much she loves me and then asks me to come home and worship. I don't believe it. She wants me for God, you know, for Heaven and all that. Where is this unconditional love bit that Freud talks about? I thought that was what mothers were supposed to dish out. Not in my world. Everyone's selling their own idea. My mother included. I don't need salvation.

———————

Fri

I can hardly write on this page, my pen sticks to the paper. It's curling with humidity, and I'm too depressed to move. I just work, get tired, drop into bed, put a pillowcase in my mouth and scream for Marvin. Guess I'm hooked. The torture rack—my backbone arches and my thighs ache to grip him. Meanwhile, he's at home playing Hubby. He hates his wife. Why do people do this to themselves? Why do they make these chains—and cling to them?

But I'm all right. Really. I'm just like myself all day, you wouldn't notice. Cracking jokes about it to my staff. You can lie about anything, and make it so. I know that. Tell them it's over. Sometimes believe it.

The only lasting truth is a new look tomorrow. The only loyalty is to change. So I should change Marvin.

Sat

He sent me a fax. "I'm desperate. I love you so much. I must see you." Audrey brought it in. "I think this is personal," she said, throwing it on my desk. Staring at it, I went from cold to hot. At the bottom he'd added, "We lasted eighteen days." Even in my joy I noticed how he said "We lasted," assuming that since he had given up giving me up, I would too. So I did. Oh weakness.

Met him for lunch at Mimi's. Fabulous to see him. Tears coursing down my cheeks. His dear hand, his beloved face, the chocolate eyes with their cat-like yellow flecks. His dear hand under the table. Oh, Marvin.

But no sex. I swear I won't sleep with him while he's still with Wifey. And it's a little different now. Subtly so. He looks so pathetic. Brought low, is Marvin. So he should be. He's so weak. Can't cut it off with her. He tells me all the gory details. How she refuses to speak about What's Wrong. She doesn't know that I am, where I am, when I am or who I am. Just senses there's *something*. Almost felt sorry for her. I would if I wasn't dying to fuck her husband.

But I felt, God, I felt *fed* when I left the restaurant. Like a normal human being, bound up with somebody like this so much it rips up the gut. Hunger for sex gnawing at me like a rat. Eyes sore red swollen under my sunglasses. Bloody fingers where he squeezed my hand so tight under the table the glass in my ring cut me. That's real life isn't it, Ruby Mason?

Sunday again

Such a bloody goddamn awful day. I hate Sundays. Everyone stays home. And I hate home. I had a fit of rage at Blair today. She never invites me over. Sitting there in her garden with her flowers, or making muffins, with her kid, or Philip—whatever the hell she does she doesn't want me around. That Ruby: a loose cannon, you never know what she'll do, she's gone for one married man after another. Keep her away from decent folks.

Marvin the creep sneaks out to buy cigarettes and calls me from Mac's Milk. Gets all lathered up on the telephone—I need you, I want you, poor me, I'm so trapped. My body fills up with bad rushes, hot stabs. Part of me wants to see him suffer in hell the way he's making me. The other part goes all hot and wet with longing. Begging him. Debasing myself. God I hate this, I hate myself! You should hear me! It's enough to make you vomit!

I have the feeling I'm being manipulated. Me! Who spent all these years manipulating women. I make them wear what I say is beautiful. Sometimes it's just somebody's bad joke, like those old vests under men's suits, with the ugly rayon backs and long points. They were ugly and they made women look like little square dwarves. But the pleasure of seeing it catch on. Of saying I invented that look. They're buying it! To change how we all look, how we all see.

Putting one over on them is what it becomes. But who is it over on, in the end? I've metamorphosed so much I've got no true shape. How did I let myself in for wanting Marvin? Visibility was what I always wanted. Not love. Money? A word I don't relate to. *Being seen* is where it's at. The only true spoil of this war. To be plastered out there.

—Can't get the boots I want for the Splash show. So I put them in Roman sandals maybe. But will have to jack up the hem. Don't know how those 40-year-olds are going to take to it.

Every now and then I look at myself in one of those long mirrors and remember, that's *me*. I'm forty. I'm ugly. I'm twenty pounds overweight, well, maybe ten. It's like until I'm forced to see the mirror I can forget, pull all my desires for beauty outside of me into designing for these lissome kids, these always young and younger models. Think I'm like them until I see myself. God! Maybe Marvin *does* want his wife. Maybe he doesn't want me after all.

Blair flipped forward, looking for a reason, an explanation for this epistle.

The pages were loose, and out of sequence. There was no sense to the chronology: it was as if Ruby—or someone—had grabbed a handful of pages and yanked them out, sent them without wanting to convey any real sense of what had happened. It was like having a look inside Ruby's disordered, feverish brain. She scanned for names, for places and times, for clues. When she started reading again the only name she recognized now was from twenty-four years ago—high school.

—I was thinking about Keith, the guy I was in love with in high school. Quarterback of the football team. Big chiselled blond from rich houses up the hill. We caught each other's eye before the nine o'clock bell. Finally said hello in the halls. We used to hang over the stairwell every day after lunch. I got out of my cousin's green Ford pick-up truck, with "Jay's Landscaping" written on the side, around the corner from the school once I started seeing him. It seemed only right.

From the first day we were into a contest: who could go the longest without wearing the same outfit. He had all these wonderful clothes—shag cardigans and alpaca V-necks, cuffed wool pants (he never wore jeans). I improvised. Used to go to the thrift shops and find stuff. Wore bobby socks with gored rayon skirt from '40s. That's how I got started.

Finally I wore something twice.

"I won," he said.

Keith had a car. A Chevy something, with fins, which he kept shined with Turtle wax to a very hard, slick glaze that made it look as if comets could strike, and bounce off. Once, in the front seat of that car, he unzipped the pocket in my stretch ski pants. He couldn't believe his luck. I wasn't resisting. Then he put his hand in, right in the soft cotton pocket. Felt all around. It was a big moment, I was holding my breath, he was panting. He figured he was going to get in down there below the waist, get a feel.

I was quiet like a mouse, waiting. His hand went around, came back to the zipper, went around again, couldn't get anywhere. The hand was caught around the neck by little zipper teeth, in the bag of cotton lining in the Borg pants I had made down from Blair's mother.

Shit! he said finally. It's a pocket. You cunt! Why didn't you tell me? You let me make a fool of myself.

I roared. It was too funny. He thought I was laughing at him. Maybe I was. But I remember another time in that front seat, under a streetlight, the lathe of white crossing the windshield, travelling past the concrete pillar at the back lot behind the gym, the peeled, cracked wood of the telephone pole. He took something off, I can't remember what outfit it was I had on, but he got it open and down over my hips quickly before I could hold it on, and stuck his cock in me before I knew he had it ready. I didn't know for sure how you did that kind of thing.

One thrust was all he got before I kneed him in the groin. I didn't know if that was enough to make me pregnant, but I thought it might. I guess that was a rape, but without the words, what did I know? I thought it was just him getting back at me for letting him make a fool of himself about my pocket. I remember him bent over himself groaning in the front seat. It gave me such a warm feeling, Keith being all emptied out over little old Ruby Mason.

————————

Wed

More stolen phone calls. Quick incognito lunches in out of the way cafés. Lovestained faxes. I'm sick of this. He'll leave her in the end. But I won't be around. This love is hateful stuff. Now he's cheating on her double. She found out, he swore off me, they're remaking their marriage, and in the midst of this, he's seeing me again. How could she stand it? How could she not know? I'm not asking him to leave her either. If he ever does, it'll be for himself. But I've gotta thank Marvin. I learned something. The crux of the problem is not his wife, it's not even him. It's my life.

"Hey I know when this was," said Blair, looking up from her reading. "It was right before she disappeared." She grasped the last two remaining pages. Please let her give a clue to where she went. But no. She was giving reasons, maybe, but no explanations.

———————

Sandwiches at the Coffee Express with Blair. She's depressed. Got to get a better job. They don't like her at work; she's too old and opinionated. Or have an affair, I told her. 'Course she says she doesn't want to.

I sat there, guilty of promoting myself and Blair out of existence. You're gone at 40. Unless you pass for 20. The ultimate vanishing act. A woman's life. We talked about Marvin. She's so judging. Pissed me off.

———————

DON'T KNOW WHAT DAY

It's pouring, bloody freezing, dark like night out there even though it's morning. I'm sitting in bed with my sketch pad. Don't want to get up. All women artists work in bed, I heard. I'm drawing a bed-jacket. Quilted satin, flared out from a tiny satin collar—what to wear while you're suicidally depressed.

I need someone to rub my back. My whole life takes place on the phone. I talk but don't tell. Not even Blair any more. The lie has crept in. Even here. I'm lying to my diary.

All right. So I'm fucking him again. And he's not leaving his wife.

Agh! I want to throw up. Want to reject/eject myself. I am rejecting/ejecting myself. Just watch me!

The diary pages ended there. Led right up to the week before it happened, and then stopped. Led you to the edge of the cliff and then wandered off. Teasing. Just like Ruby.

The more she read her words, the less Blair could see Ruby. *Ruby*. Even the name now sounded to Blair unreal. She was gone.

Perhaps she had never been amongst them, truly. Perhaps she had been biding her time with them from the beginning. Maybe Ruby had known what she was coming into, like someone with a vast inheritance playing with ordinary kids. From the start she had been destined for greater things, even if it was only to be a famous missing person.

10

The Last Safe Place in the World

Blair sat on her front porch. It was three o'clock in the afternoon, on Hallowe'en. She had called in sick to work. She could not bear to miss Sissy's Hallowe'en parade.

Two petunias survived in the window box, long and straggly, and one pansy. The porch floor, which Bernie swept clear yesterday, was again dotted with curling orange-and-green maple leaves. From the corner of her eye, Blair could see the sad downward incline of yet one more.

She picked it up. Its red, rubbery stem and veins stood out against the shrinking skin. The underside was faded, duncoloured; the top was brilliantly coloured, green and yellow and red darkening to the sharp, curling, brown tips. She held it up to the light and it glowed greenish-yellow, translucent, like the large, weightless paw of some air-stalking, mythical beast.

Every day now more light fell on the house, the lawn, the windows, as the elm tree and the maple thinned and thinned. Still there were others: the oak, holding on to a shaggy yellow mane, the pine.

Bernie came up the stairs; having cleaned two houses, she

looked a little tired. "There's mail for you," she said, taking a handful of envelopes from the box.

Blair's inamorato had gone to Greece, apparently. The postcard stood out in her hand from the flutter of unbleached envelopes stamped all over with red ink: **LUCKY READER,** *you are a big winner,* **We are holding for you one **Cartier Watch!!!!*** you hold in your hands one free ticket, all you need to do is read the enclosed . . .**

She picked out the glossy picture from the junk mail, glancing first at the writing on the back. The familiar peacock ink and baroque calligraphic style told her it was him. But the picture was a trick; the postmark was Toronto.

She didn't read the words right away, but turned it over to see the image. That unmistakable Greek blue sky was forced up into a corner, nearly out of the picture. Pressing in at claustrophobic angles were the white stucco walls lining a narrow alley. In their shade were three black-shrouded figures, women in mourning, presumably, feeling their way with crabbed fingers along the wall, sightless and bent.

It was a shocking image. Their wrapped and covered heads, their almost blind progress, their stooped, thick forms were ugly and pathetic. They made their way toward—what? A light, possibly somewhere near the photographer's feet.

Blair turned it over. She read it quickly, too nervous to absorb the words fully. It was still saturated with lust and longing, but there was something else—bitterness, disappointment. She did not know what she could have done to offend him, just as she had no idea how she had attracted his devotion in the first place. Perhaps he assumed she knew who he was and had expected her to be on his doorstep by now, ready to be claimed.

She turned it back and studied the Greek widows again. There was an implied threat in the image. What did it mean? *You'd be lost without me? A woman without a man is blind, and helpless?*

Blair wondered if she would like her secret lover. While he had thrilled her with his protestations, she had been getting to know him. Now, suddenly, she felt she understood him; it was not a pleasant experience.

Reluctantly she turned the card over and began to read.

"You are dying in your present life. It is not even a life, it is a half-life. A second-best. You need me. You need to be living on the edge, to risk all. If you do not follow your instincts, soon it will be too late. We can be beautiful together, but only if you have COURAGE! You must find me—Where is the wild girl in you?"

What a nerve! Blair separated the postcard from the other solicitations. But the unknown lover's questions nagged. Follow her instincts, yes, but what were they? Where is the wild girl, indeed?

In the kitchen the coffee, which had been on the element, had turned bitter. Blair poured a slug of milk into hers. Bernie took it half and half. Before noon they met here and discussed the intricacies of the day: when Sissy had to be picked up and where taken, what shopping there was and who would do it, who needed the car more. Usually Bernie got the car.

"Was Simplicity all right this morning?"

Blair looked up, startled. "Of course she was. Why?"

"Oh, just because I dreamed she was dead."

Blair was rattled. "Don't you think you're a little blithe with your premonitions!"

"*Blithe?*" said Bernie. "How do you spell it?"

"Have you seen my black dress with the net and sequins?" said Blair. She had no time for words today.

She needed a dress to go to a black-tie dinner with Max. It had been a year or more since she'd worn it. It was not in the back, left-hand side of the cupboard where Blair had seen it before the summer. It was not in the ancillary cupboard in

Simplicity's room, where Blair stored her less frequently worn and more fragile clothes. Nor was it in the cedar closet in the attic. It was an important dress. Ruby had made it for her.

"Did you look upstairs?"

"I looked everywhere." Blair had pawed through old black garment bags with zipper fronts from shops she'd forgotten had ever existed. She had drawn out—creased, diminished and much smaller than she remembered—dresses and suits and pants that belonged to the distant past. A grey silk pant suit with red trim, which she'd worn when pregnant with Simplicity over six years ago. A dinner jacket she had cut over for herself, which had come down from her grandfather. A lot of hippie clothes, thin cotton dresses with tie waists and ruffles at the hem. Navy fitted pants, when she'd just bought a new pair this year, saying to herself, I don't have, and I desperately need, a pair of navy fitted pants.

There were clothes in there the very existence of which was a revelation to Blair. Each brought back with it, emanating from limp folds of blue linen or cotton with sprigs of pink flowers, a time and place where it had been bought, where it had been worn. That one was a shower, a wedding shower in Medicine Hat, for she couldn't remember who, and she'd worn it with a pink straw hat with a brim. For some reason she had felt inadequate to attend this shower in the clothes she owned at the time.

"I can't go to this shower. I don't have anything to wear," she would have said, which meant, "I don't have the thing to wear that will project the image of myself that I want to project."

So she had gone out and spent money on a dress, worn it once, and then it had gone into the closet. These purchases, usually last-minute, panicky and full of an unsure triumph when the thing was found, would be found wanting in some yet unforeseen way. Going through her closets, Blair took hanger after hanger in her right hand and jerked it a foot and a half to the right, against the rest of the dresses, going down the ranks, like a sergeant inspecting drill. *Look at those twill pants with the cross-over front, I remember those. Oh the black silk spotted summer dress—how small I was! I was so thin then!*

As she went through this phalanx of fashion, she realized that the parade had stopped, that she no longer ran out at three o'clock in the afternoon to buy something to wear that evening at seven. She no longer wished to shop. She no longer needed to shop. She was content with the costume she wore.

And the black dress was not discovered.

Blair and Bernie took their coffees in both hands and moved together, in sympathy, toward the kitchen table.

"You didn't take it to the cleaners?" said Bernie.

"It's covered with sequins. It can't be cleaned. I'd never take it to the cleaners," said Blair.

"You checked in Simplicity's closet?"

"Yes, and the attic. It's not there. It's gone."

"I can't picture this dress," said Bernie. "Tell me more about it."

"It's black tulle in the front and the sleeves and the back and it has a satin butterfly in front, with sequins all over the skirt. You liked it," said Blair. "I remember the last time I wore it you said you liked it."

"If I can picture it then maybe I can dream where it is."

"I think we should give the closets one last going over," said Blair.

Bernie looked into her coffee cup.

"When I lived in Philippines a ring was lost. It was a very special ring to my mother, which my father had given her, not a wedding ring but for an anniversary. And it was lost for such a long time."

Sometimes Bernie liked to talk about home. Blair looked out the window to listen. A trio of squirrels chased up and down the trunk of the Norway maple in the back yard. Its leaves, yellow splashed with vermillion, were drooping and lying in drifts around the bottom. The blackness of the squirrels was like a moving eye, a point of reference, life pursuing its own ends.

"And my mother said if I could find it she would be so happy. So one night I dreamed of a high place and a little cup and the ring there just inside the cup. In the morning when I got up I looked up on the wall. Our house, it was not very big, but there was a high shelf where no one ever reached or could reach, and I saw this cup which was in my dream. So I climbed up there and I found the ring," said Bernie. "Always I see things in my dreams."

"Amazing," said Blair. "Well I wish you could find my dress."

She was thinking that not only Ruby but everything Ruby made would disappear now. Her designs, even her memory. Sometimes now Blair wasn't positive she knew the voice; sometimes, when she saw Ruby's face in her mind, there was a blur over the eyes, the mouth; part of it was obliterated.

"And while you're at it you can dream where Ruby is."

Bernie closed her eyes and hummed. She hummed her high, intermittent hum, which meant she was worried. She never said anything about Ruby. She was superstitious. Death came in, if you left the door open for it. Blair stared at her coffee and thought irritably of having to find another dress to wear. Getting all dressed up and going downtown. Changing her clothes in those desperate little rooms with the cellulite-searchlights in the ceiling. Not to mention paying for a new one. Maybe it wasn't worth it, going out on dates with Max Ostriker.

"Where do you think your dress has gone?" said Bernie.

"I think someone must have taken it. I think it's been stolen," said Blair, who hardly knew she thought this until she said it.

"Maybe one of those people who stayed here this summer, when we were away," said Blair hastily, to dispel any thought Bernie might have that Blair suspected her. Bernie would be the last person on earth Blair would suspect.

"Who? Why?"

"Remember I gave the key to my friends from Vancouver? And then their friends came too. And there was a key left with that student who watered the plants. I was careless about who I gave keys to. But someone must have found my dress. Admired it."

Bernie looked distressed.

"What bothers me is that it's not out of need. None of these people needed that dress, they just took it, as a gesture," said Blair. What bothered her most was that Ruby made it for her.

"At home," said Bernie, "we hang our washing on the line outside the house overnight. Right in the open. Not like here. It's very bad, isn't it?"

"It's not bad," said Blair. "It's nice. If you can trust people."

"Nobody has washer and dryer because they are so poor. I remember one day I hang my shirt on this line and I woke up in the morning and looked out and this top was missing. It was very nice top too, with a line, like this"—she drew a diagonal line across her breast—"and stars around the neck. I like this top very much. And it is gone because someone takes it off the line."

"There you go," said Blair, "that's the feeling. Just gone. It's hard to fathom."

Fathom. Bernie wondered what it meant. Find, perhaps. Or get back. "Yes," she said, "it's hard to get it back. I remember what happened. I was so upset because I like this top very much. And then I saw it on the person. I know it is my shirt because this is not a shirt that can be buy in Philippines, it's from State-side."

"What did you do when you saw it on the person? Did you

confront her? I assume it was a her."

"No," said Bernie. Her cheekbones tipped to one side; the light fell from the window to the front of her face, removing the planes. Now it was a flat heart. "No, I did not. I don't know why but I couldn't. I have a feeling of—I don't know how you say it—like I wanted to stand back, it is enough just to see, and to understand that this is the person who takes my top. I feel like—when you see a ghost?"

"Freaked out?" said Blair. "Aren't we in the Hallowe'en mood."

"You're going to see that dress. One day. You're not going to have it back but at least you're going to see who has it."

"I wish it was a poor person who took my dress," said Blair. "Then at least I could figure it was because they needed it."

"Poor people don't need dresses with no back and sleeves made out of net," said Bernie.

"You're right," said Blair, glumly. She stared out the window some more. "Stealing when you don't need something is different from theft, it's an act of"—she paused a moment for the word—"an act of revenge. It's like someone is angry with me." *But who*, she thought. *Maybe Ruby herself.*

"I know *revenge*," said Bernie. It had an exact equivalent in Tagalog. Getting even. People killed to get even.

Blair pulled herself out of her reverie. She saw by the look on Bernie's face that she was frightened. "Don't listen to me. I'm dreaming in technicolour. I don't mean revenge," said Blair. "That's the wrong word." She laughed. "I have to be careful about my words around you, you're such a good student. You're going to go and look it up."

Bernie did not answer directly.

"Do you know what we do in Philippines on Hallowe'en? We go to the graveyard to visit the dead. We have a party. Everyone brings lots of food, and eats it there. It's like a big—" she stopped.

"Festival?"

"Celebration. Do you think that's strange? To visit the dead?"

"No, I like it. I think it's a good idea."

The long stretch of perfect fall days that had lasted since early September was coming to a close. At three o'clock the sky began to cloud over. At the Simcoe School Miss Rushton, who was dressed as a genie, rubbed her lamp and requested that it not rain for the dress parade.

In the gym, the children began to struggle into their costumes. Those who lived nearby ran home for help with make-up. Mothers arrived to help.

Blair carried the egg-head Philip had made, with the shoulders attached, the stuffed blue waistcoat and red shorts, the white tights and black shoes. Simplicity did not want the others to see. They went into the upstairs washroom to get her dressed. This was a serious disguise. She did not want to look pretty, like the other little girls, in princess and fairy outfits. She wanted to be Humpty Dumpty, truly; no one must know who was inside the egg.

Dressed, Simplicity stood alone beside the school door, waiting for the parade to start. Blair sat on the picnic table with a half-dozen other mothers. Two men joined them.

"Look, a parent," said one of the mothers. The others laughed. When the call went out for parents, only mothers responded. However, to ask for mothers, or to admit that only mothers did this, would be sexist.

Miss Rushton led the parade, in purple harem pants and a flowing gold-chiffon top, holding her lamp high. She had taken tremendous pains with her costume, quite outshining the children. Following her was a dinosaur made of pink plush with spines on his back made of stiff tulle. Then came a body builder, in a flesh-coloured body suit with muscles made of satin appliqué.

"His mother works on Hallowe'en costumes all year," said a mother. "She'll start tomorrow for next year."

There was a boy in a man's fedora and long trench coat, who held up a sign that spelled out S-P-Y. If he didn't tell you, you wouldn't know. After him, a Rambo, with blood on his cheeks.

"I'm horrified," said the mother. "I let his father take him out and this is what they came back with."

There were three Phantoms of the Opera, two Batmen, one three-legged, two-headed monster shrouded in fuschia, which was two best friends together, Clara and Sara. There was a clown with a bald head, a fringe of orange wool above her ears and a red ball on her nose. A passel of princesses and fairies, a doctor in a white jacket covered in blood, a gorilla in a thick, furry suit. Pebbles, in a white diaper. A Ninja Turtle, a bunny, a pussycat, two witches. And Humpty Dumpty.

"Look at that Humpty Dumpty, isn't that magnificent. I wonder who it is?"

Simplicity's skinny legs protruded from the round, blue, stuffed waistcoat and red shorts. The egg sat neatly on her shoulders, with eyes and nose and smiling mouth, screened so Sissy could breathe and see out. The crack was a jagged line running crosswise across the top of the head.

The parade continued in a circle around the schoolyard. A robot. A unicorn. Superman. Miss Rushton in her Turkish trousers and streaming chiffon, revealing a suppressed desire to be a dancing girl, all waving to the onlookers. Humpty Dumpty soldiered on, mysterious, unclaimed.

"It's a wonderful costume," Blair said. Humpty's head turned slowly toward her. His eyes seemed to glare: do not give me away. The other little girls waved and simpered at their mothers. Blair was suddenly unnerved. *She is so serious, so deadly serious.* She stopped cheering.

"Is that Simplicity?" said a mother.

Blair put a finger over her lips. "We're not supposed to

know." Then she felt she had betrayed her.

After the parade they all went inside to sing Hallowe'en songs and eat popcorn. The gym was dark, the windows draped with black crepe paper. A boy was in a garbage can with a flashlight, making swaths of light cross the ceiling. When the little kids came near he shone the light on his face and jumped up: he wore green make-up and pointed false teeth.

There was a table where you could put your hands into bowls. When you put it into the spaghetti, a voice said, "brains." A peach pie was "dead ears." When you put your hand into the bucket of peeled grapes, the voice said "eyeballs."

Simplicity opened the top of her head, forgetting herself. "Mum, I know what it is," she warned. "It's not really eyeballs."

The rain began as they ran back to the car. Stopping to buy more candies to give out at the door, they found only plastic bags of peanuts sold in aid of the Kidney Foundation. Rain continued hard for half an hour while they drove to the supermarket and back, steaming up the car windows and causing major swamps to form at the corners and in front of the house, where the road dipped. The water ran down the hill from the reservoir, in sheets, down from Poplar Plains Crescent to MacPherson at the bottom.

Until six o'clock it rained, soaking the patterned leaves piled thick against the fence. People began to complain, over the telephone from their offices, as the dark conglomerated over the city. It wasn't fair to rain on the kids for Hallowe'en. Why couldn't the beautiful weather last one more day?

The rain was still spattering when the streetlights came on. Blair came out the door carrying two carved pumpkins, set them on the steps and lit the candles inside. She covered them with a tin plate to keep out the rain.

Simplicity, much reduced without her eggshell, ran around

the house and could not sit still to eat dinner. Blair searched for black rubber boots to replace Humpty's shoes. At six-thirty it was dark, warm and windless, and still raining, but not so hard.

The doors along the street began to open and release small costumed creatures, most followed by a parent with an umbrella held up. Simplicity was dry in her egg-head. Blair stood on the street in front of the house, waiting for Philip. He had promised to come and see Sissy in her costume.

In the window of the antique shop, a giant black spider web hung on a fluorescent skeleton. On the lawn of the pumping station someone had erected a painted cardboard gravestone with "R.I.P." carved on it. The house across the street had gone in for the total environment. A spotlight placed in the tree shone down on a grotesque, green-faced witch collapsed in an aluminum lawn chair; the door was draped with candy-floss spider webs.

"I'm going there," said Simplicity. "Don't come with me."

She walked falteringly past the witch. She got to the door and pressed the button. Her thin voice calling "Trick or treat" was barely audible. She waited.

"Say it again!"

She said it again.

Two witches opened the door. Simplicity screamed, but held her ground. The witches giggled and cackled while they reached for candy to drop in her bag and pennies for her UNICEF box. Sissy turned her back on them. As she walked away, their otherworldly cackle came out loudly from a loudspeaker in the trees. She ran.

Blair wore a witch's mask. Wearing false noses, neighbours were able to speak to each other easily in the street, the way they usually didn't. It was something about the city. Hallowe'en loosed some inhibitions.

"Last year we only did two blocks, but this year we'll try for three."

"The pumpkins were good, aren't they?"

One was cross-hatched, one an owl. There was some very tiny ones, like babies, piled together. Some houses had large orange garbage bags with faces on them hung over the front door, like a piñata. But when you struck them they were soft; you could tell it was only leaves inside.

At home, Simplicity took all of her candy out of the bag and looked at it. She had not eaten any yet. She had: Smarties, suckers, popcorn, freshly popped. Stickers, McDonald's coupons, Coffee Crisp, peanuts, licorice, small chip bags, even a tiny book. She began to collect the candy kisses.

"The librarian at our school loves these. She wants us to bring them all to her."

"Don't you want to eat any?"

"No," said Simplicity. She had taken off her egg-head and wore only her padded trouser suit.

"You were a very good egg."

"Yes, I was."

Philip arrived on his bike just as Sissy was going to bed. Blair took photographs of them together, Sissy wearing her Humpty head.

"Hate this Rosedale stuff," said Philip, miserably.

"It's not Rosedale, not by a long shot."

"Anything up here."

Bernie came in, silent and dark-faced, and went upstairs to bed. Perhaps she was homesick, Blair thought.

"Now we can go out for a ride," he said.

"It's dark. It's Hallowe'en. There's all sorts of crazies out there," said Blair.

"Even better," said Philip.

They went across Summerhill to the end, where the wooden steps descended into the ravine. There was a wooden picket sign pointing down that said "Nature Path." They went, one after the other, sliding their bike wheels over the wooden steps, which were slimed and broken and thick with leaves. On the pylons of the concrete railway underpass were written the words "Kill Faggots. Death Tally, 5." Philip flashed his light at the words for a moment, and then continued on.

"That's new." He laughed.

"You'd probably laugh if two skinheads jumped out of the bushes, too," said Blair. "It's the large white male syndrome. You feel safe anywhere."

The bottom of the ravine was deserted, eerily lit in the mist with lamp posts, spread out along the curved path. At the top of its steep sides the backs of big houses were revealed, now that the trees were bare. They could see big rooms glaring with light, the lost modesty of summer.

"I like Toronto in the fall. It's all exposed. People strut their stuff. I go to the Eaton Centre and Chinatown and Queen Street West to observe. It is a disease, Toronto, a very flashy, elaborate disease. And one cannot help but be fascinated," said Philip. "I am, however, very careful not to catch it."

"What's the disease?"

"Materialism. The mirror disease. To me, Toronto is the glass-sided skyscraper."

"I still love skyscrapers. I think it's from growing up in Medicine Hat. I go down there to stand in front of them, when they are all yellow and pink at sunset. I feel lifted into a world that's ten-times life size."

"And you're taken into the mirror. That's what happened to Ruby, you know."

Blair watched the light on Philip's front wheel as it skimmed the crusted sides of the trees ahead. "What do you mean, it's what happened to Ruby?"

"You look in the mirror and see yourself, flattened, part of its surface. You and all the crowds going past, and the buildings across the street, the potted trees and awnings, the trappings. Trapped in the mirror."

"Not trapped. You can walk away."

"If you walk too far away you disappear. And no one wants to disappear. That's why they all have to stay close to the centre. Without the mirror they aren't real."

"They?"

"We."

They rode along in the silence. The light faltered on the side of the hill. The path began to slope up, under the St. Clair Avenue overpass.

"It's been too long. Seven, nearly eight weeks. Everybody has a story. People say it was drugs. Or debt. I even heard she has AIDS."

"I don't believe she's dead," said Blair. "I feel her presence. I feel her now."

It got darker all of a sudden; the streetlights no longer reached down. The path led over a sewage run-off stream, and then in under the west side of the hill toward the Mount Pleasant Cemetery. They turned their bikes north. Blair was happy. She felt Ruby had come down to her, from somewhere, spreading a balm, a healing balm. She had such power.

Philip looked up at the sky. The cloud had cleared off, leaving a generous patch of clear black. A long way up, beyond this zipper path through the valley of shedding trees, stars were beginning to emerge.

"I told you. I think she vaporized on account of excess upward mobility," he said. "Those mirror towers are slippery and cold. When you start to fall down they let you go awful fast."

They tottered along slowly, the path narrowing now and becoming more precarious. They stayed near the rocky side of the little stream. It was still, and silent. Slowly, Blair felt Ruby slip away. They were surrounded by a portrait of trees; the litter of smashed gold was everywhere. From moment to moment there was the small gasp of another leaf falling, or a squirrel in the thickets.

"We can go in here," said Philip, stopping before the fence at the cemetery.

"Hey that's what Ruby said they do in the Philippines on Hallowe'en," said Blair. "Have a party for the dead."

There was a gap in the chain-link fence, and they slid their bikes through. Now the lights and cars of Yonge Street rubbed up against the edges of the dark. They passed a grave for a cowboy; it had a cactus and a drawing of a hat on it, and some bars of music.

"We can cry," said Blair. "If we want to."

"It's no tragedy. Perhaps it's a comedy," said Philip.

They had to walk up close and shine their bicycle lights on the stones to read the writing. There was Captain Fluke, locked in or out of his little black stone mausoleum. And George Lissant Beardmore under a twenty-foot obelisk, with his wife Elizabeth. Even now, nearly one hundred years after death, the possessives rang out: BELOVED WIFE OF, BELOVED SON OF.

Philip flashed his light: pigeons rose from the earth of the "Resting Place of Pioneers." A new sign explained that in 1841 the pioneers had been buried at the corner of Bloor and Yonge; they were moved in 1860, and moved again here. They had been buried in three places so far. A clutch of red plastic flowers was affixed to one of the graves.

"They didn't rest very long, did they?"

"That's what you get for dying in a new country."

"Talk about upward mobility."

As Philip stood reading the sign, Blair's radio voice started in her head, working up an item on it.

Who were all these pioneers buried by public subscription? What did they think to build, and what to leave behind? The last safe place in the world? Possibly. The dark fir skirts that children could crawl under, the black, opinionated crow high in the branches of a tree, suggested otherwise, an unexpunged devilment in this country.

They got on their bikes and rode. The road was wide now, and clear. Taking the curve fast, Blair and Philip sailed over the crest of a hill; all the trees beyond here were bare; their branches scratched the charcoal sky. In her head, Blair went on writing commentary. *Fall used to be my favourite season. But now it's too much like death. Is it just because I'm getting older? Is that why it's never possible any more to be sure of another spring? It is not my own mortality I fear, but somehow the death of all this, the death of life itself.* That would never do for CLIK-FM.

Another curve in the road and they were nearly at Yonge Street. In the glow of the streetlights a waste of brilliant yellow leaves spread over the road; the groundskeeper's red rake had been left propped against a tree, as if overcome by the size of its task. Blair skimmed through; the gold crunched beneath her tires. Philip sailed ahead of her, shouting his greetings to the spirits of Jessie and Fannie and George and Annie Couch, of Frances and Euan. The smell of maple leaves drying—a dusty, rich odour, must and perfume strangely combined—followed them.

Now they sat in Blair's living room having tea. She told Philip about the diary.

"She's around somewhere. I think she wants me to look for her."

"Be careful," he said.

"She's my oldest friend."

"Hardly."

"Well almost. We come from the same—"

"You think because she came from Medicine Hat you know all about her. You don't. She hung out with some desperate types."

Blair sipped slowly and deliberately, disagreeing.

"Besides, she has a right to disappear if she wants to," said Philip. "A right to be dead, too, for that matter."

She set the cup on the glass table; it steamed slightly. "It's not your job to protect me. You're not my husband. You're not even my lover."

"And what am I?" said Philip in his tired voice. "Whatever it is, you haven't let me go for twenty years."

Blair's eyes smarted, reddened. "Not fair," she said. "You've been in California for twenty years. I hardly ever saw you."

"You never let me go," he repeated sullenly. "And now you ask me for help. So you have to listen to me. You don't know what you're getting into. I don't care if you resent being told."

They sat in silence. This feeling of ownership made them stiff-mouthed; they could not get to the bottom of it. Philip had invented Blair, or so it seemed. Her perfection held him off. It was not desire, in the average sense; more like a childish need for access. To have, to prove the power of their connection.

"You'd think I was some kind of complete naif who never went anywhere or did anything," she complained. "You act like I can't look after myself."

"Well?"

"Well what?" Blair thrust her jaw forward and up. "I'm a mother. Who can you say you've looked after?"

Two, three, four soft footfalls came. At the top of the stairs, Simplicity stood. A small, dark shadow in the tunnel of light that led to the windows. Like one of her own drawings, with a large head and thin stick legs.

"What are you doing up?"

"Are you eating my candy?" said Simplicity.

"Yes. Do you want to come and sit with us?"

"I can't go to sleep."

"Come down and I'll give you a hug."

The girl was quiet and thin, part of the darkness. She tucked herself into Blair's side.

"I don't like it when you go out at night."

"I know, but that's the time when I can see my friends too. I have to see my friends," said Blair. "Like Philip."

"But you're out when I come home from school, too."

"I have to work."

"Why can't you get a new job? One that you go to in the day? Then you can have dinner with me and put me to bed."

"Don't you like staying with Bernie?"

"I get scared at night."

"Just because it's Hallowe'en," said Philip. "She ate too much candy."

"No I didn't," said Sissy with dignity. "I don't eat candy."

And now the cold had moved in overhead. At first, purplish storm clouds gathered at the lakefront. Pelts of rain struck in waves, across the slick black streets, through the stripped branches, driving everyone inside. The days were dark, and darker nights closed in early. The cold deepened steadily, crisping the remaining leaves; the clouds grew opaque, heavy with their burden. In the Simcoe schoolyard, the last leaves, caught between chain fences, flew from one side of the asphalt to the other, like refugees who had missed the last boat.

Then it happened: the low, solid, pearly-grey clouds burst, and snow fell on the city. The flakes were large, dry, perfected. They landed lightly, sitting lightly on lawn and rooftop. The black, empty arms of the great old maples were whitened on their upper side. The sky cleared, in patches, and more flakes came, dancing in the sun. Then more clouds moved in: the snow fell thickly, straight down, all through the night.

Blair and Sissy stood by the school door waiting for the bell to ring. The children were in purple, green and blue snowsuits, padded; weightless as space men, they fell and rolled in the shallow coverlet of snow. Sissy put her face up, tongue out, to taste it on her tongue, her eyelids. It was

Friday.

"Mummy, we can go skating? Tomorrow?"

"We'll see if your skates still fit you."

She had promised to see Max. After she finished work tonight he might come over for a drink. She might even let him stay over. She hadn't, so far. She didn't want Sissy to find him in her bed in the morning. But every day Sissy came to wake her with the same question: "Mummy, was Max here last night? Did he come to my room to say goodnight?"

Sissy had no father, not to speak of, no man on whom to fix her love. Only this unremembered, absent figure who sent cheques. There was no one to whom Blair was being unfaithful, except Sissy herself. But that felt, to Blair, like the deepest betrayal of all.

The girl stood, motionless, like a little pillar of salt, face to the sky. Snow was melting on her eyelids. Blair felt like the original pillar, solid with regret. She could not melt. She was the tree in whose shadow Sissy had to grow. It seemed a solemn undertaking. Too solemn. If Blair began to break up, to dance like the tree shadows on the snow-whitened roof, then Sissy must stand alone. But it was happening. Blair was melting. Max was melting her.

The bell rang. Sissy waited as the children ran into place. Then she let go of her mother and walked slowly to the end of the line. Blair waved her off, a solitary figure swallowed by the doorway to the school. She walked home, her feet moving in the footsteps of others at first. As she approached her front door, they made new marks in the feathery coat of snow.

To love: to make love. Two contradictory, opposing acts, to Blair. Love was for Sissy: tender, fierce, protective, tireless, drawn from a spring-fed pool. Love was what Sissy gave back, with little white arms and printed messages, all the "b"s and "s"s and "d"s and "r"s reversed. "You're the Best in the Univurse." Mirror writing.

When Max lay heavily on her arm, his back wet with sweat,

and said I love you, he meant something else. Blair did not know what he meant. Perhaps it was only some internal force released, a valve opened, a hiss of steam, the pressure of words. Blair thought of her father, in the chemistry lab. All those shining tubes, faucets to open and shut, the smell of ammonia, liquids light and dark in measured flasks. A man's words were dark and complicated. Like money. Before you took it, you got a warning. Don't put it in your mouth. You never know where it's been. Something is expected if you accept it.

What obligations, what exposure did she have now, to this man? Blair went up to make her bed. The telephone rang. She did not pick it up. The machine began to whir. "I'm not available. . . . Please leave a message." She watched. Out of the little slots which were a speaker came Max's voice, a morning voice.

"Hi. It's me. I know you're not there, you're probably still walking back from school. I just wanted to say I miss you. I need you. I'll see you soon? Call me."

The pit of her stomach responded. The purr of his voice started up the longing. It came too often. She pressed the rewind button and listened again. This time she expected it. This time her blood woke up, warmed. She stopped the tape. She had choices. She could kill the feeling. Sit now and play the machine over, until his voice was dead to her. Until the love was disciplined, put out of its misery. She'd done that before.

Ruby's words—"What you need is an affair!"—rose up unbidden. Yes, but how to make room, in my heart and my life? thought Blair. How to find the courage? Ruby was dead, or gone. She had left messages, left them imprinted in Blair's mind, so that they played, over and over. She had left her Max. It was uncanny how Ruby, so selfish, in such a constant buzz of nerves, had still managed to speak directly to Blair, to give Blair more than anyone.

Max and Blair and Sissy went skating, on Sunday, at Ramsden Park. The rink was just like the ones in Alberta, thirty years ago: the rubber-mat path to the change room, the narrow benches all around the sides, hockey skates and figure skates and bobskates on babies. People perched with backs curled over to tighten the laces. Blair stood in front of Sissy, taking the blade of her skates between her knees, and did her laces, tightly pulling them under the hooks.

The rectangle of ice lay at the bottom of a valley. To the north were the backs of the houses on Roxborough Avenue; to the south-west, on top of the hill, two apartment towers made a gateway. A scratchy record played "A Summer Place" over the loudspeakers. A man in a toque with serious black figure skates, hands clasped behind his back, stroked around and around. A mother pulled a tiny child with a crash helmet, her hand on her aching back. Two Chinese women were learning, holding hands, next to the fence, making slow steps along the stretch. On the hockey side, a boy played by himself, circling over and over and shooting on the goal. Then the rinkmaster blew the whistle and the bigger boys flooded in the gate; the smaller one ducked away.

Sissy hung back at the edge of the ice.

"You know how to skate."

"That was last year. I forget."

"You don't forget," said Blair. "Look at me. I haven't." She stepped off the worn wooden tread to the ice. It was soft, and scored with many blades. "It's not too slippery. Come on."

Max stood behind Sissy, waiting. When she wouldn't move, he picked her up in his arm, walked onto the ice and began to skate around the rink. She screamed.

"Put me down. I'll fall. Put me down."

He put his face down to hers and spoke. She stopped screaming and began to laugh. They circled the rink and he put her on her feet on the ice. She protested. "I can't carry you any more," he said. "I'll hurt my back." He took Blair by the hand and pulled her off around the rink.

"Don't look back," he said.

Around and around the rink they went, hand in hand. Sissy stood scowling. Blair didn't look for three more circles. Then she did. Sissy was walking on her skates, and then she was gliding a little, and finally she was racing a little boy down the centre of the ice.

At the corners, Max and Blair did crossovers, just the same way, in rhythm. Over the scratchy loudspeaker the music was ancient. "Love Is a Many-Splendored Thing." "Chitty-Chitty Bang-Bang." Songs they knew the words to, from times unremembered. The ice made it easy; it was as if they were not covering ground, but stroking it, allowing it to pass, allowing them to pass.

The music stopped. The ice-machine appeared at the gates: the rinkmaster, in his orange neon pinnie, opened the gates and they all had to clear the ice. They waited, on the wooden steps, stamping their feet, while the machine wheeled around the corners of the rink, scraping the surface clear of snow and slush. Then the water. They had a new, fresh, glassy coating.

As the machine backed out the gate, the skaters hurried to make the first marks on the fresh surface. Blair and Max took Sissy between them. They made a train, with Sissy in the front. They played tag, and let Sissy catch them. Max caught Blair in his arms. She pressed her face into the rough, damp wool of his coat. Sissy was cold, then, and wanted to go home for hot chocolate.

In the kitchen, Max and Blair hovered over the counter. Sissy had found a book and gone upstairs. "She takes my hand as if I am her friend," said Max, very pleased. Blair felt a jolt of alarm. *She's only pretending; she's waiting to see what I decide*, she said to herself. She did not need to tell Max that. She felt the strong pull again, toward him, to be inside those arms, to rest her head against his large chest. She resisted. He came up behind her and put his arms around her ribs.

"I think I've been missing something all these years," he said.

Blair laughed. "I doubt it. You've been free. You don't know how hard it is, alone with a child."

"I can help you," he said. "If you let me."

The milk began to boil. She snatched it off the heat, then busied herself lifting the skin off with a spoon.

"How can you help me? Oh. I guess you can make love to me."

She stared at the white, steaming liquid.

"That's no problem," he said, hurt. "Anything else?"

"You can understand me. Try," she said, relenting a little.

He dropped his arms and moved beside her, holding the cups while she poured.

"That's a little bit difficult. You keep many secrets."

Max loped up the stairs two at a time to Simplicity's bedroom. Her door was ajar. He pushed it open farther and stepped into the room.

The red poppies on her wallpaper were dusky in the night, and the sand-coloured ruffles at the bottom of her curtains and her bedspread seemed to move gently, as if her bed were floating over a lake. The charcoal gloom evened out the background of her dresser, her jars and baskets of treasures, her shelves of books and stuffed animals, her desk, with its flower-trimmed blotter. The curved headboard of the bed with its two slender posts had the look of an Oriental temple. There, in the centre of the bed, sitting up, was Simplicity.

"Hello Max," she said.

"Hi Sissy." He moved toward her, bent and kissed her, and then sat on the edge of her bed. "You're still awake. Good. I wanted to say goodnight."

"You stayed for the whole weekend," she said.

"I'm going now," he said.

They sat for a few seconds in silence. How different the silence was, with Simplicity, from other silences. This was sympathy, a sharing of things not said; most silences he knew were stand-offs, shields against the attack. He could sit here for a very long time.

"Max, are you my daddy?" she said.

"No, of course I'm not. You know who your daddy is."

"He sends cheques," said Sissy.

Max knew about that sadness. Money for love. No fair exchange. "It helps your Mummy," he said.

"I liked you telling me about the kind of music Mummy sang before, before I was born. When she was a singer."

"She was a good one, too," said Max.

"Why are you going?"

"Tomorrow's a work day."

"Do you work hard?"

"Sometimes I do. But other times I think I don't work hard enough. Or else I don't work hard at the right things."

"Oh," said Simplicity. "Mummy is sad a lot. I think it's because she misses you. But when I don't see you, I don't care."

"I don't know that your Mummy misses me," said Max.

"She doesn't know it either. Only I know it," said Simplicity.

"Oh dear," said Max. "Nobody's very happy with me. Maybe I'll have to try something different."

"Who's not happy with you? We are," said Simplicity.

"Well, sometimes I'm not happy with myself," said Max.

Simplicity smiled in the darkness: her small, even baby teeth were faintly visible in her face. "How?" she said.

"Well, I might start doing a different kind of work," he said. It was easy to talk to her.

"What different work?"

"Just a different kind of law, more the fighting kind, not the paperwork kind."

"Are you going to?"

"I don't know. I think of it, but then I imagine how hard it would be, and I get a little intimidated."

"What's intimidated?"

"Sort of—scared. I don't know if I could do it very well."

Simplicity thought about that for a moment. "Well," she said, "have you tried?"

Now Max was silent.

"No. Not yet," he admitted. "Goodnight, Sissy. You should lie down now and sleep."

"Goodnight, Max," she said, and she slid down so that only her cheek and the top of her blond head protruded from under her clown blanket.

11

Mirror Writing

Heavy feet stamped across the porch. Something dropped; the storm door creaked shut. Blair ran downstairs in her tattered chenille robe. It was before eight o'clock on Tuesday morning. The package, in plastic over a brown envelope, lay between the doors. Whoever delivered it was gone.

The first thing she did was scan for dates. But there were none. The entries were from last summer and spring, getting no closer to Ruby's disappearance than the last one. They were bits of her life marching in a rhythm that did not know the calendar, seemingly ripped out of her diary at random.

Saturday

These two guys, Richie and Don, came to see me about the drag queens. They come every summer, gearing up for Hallowe'en. Want to borrow some gowns. "Hey," they tell me, "couture drag is in. The taste level is very high." They're so immersed in fashion they don't even breathe.

Their party is at the Lizard, and they invited 300. They've

promised to pick up all the queens in limos. Last year no one was ready; they sent the car around and these guys would send their sister for a ride because they were still working on their wig or their sequins or whatever. They had a runway out front, and a Hollywood wife at the door, in a terry-towel robe with a towel on her head, turning people away if they looked too tacky. "We turned away 30 percent," he says. "If I had my way it'd be 60 percent."

Richie will go as Ivana Trump, he said, and Don as Marla. They were going to have a fight in the middle of the floor. But then Don decided it was too tacky. So he'll be a baton-twirler, with little crystal balls on all his tassels. He'll wear thick, thick, thick fish-nets, he says.

So I must have been looking slightly chilled, because he suddenly got huffy. "We like to have a mix," he said. "It's good if the girls come too . . . . Last year some of the models dressed too, they came really decked, decked, decked. One came in period. One was Marie Antoinette. It was very cheeky."

For these guys, fashion is a religion. Their eyes have replaced their brains—maybe everything else too.

I asked Richie how he got into fashion. He said he was the baby of the family, out there in Orangeville, and when they all went out he'd get the sheets and go into the closet and wrap them around him. He's a perfect six, and he just loves to try the stuff on. Every male designer does. I know, I can tell when they look at my dresses, they're dying to. So why doesn't he design for men? "I know the way I want women to look," he says, "but as a man I want to look different all the time."

I'm getting my back up now. Why is it easier to tell a woman how to look? I say. Not that this is news. Hate to admit it. I've fought it all this time. But now I feel—this is death for women. If not death, life as a stool-pigeon, a decoy—to draw them in to satisfy the enemy.

All right, it sounds extreme, but I'm going to extremes. I used to watch the streets, sit at some sidewalk café with my sketchbook and my paints, and turn out new, original, "look at me" designs. But nothing was as beautiful as the vintage stuff, except maybe evening dresses. People are dull in the day, they only fantasize at night. At night, they were ready for me.

I got typed. I got labelled. Nobody's interested. I see the faces of the photographers when they come up to the studio. My dresses don't have much hanger-appeal. That's why I had to have Ramone hanging around. "Am I gonna have to shoot this and make it look like shortcake?" The critics, such as they are, only want to know if I'm serving champagne.

But they love Sue Gosh. As far as I am concerned, SG should be in bric-a-brac. Her great contribution was she brought giftwrap to town.

Richie showed me some sketches of his new line. It's late '50s. "We call it 'Mama,'" he says. I croak. "That's me. I wore that."

"Ruby, you're jaded," Richie says, carting off a couple of sample gowns. I say sure, Richie. I guess you're right.

I remember after I'd been in the business about five years I got lonely for my designs. I drew them, and I had them made, and I sold them, but then I never saw them. I'd go to the clubs—they weren't there. The people who could afford them didn't go out, not where I was. Because I wanted to make clothes I'd see, I decided to do a lower-priced line. I had it all worked out, I had a name—it was a good name, I never told anyone because I didn't want it stolen. And I had it all figured out—the price points, and what I was going to compete with, and getting the fabric from Italy and the buttons cast in Korea.

Then I went to the bank and couldn't get the money. I showed them my orders and they said it's not hard collateral. How hard do they want it? . . . Harder than silk and lace, I guess. My backers were keen at first but then they backed off (hey, that's what they do, back off, what else are backers for?). They said I needed more of a track record. Isn't five years enough, I said?

On it went. Losing out to the Philistines.

I remember the shoots for magazines. I'd give them the look, the hair, the shoes, the earrings, to go with the dress, and they'd start changing it. Bring down the height of the heels. Change the earrings. I had to fight every step of the way. If these folks hadn't seen it somewhere else, they wouldn't shoot it. People don't want to do anything they haven't done before.

Wednesday—Late

I seem to be revising my past life. Something's pushing me. I got into retro because I had more taste than money. I like the stuff, liked the fabrics especially, and the weird old tailoring, how the seams went all over the place. After Hearts of Flame. In the late '60s, the clothes I wore, and everyone else wore, were all of a sudden Language. Politics. Spirit.

I combed the estate sales, all the old homes from here to Ottawa, and down to Windsor. The stuff got harder and harder to find. Everyone started doing knock-offs of old designs. Before long I was designing new stuff to keep ahead of the pack. All those days I spent sketching, waiting for fabric to be delivered, ordering buttons and zippers, paying the pattern-maker, the sample girl, running over to the factory ten times a week to make sure they weren't ripping me off.

Of course half the time they were. Stashing away half the bolt of fabric—I'd say you can cut 25 from this and they'd tell me, you made a mistake, it's only 15. Six months later you see the knock-offs they'd made, your whole line hanging up in somebody's garage.

By then, fashion had begun to swallow its tail; retro moved so fast it caught up with itself. The '80s was full of the '60s and '70s. To see these kids now thinking they've invented the past! They find a little A-line polyester dress and lose their minds. They *live* to look so good they get called to the front of the line at the Big Bop. We at least believed. Retro this and retro that, they've retro'd everything right up to last year. Instant nostalgia. It's obvious that no one has created anything worthwhile for 20 years. You can't change anything that fast, not even your mind.

———————

Saturday—Lying in bed a.m.

I want to design beautiful things, but not to wear them. I'd rather spend four thousand dollars on a garment and hang it on the wall than hang it on me. Maybe I think I don't deserve it. Maybe I'm past wanting to be looked at. The Shaker idea of design: beauty from dedication to function. Nothing to excess. Simplicity. I've been thinking this for a long time. Aren't I nice. I gave Blair the name for her baby.

And if she doesn't fit in with her times, then she's just like me. Always the misfit. I'm never on time. Retro, but not past: restless, but not future. This is how my energy works. (So Oswald says.) What I am is today. Today is uncertain. In flux. Today is always disappearing. I want to disappear.

I thought fashion was about an open mind. After all, it accepted me! But everything becomes subject to season. Green is so in it's sickening. Peace and war have always been fashion trends, same with black or yellow faces. Colour an idea. Intellectuals take their ideas so *seriously*! But I know it all now. Any idea, no matter how profound, *will go out*, as it came in. Amen.

Sunday night

I seem to be obsessive—I am. I'm swimming against a whirlpool, trying to pull myself out. On the edge looking down is Marvin. And he's not reaching out!

Clothes are ideas in solid form. Right now people dress to punish themselves. The future is jumpsuits. Self-incarceration. The future is unisex—uniforms. The future is polyester and meltdown seams. Let me out.

People who dress fashionably, do they buy it all? The thinking too? Some do, and some don't. What about people who *don't* wear fashion? They don't show it—they're wearing an old uniform—but they're fashion victims inside. They've chosen MAINSTREAM, the ugliest word in the language. Happy little fish swimming with the flow, no need to look where you're going.

Hockey games, movies, videos, they buy it all. Hey! You don't argue with success. If you don't like it you're a poor sport, unpleasant, unpatriotic even. These are the real fashion victims, the ones who can't even choose a look, much less a thought. People who can't take exception. Happy children, happily consuming the food they are given, because it is given, and because the others are consuming it, insisting that it is good, it is right, it is just how food should be. I could never swallow it.

Here I am again in my vacuum of the present. I think I *am* disappearing. I think I have disappeared. I hate androgyny. I don't like skin-tight. I like to see movement, the flesh beneath the cloth. What happens in that slipstream of air, between what you wear and what you are; the way your body moves the fabric and moulds it. That's fashion. Good models know that.

Models make me weep. Why is it the designers in this country are all unknowns, while we export the biggest models of all time? "We don't wake up for less than $10,000 a day," say Linda and Christa. If that were me, I guess I'd be in a permanent vegetative coma. While I can't get through my seasons without turning out those custom wedding gowns. Wedding is the only part of the industry that never dies. It's a bit of Shakespearean tragedy; the great virgin frigate, her sails getting trimmed. Nobody looks herself in a wedding dress. Human sacrifice: the young virgin thrown down the pit. Only now the pit is matrimony.

Maybe that's why I never married. I didn't want to wear the uniform. White: a blank page. A nurse, with barriers against infection by life. An angel, in her virtue package. But angels are supposed to be men, right?

Now that's a drag.

O.K., love I understand. Marriage is another matter. I could design a wedding, a real one. For Marvin and I. In body-paint, with filmy layers, sort of Mary Quant. Huge, heavy headpieces to mark the occasion regally. Sex with hats is something I approve of.

But I missed out on that one. Marvin, I mean. He's got that wife, and she doesn't make him happy, but she keeps him off the market. Maybe one day he'll be free, but he's not for me. Bad timing. When everything is fashion, the only genius is timing. And I haven't got it. I fell between yesterday and tomorrow. Inhabiting the present, there's nothing but din and clatter, what was it Blair always used to say, sound and fury?

Blair walked up the short sidewalk on Montrose Avenue. It was warm again, Indian summer in November. The little house squatted on a table-sized lawn; rose bushes and wisteria, reminders of more domestic previous owners, straggled up a lattice. She rang the bell. She shifted her feet. From up and down the street, through wrought-iron railings and vine arbors, she was watched. Watched by Portuguese mothers. Watched by two teenage boys fixing a motorcycle. Watched by a crowd of little girls playing Chinese skipping.

The door opened with a jerk. Arthur, Ruby's brother, glared out at Blair from red-rimmed eyes.

They didn't look alike. They never had. Arthur was darker, thinner. His skin had been bad in high school; it was still scarred. He had a long, narrow head, a sharp, marauding face. In high school he had been an army cadet. He was off-duty, no uniform, but his chino pants and white T-shirt neatly tucked into a black leather belt still looked like a uniform.

"Arthur," said Blair, extending her hand.

He lifted it casually, and then dropped it. They had not been friends, apparently they were less so now. He would brook no pretence, nor any expression of grief.

"This is my wife, Mary." The small woman sat on the edge of a stiff, velvet-covered sofa like a hungry, red-beaked bird. "My mother is coming down."

As Blair stood awkwardly in the small room, the lengthening afternoon sun retreated a little farther across the flowered carpet. The stairs creaked, as someone heavy moved slowly down them. She searched for anything in the room that resembled Ruby; there was nothing.

"Hello Blair," said a low voice. "It has been a long time since we've seen you."

Ruby's mother Martha was massive; short and powerful, with grizzled hair shaved at her nape like a man's. She wore a wide, floral-print dress that came nearly to her ankles. She had raised her kids on a useless piece of land, working as a waitress first, and then managing a trailer park. She had always been in the doorway, watching Ruby come or go.

"It's not a good time for visit. But sit down."

They all sat down and looked into the empty centre of the room. It was a long time since Ruby had gone, over two months. Blair had not come earlier, mostly because she'd been afraid. Everyone talked about Martha Mason's anger.

"Why don't you tell us what you want?" said Arthur. His voice was low; whether it was from suppressed feeling or an attempt to threaten was unclear. Blair had imagined this was what they would say: what do *you* want, making the need hers, denying theirs.

"I want to know if there's something I can do to help. Maybe just to talk about Ruby and her problems."

"Ruby has no problems," said her mother. "And God will help us."

Mary's head inclined this way, then the other, sharply, as she devoured every word. Arthur looked at none of them.

"I feel bad. I wish I'd been more attentive. To know she was in trouble."

Martha raised her chin off its wattles. "Some other people have trouble with Ruby, that's why she disappeared, but my girl had no troubles. She disappears, maybe kidnapped, maybe murdered, you gonna say she had problems? You're as bad as all the rest. You know she's a big success. She works too much maybe, but *she's* got no problems."

"The last week nobody heard from her," said Arthur quietly. "Not one of us."

"I talked to her! I talked to her on the telephone the night she went!" Martha countered. "She called me and said Mum, I paid the bill on my phone card so we can talk. She was in some big public place, like a hotel lobby. Or an airport. I heard a P.A. system in the background."

The others obviously had heard this before.

"Do the police know this?" said Blair.

Martha waved a limp arm. "They know, of course they know. Mr. Big Investigator Dick Nolan, all he does is see a psychic. She told me some things were not going so well, okay. She had a little problem with her business, I think. She told me, 'Marvin's angry because I told him I didn't want him as my partner. And I don't *want* to marry him.'"

"But he's already married," said Blair. "That's not what—"

Martha's voice was gathering force now. Nobody was going to get her off track. She had kept her family in line this long with the weight of her expectations. She unfurled her powers, like a diva.

"And we had a nice talk that night and I said, you know, Ruby, what about God in your life? Let us pray. Because if things are not going well we call on God. So I said, Ruby, let's have a time of prayer. And we had a time of prayer."

"On the long-distance telephone?"

"And when we finished, she seemed very happy and she said I wish I could come out and spend a little time with you and so on."

"Aw, Mum, she always said that."

"I'm talking about that night! And then some man came along at that time and I heard her say, 'I'm talking to Mum!' As if she were in-tim-i-dat-ed." She said the word in five syllables, each one equal in value. "He didn't say hi to me. He took the phone and I said—I thought it must be him, Marvin—'Marvin, Ruby seems upset, what's wrong?' And he said, 'It's not Marvin and nothing's wrong, I'm in charge.' I said, 'No you're not, God's in charge.'"

"He took the phone, which I found odd," said Arthur, slowly. "But you don't know it was Marvin. You said it wasn't his voice."

"If it wasn't Marvin it was someone he sent. I know it! I feel it!"

"He took the phone," said Mary. She had found her place to enter, delicate and determined. Martha reluctantly settled, head vibrating side to side in denial. "I wouldn't let my husband take the phone when I'm talking. And they aren't even married."

"I phoned Ruby that night; she wasn't there. Or she wasn't answering. I didn't know which. I figured Marvin was there. All the time when I call her when Marvin's there and I say I'm comin' over, she says, 'Mary don't come, Marvin's here. Marvin's here.' So I left her alone!"

Now Mary's voice, which had been soft and precise, began to rise, like the sounding of an alarm.

"I wanted to help. I wanted to talk to her." Mary was crying now.

"She didn't tell you nothing, she never would, Mary," said Martha.

"We didn't talk about her problems. She was always concerned about me."

Blair nodded. "That's Ruby. She could be going bankrupt, or have lost her last friend, but she'd make a point of zeroing in on your problems. . . . It was how she kept her secrets, I guess."

"Don't you go criticizing my daughter! I'll tell you," said Martha, shaking her fist, "if you're looking for excuses to blame this disappearance on the family, you better get on out of here."

"I'm not, I'm not."

"Do you hear what that Dick Nolan said?" said Mary,

"'You never find a nice girl in a trunk.' Like this is *her* fault, and she must be up to bad, evil doings. People say terrible things about Ruby now."

Arthur appeared to be tired. His eyes connected with Blair's.

"Now, Mum," he said. "I think Blair is a friend, you know. She's not launching any investigation. Are you?"

Blair shook her head. "It's too late for that."

"She just wants to talk to us. We all have feelings."

"We do," said Mary.

Martha's face held on to its massive glower. "We know," she said to Blair, more calmly, "we *know* who's done this thing. It's Marvin."

"We never liked him," said Arthur simply.

"None of us did."

"But if we said something to her about it—"

"—she just went straight back to him with it. I don't know why."

"Arthur never liked him. Not from the first. Tell them about when you met him."

Arthur's voice was low and slow. He sat back with his ankles crossed, his long, narrow body still military even in repose.

"He parked his car in front of the house here. Flashy red Camaro, white interior, about fifteen years old, perfect condition. And his licence plate was expired."

The women in the room fell silent as his voice went on; it had a settling, mesmeric quality.

"So I asked Marvin about these plates," Arthur went on, his deep, soothing voice again casting out the scattered interjections of the women. "And he says to me, 'Oh, I never gets those things. If a cop stopped me it'd take him all day to write up all the tickets and summons I have.' And I said, 'Being as she's my sister I'm really interested in why you'd be driving a car like that. And how did you meet my sister?'"

"I was embarrassed," said Mary. "I wasn't ready to come down hard on him."

"And he answered that they met in Jamaica down on the beach."

"Well that's not true 'cause they met at a reception. Mayor's reception for the designers. Turns out he's some culture bigwig," said Mary.

"Slumming it," said Arthur.

"Not at all! He can't believe his luck she looked at him for five minutes," retorted his wife. "You've got it *wrong*," she dared.

Their words were a kind of chant; they'd been through the verses a hundred times in the past weeks. It was the chant of what they knew, to drown out the roar of what they didn't know. A chant of anger, to drown out their powerlessness.

"He wasn't Ruby's type."

"She picked up people like that. She thought she could help them. That was Ruby. You know she was so generous—"

"So loving."

"She saw him as a challenge, as somebody she could help."

"People latched on to her. Ramone was the same," said Mary. "She wanted to be like Ruby. She wanted to *be* Ruby. That's why she stole Ruby's clothes. That's why she ran off with Marvin. I warned Ruby, that woman—"

"She was so good to people. You know Ruby. She was always like that. She was on her way to success and she was gonna take everyone with her."

"The type of people Ruby gravitated toward really bothered me. You know, I'd been working with kids, in the force. When I meet someone I automatically size them up."

"We're talking about Marvin, aren't we?" said Mary anxiously.

"I'm talking about the *type* of people. Other people, too."

"Don't talk," said Martha. "Just don't talk. We're not telling her everything."

An open pause, then, while Blair pretended she hadn't caught their meaning. They weren't telling her. But she wasn't telling them, either. Not about the diary. It would be too cruel. She had hoped the family had news.

"I didn't know her friends," said Blair. "Just the model, Ramone. And Audrey in the office. But some people say she kept dangerous company."

The family said no more; lips firmly pressed together, they sat over their secrets.

"Witchcraft," Martha burst out, breaking faith.

"Not witchcraft! Maybe drugs," said Arthur. "This Oswald. He told the police Ruby wasn't dead but her energy had been transferred somewhere else."

Blair laughed. "That's just Oswald," she said. "He's harmless."

As abruptly as it began, the chant stopped. Martha relaxed in her chair, her eyes closed. Mary moistened and pursed her lips, repeatedly. Blair let her breath out in little jerks. Children's shouts from the street came in through the open window.

Mary Mason stood up and offered tea. It was a signal. Arthur excused himself. He clomped up the stairs and came back down with a piece of white paper frayed on the side, as if torn from a notebook.

"Look at it. Read," said Martha.

It was a poem to Ruby. Something about the night in her hair.

"Where did you get this?"

"It's Dick Nolan's report."

"You're not serious."

"Police!" Martha exploded. Arthur stood by the window, watching the sidewalk.

The sun left the room, suddenly dropping behind two housetops on the west side of the street. Mary moved around the room, setting down the tea, turning on lights. Martha and

Arthur sat, silent, in their chairs.

"Shall I come and see you again?" said Blair, as she stepped down the front steps. The family was crowded in the doorway, delivered of their anger. Now they looked helpless.

"You tell them that Ruby Mason's mother says somebody did this to my child because she was in their way. You tell them Martha Mason says my daughter's been kidnapped. Maybe murdered."

"Mrs. Mason," said Blair, "I don't have anyone to tell. I'm not a cop, I'm not a detective."

Blair turned to walk away. At the street, she looked back at the house, the faces in the square glass of the door, like faces caged into a photograph, where they didn't want to be. They were bewildered. Pushed aside, behind the door, like she was, by Ruby and her mysteries.

"Call me, if you hear anything."

"We're trying to find out where she is, that's all."

"If I can help . . ." Blair repeated.

They didn't ask her any questions. And they didn't say they'd call her again.

Blair walked down the street toward the subway, her purse over her shoulder and a scarf on top of her winter coat. It was cold now, late November. The passion of the Masons' denials felt like a wind at her back. They had not accepted that Ruby was gone, but how could they? And Blair walking away with her secret.

The only one who knew about the diary now was Max. That was all. Blair figured it wasn't her news to tell. Besides, she did not know what the diary meant. It could mean Ruby was dead, that someone had her effects. This diary was being sent back like a macabre joke, by a kidnapper, like a chopped-off ear. Or she might have sent it herself, being unable to explain herself. *Here is something to understand about me.* "The ultimate vanishing act." Ruby had reason to be angry: here, take me as I am, or not at all.

"We don't listen to this talk of suicide. We don't even consider it. Ruby was so beautiful. She took such care. She would want to preserve the body she worked on."

Blair remembered sitting beside her at the Coffee Express.

"Squeeze my thigh," Ruby said, pressing it out from the chair with her tight skirt spread over it. "Is it not perfect?"

"It's perfect."

Suicide was possible, but it didn't seem likely. Not because she loved her family and friends. She was not above hurting them. And not because of her beautiful body. But because she wanted too much. That day at lunch, when she talked about Marvin, she was like someone pleading for a better deal from the gods. Yet she told her family *she* wouldn't marry *him*. It was Ruby's backwards code. Mirror writing: the opposite of the truth. And there was a man with her when she called her mother. Probably not Marvin. Had she found another one already? Ruby usually got what she wanted.

She knew what Max would say: Show the diary to the cops. They might be able to get fingerprints. Or find out where it was sent from. She would. But not just yet. She wanted to hang on to it a little first.

Max. Now everything reminded her of him, connected her to him. How strange, when only the misleadingly reassuring fact that he had had a walk-on part in her life twenty years ago had persuaded her to go out with him in the first instance. She had not wanted him in her life. This suit-wearing Bay-Streeter, suspect easterner who (she thought) killed Hearts of Flame.

It was early yet. She reminded herself that she could stop the feeling, if she wanted. She knew how to put love aside, to shut it in a cold chamber, make it die like an abandoned child. She had done that before. It was how she maintained her footing these slippery years. But perhaps—her mind wandered to Max's coarse grey-shot curls, his loosened tie, his wide and capacious chest, a place to rest her head. Perhaps this time she did not need to perform the murder. Perhaps she needed *not* to. The balance had changed; Ruby was gone.

Blair ran down the subway steps and boarded a train going east. She sat on a sideways seat looking across the empty car at the advertisement across the top of the windows. It was a photograph of six good-looking young professionals: three men and three women. They all wore suits. The women's suits had discreet V-necklines which suggested that voluptuous breasts needed little encouragement to emerge from the crisp corporate lines.

"Each week they embrace the law. Leon and Alana. Olivia and Chuck . . . Each week they embrace the danger, the pain and the passion of practising their own brand of law. And so can you. Just watch."

The men and women in their business suits were hanging on each other's necks, pressing up against each other's backs, nearly reaching into each other's clothes. It was an ad for a television show called "Street Legal." These women and these men were all lawyers. They worked together. They played together. They had sex together, the ad implied. What fun it was and what a good package it makes, what good sense, when you can do all that with the same people in the same place.

Blair looked in her purse for a piece of paper to write it down. There was nothing, so she tore a cheque out of her chequebook and scribbled it there. "Each week they embrace the law . . ." It was something to sound off about on her show. She already knew what she was going to say. According to this ad, in Toronto, wife-life was becoming obsolete; the office had taken over as emotional-sexual satisfaction centre.

People talk about pornography, like it's those magazines in plastic wrap, and videos that people smuggle across the border. Well, I'll tell you what I think is pornographic. An ad in the TTC for one of our very own CBC television shows . . .

Blair's lips were moving. She looked around the car: no one else was there except a narrow-faced young man with a pair of earphones on, slunk down in one of the back seats. The subway train raced around a curve and began to slow to enter the St. George station. Blair had to get off. But not yet. She was not delivered from the ad yet. The message was an old one. We Give at the Office. We Take at the Office. With a new addition: We Fuck at the Office. This self-contained, self-sufficient little tribe of lawyers, with their well-tailored outfits and their fluffy hair and perfect teeth, was a new breed of people, efficient as clocks, output and input all rolled into one, all billable hours, as Max would say.

Max again. They made her think of Max.

Blair sat neat and straight on the sideways-facing seat, shocked. If Ruby were there she would have laughed: "It's your punishment for not believing in love," she'd say. "You've been bitten." "So we're back to love again, are we?" *We're back, Ruby, and you're the one who set it up.*

So was that the message? She needed a man to connect with life? But what would Max (or her anonymous lover, for that matter) be able to offer but a place to stand, a thing to be called ("wife"), invitations to dinner parties, where she could stand with Marsha and Sal and talk about kids. To be a wife was to be cut off, too, but in a different way. It was to be joined at the hip, paralysed, marked, tied down, *un*free. Blair wondered where the world was in which women participated, truly, on their own. The best time had been when she was twenty, and Hearts of Flame, her "family" of four, was at the centre of the world, its members tied only by the things that mattered—time, place, friendship and creating.

The train's brakes shrieked as they pulled into St. George. Blair turned her back resolutely on the advertising.

Andy stuck his head around the corner of Max's office door.

His pale face and thinning, mouse-brown hair neatly blended into the wallpaper; he'd be invisible were it not for the dark purple of his lips and the tight, navy noose of his bow-tie. Perhaps the two were related, Max thought for the first time, the pale face and grape-coloured lips being early signs of strangulation. Max was leaning back with his feet on his blotter, dictating into a hand-held tape recorder.

"You busy?"

Max stopped the tape and raised an expressive eyebrow. "I'm always busy, come on in."

Andy slid around the door, light on his feet and so graceful as to appear apologetic for intruding on the heavy teak furniture, the fat, leather-bound books, the stacked and bulging files on Max's side tables. Andy's own office never looked like that; it was picked clean of work. Because he avoided paperwork, Andy's secretary was never as busy as Maureen, a sore point in the office. Now he had something in his hands, a piece of yellow foolscap with writing on it.

"Want to talk to you about a call I got," said Andy.

Max's eyebrow shot up farther. Andy never consulted him. Andy didn't need to consult, and if he did, it would be someone else, one of his other pro-bono friends out there who specialized in these off-beat cases, like the right of a wheelchair-bound primary student to have playground facilities especially designed for him; the single father who stayed home from work and wanted to collect mother's allowance; the video store owner who refused to put classification signs up on his tapes. All those little freedoms we take for granted, as Andy said, are being whittled away even as we speak by government memoranda and poor judgments in court. Eternal vigilance and all that. It was up to him to fight the battle.

Not that Max minded. He and Andy were in harmony, politically; their eyes rolled on hearing the same things. It was only this grandstanding, this love of attention, that made Max leery of his partner's schemes. He pulled his feet off the blotter, sprang up and ran around the desk. With a footman-style sweep of his arm, he pulled out the chair for Andy to sit.

"It's a great honour to be consulted," he said, "by the defender of the weak."

Andy squinted at his foolscap, trying to read his own handwriting.

"Got a call from a fellow named Hugh Mensa. It seems he was a friend of this woman Ruby who disappeared," he said.

Max retreated around his desk again. He sank slowly back into his own chair. Ruby again. She had never been in his life so much as since she'd disappeared. True, she'd led him to Blair. But even that was a mixed blessing. Any reference to Ruby now tipped Blair off into moaning and wailing about her lost youth, everybody's lost youth. Now Mensa, the fashion critic—what did he want?

"You remember about Ruby," he said, casually. "That she's a friend, a slight friend of mine? And a great friend of Blair's?"

"Oh. Right," said Andy. He did not give away whether he remembered this or not. "I'm sure it has nothing to do with Mensa's calling me. I'm sure he doesn't know the connection."

Max shrugged.

"Well this is the thing. Hugh Mensa, fashion critic, *Metropolis*. Here's his card." Andy said the name with a relish. "Mensa says the cops are doing nothing. Tapping a few phones. Trying to pin a murder rap on Marvin. He says he's not sure the woman's dead, and if she is it wasn't murder. He wants to know if there's any way he can launch an investigation himself."

"And what do you know about Mensa?" said Max.

"Not much," admitted Andy cheerfully. "But I liked his style."

"They're all in the business of style," said Max.

"You know this guy?"

"No, no. Never met him. He was not considered to have been, I think, an altogether benevolent force. He's the one who wrote the first piece about her." He folded his hands on his desk and smiled. "You know I've already spoken to the police about this. And the family. Had them upgrade it from Missing Persons to Homicide."

Andy put both his hands up over his head in a gesture of surrender. "I didn't know you were on this one."

"I'm not on it," snapped Max. This thing stuck to him; it would not let him go. "The family called me and said they were concerned. The cops figured she was a flake and wouldn't put any men on it. I spoke to the officer in charge, as a concerned citizen and friend."

Andy smiled. "And now, of course, you're under suspicion yourself."

"I am not!" But Max had felt this; he knew. This pre-dated his already advanced sense of guilt. How thoughtful. A friend calls up to assist the cops—like, I killed her myself. Why don't you hurry up and catch me?

"Sure, why not?" said Andy. "But it won't hurt you. Unless you mind your phone being tapped. So what do you want me to say to Mensa?"

"Find out what he knows and tell me. I'll tell the cops," said Max.

They both laughed.

"I can't do that."

"Of course you can't."

They sat together looking out the window. Max tapped his fingers on the desk. "Wait till he starts telling you he's been communicating with her from beyond the grave. Like Marvin. They're all a bit wacko."

Andy said, "Hmmm," in his way. Then, "What'd Ruby want to see you about in the first place?"

"Isn't that privileged?"

"Privilege goes when you're dead. This is an investigation."

"I thought you said it was a consultation."

Andy laughed merrily and waited. He knew Max.

"Since you're not going to represent this guy, I'll say that, as far as I could tell, she was seeking ways to get rid of her boyfriend. She didn't want him involved in her business, he was a user and had a lot of debts."

"Hmmm," said Andy again. "Doesn't make him a murderer, though."

"I must say I agree with this Mensa. I figure she killed herself," said Max. "I keep thinking they're gonna find the body. Maybe Marvin's a factor. Maybe he pushed her. I blame myself a bit for not seeing how bad she was, but who would have thought . . . I just don't want to get involved."

"Sexy and successful," said Andy crisply. "What more could you want? She had it all. She made Toronto people feel glamorous. What a gift. She's vanished, and nobody has really stirred it up. I'm amazed. It's such a waste. When someone like that gets done in, or maybe done in, there's no end of interest. Look, you're in on it already. Let me give you Mensa. You could really run with this, Max."

Max grimaced inwardly. Andy had instincts. While he, Max, had steered away from this case, listening to his mole-like instincts, telling the family he didn't want them to use his name, advising them to get a detective and then hoping they wouldn't come back, Andy went for the jugular. Trust Max! Wrong again! He could never figure the way these stories would play. It took one of those old WASPs to understand the jaded, childish, prurient taste of this town. He, Max, would just have to carry on with the wills and the trusts until he had it inside out. His best hope for fomenting revolution was the Family Law Reform Act. He would leave it to the more securely fastened down, like Andy Mugwell, to take on these risky manoeuvres.

"Well she was beautiful, but she's gone, Andy. You won't be able to get your picture on the front page of the paper holding her hand," he quipped, nastily. He jerked his head toward the newspaper photo he kept on his corkboard. There was Miss Budd looking like a movie star after she reconciled with her boyfriend and called a press conference to say that she was sorry, and that she was henceforth going to support the pro-lifers. It had been a remarkable transformation, from bedraggled innocence to canny (and photogenic) bravado. Still, this little humiliation didn't stop Andy from getting more calls than he could handle in his role as defender of the innocent and the perverse.

"How insensitive and tactless of you to point that out," said Andy, putting on his prissy face. "Besides which, you should never underestimate what I can get into the papers. But this one's for you. My little gift. Call Mensa and talk. Just remember, they're listening to you."

He put the piece of paper on the desk. "See you later tonight?"

Andy was having one of his parties.

"Yeah, see you," said Max.

Max picked up his tape recorder and tried to remember where he was in his letter. He pressed the button and wound it back a little. ". . . and whereas if the aforementioned second Mrs. Bothy should *pre*decease the first Mrs. Bothy, and indeed should predecease Mr. Bothy himself . . ." But the magic was gone. He couldn't roll out the phrases as he had done. He was destabilized.

He looked out the window. The sun was low in the west, though it was only four-thirty in the afternoon. South of him, the Royal Bank Tower shimmered pink and gold, like the inside of an oyster shell, as the sky cleared and deepened. Lines of cars already plugged the underpass on lower Bay that led to the Gardiner Expressway; all those office workers fighting through their own fumes to get home. He, Max, did not have to drive to the suburbs. By virtue of a little foresight and a little family mortgage, he had bought his condo on Charles Street before the boom. This meant he could sashay out now, get a game of squash or do a set on the step-machine, go to Simpsons menswear and see what was on sale, wait till the traffic was out of the city at six-thirty and then fly up University and be home in ten minutes.

Similarly, he did not have to log four thousand hours a year like lawyers in big firms; Andy set such standards for leisure that overworking would only make Max look bad. He did not have to be responsible and hard-working. He too could take up with flakes. Why didn't he? He was safe, he was financially secure, despite having no social pedigree, he was perfectly adequately placed in Toronto, Canada, in 1989.

Still, there was a provisional feel to his security, a feeling that he was on sufferance, that he could be turned back from the shores of prosperity for some minor infraction of the code. Max did not like to break the rules. Andy liked to tweak the nose of the Establishment. By doing that, he stressed his distance from it, how far he had travelled. Fine for Andy: he was a third-generation Conservative lawyer on his father's side, while his grandfather on his mother's side, a dollar-a-day man for the war effort, descended from United Empire Loyalists in Nova Scotia.

Max's grandfather, on the other hand, had come to Toronto from New Jersey, where he had resided two years after coming off the boat from Poland. He never learned to speak good English and was working himself to death laying bricks when he married Elsie Towbar. They just had time to have two kids before he died. Con Ostriker, Max's dad, was the younger. Con had fond memories of being dragged up before magistrates for breaking the blue laws, short and grimy and smart, being given a fine and let go, turning his back and sticking out his tongue at the pastry-skinned and self-righteous guardians of Toronto the Good. As a boy, Max had been ashamed of Con's tales of survival on the streets of Toronto in the '20s and '30s. Now he was ashamed of himself for being ashamed.

And what did all this have to do with Ruby, with his desire and his fear of getting involved in the search? The word guilty formed in his mind, along with the image, which still sprang on him at odd moments, of the black woman's athletic leap, not from the train platform, but her second leap, from the floor of the tunnel into the iron arms of the train.

He stood up to leave. He had to go to Andy's, but there was something he was going to do first. He closed and locked the top drawer of his desk. Not that he had anything scandalous in there. Just the old copy of *Playboy* with the Jessica Hahn interview in it, which he'd won in a raffle at the squash club, and a bottle of Valium pills he'd got years ago. And some dope, so old now it was dust. He took a bit of heat from Maureen about this locked drawer, but so far he had resisted her prying.

Prying was exactly what he was going to do. Taking action was the only way to lift himself from this hook of guilt and imagined collaboration in a death that may not even have happened. But he couldn't do it directly; he was a suspect already, as Andy pointed out, and besides he felt foolish as one did, chasing a private fantasy out into public.

He looked up the name in his calendar. He'd called the TTC once, posing as a sociologist, and asked a few questions. The inspector said he should drop up to the Transit Center for a visit, and now he was going to do it. There was the name—Ron Welsh.

12

Be Odd on Your Own Time

Max drove up under the concrete pylons of the Allen Expressway and let the road swing him around onto Wilson. Only the pages of a newspaper, caught up against the chain-link fence, and a cold scattering of leaves graced the landscape around him. Overhead, the green-and-white signs were huge, the arrows unambiguous. He pulled off Transit Road to the gates of the Wilson Complex. The enormous paved area was full of buses—buses parked in rows, buses coasting out of the garage, buses curving in from the road. A man in a pinky-brown TTC uniform gestured him impatiently out of the way; Max hesitated, his car dwarfed and made vulnerable by these mammoth vehicles with their high-perched drivers.

"What are you looking for?" said the uniformed man, striding up to the car window. Max unrolled it; the November wind blew into his mouth as he tried to answer.

"Here to see Inspector Welsh," he said. He had his alias prepared, his reasons too, carefully rehearsed, but already the man was waving him to a parking space beside the two-storey brick building.

"Put it there," he said. "Use the main entrance."

He entered a vast room the size of a high school gymnasium, where throngs of men in the same pinky-brown uniform lined up in front of vending machines for coffee, Coke, sandwiches.

"Inspector Welsh?"

"*Mr.* Welsh now, he's moved up," said one guy. "Over there." At least fifty pairs of eyes watched Max as he backed out of the room and headed across the hall. There were a few women drivers, but they wore uniforms too, and made him just as nervous.

Today, Max was a researcher for a sociologist who wrote about suicide; what he hoped, privately, to discover was if Ruby had jumped in front of a train. Could it have gone unnoticed? Was it possible her body was never found?

"Bit unusual, having someone like yourself out here," said Welsh. "Have to excuse the guys. They're on their break. Go back out there to rush hour."

Max said you could excuse them anything if they had to drive in rush hour. He was given a styrofoam cup and sat at the edge of an arborite table. Mr. Welsh, Ron Welsh, sat opposite him, one leg crossed over the other knee, keenly anticipating his questions. He was a short man with glasses and a genial, puffy look. He was in shirtsleeves with arm garters.

Max felt duplicitous. "It was good of you to agree to see me. I won't take much of your time."

"You're interested in . . . ?"

"Suicides," he said.

Welsh looked displeased.

"I mean, I'm interested in the TTC's safety procedures. What happens when you have a suicide—"

"—say attempted," said Welsh. "Most of them are just that. If someone you know is thinking of it, tell them it's a poor idea. The success rate is very low."

Max got out his pad and his pencil.

"And you want this for . . . ?" said Welsh. "I just got the

message from public relations that I was to see you. We don't like to talk about it much. We dealt with this suicide-prevention group, you see, and they advised us, the more you talk about it the more some unstable person is gonna get ideas. We don't want copy-cats."

"Of course not."

"It's a very poor way. Pills, much better."

"But not so public."

"That's it. Some like to go over Niagara Falls. I've heard of that, too. You see it's a kind of public statement. Hangs people up for a while, too, if you're interested in that. I mean if someone is."

He didn't really care what Max wanted the information for, because he had not stopped speaking to listen to his answer. Max decided to go right for what he wanted.

"Can the driver see? Does he know the minute he pulls into the station that someone's going to do it?"

"The driver can sense something is wrong, eh? There's a person right at the edge say when he pulls in. The worst is when they're in the tunnel. Sometimes they've gone way in the tunnel and you just look down and they're on the tracks in front of you and they put their head down and that's it."

"You can't stop?"

"You've got fifty tons of metal in a six-car train. You're going forty miles an hour. You put the train into emergency, eh?"

"Emergency?"

"It's a dead-man feature, we call it. Train stops automatically."

Max wrote this down. "Dead-man feature."

"So then what happens to the body?"

"It's like I told you. The success rate is very low. Only about one out of ten dies, okay? I tell you it's not a good way. But what happens is, okay, the force of the train usually pushes you up under the lip of the platform. Train stops, operator gets out if he can. Sometimes he blacks out. If he's conscious, he pulls the lever on the wall of the station to cut power."

"If he can't?"

"There's a second guy on the train. If the power's cut and he doesn't hear the operator on the buzzer system, he'll say, "Oh no, it's a jump.""

Max wrote down, "Oh no, it's a jump."

"So the power's cut, it's dark down there, and the alarm's going. Priority One comes up all down the line. And the person under the train is sometimes wailing and screaming." Ron Welsh was a bit of an actor. He created his scene. "It's quiet. People are fainting on the platform, eh, if they saw it. Strange what people will do. Some will turn and walk away. Just like that. Don't want to have anything to do with it. Others—we had a nurse, last time. Just pitched right in to help."

Max wrote, "Priority One. Go down and find them—who?"

"We get the fire and police and ambulance all there once the Priority One goes out. But still, they always let the TTC go down first."

"Go down?"

"Under the train and find out what's there." Ron Welsh got off his chair to demonstrate. He got down on his haunches, waddling like a duck. He lifted one arm up.

"We've got a lantern, eh, 'cause it's dark, and a fluorescent vest, and a gown, and gloves to protect yourself 'cause of AIDS, right?" He paused in his acting. "I would not be amused if I went down there to rescue some guy and ended up with AIDS, you know? You're nervous, right, you sweat, you don't know what you're gonna find."

Max was writing quickly.

"Well most of the time they're alive, like I said. Sometimes you hear them but you can't see them. Once I found a guy way over on the other track. Sometimes they just get spun around and lose an arm or something. Have to look around to find the arm, too. Once I found one, a woman, she just had one cut, straight across her middle.

"See it depends on how you jump. If you're lucky, that is if you really want to die, if you're lucky and you take a running jump and hit right about in the middle of the train, you can get killed. But otherwise—"

He got up off the floor, dusted the knee of his pants. "—no telling what it'll do to you."

Max let him talk some more. It was easy to get information, even when the people who had it claimed they didn't want to tell. Almost too easy. Finally Welsh began to slow down a bit.

"The bodies get pushed under the lip of the platform, see, there's space in there, and they spin. Spin and spin till they're just about unrecognizable." Now Max made his move, asked the question he'd really come to ask.

"Any possibility of a body getting lost altogether? Any possibility of someone jumping in front of a train, and no one ever knowing?"

"Naw. Naw, the driver couldn't miss it."

"If he passed out?"

"He'd feel it. They walk the tracks anyway, to clean up, the maintenance guys, on a regular basis. But the driver would know, you'd know, if someone jumped. You can lose bits of bodies. Get decapitated. Sometimes they find the body way over on the other track. Sometimes they can't find it at all, at first. But then they do. You can't lose anyone down there."

"Any missing persons ever turn up in there?"

"No no. It's not like the ravines, eh, or the lake, this big wilderness. No, it's a comparatively narrow tunnel, it's our lifeline, eh, we keep a good look-out."

"Are there any jumpers you don't report? Do you always work with the police?"

"Have to. *Have to.* Just because we don't tell the public doesn't mean we keep secrets. Hey, what would we do that for?"

Max rang the bell on a darkened porch. Andy opened the door wordlessly in his shapeless Harris tweeds and quickly withdrew into the interior. Andy, being a small-l loyalist, small-c conservative, small-h homosexual—lower-case, upper-class Andy, with his houseful of relics of faded belles and stiff regimental soldiers, bachelor farmers and eccentric matriarchs who hung on to their farms—was getting the guys together tonight. Perpetually amused, unpretentious, without need to demonstrate purchase power; rooted, perhaps root-*bound*: that was Andy.

But no doubt this was the end of the line for the Colonel, thought Max, rubbing his hands in the cold living room and eyeing the portrait. Andy was unlikely to procreate, more likely, in fact, to leave the place to the Coalition for Innu Rights or a persecuted publisher of erotica. Unless Belinda managed to hang on.

But there was no sign of Belinda tonight. The living room, with its strange, green-tiled fireplace and twelve-foot ceilings, its wide window ledges and thick doorways, had returned to its normal dusty state. The silver winked sullenly in the cabinet. Max knew there was no point asking after her. Andy was occupied setting out pink crystal glasses on a sideboard.

The party was for one of Max and Andy's old law school friends who'd come back to town. Cal Sorokin was a big, shambling man who carried his head tucked slightly to the side, chin in, anticipating blows. So opinionated had he been at law school, his sense of fair play so large, so *immature* (as they said), that he had held up every class in long debate. He was graduated, it was said, only because they couldn't stand to see him in class any more. Eventually he fetched up at a university in Newfoundland, from which his books had emanated over the years: fierce, dense continuations of the same old arguments.

Max took a beer and stood to the side, watching the others come in. Cal arrived with his wife Dee-Ann, both appearing much put upon. Dee-Ann was large, phlegmatic and pale. She shed her cape and looked suspiciously around the room, as for a trap. Cal stood with his head tucked down cornerwise, as usual, like a large, troubled bird.

There was Sue Cantor, now a judge; Dennis Strachan, who taught legal history; noisy, obnoxious Stretch Burr, who had wanted only to be rich and now supposedly was. John Beaumont, large, fleshy and aggressive. The best anyone ever said about him was he'd never get you in the back. He was a "front-stabber." People feared him, but they needn't have; he said his worst to your face. Everyone looked older, even Stretch, who, for training fiendishly and losing forty-five pounds, was Man of the Year at the Cambridge Club. Dennis looked simply faded and purse-lipped; he'd brought his wise-looking twelve-year-old daughter, who listened intently and ate quantities of melon squares on toothpicks. She went to an alternative school where the teaching was accomplished by contracts; she had two weeks to do a research piece on what she wanted as a career.

"My dad said if I came here tonight I'd probably decide never to take up law."

Sue Cantor was the only judge among them, as she had been the only woman in their group. Max liked her then, he liked her now, but she was distant, serene, a manager, with her children and her nanny arrangements, her careful marshalling of time to allow for participation in the Cub pack and the swimming lessons. She was inhumanly *good* at all she did. How did men face such wives in the morning? he asked himself. She made him feel like an unrealized meatball. He couldn't figure out why she seemed so glad to see him.

John Beaumont, now so fat his progress across a room could only be described as a billow, began to harangue Sue about his bad experience with a judge. She nodded, sympathizing, her smile drying and stiffening as he went on.

"He was obviously against us from the beginning; I was too junior to figure it out. If I'd known more, I would have provoked him into saying something outrageous so we could get a mistrial."

"Making dough?" called Stretch Burr. He had four children in private school; he'd been with their mother for ten years and never married her. "How're you guys doing, anyway? I'm printing money," he said. "*Printing* it. I act for developers. It's simple. I decided I could either choose to enjoy what I did, or choose lifestyle. I chose lifestyle."

The rest of the guys began to rib him about how he hadn't married his wife.

"Why would I marry her? Matrimonial Property Act, she gets half of everything I own if I marry her," he said in his braying voice.

"Family law reform, it's all the same anyway," said Sue. "After two years living together you might as well be married."

"You have to give 'em support, and half the house, but nothing else, if you're not married," said Stretch, grinning.

Andy stood up to make a speech.

"We're here to honour Cal Sorokin, who we all remember as the biggest pain in the ass in our year. How many of us remember how incensed he got when old Beals explained in class it was cheaper to kill a guy than to maim him?" Reminiscent laughter filled the room. "I was standing with Max and Stretch in the hall, later, when old Beals swept by and said, 'Sorokin, come up and see me.'"

Max laughed; old Beals used to try to befriend them. He could see him now, long-faced and lean, slouching against the walls. His favourite saying was "My door is always open."

"Remember, we waited for him in the lounge 'cause we wanted to see what he'd say? Sorokin was in the office for two hours. When he came out he was *apoplectic*. Apparently, old Beals said to him, in a nutshell, 'When you go to law school, leave your social conscience at home.'"

The laughter increased. Andy waved his arms to quiet the group. Having an audience brought a slight flush to his always-pale face.

"And there are two things we're here to toast. The fact that the law school has asked Cal back to teach, after nearly throwing him out on his ear. And the fact that he's got a chapter on old Beals, putting him in his place. To Sorokin. A man who was relentlessly, obnoxiously, out of step."

They all raised their glasses.

"Too bad old Beals isn't here to read it."

Beals had been hit in a crosswalk and killed instantly, provoking many remarks implying that it had been a lawyer who hit him, because he understood the liabilities.

The men began to talk to each other again. Max found himself standing beside Sue after her tormentor had moved on.

"Well, I hope he feels better now," she said mildly, looking after John Beaumont, who was now wagging his finger in Stretch's face.

"You've got power," said Max. "I guess you've got to answer for it. Yours and everyone else's."

Sue gave him her perfectly composed smile. "Andy got me thinking about you guys back then. You and your long hair," she said. "Your guitar."

Max smiled. He had a cloud of curly hair in law school. He carried his books in a fringed leather bag and wore jeans that frayed under the heels of his shoes.

"Speaking of Beals's little aphorisms, remember what he said to you?" Sue said. "When you used to sit on the stairwell picking songs? Remember?"

Max thought back.

He used to go in to see old Beals, in the room with the always-open door. There were all those heavy, leather-bound books, the ashtray overflowing with bits of shredded tobacco, some heavy, aromatic smell turning your stomach, old Beals with his jowls and his white lips, his sharp, pouchy eyes and long nose, the vast and overwhelming stomach of the guy, his gross physical unattractiveness made more obvious by the thick, sonorous and elegant tones of his voice.

One day after class, Max was fixing a guitar string on the back stairs, planning to go over to Meat and Potatoes to play a set. Beals made him come into the office.

"Non-conformist, is that it, Max my boy? Love-in on the steps of the law school, is that it?"

Max shrugged. "Like to play a few songs," he said.

And old Beals leaned forward and sucked on the pipe. He waved his giant head back and forth a little to let the smoke clear. "Let me tell you something, boy," he said. "There's no law against it, that's true. But it won't do you any good, hear me? Not only will it not do you any good, but I'm telling you to leave the guitar at home and stop dressing like a hippie. This is a profession we're training you for, boy. *Be odd on your own time*."

"Sure, I remember," said Max. He'd gone out and told them all and made a joke of it.

"Be odd on your own time," said Sue reflectively. "The man had a way with words."

"We got a lot of mileage out of that one." The jokes had gone on for months.

"So are you? I mean, can you?"

"What?"

"B.O.O.Y.O.T.?"

Max grimaced reflectively. "Maybe not odd enough," he said.

He made excuses about work and left early. On his way

back to the office, Max wondered. Could it be that old Beals had had his way? He certainly wasn't being odd on *their* time (whoever *they* were), on company time. But he still had his own time, didn't he? And he could be as odd as he liked. If he liked to be odd.

Max sat in his office. It was now late. He had turned the lights out. It was snowing, a serious winter snow. The snow made the sky bright, and stray bullets of light from neighbouring towers crossed the windows, white through white. He could feel the tower sway in the wind. He liked it when he could feel that. It was as if he were in a control tower, unseen, and waiting, and watching.

He thought about Ruby. Ruby always gave him her great big lipstick smile. But had he known her at all? There had been a slight *frisson* between them, but she came loaded with all kinds of freight from the past. How pathetic and desperate she'd been that night he first saw her in Banff. What a lot of damage she could do, and what a dangerous weapon she had in herself.

He wondered if he was right about what Ruby wanted from him. Lots of people wanted to get a bad actor spouse out of their life. Talked a big story. But when it came down to the hard work of actually reading the riot act, getting separate accounts, dividing up the spoils, or whatever was necessary, they wouldn't. People liked to complain, but they didn't actually want to be free, to simplify, to *let go* the strings they held on other folks, and the strings those other folks held on them.

From the little she'd said about Marvin, he'd pegged Ruby for one of those, rightly or wrongly. Involved with a guy who wanted in on her business, which was no prize anyway, but he had debts and she was leery. He couldn't have done much for her. Then the suicide in front of the train, the cancelled lunch, that little explosion of emotion made them seem, for a couple of days, more intimate than they were. Then she disappeared.

"Whatever that was all about, Ruby dear . . ." he said aloud. "And you left me Blair."

Left him Blair, like a legacy. Because of Ruby, Blair came here, to this office, obediently, like a package that had been sent. For no reason. With no strings attached. Carrying that stupid dying bird and with her face all pink, she really rattled him badly, and, in the end, charmed him totally.

The trouble was, Blair was not so simple as all that. She did have strings attached. No lovers maybe, or ex-husbands—at least not in town—only that small, intense child. But she had Ruby. Or rather, the absence of Ruby. She was obsessed by the loss, by some kind of memory search, as she tried to find a cause, to understand this (to Max) ultimately selfish woman and her selfish act—if it was her own doing—of subtracting herself from all of their lives.

Now he, too, was stuck thinking about Ruby all the time. About her absence at least. He wanted it settled, for Blair's sake. He wanted Blair to be obsessed about *him*. He didn't know any more than she did whether they could last. But he wanted to try. And Ruby was in the way. She had stopped time, arrested them all where they'd been, where she'd vanished. She had them hostage.

He had to solve the riddle of Ruby. He'd shied away from getting involved, for no good reason. But he could do something. Even if it meant making a fool of himself. Even if it meant being odd on company time. Who was watching, after all?

Dick Nolan had been down to visit Max. Stood around in the waiting area in his obvious plain-clothes cop outfit, unnerving the Family Compact types, as Andy's clients so often did. Cheap trousers with several creases ironed in, the shapeless jacket of some synthetic weave and the shirt that looked too tight, a long, thin tie that looked as if it had been pulled and pulled like a pigtail. Max didn't let him linger. They went for coffee down in the mall.

Breaking bits off the edge of his styrofoam cup, Dick casually asked a few questions. Had Max been in touch with Marvin or any of Ruby's friends? How had he met Ruby? What did he think she wanted a lawyer for? Dick was surprised Max didn't patronize Oswald. All the rest of them did, didn't they?

"And did Blair tell you anything about energy transfer? Or destiny reform?" said Dick, fishing.

"Blair's not into that sort of thing," said Max, with dignity. He hoped not, anyway.

When Max turned the tables and asked what was going on, why they hadn't been able to find out anything, Dick hemmed and hawed and said that people were under surveillance, and he didn't want Max to throw off any of their carefully laid plans. They still had absolutely no evidence of foul play.

"People disappear," said Dick. "Sometimes you just gotta wait. They show up when they want to, alive or dead. Sometimes they never show up."

"This case is a bit different," said Max.

"They're all different."

"So many stories," said Max. The rumours were getting more complicated. The latest were that Ruby's disappearance was due to voodoo, that she had been kidnapped by Marvin's friends, and that she had committed suicide while under hypnotism by Oswald. And the amnesia story still had currency in some quarters.

"And any of those tales might be the right one," said Dick, with some satisfaction.

"And then there's the diary," said Max. He hoped to surprise Dick, to demonstrate his knowledge. Blair had told him first, then she'd told the cops.

"Oh, that's another wrinkle," said Dick. "Quite a life she was leading." He smacked his lips reminiscently. "Good reading. But I could have done with more facts. Too many feelings. Not much you can do with feelings, after all. 'Course they were written a bit carelessly, on the run, like." He almost, but not quite, smiled.

"You moonlight as a literary critic?"

"My first opportunity," said Dick. "I never had a writer-type go off on me before. I just think she coulda given more leads."

"You think that's why she wrote them?"

"No, no," said Dick. "No. But they put—ah—a twist on the case. Somebody's sending them. We don't know who. Did a forensic work-up on them. The envelope is useless, too many prints, couriers and what not. On the pages inside we thought we'd get something. But it's only her fingerprints, unless whoever has them used gloves. You can't get anything off them." Having destroyed his cup totally, he leaned away from the table, his lips smeared together in a grim smile.

Max had a funny feeling about Dick Nolan. His feeling was that Dick didn't want Ruby to be found. He was possessive about her; holding a couple of well-thumbed pictures between tobacco-stained hands, he seemed too familiar, proprietorial of the woman whose trail he was on.

"Only possibility is Marvin Arbat," said Dick. "And if it has anything to do with him, eventually he'll slip, and we'll catch him."

Max said nothing, but he didn't think Marvin was the answer. And waiting was not good enough now. In his office, in the eye of the snowstorm, he pulled Andy's piece of foolscap across the desk and dialled Hugh Mensa's number.

A dazzle-painted van with "Kid Gloves" scrawled along the side pulled up in front of Blair's house. The driver handed her a package. His hands were rough and dirty.

"Courier from where?" said Blair, as soon as she saw the

envelope. Her heart was thumping.

The driver was tall and raw-boned, his hair shaved close over his knobby scalp. "Doesn't say the sender," he said, consulting his clipboard. "It was a drop-off at the Cleveland office. Paid cash."

She signed for it and went inside.

Now the package sat on a footstool in the living room, in front of the old corduroy chair by the window. Blair made herself coffee. She made a telephone call to Sissy's doctor. She saw the sink full of dirty dishes and washed them. She could avoid it no longer; now she held the diary pages in her hand. They were yellow, with a ruffled top edge where they'd been torn from the binding. She longed to be—and dreaded to be—immersed in Ruby's world again. She took a sip of the hot, strong coffee, for strength. She ran her fingers over the writing on the envelope. "Useless," Max had said. "They did a forensic work-up on them and got nothing."

The first thing she did was scan for dates. And this time she was rewarded. The first entry was dated September 9. Three days after she disappeared. This was what Blair had been waiting for.

I got out of the cab at the Royal York. I paid the kid well—he was a sweet kid, and he felt like my last contact with humanity. I had no real plan; my connection to the world had simply been slashed. It was an effortless cord-cutting. I was a kite on a string that had been tugged at and strained for years on end. For no reason, today, a little wind broke it.

I felt light and giddy. Could have gone anywhere, flown to the top of the BCE Place. I had nothing, my purse only. I thought about taking the bus out to the airport, but it was too soon for that. It would have meant using credit cards. I hadn't planned this escape, not consciously, but I already knew that I didn't want people to follow me. People and things: they were the same. They held me down in that old earthbound, unfree life.

I always carry a little razor knife in my purse, one of those little plastic sliding ones, in case I want to cut a picture out of a magazine. I got it in my hand and went into the hotel lobby, skirting the edges. The place was jammed with guys in cheap suits and women in polyester travelling knits; I figured I wouldn't be recognized. Found myself a Ladies. Waited in the john until it was empty, then took a chance and went to the mirror, starting slicing off my hair. I had the bowl half-filled with these hennaed strings (whoever said "silken" in regards to hair didn't know me) when I heard the outside door open. I fled back into the cubicle, heard some lady approach the sink and shriek to her friend: "It's a rat!" Their heels clattered backwards to just in front of my cubicle. The friend said it couldn't be, even Toronto wasn't that bad, and eventually, clinging together (or so I gathered from looking under the door), they made their way back to the sink.

"It's just hair, see?" said one of them.

"But that's disgusting!"

"Think how dirty everything else must be!"

"I don't think we should use it, do you?"

"We'll go and COMPLAIN."

I could tell the idea of complaining was one that had a lot of attraction for them, and they'd be back. I probably didn't have much time. As soon as they were gone I finished off my hairdo in the cubicle and flushed the pieces down the toilet. I ran my hand over the ragged ends, it was all standing up. Not too bad, I thought, as I grabbed a glimpse of myself rushing past the mirror. I did look wild.

The next thing was sunglasses—obvious, but easy. Luckily there was a drug store open in the hotel. I managed to get a pair of neon reflectors that curved around the sides, put them on right at the cash. I was getting off on this. It was dress-up, but it was terminal: there was no being Ruby again. It was fun to see the different way people looked at me. It used to be with a detached admiration—oh, stylish. Oh, confident. Or, from men, sexual assessment, overt or not so overt, depending on their mood, but always measuring, testing out their hormones against my presentation. Always with the subtle undercurrent of—you're offering, and I'm thinking about it.

Not now. I was a renegade. They still looked at me. But now with open hostility. I dared not try to attract them. Was I dangerous? Not yet, but I might get that way.

But hair wasn't enough. I had to do something about my clothes. They marked me. They tied me. At the side door of the hotel I saw a bag lady with her metal shopping cart, stuff all tucked in there in plastic. I went up close. She didn't smell bad. So I asked her, how would she like to trade? She looked me up and down and said, what would I do with that get-up? (My black '40s rayon suit with the red buttons.) And I said it was worth money, maybe she could sell it. No one would buy it from her, she said. She'd have to have money. I said I had to ditch somebody and I didn't want to be recognized. I figured she had something in those bags that would help. She said she couldn't turn away a sister in need, could she? So we went off to the corner of the building and tucked up against the wall and went through her stuff. There was a not-bad pair of jeans, men's, still strong, and a sweatshirt, so I took them.

She trusted me while I dodged back into the Ladies, which was empty now, and changed. I came back, gave her the suit and tights. Meanwhile she had dug out a couple of items for me to keep. One was this great hockey jacket and the other was a grey woollen toque. "If you're going to live rough I'll give you a start," she said. I kissed her and gave her forty bucks. I only had sixty more.

I started walking up Yonge Street. It felt good to be out, no dress code, mixing in. The only problem was my shoes. I had to find some track shoes to walk in. These pointed-toed, jet-heeled numbers were definitely trouble. I kept on going till I hit Bloor, bought a take-out coffee and stood under an awning, looking out at the world.

I was in the midst of my own disappearance. What a viewpoint. It was unfolding in front of me. I was fading into the background. It felt like a relief. I was less the active than the passive participant. Foreground was forming in front of me, wiping me out. It was going to work! Oh sure, I could see problems. I'd have to get money. And I needed one completely trustworthy soul to act as anchor. So I could pull myself back if I needed to. I knew who it had to be. Oswald. I went down to the concourse under the Bay and called him. He was still at the office, my workaholic psychic.

"Oswald dear, my old friend," I said, very merry, "it's Ruby and I am doing a vanishing act. Come down and see me one last time." He made a bunch of excuses but I knew he'd do it. "And bring cash," I said. "I'll have to owe you." After that I hung around watching the crowds come out of the movie. Teenagers were milling and smoking and getting sent off by the security. Oswald twisted in, impeccable as ever, looked around for me, didn't see me, gave an exasperated sigh and then leaned up against the window of the tobacco store. He got out his electronic diary and started pushing buttons. I gave him a minute and then sauntered up.

"Hi there," I said. "Don't faint." He pulled himself up like to brush off a panhandler before he recognized me. Then he pretended not to be surprised. This was my husband, after all, from a previous life. King and Queen of Egypt, right?

"You've cut your hair," he said, always the master of understatement.

"I didn't get a good view of the back," I said, turning around, "how is it?"

He eyeballed me, getting the general idea. "Not bad," he said, "it might catch on. And now I'm going to take you for a drink so you can tell me why."

He took me by the elbow and steered me up to the street level. We ended up in the top of the Park Plaza, where I was treated with exaggerated courtesy, like somebody's runaway mentally deficient wife or else a rock musician Oswald was trying to snag for one of his bands. I told him there weren't really any reasons but insisted that, as my friend and consultant and husband from a former life, he was absolutely compelled to assist me in any way he could, and that if he didn't I'd blow the whistle on him. He didn't ask for what and I had my ally, easy. Also, I have to say he began to fall into sympathy with the project. The project was, essentially, getting the hell out of my life as it was, and into something more rewarding, without having to die first. Reincarnation was fine, I said, I gather I'd already done it once or twice. But I'm ready for the next, and don't want to die, and take the risk that this was as far as my ticket went. "I can go it alone, start over, invent myself," I said, "and I don't need a single, solitary soul." I didn't know exactly yet where I wanted to be or what, just that nothing and nobody was coming with me. I was cutting up my credit cards, and I couldn't use the bank, so I was going to need a little money from time to time. And maybe a hide-out from time to time, and maybe a little friendly consolation. But it was going to be my journey.

So Oswald said, essentially, okay. What choice did he have? The only thing was the cops would be onto him before long because of course there would be a search, people don't just walk out of their lives and close the door behind them; families and friends and lovers tend to make such a fuss. I told him fine, you're doing nothing wrong, and you honestly won't know where I am. You'll only hear from me once in a blue moon and we'll have a rendezvous.

I drained my Courvoisier, figuring it was the last one I was going to get for some time, and we went back outside. From the lobby I called my mom. I just wanted to. OK, a slip-up. A weakness. When I started to get emotional, Oswald took the phone. "Martha, don't worry, I'm in charge here," he said. And he went on and gave her his destiny reform rap. That's when I knew he was really on my side.

13

Subject to Season

Bernie pulled the heavy clump of keys out of her pocket, sorted through them with expert fingers and found the one— a Schlag with a green-plastic rim around the head—to open Blair's door. "I'm like a jailer," she always said, jangling her key collection. Her heavy key-chain was the secret of her success in Canada. She opened a dozen houses in the neighbourhood in the course of a week, to do her cleaning. Most days by this time she had already cleaned for Walkers and Sandersons, each of whom paid her for half a day, although she could do it in an hour and a half.

She was a fast cleaner, and she worked on a system: first a run through the rooms tidying, taking out the wastebaskets, carrying unplaceables and miscellaneous to the kitchen. Then dust and vacuum including stairs. Last, clean the kitchen. Those left-aside items—kids' art, odd earrings, library books and rubber boots—she put in plastic bags and hung in cupboards, or folded them behind the canisters on the counter. Blair called it the Third World filing system. Items bagged were sometimes lost forever. But what could Bernie do if they insisted on leaving these unplaceable oddities around the house? she asked. It was not her job to sort, to create order and reason. It was her job to clean what was there. Her last act was to go back over the house with a damp cloth and polish, and make all the surfaces shine.

But today she had not done her other cleaning jobs. Instead she had gone to Immigration. Got up at six o'clock and stood in a line until nearly noon; they let her in just before lunch. It was her final assessment. She was on her way to becoming a citizen. All that was left now was to wait, perhaps for one year, perhaps more, for the hidden machinery to whirl and cough and finally spew out a paper saying Berenice Serapion was a Canadian citizen.

The house was empty. Blair had gone off to exercise, no doubt, and then to work. Because it was not a normal day, and because Bernie had many things on her mind, she slowed her program. She dropped her ski jacket on the hall bench and went to the kitchen, where she poured herself a cup of coffee out of the drip machine. Once she had taken her coffee, she switched its cheerful red light off: Blair tended to waste electricity, though Bernie warned her every day, and Sissy had begun to do the same thing, because she was learning conservation in school.

She drank her coffee standing, with one eye on the stove clock. She had two hours to clean, and then she had to pick up Sissy. The coffee was thick and a little stale. She rinsed the cup and put it in the sink, and then ran lightly upstairs to her room. She threw her ski jacket on top of the bed and felt under the foot for her slippers, the old, frayed, floppy slippers from Chinatown that she always wore in the house. Jesus beamed down from the wall; Berenice herself, head over her shoulder and one leg slightly bent, gazed seductively if redundantly from the other side of the room. On the table were two piles of airmail envelopes, some used and open, with letters from Dugale tucked in, the others fresh, thin, waiting for Bernie to insert her pages of careful writing and money orders.

Hello, hello, said Bernie to these fixtures in her life. I haven't got much news, have I? Still the same every day, running in, running out. Many jobs, good money, send much home. Give, give, give, and what do I get? What is for me? If I am to have this power, to be this strong and wonderful thing, a Canadian citizen, then what will I do for myself?

These words came newly to her mind, with such clarity that she stopped to listen, as if it were someone else talking. Perhaps she had thought them before, confusedly, angrily, as she rinsed the dishes or drove the car. But today there was only the simple logic of the language. It followed. Bernie had gone this far; she had worked hard; she had helped other people; she had made herself a new person in a new country. And now, the question was obvious: once she had looked after the others, what would she do for herself?

Bernie's book, *Dreams and Their Meanings*, lay on the bedspread, open and flipped over where she had consulted it as to the meaning of a dream. In her dream, her teeth were swimming in a little lake of blood. Something to do with sex, she understood from the only reference to teeth she could find in the book. That rang a bell. Physical love was one thing Bernie wanted. It was life after all; it was natural, a woman's right. Bernie wanted many things, she said to herself. Some things you can work hard to get. Sex was different, you can't arrange it. Or can you?

Leaving this question unanswered, she ran down the stairs and into Blair's room, picking up old coffee cups, folded newspapers, a damp towel. She stripped the bed and dropped the sheets at the top of the stairs. Beside Blair's bed, on the rug, was a pile of yellow pages with handwriting all over them. Bernie picked them up. She flipped through the pages. The paper was sending a buzz into her fingers. Her fingers felt as if she had been lying on them and now they were coming back to life. It was so bad she had to put the papers down on the bed. As she dropped them she saw the word "Blair" in the writing, and then "deBoltz."

So Blair had received a message from Ruby. A very long letter, perhaps, telling her where Ruby was. Bernie's fingers were burning. She wanted to pick the papers up again. The papers would tell her something. It was like the time when she picked up the fishing net and knew her father was not coming home that day. He was dead already. It was an accident, they said. He had died in the water, lost over the side of the boat.

After that, Bernie was special. People came to her to ask questions, to find lost relatives. People wanted Bernie to help them. It was the beginning of Bernie leaving home. Because she was special, she was alone. They did not trust Bernie any more.

Cautiously, Bernie picked up the pages again. Her fingers began to buzz. Her eyes closed and the lids flickered. She could see Ruby. Ruby was on a train. A subway train, or a big train. She was travelling into the sun. She looked different, she wore a cap like a little boy, but it was still Ruby, and she was dozing in her train seat, and the train was driving straight into a great ball of sun.

Bernie screamed and dropped the pages on the bed. The picture went away. Her eyes opened. She felt the way she did when she got an electric shock from the vacuum cleaner. She did not move for a minute. Then she shook her head. She would not remember what had happened. She put it out of her mind.

She darted through Sissy's room, picking up, taking out, and dropping her laundry at the top of the stairs. Speeded by fear, she went back in to tidy. Sissy's room was littered with clothes and popsicle wrappers and pencil shavings. Bernie did not mind cleaning for someone she loved. Conchita always fought Bernie over this. She told Bernie she was mixed up and backwards, that she was emotional where she should be practical and practical where she should be emotional. She was shocked by Bernie's attitude about Dugale, for instance. Bernie said, Dugale cannot work; he earns no money. I don't love him because it's not *practical* to love him. I need a man who earns money.

Conchita did not agree. For a man you must feel romantic, she said. That kind of love is not to do with money. But Bernie just laughed. Romantic is to keep women poor, she said. I stay with Blair because I love her, and I love Sissy. Blair is my friend. That makes me happy. Conchita shook her head. You are romantic about your work, but practical about your man. You are crazy. Backwards and crazy.

Today Bernie could feel unhappy waves lapping around Blair's house, licking at the staircase, flowing thinly from the bedrooms across the hall. She blamed Ruby for bringing un-happiness in. Ruby was a witch. Bernie crossed herself in the bathroom mirror where she was cleaning out the sink with vinegar. Killed herself, or maybe murdered. People said she had bad friends. But Blair said it was not true. Blair cried at night and did not sleep well. Sometimes in the morning, early, she tapped on Bernie's door and whispered: "Can you get up with Sissy? I have to go out walking." Bernie knew what she did when she walked. She looked for Ruby.

But why had Bernie seen Ruby? Seen her on a train going into the sun. She did not know if she could tell Blair. She was afraid Blair would try to follow, or Blair would get hurt. She tried to forget the image of Ruby she had seen. The bath-room finished, she sped down to the main floor. She tidied the narrow hall, the dark-green papered dining room, the liv-ing room with the books and magazines spread everywhere, tulips dying in vases, tulips Max brought, arched in agony, their petals curling back and the blackened stamens exposed.

"They die so beautifully," Blair had said, when Bernie tried to take them away the day before. "If we have to die, we might be proud to do it with such grace."

They worried Bernie, these thoughts of Blair's. In her

opinion they were all because of Ruby. Bernie did not love Ruby, as Blair did; in fact, she hated her. That was why she would not look for Ruby herself. You could not see into the life of those you hated and feared. If you could, it would be too dangerous. There would be many murders. It was a powerful, very powerful thing, this seeing.

Canada was such a large country, too. In Philippines hardly anyone was murdered, only a few lovers of married women, or married women themselves, when people ran *amok*. "Amok" was a Tagalog word that had come into English. At home, thought Bernie, no one disappears. No one runs away. There is nowhere to run to. If you want to get out you can go to Canada, if you are lucky. There you are so far away that no one can find you, even if you tell them.

But sometimes in Canada people disappear. Bernie knew some immigrants who did. They go underground. They just have night jobs and no documents. Borrow another person's card for the health care, live in somebody's basement, save money at home under the mattress, or maybe, if you trust them, in a friend's bank account. It is not so difficult. But you must be careful. Careful that you are never stopped by the police, for jay-walking, or riding in a speeding car.

Maybe Ruby was not dead, but she had gone underground. Maybe that was what the picture she'd had of Ruby, in the boy's cap, sitting in the train, meant. It is not easy to understand why she might do such a thing, Bernie thought, stopping to dust the photo of Blair and Sissy that stood on the mantel. Why a Canadian woman with a good business and many nice clothes would do that. But she could have. She could be still living, just hiding and waiting for her moment to reappear, to frighten them all the more.

Blair sat in the studio, facing the technicians through the glass. A thin, spoon-shaped microphone reached in a curve from her ear to a spot somewhere in front of her mouth. Her headset nicely blocked out the sound of the world outside. She could see the back of her guest's head reflected in the pane of glass behind him. The sign of the studio wall read SILENCE. It had always struck Blair, that sign. Sound studio; silence. The sound depended on silence.

The man sitting across from her kept his eyes on her, as if he were about to sink underwater and she were his life line. The producer occupied one ear, the guest one eye, the technicians the other eye. Blair was adept, amphibious. She had learned to carry on two conversations at once, to do intros and extros in the allotted number of seconds, to think ahead and talk behind. She signalled the nervous guest with her eyebrows: we can do this. She wondered if he would talk. You never could tell about people. Some of them were great on the phone, but the minute they were on air they clammed up.

"Not half as bad as TV or film," she said. "There's nothing much to worry about. Just don't jerk your head forward. And don't be afraid to repeat yourself," she said. "You may have said it all to me, but they haven't heard you out there."

The man opened his mouth and whispered, "Yes." He wore a black leather jacket and was unshaven; one ear was hung with a skull-and-crossbones, and his wrist, extending from the sleeve on the table, was tattooed with something that looked like an eagle.

The technician spoke in Blair's ear. "All right. We're set. Any time."

Blair drew in her breath, opening the back of her throat, yawned, once, and then again, to allow the voice to come out. She turned her head from one side to the other, let her jaw drop down, then put her hand on it and pushed it in circles, letting the tension out. Normally she didn't get nervous. But this was her last day.

"Good evening everyone out there," she began, "and I hope it *is* a good one for you. For me, it's a little sad. I'll be leaving 'Driving Home' after today. You won't hear my plummy tones any more coming across the airwaves as you struggle down that long road home from work.

"I'm going to play a lot of my favourites today, so look out," she said. "After all, this may be my last gasp as a deejay. Look for me in other lines of work. Not that I haven't enjoyed sounding off. I have. Now here's the Band."

She gave her guest a sign as the music began. Just two minutes of this and then he'd be on. He grinned under his overhang of hair. On the table, his fingernails, clipped down nearly to the quick, shone a bluish white in his raw, red hands. He wore thick glasses and had a moustache of a reddish colour, although the hair in a ponytail at the nape of his neck was dishwater blond.

"I'm not happy with the mix," said the technician in her ear. "There's not enough bass. I'm adjusting it."

Blair waved her hand at the technician that he could do what he liked. She looked around the studio she'd taken for granted these few months: the walls of acoustic tile, hung with circles of wire and speakers; the technicians, like giant insects with their headsets, the wires curving overtop their heads, joining ear to ear; the corners where old music stands were pushed up, their brown, flat angles covered with dust; the chinless researcher drifting around on the other side of the glass wall; the receptionist who yawned and slid down in her chair, in black leggings with a transparent, patterned chiffon skirt drifting around her knees.

"Okay, you ready?" said the technician in her ear.

The music was abruptly turned down—they never allowed a song to finish in this place, it was one of her grievances—and Blair's voice billowed up to fill the silence. The guest began to talk about the heavy metal fans in town, what he called "head-bangers." But he was dull. Blair wasn't doing too well either. She was distracted, sad. The interview stumbled to an end, and she cut to music. The head-banger made a noisy exit. The song was about love, and lying, and crying. She hadn't planned what she was going to say; it just happened. When the music finished, she started.

"More romance," she sighed. "You know, women are liable to forget what they're doing and drop everything else in life, just to fulfill a romantic destiny. At least that's our reputation. You understand I'm not saying women do this out of an innate propensity. We're taught. We're led. We're very nearly *forced*. It takes considerable effort to resist the pull. I'm quite passionate about this," said Blair. "But we're going to have to break off for some weather and sports—"

She turned off her headphones, took a sip of water and avoided looking up, so as not to receive any messages she didn't want. She was angry today. At Ruby, and at Max, too. And at the fat producers. Angry at everyone, including herself, perhaps mostly herself, and she could not understand why. What was it one of her callers had said about Toronto? "The last safe place in the world"? That's what this job felt like now. A safe job in radio, where they couldn't see her wrinkles. That's what it had been. A place to grow old gracefully for Blair, the acquired taste. Maybe there were no safe places in the world for her. Her mother used to tell her she always took the hard way. But the easy ways didn't work for her. Blair didn't understand how people did it. It was a stamp on her, perhaps. Scarlet letter—D for difficult? The stamp was the stamp of her time. She was made in an earlier time, suited to it. Why did everything have to change? If history had stopped twenty years ago she would have been fine.

The break ended and she was back on air.

"Life was not meant to be sliced up in decades, like a parsnip in the Cuisinart," she said. "But since we've been doing that, it seems as if there was one disc that got caught under the blade and wouldn't go away. The '60s."

The technician smiled.

"Any idea how to move on from that?" she said. "Keep

those calls and letters coming."

During the next song she signalled the technician. "Do you know who's coming on to replace me? I might as well give them a great build-up."

The technician looked sheepish. "They couldn't hire outside. I guess it's Lenny," he said, "if it isn't Bart. I know it's one of them."

The fat producers. Blair struck her forehead with the heel of a hand. Of course. Why hadn't she realized? They wanted her job. "Thanks, pal," she said into the headphones. "That's a weight off my mind." As she went back to air it all fell in place. That was why they criticized her. That was why she was always wrong. It made her feel better. Better to fall victim to someone else's ambition than just to be no good.

"I have a big surprise for you listeners out there," she said. "And I want to give it to you easy, so you don't run up on any curbs. Your new host is going to be someone you already know, even if you don't *know* you know him. He's been working off-air all this time, guiding yours truly in her choices, making it palatable for the folks out there." She managed a giggle.

"Hey, I know you love me—you'll miss me. But you never write, you never call. Give us the benefit of your views, I beg you. I'll catch you later."

Several hours later, Blair packed her briefcase full of interview notes and tapes, old sweaters and an umbrella, and the coffee cup that read "To dance is to live, to live is to dance." She said goodbye to the technicians and tiptoed past the door of the fat producers. Bart, not Lenny, followed her. "All the best," he said, with a weighty grimace. His long, grey hair ran under his ears. "You were coming along. And you never know, we might call you again. I'm impressed by all the response you got, anyway. Even though it was mostly negative."

Once again, at eleven o'clock, she was pitched into the cold black vacuum of the city on a November night.

The kitchen was dark. She filled the kettle by feeling her way to the tap, and plugged it in. The red light on its side shone like a sullen eye at waist height. There was a note, painstakingly printed.

Dare Mommy I need sholases becas my old ones broke. Tomurro can I have 2 dolrs for pzza? Love Simplicity.

That was someone who did not find her services unnecessary. Someone who needed Blair: indeed she had no one *but* Blair, unless you counted her father, who paid, and Bernie, who was paid to look after her. For her father, it was an investment; one day he'd come inspect what his money had earned. For Bernie it was a job. One day she would be gone. Neither of these eventualities bore thinking about. If Blair didn't have a job as Simplicity's mother, if that weedy old Englishman, her ex, didn't send her those cheques, then what? She wasn't doing very well on the employment front. She had liked the radio job. It suited her. She pretended she didn't care, but she did. Now she'd lost it.

Max met Mensa in a small Israeli restaurant on north Avenue Road. Mensa suggested it: he said anywhere south of Bloor he might be recognized, and anywhere between Bloor and Eglinton he considered too yuppified. They ordered beer and sat in the back in a dark corner. The only other people in the place were the owner, a man, and a woman who waited on the tables, who whispered intensely and constantly behind the cash register.

Mensa was cool, with an air of lending himself to this escapade. At first this rather annoyed Max.

"You called," he said. "You must have had something definite in mind to do."

"No, no, nothing definite," said Mensa, his lean, slightly freckled face rearranging itself into a rueful smile. "I am not an expert, of course, in law, or in searches, for that matter. A mere scribbler, you know. Noted for my impracticality, you might say. But still . . ."

"Still," grinned Max.

Mensa held up his hands and let them flop outward from the wrist. "A journalist has a feel for things, a nose, you know?"

"And what does your nose—" Max swallowed his beer and wiped his lips with the back of his hand. "—tell you about Ruby?"

"My nose doesn't tell me anything directly. It is a sensory organ. It just gives me a sense. My sense is the cops aren't doing much, and the trail is going cold, and we might be losing any little chance we had of finding her alive."

Max made a nasal sound like a harrumph that signified agreement. "You don't have to be a genius to know that," he said, "if you don't mind my saying. Why did you call Ostriker, Mugwell?" He figured he knew already. "Andy being a headline-grabber have anything to do with it?"

Mensa smiled graciously. "We have such a powerful tool in the press," he mused. "I wonder if any of us really understands it. I wonder if any of us really knows how to use it."

"Well, Mr. Mugwell does a pretty good job," Max said somewhat pugnaciously. "I'm not like that. I don't work that way. It doesn't interest me. My interest in this is that I knew Ruby." He didn't know why he was being so gruff with Mensa. But it did seem to be the right tactic. The ruder Max was, the more ingratiating Mensa became.

"Ruby had many friends. I did not realize she was lucky enough to count yourself among them," he said.

"Cut the crap," said Max. "What do you want? To write an article? You should talk to Dick Nolan."

"Oh, Dick Nolan," said Mensa, waving one of his long hands again. "He's the whole problem. All of Queen Street is laughing at him. He's fallen in love with Ruby. He writes her little poems. He moons around the Cameron House and talks to anyone who'll mention her name. He's worse than Marvin."

"Maybe he figures that if he just talks to enough people he'll eventually find the clues to put this thing together," said Max.

Mensa had hardly touched his beer. He bent over the table now and looked deep into Max's eyes.

"Maybe he does. And what do you think?"

Max had decided ahead of time he wasn't going to give anything away. But now he'd given Mensa his opportunity.

"I think . . ." said Max. "I think—I don't see how you're going to get a better investigation unless you can start up some kind of uproar. Find a hook, you know. Just like you need for your stories. An *event* that can mobilize people . . ." As he spoke, he realized there was just such an event. But it hadn't worked. It hadn't worked for one reason, and that reason was that the right people didn't know about it.

The event was, of course, the arrival of the diaries. Dick's reaction had been disappointing; he didn't seem to make much of it. When the second one came, it was only more of the same. "We've got to get some action," he said. "It's no good to us unless it tells us what happened on September 6th." Now the third one had arrived, and it did tell what happened on September 6th. Why hadn't anyone thought of leaking that to the media? Andy would have done it in a second.

Max drained his beer all at once. The place was dark, and the whispering was giving him the creeps. Outside it was a rare, sunny midwinter day. He was restless to go.

Mensa could tell something was happening. He was making himself as unobtrusive as possible on the other side of the table. He did have a nose, obviously. He could smell secrets. He could tell the moment their holder wavered: would he or would he not tell?

What was to lose, Max thought, standing up and putting

five dollars down on the bill. The two men walked out into the sunlight together. The bare, ugly, two-storey storefronts stretched up endlessly northward, and equally far southward. There were a few small trees embedded in concrete boxes, three feet high. At the curb, a thick slab of gravel-encrusted ice inhibited parking. Max wondered if Ruby, that is, if Ruby· were still alive, if she had managed to find somewhere halfway warm for winter.

"Actually there is something," Max said. "Something I could tell you. Something we could use to get a search geared up. But if I tell you, you're going to have to promise you'll deep-six it until I say so."

Mensa had his hands in his pockets, as if to portray his own harmlessness.

"You mean it's off the record?"

"This is all off the record. You're seeking legal counsel, re-member?"

"Oh, right," said Mensa.

Max nearly didn't tell. But then he was tempted. He could not resist.

"Diaries have been arriving, you see. In her handwriting. Regularly. To Blair."

"Oh," said Mensa. He swayed, tall and without hands, on the cold sidewalk. "Diaries of her life before—or since?"

"Before," said Max. "Unfortunately. Except that—" Oh now he had really told, hadn't he? He had really given it all away, the most recent, the most vital information. "—except that the last one was dated September 9th."

Mensa's eyes popped. He struggled to keep the grin off his face. The mere mention of such a scoop gave him a jolt of pleasure. Even if he couldn't use it.

"You've seen it then?" he said to Max.

"Oh sure, I've seen it." They were walking south now, to-ward Max's car.

"I don't suppose I could see it?"

Max laughed. "Like I said, absolutely not. It's in police hands now anyway."

Mensa was indignant. "You know, that's not very clever of them, to lock it up. If you asked some of us we could throw light on it, I'm sure. That last night I expected to see her, at Sam Chow's wake."

Max said nothing. He found the keys to his car and unlocked the passenger door. None of these Queen Street people drove cars—that was his experience. He'd drop him at the subway at St. Clair. He wondered if he'd made a big mistake, telling. He tried to fix it, if he had.

"The thing is, Mensa, I can let you know what's going on, and you can be the first to get the story if we ever learn the truth," he said. "But if you let a word of this slip out before I say so, you're dead in the water. Think of the possibilities. These may be being sent by a kidnapper. She may be trying to get our help. Anything could be going on. You could seriously endanger Ruby if you breathe one word of this."

Mensa got obediently into the passenger seat. His face was a mask. He was suffering agonies. The agony of having extracted information, but only on the promise that he wouldn't use it. It was a pain that went right through his head to his heart. He was going against all his principles here. He was making a promise, and he was going to keep it. He could actually imagine what an extract from the vanished Ruby Mason's diaries would do for his career. It made him tingle all over at the thought of all that glory coming to him. But he knew, with a sick, sinking feeling that what Max said was right. It might harm Ruby to publish now. She might be in danger. It might throw off any plans Dick Nolan had. Mensa's head began to ache, suddenly and splittingly. What a tragedy. A perfect story, and he couldn't use it.

Mensa turned right at Avenue Road and headed down the hill. After Max dropped him, he'd poked around on St. Clair till dark. This was a vista he loved: the broad strip of road heading over the crest of the hill and south, between increasing heights of buildings, cutting through Bloor Street's milky way to where the dark, nested crown of Queen's Park, plugged the thoroughfare, its two small turrets seen as darkness against the illumined night sky. Further down, the real explosion of lights came, and then the dark pool of Lake Ontario. The city was laid out, readable. You could penetrate its latitude and longitude. Night took away the murky bits and made it definite: black or white or colour, compass directions only, a grid-work, clean and without doubt. He walked straight down, almost to the edge of land, and he was home.

The lobby of his building was freezing cold, with wrought-iron garden seats and many hanging baskets of artificial flowers. The rooms smelt of one man, living alone; a woman came in weekly and dusted, but Mensa did not allow her to adjust the piles he made everywhere, of papers and boxes, of sweaters, of shirts in dry-cleaners' wrap. He poured himself a soda water and turned on the television. It was a football game, but that was incidental. He had a habit of talking out loud to himself; he did it while the television was on because it felt like company.

"I'm doing some investigating on a case. You'd like it. Fashion designer disappeared. Cops aren't doing their job," he said. "But I can't use the story. Not yet."

The announcer blared on about yards to go. Mensa went on himself, reviewing the facts, as he knew them, of the case.

"You know," he said finally, standing up to turn down the volume. "You know I've been thinking of writing a book."

Silence.

"Thinking of it. I didn't say I would. The trouble is I kept no notes. I can't remember it all, exactly. And I don't know how to involve the reader, long-term," he said.

He looked at the television screen. Men with shoulders like orange crates cantered about on the field. The story was about Ruby and the world they shared, he knew that. But he didn't know what happened. How could he know, when it wasn't over yet? Unless he decided to make something happen. That was what you called a plot.

"Trouble is I guess you have to have a plot. I guess that's it. Well, maybe not. I may not be making a clear distinction between fiction and fact. If it's just about life, maybe you don't need a plot, he said, after a moment's reflection. But he wasn't at all sure.

Max and Blair sat at a table in the breakfast nook. The back-porch light shone outside the window, illuminating the cold, frozen ground and the scrubby, bare bushes. A few narrow gold leaves clung to the branches, tugged at by wind. Yesterday's snow had gone, leaving a hard, thin ice-coat on the dead grass.

Their plates were pushed to the side. Spaghetti with mussels had left an oil-and-wine glaze on the plates, and a heap of opened shells, as if a feast had been had by seagulls. It was a light meal, in fact, and they still picked at the remains of a green salad, dipping bits of French stick into the oil. A wedge of white cheese slowly diminished as they sliced off bits and ate them.

The house was quiet. Bernie was gone for the weekend. Simplicity was in bed. Blair draped herself lethargically over the tabletop and gazed out the window. Max didn't need to ask her what was wrong. He knew.

"Are you thinking about Ruby?" he said. He put out his hand across the table, touched hers. "Again?"

"It bothers you," said Blair.

"I'm tired of living with a ghost. She's gone. Stop worrying."

Blair jumped. "Who are you to tell me what I should worry about?" Then she relented, resting her cheek on his hand. "I keep thinking she's out on the street somewhere."

"She wouldn't be. Why would she be?"

Blair shrugged, elaborately. "Why any of it?"

"Worry just makes you feel useless," said Max. "If it's so important you should do something. We should do something. Investigate."

Blair rolled her eyes. "That's Dick Nolan's job."

"But is he doing it?"

"Whatever I do is wrong," she said. "If I worry about her you tell me it's wrong. If I don't think about her that's wrong too. I have to imagine her. Otherwise we'll all just forget and she'll never be found."

"You sound as if she's your creation. As if it's up to you to keep her alive."

"Utterly selfish, okay? I just want to be able to call her up on the phone. I want her to be there, down in her studio, even if I'm not on my way down for a visit." Blair lifted her pointed chin off her hands. She stared at Max across the surface of the table. Its blue paint gave her skin a grey cast. Her eyes burned in the midst of the ash, red-rimmed.

"Maybe I can help," he said.

Blair shook her head.

"You never want help. But you launch these appeals," he said. "At least we can talk about it. Reason it through."

"Oh lawyers," said Blair. "I know you and your lawyer tricks."

He promised himself he would not take offence. He pulled her by the hand into the living room. They sat on the wine-coloured couch. Its cover was torn in two places. The cushions were squashed permanently out of shape.

"Listen," he said, "here's a woman who was strong and successful. Her friends are dedicated to that vision. Her family, too. Worked for years to build up a business and made it. Seen as a mentor by many, well-liked by all in her field. Nearly forty. Classic case of having it all."

"So they say," said Blair, grudgingly.

"But we know more. We know fashion's a mean business. You gotta have a new skin every day. You gotta be perfect all the time, which isn't easy, especially when perfect means something different every few weeks. We know now, because of the diary, that she felt just as bad inside as she looked good outside. Her new line was ignored. She was involved with a married man. Maybe she even wanted a kid."

"Max, this is so simple-minded."

"Hear me out," he said. "When Marvin's wife found out about their affair, she thought he'd leave her. But he didn't. So here's when it started to get interesting. Pushed to the limit, proud Ruby finally started making signs she wanted help. Tells her mother over the telephone that she's in trouble. First mistake—the family's star performer isn't supposed to *have* trouble. Mother recommends God—Thanks, Mum. Tells Blair how desperately she wants Marvin. Second mistake—Blair acts shocked and disapproving—Thanks, Blair. Max cancels lunch, and instead of his company offers a little horror story about a woman's suicide—Thanks, Max."

Blair moaned.

Max held up his hand. "Point is not to feel guilty. We're just reviewing facts. Let me continue. She can't turn to Marvin because first of all she's not allowed to phone him, and second of all he's half the problem, so he's not going to be much help solving it. Business problems, like you said. Hard to quantify. But suffice it to say, the lady is not getting what she wants."

"You said it," said Blair.

"So here's the point when she disappears. Either it's done to her, or she does it to herself. Two possibilities. Either it was her idea or it wasn't. If it wasn't, then whose was it? What did they do to her? Where's the body, or at least the ransom note? In the case of foul play, the chief suspect is Marvin. He was tired of her. He was not getting her money, which he wanted. He had money problems, drug problems, maybe he was being hounded by bad characters. But the cops can't find anything on Marvin. Sure he acted like an ass when she disappeared, sure he goes in for flaky therapies, but you can't arrest him for that."

"You've got to consider the diaries, Max."

"Okay, but what do they mean? They might mean she's alive and someone's got her as a hostage. They might mean she's sitting pretty somewhere having a laugh on us. Stranger things have happened. They *might* mean she's dead and the murderer stole them and is just sending them back as a tease. I'll tell you one thing, those diaries have got Dick mad. He can't figure it out." He felt guilty even mentioning them. He hadn't told Blair he'd told Mensa.

Blair smiled ruefully. "That's just what Ruby would like."

"What do they tell us?"

Blair scrunched her eyes shut. The diaries were alive in her head; in Ruby's hoarse, penetrating voice they came back to her at any time, day or night. But what did they say? "The first ones say that she was going through hell, or a breakdown. That she couldn't let anyone know. That she'd lost faith in what she was doing. It's almost as if she was building a case, building a case for—" She stopped.

"Building a case for what?"

"For getting out of it all. Which came next."

"Right," said Max. "But that seemed to be totally spontaneous. And what we've got so far gives us few clues where to look for her."

"Obviously, Oswald."

"But if we talk to Oswald we tip Ruby off. And if she's hiding she'll disappear again. Besides, if the cops haven't got to him yet, they're tapping his phones at least. He's actually in breach of the law, withholding what he knew all along."

Blair sat with her chin her hand. "I still think Oswald's harmless. She just used him for what she wanted and then split."

"You never talk about him. But he was one of you."

"We haven't seen each other for years. There's nothing strange about that."

"Have you been to see him?"

"No," said Blair.

Max waited. She said nothing more. "I think you should go," he said. "To put your mind at rest, if nothing else."

"To see Oswald?"

Max nodded.

Blair sighed. "I think she's out there somewhere. I think I can find her. I don't want to deal with Oswald's psychic fields or whatever."

"In some ways she's more obvious than ever. Marvin claims he's communicating with her regularly from the grave. And the gossip keeps up. Only last week there was a tidbit in Mensa's column. 'Where is Ruby now? It's been six months?'"

"That's Ruby. She's always been useful to people—people with no imagination, people who want to lean somewhere. She wasn't going to get off the hook just by being dead! She still has to be useful to them. So she'll have to provide a story, a vehicle for their fantasies. Become a victim of a man. Or of fashion. Or of life in Toronto," said Blair. "She's not going to get off that easy." Ruby could disappear but she couldn't escape: a depressing thought.

"If there's anyone we should see," she said, "I think it's Marvin. I'm not convinced that he's in the dark. I really want to have a good look at him."

"Well, that's easy," said Max. "We can ask him to come to my office to talk. If we do, you've got to promise me something. You'll try Oswald, and if that comes up a blank, say you've done your bit and lay off. Is it a deal?" said Max.

"Deal," said Blair.

Blair woke up early, at six o'clock. It was dark. She dressed and went to knock on Bernie's door. "I'm going out," she said. "Can you get Sissy to school?"

Now the sky was a twilight blue, infused with promise. The city had the eerie, hectic feel of recovery from a storm. There had been a thaw, the snow had gone, and now rain came in splattery shifts of wind. Blair walked. Her legs had an agenda of their own, to take up the streets, to consume the pavement. She went down Avenue Road. On either side of the wide street, lights were still gaudy. Night-time neon lettering was still alive on buildings; fluorescent lights stared out of empty shops at blank sidewalks. Car lights smeared double in the slick, black, mirror streets.

As she walked, the warm, dark folds of her bedsheets retreated. She imagined other people—their destinations, their mental preparations for meetings, their machinery warming up to meet the barrage of wants. She rounded Queen's Park, fetching as a candy heart. She walked without wondering why, without meeting anyone, without seeing faces, without thinking. She only wanted to cover the ground, to outstrip the rolling anger within her.

Ahead was Canada Life, its weird barometer probe lit, circles of red and white lights running up and down, sending hectic signals from its stout, conical head. Now came the great stone walls of hospitals. Sick Kids', with a perennial cry for money scribbled on its face. From the glass front room of Mount Sinai, crumpled white figures in wheelchairs seemed to be contemplating escape. A thin stream of cloud had been tossed around the towers farther down. The top of the CN Tower was lost. She walked on. It was still early.

At eight-thirty, a frenzy of workers escalated from the subway, pushing Blair back against the windows of shops. She passed the foot of Max's building, but she did not go up. Instead, she walked across to Yonge and headed north. At College, she took refuge in the Happy Face restaurant, open twenty-four hours. There she drank three cups of coffee. Ruby might have done the same. She liked that idea.

Out on the street again she stared across at the corner of Yonge and College, where a great hole in the ground was surrounded by hoarding. A green-shingled clock steeple, survivor of another era, protruded above a mirrored storefront to which it bore no relation. The combined structure looked like one of those folded-paper drawings kids made at pyjama parties. You drew the head, folded the paper, leaving only two lines for the neck visible, and passed it on. Someone else drew the chest, leaving a waist, and so on. Two doors north stood the Zanzibar, a strip club. "The show that never stops. No cover." A painting of a nude woman on the side of the building. To go without cover: Ruby's adventure. Maybe Blair could try it too.

The Zanzibar was the last lapse of taste in a northerly direction. College was a kind of boundary. Buildings were lower here, two or three storeys only. Up the hill, the proprieties of Toronto became visible in Laura Secord shops, tame lingerie displays, men's furnishings. On toward Wellesley the niceties took hold, until, at St. Clair, they would have completely eradicated signs of sin or exuberance. Beyond was the country of Max and Andy's friends, the dread North Toronto. No Ruby there.

She turned her back and walked south again. Now light from an invisible sun mixed with the cloud over Toronto. By the time she reached Queen Street, pink and gold swirls had appeared, a higher, lighter version of Turner's sea skies. Up there were the glass towers which now said Max to her. His world. Gold fronts pleated like fans miraculously held up against the twisted winds that worked their way amongst them. Near the ground, blue windows gave out square white workaday tiles of light. But in the darkened upper floors clouds still moved in and out.

It was nine-thirty now. She was supposed to go up and see

Max, get ready for meeting Marvin. She looked up, into the darkness. Maybe it was always night up there. Maybe howling winds and moonlit clouds sailed in and out of boardrooms and cubicles all day long, thought Blair, but only someone like me, standing on the street, can see them. She crossed the courtyard of the TD Centre, where the two metal cows grazed in sublime indifference. Above, one tower was reduplicated in the glass of another. Down here, her coat swirling about her knees, a young woman walking quickly cut a path across the courtyard: the shortest distance between two points. No more wandering.

She sat on the stone steps. She had tried to walk around it, away from it, but she had come back. Back to Max. Back for a purpose at least for now.

Blair sat in her chair in front of the open door, between Marvin on the couch and Max behind his desk. She was wearing the body-pack Dick Nolan had supplied. She felt improbably brave, and somewhat uncomfortable.

Marvin turned his head to take her in. "I remember you," he said. "Ruby introduced us. In her studio one day. You're the singer."

"Was," said Blair. "When she was. We were together. Yes, we met last fall. Just before she—went."

Marvin looked different now. Then he had been the perfect television executive, in a soft, well-cut suit, his face in profile self-possessed and strong. Only when you looked straight into his face did he seem to fragment, to fall away into pieces. His eyes, mouth and nose were on different planes, like a Picasso face. He wore baggy corduroy pants and a leather jacket, an open-necked shirt. In bleeding earnestness, he looked like a convert to some new age philosophy, which perhaps he was.

"We wanted to ask if you had any hints that Ruby might

just, say, up and disappear?" said Max.

It was hard to tell if Marvin was on anything. Perhaps he always gave the appearance of being in an altered state. He was pale and he sweated; his pupils were hard and dark and agitated.

"I thought you said you knew her!" Marvin's spume flew across the rug. He dipped his head, trying to get his long forelock out of his eyes. "This woman was so beautiful. She was so good. She was such a talent. She had everything going for her. And we were getting married."

"I said I met her. I didn't know her well," murmured Max. "You said you planned to marry. Was she having second thoughts?" It was a provoking remark.

Marvin jumped off the sofa and strode up to Max's desk, seizing the edge, as if he might try to flip it. "We had picked out a house! We were going to make an offer on it."

"Why didn't you?"

Marvin let go of the desk. "We had no money."

Max shrugged. "You set a date?"

"We had a problem. Problem was my wife." Marvin suddenly started chewing a fingernail. "Oh God," he said brokenly, "I'll never get over this. I loved her so much. I loved her." His voice disturbed the still air of the office. "I can't—I can't go on." He went back and dropped on his seat.

"It hasn't been very long. Time will . . ." said Max, wondering what it was he intended to suggest that time would do. Love! What was he talking about? People didn't talk about love in here. He was not a grief counsellor. He dealt with a lot of people after death, but the kind who had trusts and wills were seldom overcome in this way. Calculating and pragmatic, they had spent half their lives in contemplation of the permutations and combinations that would attend the death of their parents or siblings. They tended to fold themselves down on the couch and watch intently the movements of the other relatives in the room, seeking any evidence of advantage or preference. This was different. Everything had prepared him to despise Marvin. But how could he hate someone who was so sad?

Marvin sobbed.

"There, there." Max said the only words that came to mind. He got up and went to the door, grimacing at Maureen to get him a glass of water.

"She would never go away from me on purpose. She never wanted to leave her life. She was never even *sad*." Marvin was now at the window; he put his fist up and pressed it against the glass. Max leaned tensely forward in his chair, praying the man wouldn't punch his way through. As in an airplane, suction might draw him out. It might draw them all out, and down twenty-two storeys.

"What people are saying . . ." Marvin moaned. He turned dramatically, suddenly, from the window to face him. "It's a bloody character assassination, if you ask me. Cops spread all kinds of rumours. About her. About me. They don't do that much searching. That cop is so dumb he can't find evidence of murder so he's claiming she's a runaway, or suicide. *Suicide*, Mr. Ostriker. You gotta understand what that means in her community. When you've found God, you do not do such a thing. *Nobody* believes it's suicide. And if it was, *they* drove her to it. Isn't there a crime like aiding and abetting self-destruction?"

"Who do you mean when you say *they*?" said Blair.

Marvin flicked his head, first to Max, then back, quickly, to Blair. "These people who were after her. Her backers, maybe. I don't know. If I knew who they were I'd go out and kill them. Ruby never told me who they were. She wouldn't. It made me very angry. But it's obvious they're out there. Who? That's for the cops to find out. Why don't they? Put an end to all the rumours. Clear her name."

Marvin was agitated; he fled from the window and dropped into the couch. It was low and the back slanted away. He reached for the coffee table and pulled himself to his feet. His knee banged on the edge of the glass top.

"I just wish the cops would get them," said Marvin. "The guys who've done this. Find out who's done this and *get* them. I can tell you who to start with. Guys she borrowed money from. It's tough to get money to start a business. What do you think? A woman? Selling your own fashion designs?"

Blair knew how Ruby got started. She remembered the bankers who had turned down the loan, three of them. And then the fourth, a woman, gave it to her. Her current backers were a couple of deeply religious Iranians who didn't want to go to parties launching her spring lines. Somehow Blair doubted they were involved. But she said nothing. She was pleased to think the tape was rolling.

"Right, well that's it, isn't it? You start with them, and you find a straight line from them to the drug barons, and a straight line from the drug barons to the cops. Some of those cops taking kickbacks. That's what you find."

"She didn't discuss her finances with you?"

"I knew they were after her. I knew they were pressing her. But she never told me, never told me their names. Who she borrowed the money from."

Max tapped his pencil on his blotter. "Why do you suppose she didn't want you to know her backers?"

Marvin gave an elaborate shrug. Max had asked the question a little too pointedly.

"It's a competitive business. You're getting money from someone, you don't tell the next guy, even if you're about to get married. That's the business. A lot of secrecy. Designs and all. People can steal things. Not that she didn't trust me. But it was a habit by then. She was proud, this lady. She was independent. She didn't want her lover going down to her backers and fighting them off for her."

"I still don't understand who was after her, in your view, and why," said Blair. "Why her backers would be."

"They're ruining me," said Marvin suddenly. "Don't you understand? They got rid of her and now they're using her to get at me! I could sue! The damage is total—personal, professional. I'm ruined." His angry voice slowly became quiet. "I'd like to just get hold of them and sulk them for everything they've got."

"Soak them, you mean?" said Blair. "You see her as a victim. I'm just saying, isn't it possible this whole thing is her idea?"

Marvin didn't answer.

"Let's back up a little," said Max. "You said you wanted to 'clear her name.' You didn't say 'find her.' And maybe you can tell me—what's all this about communication from the grave?"

"She's crossed into spirit," said Marvin. "Energy never dies." He turned a pleading look at Max. "I never understood this stuff until now, myself. But I *have* been able to communicate with her. It's been a great comfort."

Oh dear, thought Max. This was proving to be a challenge. First love. Now spirits. Another difficult subject. He felt a new respect for Andy. Andy regularly handled this kind of work. He walked over to the window and stood as close to it as the toes of his well-buffed oxblood brogues would allow. He pressed his forehead against the glass and tried to look down. He tried this often, mostly when he was alone. This was what it was like to be odd on his own time, apparently. You enter a world of loonies. Where did other people find sponsors for their oddness? The media, apparently. How did you go about making a living being odd? He should ask Marvin. Ruby. Even Blair. They all knew.

"What does that mean? From beyond the grave?" Blair's voice was acid.

Marvin kept his eyes down. He appeared at first not to have heard.

"We're not mocking you," said Max. "We're really, truly

curious. Not totally unspiritual myself you know, even though I am a lawyer. When you want something bad enough, you've got to be prepared to go to any length to get it. I can appreciate you going to that length."

Max raised an eyebrow in Blair's direction, while Marvin opened his cigarette case.

"We have been in contact," he said, "but as I told your friend the cop, we don't talk details. We don't get into arrangements, you know. Spirits can be rather evasive."

"I guess," said Max.

"Is she happy?" said Blair.

"I would say." Marvin smiled at Blair. His was a face like none other. It was not handsome, strangely put together, made of improbable nose, eyes, mouth, all of which seemed to have been looted from other, more attractive beings. But there was a power in it, the power of hunger. Like Ruby's.

Max watched. He began to *see* Marvin, to *know* Marvin's mind. Soaked in dope and booze and suspicion, glazed with sweet talk and manipulation skills, it was still a mind Max knew. It was a draft dodger, a '60s person, displaced, re-treaded, reupholstered—the same mind he'd met at protests outside the U.S. consulate, in soup kitchens, even in jail. Stubborn, self-righteous, cunning: a survivor, with a good line of chat and adjustable principles.

"I'm careful what I say about this. People misunderstand, okay? There's a lot of talk about voodoo. How Ruby went through a voodoo ceremony to make me fall in love with her. How I used witches and curses to try to get my wife to leave me. It's all crap."

"But you do use a medium, or spirits, or—I don't know," said Blair.

"Oswald," said Marvin with dignity.

"Oswald?" said Blair. "Somehow I can't think of him as a spiritualist. To me he's just—a crazy pianist."

Marvin was on his feet now, moving restlessly. "I can't

explain it to you," he said. "You've gotta see for yourself."

Max pressed his fists behind him against the window pane. He pushed himself away from the edge. He thought about all this searching and scouring and calling of names. It was all going back to the beginning. Oswald, Blair, Ruby—even himself. Next would be Philip. It was a circle. Back to the beginning. Events had their own direction. He felt quiet inside, resigned. Maybe the story of Ruby didn't need their detective work. Maybe it would tell itself.

"You know what we've gotta do, Marvin? And Blair?"

"What?" Marvin barely paused in his prowl around the office.

"We've gotta give up."

Marvin did not look receptive to the idea. Neither did Blair.

"Give up, let down, give in. She's gone. Let her go. And then maybe she'll come back." He hoped it wasn't Kahlil Gibran he was quoting here. "You know? Hey, just accept, for the moment, that this is where we are. All your agitating and gyrating and talking to her from the grave is just fighting it. Talk about energy. Your energy should go to healing yourself, since you're suffering. Then, if she shows up again, you'll be there for her. You owe it to Ruby. Let it go. Until something happens. I have a feeling something will happen." Max looked around. No one seemed to like what he said.

Blair watched Marvin stalk out the door.

"I feel I should go right out and wash my hands," she said.

"He didn't kill her," said Max. "He may be a sleaze, but he's not a murderer. I read him clear as a bell. He doesn't know anything. He's just trying to get people off his tail. He's a harmless, classic, double-life character, what do you call them?"

"Dissembler?" said Blair. "We'll see what Nolan thinks." She pulled the body-pack out from under her shirt. "Maybe I am too. Dissembling was surprisingly easy."

"Yeah," said Max. "Yeah. We can play detective. We can make ourselves feel good. But I have a feeling. We're not going to find her. We're not going to find her this way."

"I don't know how you can be so sure."

"Call it my woman's intuition." Max had said what he meant to say. He was satisfied. He'd done the investigating he wanted to do. It hadn't lasted long, it was true. But he knew, he felt, and he trusted his feelings, that this was not the way. The only problem that remained was to convince Blair of the same thing.

"There's one more thing I want to do," said Blair slowly. "I don't know why it's taken me so long."

"What's that?" He knew what she was going to say.

"Oswald," she said. "I'm going to go see Oswald."

14

Where Were You When the Parade Went By?

Rachel, Jessica, Kate, Maria and Leslie, you go with Ms. Bowker. Simplicity? Do you want to be in your mother's group?"

Sissy nodded mutely. She slid sideways through the group of jostling, giggling children to lean against Blair's leg. Across Miss Boggs's forehead, a fine line of displeasure appeared.

Blair looked over her charges; they all had scarves and mitts, their snowsuits were zipped up. Four similar groups, led by other parent volunteers, set off toward the St. Clair streetcar stop. Hers was noisy and out of line. The other mothers were clearly more authoritative.

"Hold hands with a buddy! We're going!" she cried.

They paired up, leaving Simplicity alone. Mother and daughter grasped each other's hand. Rachel and Kate began to run ahead, sliding on the icy parking lot.

"That's not a good idea," cried Blair, futilely. She dragged Sissy as quickly as she could. An outraged howl rang in the cold air; ahead, Rachel had fallen on her back. Blair ran to help her up. It was field-trip day; they were going to Riverdale Farm, where they would have a sleigh ride. It was the worst day of winter so far; snow was already falling thickly and the wind was rising.

The streetcar slid nobly out of the white whirls and clanked to a halt. Twenty-five kids ran down the aisle and scrambled into seats. Their breath clouded the old sliding windows. Blair's section began to quarrel over seats, who got to sit next to whom. Blair saw Miss Boggs's serene profile riding up next to the driver, staring across the car, without reference to where this noise was coming from. Clearly, today she regarded all problems as the mothers' responsibility.

"What seems to be the trouble?" said Blair.

Leslie stood in the aisle, weeping. "Maria took my seat! I wanted to sit beside Rachel."

Maria, victorious, bounced gleefully in the seat. Her hat and gloves and scarf were in a puddle of melting snow on the floor. Meanwhile Rachel, prim and ferocious, maintained her position, one hand gripping the window ledge, the other the seat in front.

"Leslie, you come and sit with us," said Blair. She put the child between herself and Simplicity: perhaps the two could be buddies today? But Leslie was resentful of being reft from Rachel. And Sissy gave her an evil stare and then covered her face with her hands.

"Please, only two people on a seat," Miss Boggs called over the heads of the girls. "You'll have to move one of those girls! Or yourself!"

Blair stood up and gripped the pole. Two more stops to Yonge Street. She looked out at the traffic. There seemed to be very little of it. There was ice on the road, too. Some cars were spinning their wheels. One lost control as she watched, and slid across the streetcar tracks behind them, settling gently against the curb. Her eyes met those of another "parent" volunteer.

"Do you suppose there's some kind of storm warning out? I didn't catch the weather this morning."

The other mother nodded. "Miss Boggs seemed very determined to go."

When they emerged from the underground stairs, the wind struck harder than ever, whipping small, damp snow beads into the children's faces. The mothers stood around readjusting mitts and toques and fur-trimmed hoods. Then they all set out, like soldiers into the frozen waste, on the four-block walk to the farm.

"Most of it is inside," insisted Miss Boggs, puffing in the wind. "There are chicks and little lambs and hot apple cider. And of course the sleigh ride."

"I want to go home," said a child, clearly. Either snow or tears made tracks down her face.

"Me too."

"No!" exclaimed Miss Boggs. "This is an excursion! It's exciting!" The children turned doubtfully into the wind again. "We're not going back to that school," asserted Miss Boggs. Then she marched up to walk with the children in the lead.

"She just wants to get out of that classroom for a day," one mother said.

"Wouldn't you?" said another.

The twenty-five children and six women plodded, face down in the gale, toward the entrance to Riverdale Farm. Each street they passed was plugged with stalled cars and devoid of people. Jessica had come away with no hat. Her hair was frozen stiff and picked out with beads of icy snow. Miss Boggs produced a plastic bag from her purse and tied it around the child's head. The sleet as it fell rattled mercilessly on the stiff, cold plastic.

When the gates of the zoo came into sight, the hardier children began to run. The others simply trudged, not fighting or laughing any more, animated only by the sight of the end. Sissy clung grimly to Blair's hand.

Inside, the little stable was warmed by an electric heater. There were lambs and pigs and chickens; old-fashioned cornhusk dolls and cardboard crèche figures. The cows and ponies lent their thick, bristled necks for petting. There was nowhere to sit but in the straw. Everyone opened their coats and tried to warm up. Blair took her woollen mitts and tried to dry Jessica's wet hair. The child was flushed, and her nose was running. Through the wide stable doors the snow was visible, blowing in long, horizontal sheets.

"Perhaps we should be heading back?" Blair ventured to Miss Boggs.

"Oh no, we've got the sleigh ride!"

"Sleigh ride? They'll freeze."

"No they won't. They'll be cosy as can be, tucked in the hay." Miss Boggs's face glowed as she cherished the image.

With scarcely a murmur, the mothers divided the group in two. Sissy was to go in the first half, with Rachel. At the last minute, Leslie burst in and tried to push Simplicity out of the way. Sissy turned to her and put her two hands around her neck. She squeezed. Leslie screamed. Sissy squeezed harder. Leslie's eyes popped in terror. "I hate you," said Sissy. "You're mean mean mean." A nearby mother pried Sissy's hands off Leslie's neck. Both girls wailed.

"Say you're sorry, Simplicity. You didn't mean to hurt Leslie."

"Yes I did. I hate her! She's mean!" Sissy's voice had never been so loud. "I hate her and I think I will kill her," Sissy announced. Leslie was sobbing. A dozen arms reached out to comfort her. Sissy planted her feet apart and defiantly refused to be moved.

"Leslie did *push* Simplicity," said Blair. Nobody heard. "Maybe if Leslie apologized too—?" Social mores dictate against choking other children. Reluctantly, she told Sissy not to do that again.

The incident was forgotten as Sissy was lifted onto the wagon by a burly farm assistant with frost on his moustache. She rolled into the hay and buried her face. Rachel and the others started out the trip sitting on the edge, dangling their feet, their scarves pulled up over their eyes. With jangling bells and much waving, the sleigh set off. The other half of the class remained behind. Ten minutes became fifteen, fifteen became twenty. Poking her head out the door of the stable, Blair saw the grey, lumbering vehicle approach. The horse had been replaced by a tractor. The driver was covered in ice. The children were invisible, hiding under rugs in the straw.

The mothers ran to dig out their children, like so many Easter eggs in grass, neon-coloured, and stiff.

"What happened to the horse?" said Blair.

"Weather's too bad for horses," said the driver.

"This is madness, we really must go home."

Miss Boggs was standing right behind Blair. "But the second group has not had its turn!"

Blair faced her. The teacher's false jollity made her face like glue. "May I call you Jasmine?" said Blair, not waiting for an answer. "Maybe the second group *doesn't want* its turn. And we've got to think about getting back. The traffic may just come to a complete *halt*."

Jasmine pushed out her chin. She clapped her hands. "Come, children. Second group!"

Sissy stood beside her mother watching the kids laugh as they were swung onto the sleigh.

"Well, they look as if they do want to go," said Blair.

"That's because they don't know how much fun they're *not* going to have," said Simplicity, with great dignity.

Blair took Sissy inside. They stood next to the electric heater. The pigs rolled and squealed on the other side of the board partition, and they could hear the cow lowing. "You're funny," said Blair to Sissy. "You're very very funny and I love you. I should be mad at you for trying to choke Leslie but I'm not. I suppose I'm a lousy mother. But I thought it looked good on you."

Sissy smiled wanly.

"This is not a good field trip," she said. "I am not having a fun day." She kept her eye on Miss Boggs and maintained a good distance.

When the second group of children returned, the mothers protested so loudly that Miss Boggs consented to leave. But it was too early to go back to school, she said. It was only one o'clock. They struggled back to the subway and ate their sandwiches on the train going up to Yorkdale. Then they got off and went to Woolworth's, where they sat at a lunch counter. The mothers bought the kids plates of french-fries with gravy, and hot chocolate. As they trudged, finally, back to the train, the children began to fight. At least six of the girls were crying. Miss Boggs walked twenty feet ahead of them through the mall, aiming for the subway stop. Blair gathered her last atom of strength and set out to separate the brawlers.

"Well, that was the field trip from hell," said Blair to Bernie, home at last and taking off her dripping clothes. "Some school you've got, Sissy. But at least you're learning how to fight back."

"Miss Boggs is not a good teacher," said Bernie. "I watch her. She's two-faced. Always big smile up front, but when mothers gone—she's *mean*."

"I don't need to go to school, Mummy," said Simplicity. "I could stay home and be a free worker like you. And Bernie."

"Freelance, you mean." Although lately it meant she didn't work at all. "You can't do that until you're older."

Blair and Simplicity drove up to the aluminum door of Philip's studio. The van was outside, so she knew he was home. The back gardens surrounding the converted garage were exposed now, the insulbrick lean-tos behind neighbouring houses stripped of their bushy disguise. She struggled out of the car in her tight skirt and pulled up the garage door handle. The door flew over her head, revealing Philip, at his counter, polishing what looked like real guns.

With her entry came the wind and the snow. Simplicity raced up to Philip's feet and jumped up for a hug.

"Shut that," said Philip. Blair pushed the door. "You shouldn't bring her here. I've gotta get these guns ready to go."

"Can't you even give us a drink?"

He grimaced furiously over his arsenal. "I don't *let* my friends drop in here in the middle of the day. This place is dangerous."

"I need to talk. Please, Philip."

Philip groaned, and his pale eyes behind the glasses swam with irritation. But, one by one, he put the guns on a high shelf. They had coffee sitting in the front seat of the van with both doors open. Sissy took her juice-box upstairs to watch cartoons. Philip's round, gold-rimmed glasses winked in the fading light.

"Here you are plotting how to fake a death," said Blair suddenly.

"These guns are not fake. They are real."

"They are not."

"Of course they are. I have a permit to carry them. I can shoot them. In film, my dear, the people may be dummies, but the weapons are the real thing."

"Disgusting," said Blair, moving away from that side of the room.

"Hey! It's not. It's what I do."

"Doesn't it strike you as odd?"

"It strikes me as very odd that people get up and put on suits and go and sit all day in little rooms high over Bay Street. Doing people's wills."

Blair smiled at her coffee mug. She took her finger and

wiped off the smear of lipstick. "You ought to meet Max, just once. You'd like him," she said.

Philip looked artfully astonished. "Who's talking about Max? Anyway, I did meet him. Twenty years ago. I got his number then, I've got it now."

"Dear Philip," said Blair, putting out her hand to touch him. "If it wasn't you talking I'd think you were jealous. What I meant was odd was that Ruby maybe really did die, and there's no body to show for it. No death in the material sense of the word. While you're sitting here with the means to create deaths where there was no life to begin with."

"She's been vaporized," said Philip. "I can't do that."

"Why not?" said Blair.

"It's not easy to do away with a real body. Much easier to be like me, make a fake, and then destroy. The real stuff doesn't decompose that great. Hard to get rid of. Heavy. Staining. Smells. Very tough. Plus, in real life, there's always somebody watching. Not like in the movies, where you can always go to an empty set. If she got away clean like that, it was a professional job," Philip said, with something like satisfaction.

That's what Blair had said about Marvin, with his affairs. Professional. It was an evil word. There *were* these professionals, lurking amongst the rest of them, hopeless amateurs giving themselves away by their intense passions.

"Don't you think it's ironic though?"

"Ironic is your refuge, Blair. I don't brook irony. It's either a comedy or straight horror." Philip stared at a poster on the wall for *Chainsaw Workout—The Video*. It had a picture of a woman in aerobic exercise tights waving a blood-stained saw.

"I disagree. There's never just one or the other. They're all mixed together. I say it's ironic," she said, standing up and reaching for her bag, "that we were all together in Hearts of Flame, and now she's disappeared and maybe dead without a body, and you're busy concocting dead bodies to scare us, and probably we should be scared just by our ordinary lives."

Philip made a grimace. "I'm the first to admit that. Ordinary life terrifies me."

"And it's ironic," said Blair, "that now I'm seeing Max. It makes me think we're still connected. That Ruby's disappearance has to do with links we've almost forgotten. The four of us—five, with Max—"

"He wasn't one of us." Philip's voice cut.

"No, but he was *there*." Blair remembered her first vision of him, standing by the edge of the gravel parking lot in the mountain twilight, his tall, curly-haired figure cast darker before the forest. "People come into your life at crucial times. You move on, and they seem to be gone, forever. But then the surface is disturbed, and you can see them, in the running current of your life, plain as daylight." Blair felt helpless to explain. She felt they were all cast, coloured and named at the same time. They were all connected. "You hate Max," she said unhappily. "For no good reason."

Philip said, "Hmmph."

"Look what I brought." From her bag she pulled out yellowed newspaper cuttings. She spread them on Philip's table. "Hearts of Flame," she said.

She pulled out more. Publicity photographs of twenty years ago. Four people, two men and two women, with huge heads of hair and dark-circled eyes, caught in action, stilled by the camera, to some exaggerated mime gesture—a gesture of villainy, a gesture of holiness, a gesture of innocence, for all that. She spread them all around on Philip's table. He put down his charcoal and came over. Together, the two of them put their heads over the table.

Here was Ruby, outdoors, in a field by the highway south of Edmonton. Her round face was open, and streaked with sun and shadow. Her ankle socks, gored skirt and sweater set made her look like a strange visitor from 1940. Blair was a classic '60s hippie, in jeans and fringed jacket, her nearly white hair long, ironed and spread over her breasts. Philip was clutching the neck of his bass as if he would strangle it, the fringe of his hair flying around in the wind like a frazzled halo. And Oswald—tiny, perfect Oswald, the wizard, they called him—was not looking at the camera. He bent over the keyboard they'd pushed out onto the grass.

When Simplicity came downstairs, Blair was laughing, but she looked as if she had been crying. Her make-up was rubbed off and made dark smudges under her eyes. Philip was reading newspaper clippings.

Simplicity picked up one photograph. Blair was right in the centre of it, wearing a black miniskirt, black tights and a black turtleneck. The even curtain of her hair broke over her shoulders. They examined it together. Blair did not recognize herself. She could not put herself back into that body. She could not smile like that, or throw her head back and let the voice pour out. But she could feel exactly the guitar strap's tug on her hair, how she had to swing it back, to get it out of the way, sometimes swatting the next person to her with a tail of dry, blond hair.

"Recognize anyone else?" Blair said.

"There's Ruby."

Ruby's hair was long and frizzy then, left loose. She was sitting in a rocking chair.

"Didn't she play an instrument?"

"Sometimes she picked up a tambourine, whacked it against her right thigh and sang harmony. Badly," said Philip.

They laughed harder.

"What did Philip do?"

"He was our stage manager. He made sure we stood in the right place and sang the right thing. He designed the lighting and the sound. And he wrote some of the songs too. He played that big stand-up bass there."

"Do you still write songs?"

"No," said Blair. "None of us do."

"Who's that?"

"Oswald," said Philip and Blair together.

He was small and neat, his luminous, yellow-white skin, the precision of his *being* obvious. He stood a little distance from the others.

"You never talk about him."

"I saw him on TV," said Blair.

"What does he do on TV?" said Sissy.

"Talks about what he's found out in the polls. You know, found out about all of us. His research material. His *subjects*. Oswald always wanted to be a king and have subjects, didn't he? As I watched him I realized something," Blair said, and paused. "People stop speaking the truth as they get older."

Philip blinked but he did not turn his head.

"There was our Oswald, the truth-teller. He wouldn't sing political songs because they didn't give both sides. Remember how he wanted to expose all the hypocrisy, to show up all the corporate heads as liars? He was so strict about *accuracy*. He even disapproved of our press releases because he said we exaggerated attendance figures. Now you should hear him. He talks gobbledygook. He says 'change' is a 'management problem.' I remember he said something about how the recession gave us 'post-trauma aggression.'"

"This surprises you?"

"Oswald? You're the one who said he was so quantitative he couldn't even masturbate. Now he 'massages' issues to make them palatable. He 'crunches' numbers to suit his needs."

"He's no different than anyone else," said Philip, wearily.

"Well I thought he was. I thought we all were."

"At some point the desire to be famous and powerful outweighs the desire to be fair, and tell the truth."

"Did he want it so much?"

"Of course he did. That's why he got us into that bad contract with his friend, now your friend, Max. That's why our tour was cancelled. That's why Hearts of Flame went nowhere. *He wanted it too much.*"

"I guess we all wanted it pretty badly," she said. "For Christ's sake, I don't want to quarrel with you. Can't I just talk? Maybe you know all this already." Sissy was watching; she heard the voices rise. "Go upstairs, please, Sissy," said Blair.

"You're naive," said Philip, gesturing at the pictures. "You're like we were then. It's like you've all of a sudden discovered that grown-ups tell lies. Where were you when the parade went by? You were so out of it. You didn't think the way the rest of us did."

"All right, I'm slow. All right, I've finally understood the '60s. It's only twenty years later. I was young at the time," said Blair, making it a joke. "Is it too late?"

"Let's just say I'm not bowled over by your insight," said Philip, bitterly. "Like I say, the parade's gone by. Most people have rejected this lovely thing called truth themselves. But not you. You have to make things hard for yourself by discovering now what is essentially an affectation of the young." He returned to his guns.

"All right," she said, "all right. It's true. I didn't want to be a rebel. I couldn't see the world, and all that lay ahead, as evil. I couldn't afford to. I wanted it too much."

"You couldn't see anyone as a villain except the man who loved you," said Philip. He had a soft cloth in his hand; he buffed the coal-coloured barrel of a gun.

"And who was that?" said Blair, slowly. He said nothing, and she was glad. She walked backwards, away from him.

"You were all different from me," she said, lamely. Philip had seen his father as a liar for his whole life. And Ruby was determined to leave her family in the dust. Oswald seemed to have sprung up fully grown from some experimental farm; there had been no hint of background in him. He really *was* a wizard, he and his destiny reform. His first success had been himself.

"I couldn't get angry. *There was no one I could do without.*" It was true, until she had Simplicity. Then suddenly she could do without them all. She leaned over the photographs. Once again she looked into her own blank face, the face of the uninitiated. It was as difficult to retrieve the Blair of 1969 as it was to retrieve Ruby of three months ago. Perhaps they had both begun to disappear, when this picture was taken. Perhaps all of life was a disappearance, she thought, a retreat from the person we became at some early peak.

"All right," said Philip. "Why did you bring that stuff? What do you want?"

"I want us to go and see Oswald."

Philip sighed. He was putting the guns in little muslin bags.

"Oh what for, Blair? You just said she was gone, it was gone, we were gone. He's—"

"We haven't even talked to him about it. He saw her. She consulted him."

"The cops will have talked to him."

"I know, but *we* should. What's the harm?"

Philip shrugged. "Stirring it all up." But he meant more.

"Ruby probably never meant you to go through all this," said Philip.

"Of course she did."

"You take everything so personally."

"People who disappear expect to be looked for. Just like people who commit suicide expect their friends to suffer," said Blair. She stood up, walked over and kicked the bottom of the garage door. The sound reverberated like a struck snare drum. "As disappearances go, three months is a long one. Most that last longer than one month are permanent, that's what Nolan said.

"There are murders and suicides that are never proven because no body is found. Those are the most difficult, the cops say, because relatives are left in limbo. Some people spend years searching. Some do everything they can to convince themselves that he or she is truly dead, because they can't stand it any more. They burn their clothes and clean out their rooms, have ceremonies to say goodbye, to grieve, to have it over with. Then there are the families and friends who keep the kettle on for tea, acting as if old what's-her-name has just gone out for a stroll.

"Police keep telling me, I'm not the family. I should take my lead from the family. You know, like, it's *their* tragedy, not mine. As if someone could own it. But Ruby's family is not behaving in a rational way. And why should they? How could they? Today they're convinced she's been murdered, yesterday they talk like she's taken a holiday to the islands while neglecting to mention it.

"This morning, early, I woke up imagining she floated up from the bottom of the lake. The other day I thought I saw her in a telephone ad on TV. Before that, I had a perfect mental picture of her lying in the ravine on her side, having taken an overdose of Marvin's drugs. Even Bernie's dreaming about her now."

Philip wasn't saying anything at all. His face was frozen into an expression of pain, as if he were being forced to undergo surgery without anaesthetic.

"There's nothing we can do."

"We can go to see Oswald."

"Oh, Oswald! He told her what she wanted to hear. He hypnotized her, or whatever the latest new age trick was. She was a perfect sucker for transformations. She became whoever people wanted her to be," said Philip. "On the outside."

"She had a heart like iron," said Blair. "She never faltered. She only hid. And then sometimes you caught her off guard. That was what was so shocking about that lunch we had on Queen Street. Something triggered her into being her, and it scared us both half to death."

Philip was lost in unwelcome memory.

"I want to go see Oswald, Philip. Come with me."

Philip placed his guns in a sports bag. He was taking them somewhere. To make a television show where people pulled them out and threatened each other with death. Real guns, pretend death. He handled them gently, as if he loved them. His face was a mask.

"Don't you remember what happened in the end?" he said.

"Of course I remember. I just think it's been too long to blame him. Or Ruby," she said. "Maybe it was inevitable. Maybe we'd never have made it anyway. I think we were unfair to him. We were all just kids. Anyone could have been ripped off. You're so angry, Philip. Why are you still so angry?"

Philip cleared his throat; his eyebrows rose, wrinkling his large forehead, and then fell down again. He looked about to refuse her, but he never did. There was a pause in which she wondered, was this the time?

"I don't want to talk to Oswald," he said, mildly.

"Just come and watch him then. He's still a performer. That's all he's doing, just a new act," she said.

"How can we watch him?" said Philip.

"I'll find out." Blair grinned, and slapped his palm. They were on.

"The things you make me do," said Philip with resignation.

In the oval of plaster in the ballroom ceiling, a bare-shouldered goddess attempted to rein in the goose that pulled her chariot. Blair and Philip paid their twenty-five dollars, grumbling, and took seats at a table near the stage, almost under the microphone. They could look through white tablecloths on the platform tables to the sagging curtains behind. The wallpaper was mildewed, the draperies dragging with age. They were at a meeting of the Empire Club, in the Royal York Hotel. Oswald would be speaking. Philip had come under duress, with his trick handcuffs for protection.

In the audience, the club members dominated, men in blue suits and women in blue hair. In their midst were the glamourati, in skinny leggings and crushed velvet hats, black leather and dark glasses. It was hard to tell who was a follower and who was not. Both wackos and WASPs were among his clientele, so Oswald claimed. They all waited patiently for the wizard.

To a scratchy trumpet fanfare the head table filed in. Behind the cleric in his round, white collar, and in front of the grey-haired mandarin, Oswald marched; he was so short that his stiffly moussed hair bobbed beneath the shoulder blades of the man in front of him. When the head table was seated, and grace had been said, elderly male waiters in red vests ran out of the wings carrying plates of shrivelled brussels sprouts and leathery roast beef with gravy.

The clink of table silver and ice cubes in glasses was brought to silence when the chairman stood.

"Ladies and gentlemen. Today our guest is a man who has changed the course of his life. And perhaps ours. Former pollster, now spiritualist, Oswald Yakibuchi was known to us as the man who moved polling into the twenty-first century. But not satisfied to test public opinion and advise leaders, Mr. Yakibuchi followed his instincts. You are about to meet a man who has his feet firmly on scientific principles, and his head in the clouds. He is tuned to music of the spheres in more than one way—we understand he is still very much involved with the contemporary music scene and can often be found in a recording studio . . ."

Oswald stepped to the microphone in a full embrace of applause. He adjusted it downward, almost to the level of the podium. His apple-bright face, small, brown eyes and even teeth were much as they had been at twenty. Only his hair was revised. It stood out radially from his head in all directions, apparently as firm as a brush; a tiny braid emerged from somewhere near the nape of his neck and lay on his shoulder, tied with a black ribbon. He wore an Indian silk jacket, an open-necked shirt, pale-grey pants.

"Ladies and gentlemen," he began. "Where there's a wall, I leap over. Where there's a vacuum, I move to fill it." His voice was the surprise—huge, magnetic, it seemed to rattle his small frame with its exit.

"I learned, as a social analyst, that we can get information now on just about everything. Find out when Canadians make love, and how often, and how. We can get the figures accurate to plus or minus 3.3 percentage points, 95 percent of the time." There was a scattering of polite titters in the room.

"But what did we do with this knowledge? Analyse those figures, 'crunch' the data? No one could crunch numbers the way I do. But at the end, what do we know? We know how many beds we have. We know who is sleeping in them. But we don't know the dream. And so, we really know nothing."

Blair and Philip sat wordless, watching him, watching for who he had been.

Delicate hands waving over his head, Oswald played the penitent Faust. He was the rationalist reformed. He confessed to his past tricks. He described how, to get the response he wanted, he "embedded" key questions in a set of questions leading one way or another. By adjusting the phrasing he could cause people to say yes, or no. He told some things he knew about how people thought. Answers were salad vegetables, he "crunched" them, "squeezed" them and "spun" them. Sometimes he doctored them, too.

"I confess," said Oswald, "I have been a 'brain' and a 'pointyhead'; I prided myself that my scientific basis could not be challenged. But I have mastered this vanity in myself. I'm here to tell you pure numbers have no meaning for me."

The audience was rapt, titillated by his account of the powers of science, persuaded of its final impotence to deliver. Oswald spoke of the turning point in his life, away from materialism, manipulation, toward the spirit. *Now* he would poll the afterlife, do taste-testing for the beyond. He began to give examples of metaphysical miracles—conversations with the dead, recollections of previous lives, destiny reform. He spoke about music, how he had felt alien to Western sounds at first, but had learned to love them. Pure sound now, not melody, involved him. He had a little shack he went to, he said, off in the wilderness, where he was completely alone, no one around for one hundred miles in any direction, where he listened to sound, and made recordings of wind, ice, water and the spirit world.

From Blair and Philip's table, nearly under the platform, Oswald's head was barely visible over the podium. He appeared not to see them. When he drew to the end of his speech, people pushed in their chairs and lifted their coats off the racks. There were no questions. He'd been a hit, entertaining, but he appeared to have no immediate converts in the crowd. Philip made for the door. Blair caught his coat sleeve. "You're staying," she said. Oswald was autographing books, bent over an opened hardcover, seated behind a broad table. She stopped in front of him.

"Hi, Oswald," she said, to the top of his bristling head.

He did not look up, but finished the flourish on his name: *Oswald Yakibuchi*.

"I saw you out there," he said, unsmiling. Then he stood up to shake her hand. His hand was cold.

Oswald, Philip and Blair walked up Yonge Street toward Oswald's office. Oswald wanted the exercise. Philip lagged behind, unwilling, sulky. Their quarry walked so fast, the pavement flashing between his short legs, that Blair and Philip were forced to run, periodically, to keep up.

"It's been a long time," she panted. "Maybe fifteen years?"

"We bumped into each other in a restaurant, when you first came to Toronto," said Oswald. Gently reminding her, he implied that despite his apparent indifference, he remembered what she did not.

Blair remembered now. He was with an improbably tall, thin, blond woman who looked like a model. "But we didn't really talk."

"No," said Oswald. "There was very little to say." He did not seem surprised to see them, pleased or even displeased. Perhaps, if anything, he was gratified: an expectation fulfilled. He thought we would come, and now we've come, Blair thought. He's been prepared for this.

They walked on, breathing quickly. Philip scowled at the holes in the sidewalk, the orange- and red-striped construction pylons on the road.

"I'm sorry we fell out of touch. Hearts of Flame is important to me. More than ever," said Blair. "Now that the world has forgotten us," she said ruefully. Well, some more than others. She bet no one said to Oswald, "Can you tell us one thing to make yourself interesting?"

"There is a greater past than that of our small, inconsequential lives," said Oswald.

Blair laughed. "Mine may be small, but it's the only life I've got. Surely you believe in friends."

"Is that what we were?"

The question remained unanswered as they flew up Yonge Street, dodging window-shoppers who dawdled three abreast. After half an hour's exertion, hot, with coats flying open, they were above Wellesley. They swept through the lobby of Integer, Inc. Oswald asked the receptionist to take their coats. Then he gave his curious, Eastern-style bow and backed away, asking them to wait in the boardroom.

The boardroom was long and narrow, with a bare, rectangular table lined with chairs. It was like any other, except for one thing: only three walls were solid, the fourth was glass. Behind the glass wall was a one-way window and a sound room.

"This is where they sit and study people," Philip said to Blair. He had begun to cheer up. "It's absolutely ghoulish." He went out and entered the sound room. A flick of the light-switch revealed him; he turned it off and was gone. "Talk," he said, his voice entering the room through a microphone.

Blair sat at the table. "I am lost and seeking direction. Help me move into oneness," she said, in sepulchral tones.

The mikes were subtle, in the walls. Her voice was sucked away. Philip's hollow laugh returned from behind the darkened glass window. "I see you," he said. "I hear your voice. I see you isolated for examination: Blair on a glass slide. Blair as specimen."

"I'll tell you what. Oswald's not a spiritualist, he's a vivisectionist," said Philip, reappearing in the boardroom. "He's a voyeur."

Oswald appeared in the door.

"I guess you have to do this," said Blair, guiltily. "To study people? Is that it?"

Oswald inclined his head. "This is where we used to hold our focus groups. Now I use them for recall sessions. It's very useful to make a recording of what happens, whether with a medium or a channel or a trance. I can often get an image, on the screen, if another dimension comes into play. My equipment is highly sensitive. We have actually videotaped spirit mediums."

Blair and Oswald sat down at the long, bare table.

"It's ugly," said Philip. "Satisfying curiosity but blocking out the feeling." He rapped his knuckles on the one-way glass. "More mirrors," he said to Blair, and laughed with hostility.

"You say old friends are necessary to you, but this is not

simply a friendly visit," said Oswald. His manicured nails were visible, his hands laid out on the table, motionless.

"It's not," said Philip, still on his feet.

"We want to talk about Ruby," said Blair.

"Of course." Oswald dipped his head, courteously, and waited.

Philip scowled. "The great panjandrum," he said. "Knock it off, Oswald, it's only us."

Oswald cocked his head further and raised one eyebrow, as if he did not understand the language being spoken.

"We're not—you know, suspicious of you. We just—*I* just—wanted to talk about it. Because she disappeared, and maybe she's dead. We need to come together. All of us, from the old times." Blair tried not to plead. She was certain he wouldn't—couldn't—tell them what he knew.

"The Ruby I saw here was not the same Ruby from Hearts of Flame," Oswald said finally. "She was a client. You must understand. It was purely professional."

"She always liked you," said Philip, his voice cutting into the air.

Oswald acknowledged this first speech with a small nod. "We were outcasts together. That is a powerful bond." Oswald did not look at either of them. "My parents lost everything when they went to the camps. I was born after; I had to make my own way. Ruby was the same. You were different, both of you. Everything was there to make life easy for you."

"I heard you two were married in a previous life?" Philip was openly scoffing. He pulled a chair out from the table and kicked the legs of the chair beside him out of his way.

"This was a memory Ruby was able to capture, through the skills of our channel. Normally it would fall into client confidentiality, but in this case the newspapers found out," said Oswald, delicately.

"What is a channel, or who?"

"A channel is a person who can be an instrument of communication for entities from other dimensions. Like a telephone," said Oswald, with a trace of condescension.

Philip groaned.

Oswald shrugged. "It's difficult to describe what we do to overly rational people. Easier just not to mention it."

"But Marvin knew. Marvin came here too. And Audrey knew."

"I have a certain following," said Oswald, allowing the first luminous smile to cross his pale lips. He had the same intensity that had made him the most admired, but least liked member of the group.

"You always did," said Blair. "You're the biggest star of all of us. Who'd have thought?"

Oswald frowned. "And who would you have picked?" he said.

Blair stopped. She took in a short breath. So that was it.

"We all thought we'd be famous. Ruby *was* a little, Philip's got a good business at least. I'm nothing," she said lightly. "But you—"

"Perhaps I have sold out," said Oswald, politely.

"Perhaps we all have."

"Perhaps there are no buyers," said Philip.

Finally they laughed. Blair looked at the one-way glass. She wondered if they were being listened to.

"So do you know anything?" she said.

"Anything? About what?"

"About Ruby?"

"That depends," said Oswald.

"On what?"

"On the level of knowledge you're interested in. In pure fact, I have nothing to offer. But there are other kinds of knowledge. I know, for instance, that she has not been physically harmed. If she had been, I'd have heard the screaming and felt the pain. This does not necessarily mean she's alive. There's always the chance she went to death willingly."

"That's comforting," said Blair. She wasn't really joking.

"I know that she exists, somewhere, because we have made contact. Whether she has gone over to spirit, or to another dimension, I don't know."

His face was smooth and still. Lies as well as truth could be spoken that way.

"But why?" said Blair.

Oswald got up from the table and walked up and down on the other side of the room. "Ruby was very very tired. She was constantly fighting against time. She couldn't let up, she couldn't stop. She was always *on*. Always working against time. Rushing to get her samples made, ordering fabric, checking out the factory to make sure it was all done right. And thinking, planning, to stay ahead of each trend, of each season. Then, in her own body, it was the same. The fight against time. Against life, really. She needed to rest. That's why she came to me."

"I thought she'd have you doing market research on what people wanted to wear," said Philip.

"She had lost faith in her intuition. Lost faith in her inner knowledge. She didn't want to guess any more, because she'd been burned. She told me she didn't think it was appropriate for people to think so much about what they wear. She wanted *inner* beauty. Inner peace."

"Just one more fashion, in the head," said Philip.

"No," said Oswald. "She was moving onto another plane. That's why I was not concerned when she disappeared. I know she went where her creativity led."

Philip laughed rudely. "I think that's another version of 'you never find a nice girl in a trunk.'"

"You do something called destiny reform, and energy transfer," said Blair quickly. "Is that what Ruby did?"

Oswald smiled. "Energy transfer is simply a refresher for body and soul. A total release. A form of submission. We all need to submit, don't you agree? If you would like me to show you, I'll take you to our treatment rooms down the hall."

"No thank you," Philip said churlishly.

"And destiny reform?"

"That's different. That takes a long time. These are individualized programs. You confront your destiny and, if desired, alter the forces you bring to it, to change your course. It's very difficult," said Oswald. "I don't suppose you'd like it."

Blair felt very tired. "My destiny probably needs it," she said. "But I'm not sure I'm up to it. What I want," said Blair, suddenly knowing, "is for you to put me in touch with Ruby. To say goodbye, and have it over with."

"It might be useful for you," said Oswald, nodding. "A good idea."

Philip gripped her hand, his nails digging into her palm.

"You're crazy," said Philip.

Oswald went out to the receptionist and opened her book. The space for each day was filled with tiny writing on narrow lines. "Thursday?" he said. "Perhaps we can make it at three-thirty. In any case, I'll have to confirm with my secretary. Can I let you know?"

Philip and Blair burst out the street doors.

"*Such* horseshit!" Philip batted his hands away from his face, as if dissipating a cloud of smoke. "It's all him. The voices, the spirits, the channels. It's all him. Electronic wizardry. You'll go there Thursday and all you'll get is him."

"Impersonating Ruby? Impersonating spirits? Maybe I'll find out something."

"Smoke and mirrors," said Philip in disgust. "You'd better figure out if this is research or if you believe it. This guy is dangerous. I could see the seeds of it then, how it would come to this."

"Oh you, too, you're a seer now. The wisdom of hindsight,"

said Blair.

Philip set off down the street, dogged, stubborn. His empty handcuffs dangled from his pocket, the joke that he had not played that day.

Blair went alone to her appointment with Oswald, in a freezing sleet-storm that clogged the streets and made the houses haggard with frost and icicles. The building was warm, a bright cocoon. Oswald appeared at the appointed time in his miniature, mushroom-coloured suit, his face clear, expressionless. He offered her a choice—sofa, floor cushions or straight-backed chair. She chose the chair. Oswald reclined in his dentist's chair. Blair noticed there was a black window here, too, half-obscured by curtains.

"Who's out there, Oswald?" she said. "No tricks, other than your normal ones, promise?"

He pressed a button on the chair arm. The light flashed on in the little room behind the curtained window. It was empty, as far as Blair could see.

"What is it you want?" said Oswald. "I am clairvoyant, clairaudient, clairsentient. I can be a channel, read your aura—"

"Read my aura," said Blair promptly. It seemed the least threatening.

He sat up and looked at her. "That's easy," he said. "You have always been golden. Golden, blessed, singular. I step into your vibration and I feel like I want to laugh. But there is confusion, much confusion."

Blair did not laugh. She sat even more primly on her straight wooden chair. If he was going to see confusion, it was not going to be in her posture.

Oswald watched her. "One of the great things about being in a physical body in this lifetime," he said gently, "is that every inch of you has information written on it."

Blair stiffened. She made an effort to disguise the writing all over her.

"There is someone in the vibration who wants you to let go. Someone who is holding on, also. You cling to a rope, an old chain, leading you away from yourself. But if you pull it the right way, it is the way back. It is wise then, this foolish thing you do . . ."

On the right hand, on the left hand. That was the old Oswald, she remembered. Ever objective, ever seeing alternatives, never making anything clear, vacillating between the horns of every dilemma he encountered. She laughed.

"This laughter puzzles me," Oswald went on. "What is it? Bubbling up. Long-suppressed laughter from some kind of joke? Or are you covering up your pain?"

"Okay. Stop! That's enough!" said Blair. "Tell me about destiny reform. How do you do it?"

"*You* do it, not me, for a start. It is nothing more than the realization that you have free will and perfect control over every aspect of your life."

"Whoever made that up obviously never had a kid."

Oswald frowned. "Of course a child makes no difference at all. It's only an excuse."

"Well, it's my excuse," said Blair. "And now I want to talk to Ruby."

"You'll have to lie down. I must put you in a light trance," he said, curtly. She had annoyed him. "I cannot promise anything. Spirits come when they want, not when you call."

"Is this what you did to her?" It seemed so ridiculous. She concentrated on Oswald in the old days—goofy, kinetic, concentrated, playing keyboard or staring out the window of the van, Ruby's feet in his lap, unwanted. It made her feel safe to remember how he'd been put upon.

She lay back and closed her eyes. "I don't know how you're going to do this, I expect I'll be very difficult to put under," she said. "Reveen tried once, onstage at the Jubilee

Auditorium in Calgary, and he couldn't—"

Then she remembered nothing more. She was above the sofa, floating on her back, and the sound—

—her own voice, the long-ago sound, plucked guitar strings and thrum of bass violin resting on its needle point. She felt herself retreat, travel to that time again and find herself there. With ironed hair and black lines around her eyes, tuning up for the concert. The concert that was to begin the triumphant tour, launch them. The concert that was their last. It was that day, the day she hung on to, the day she could not let go of. Oswald spoke, but his voice came from the air. "Blair, you feel you have been betrayed by time. Yet the retreat is yours, not time's."

She couldn't open her mouth to answer back. She waited for Ruby to come. She saw the little motel room, and Max by the door. Philip shouting, a beer in his hand, foam floating out of the bottle neck. There she was, her back. Loose, heavy hair all down it. She couldn't see her face, but she knew Ruby was crying. If she'd only turn around. If she'd only speak.

Max spoke instead. "Goodbye, Hearts of Flame," he said. He opened the door and went out. Ruby jumped up and ran after him. Blair was closer now, to the window. She saw the large arm go over her small shoulders, and Ruby's face tip up. She could not move to stop her going.

But there was more. Ruby sharing the upper berth on the train to Winnipeg for their first out-of-town concert. Swaying in the wind on Tunnel Mountain with their first hit of LSD. Singing at Phil's Pancake House in Banff. Later, in the east, jolting down country roads, knocking on the doors of sagging farmhouses. Ruby was helping Blair into her first apartment in Toronto, with Simplicity, just out of a pram herself, pushing a doll-carriage with her mouse-cage and pet mouse riding in it.

Ruby even spoke, her old words. When Blair had her baby,

Ruby came out to visit. "Call her Simplicity," she said. "It is the most powerful thing."

When Blair left Simplicity's father, saying, "I can't be married. It was a ridiculous idea in the first place," Ruby said, "Of course it was. But I admired you for giving it a try." And years later, draining her coffee cup on Queen Street, "What you need is an affair."

These were her gifts. Words uttered so casually at the time, nearly lost amidst all the paste and glitter. Of that past fortune, her hours of talk with Ruby, a few short statements to hoard.

Now she said nothing. She did not speak to Blair.

When she opened her eyes Oswald was smiling. She imagined he was pleased.

"You cannot force her to make contact. She is reluctant," he said. "I think something else has to happen first. Perhaps you do not trust me?"

She only realized after she'd left that she had not mentioned the diaries, and that he had not given her anything but memories: what she already knew.

15

The Last
Instalment

What's that?" said Blair. From her chair on the dock she looked straight down on it.

It began as a shadow in the shallows. Slowly rising, it took on edges, turning from a rock into something alive, its wide, oval back as big as the circle of a man's arms.

"Huge old snapper," said Andy, not bothering to move. "He's ancient, he's mean, he's the size of a baby's bathtub. He surfaces once or twice a summer."

Now they could see the patterns on his back and his small, diamond-shaped head as it lifted haughtily out of the water and then sank again, leaving only his pattern, seen through the waves, a greener transparency.

Belinda walked out to the end of the dock. She saw him rising again and began to tremble.

"It's so big," she said. "Do you think we can catch it?" Without waiting for an answer, she went to the shed and got out the largest landing net and a wide enamel basin.

"Not possible," said Blair. "How could you even lift him?"

"He's very old and very heavy. Bites too." Andy exposed his stomach, fish-belly white, to the sunlight. For a man who never showed his body he seemed peculiarly unselfconscious.

"What could we do with him, anyway?"

When the sun came out from behind the cloud, Belinda climbed up to the top of the boathouse and looked down into the water. "There he is," she said, pointing. No one else could see; he was down on the mud-sand bottom.

"He's coming up again. Do you want to try?"

It was Belinda's first time in cottage country. On Friday, their first night up from the city, after they unpacked all the groceries and stuffed the refrigerator and cooler, after Sissy was washed, her teeth brushed, and off to bed, they all sat down in the screened porch for a cup of tea.

When the first cry came, Andy and Max looked at each other with satisfaction.

"Right on cue," said Max. "Always makes it worthwhile."

The first high, ululating call was joined by another. The two wove and tangled, exulting or exhorting, and then died in the still night air. Everyone sat in silence, hoping the call would be repeated.

Belinda mistook their reverence for fear.

"What's that?" she whispered. "What's that noise?"

"Loons," said Blair.

"Oh," said Belinda. "Okay." But when they started again she stood alert, trying to locate the danger.

"It's only loons," said Blair. "What did you think?"

"I thought it was the Indians. Maybe they are making war over there," she said, pointing toward the dense, treed island that faced them. When everyone laughed, she laughed too.

Andy was charitable about entertaining visitors from the city. He always gave Max his cottage for a couple of weeks a year, had done for a dozen years now, so that Max knew how the pump worked and could fix the boats himself. But this year he had outdone himself: he was letting Blair and Simplicity have it for most of August.

"The kid needs a break," he said, "and I don't mean just going to your mother in Medicine Hat." Cottage life was restorative, he said. Otherwise the place would sit empty, he being too busy to go up. It might as well be used. And Max added, "Take Bernie with you so you can have a little time to yourself." It had been a long, cold winter.

Andy wasn't so sure about Bernie. Traditionally, nannies did not fare well at the Bay. He recalled tales of English-born au pairs who broke down crying during the first thunderstorm and demanded to be taken to land. On the big island to the north, where the boathouses were painted French-blue with white trim and had window-boxes of geraniums, and the float-plane bobbed by the dock, the nanny had been told she had to wear a uniform. After refusing, she too went back to the city on the bus.

"Bernie's not really my nanny," said Blair quickly. "She has other jobs too. She helps out with Simplicity and I give her room and board and a small salary—but mostly she's a friend." Andy smiled broadly and said nothing. Blair may keep her little vanities and delusions, he thought, but a nanny was a nanny.

Monday morning was the changeover. Max, Andy and Belinda were going down to the city to work; Blair and Sissy drove them to the marina on the way to the bus to pick up Bernie, arriving from the city. They all set out at seven o'clock in the aluminum fishing boat they called the Molly. They joined a small fleet of wife-driven boats, which ultimately disgorged men in T-shirts and shorts carrying business suits in garment bags.

"You'll be all right, alone here, till the weekend?" Max said, standing with his arms around her at the dock.

"Of course I will, and I won't be alone."

"Don't forget," Andy called over his shoulder, "there's Abe in the white cottage on the point if anything breaks down."

Andy and Belinda got in one car and Max in another. They

gunned the motors, throwing up dust and stones on the un-paved road.

Two hours later, Bernie stepped off the bus with her knap-sack, sunglasses holding back her hair, her short, strong legs bared in white shorts. It was cloudy, damp, and the flies hov-ered close in the still air. She squinted at the rim of scraggy pines, the parking lot with tilting boat-trailers, the collapsed windsurf sails. Sissy ran to hug her. Bernie looked over Sissy's head at Blair. "Is this what they call cottage country?"

They set off back to the cottage in the Molly. The weather did not improve. Bernie sized up the place and got Blair working, clearing out dead branches where they wanted to hang the hammock. Side by side they laboured, lending and borrowing the hoe and the mosquito-repellent. There were no telephone messages, no couriers at the door, none of the thousand material possessions to be altered, polished, dry-cleaned or repaired. They worked until four o'clock, and when they stopped they compared the bulges of their biceps.

Bernie not only survived, she thrived. She found wild things—flowers, leaves, snails, minnows, crayfish. She could see a tiny, thin stalked mushroom with a tacky, beige um-brella top. When Blair and Sissy got down to look at it, Bernie showed them an entire miniature forest. She caught frogs and fished in her black peaked cap with her ponytail sticking out through the hole in the back. When the strange, creaking sound of the trees in the wind came she said, "It must be a *lee*-zard."

"We don't have lizards here," said Blair. Bernie didn't be-lieve her. She was afraid of only two things: deep water and bears. The berries were good this year, so the bears stayed out of sight, unless you happened to be at the dump in the evening. Deep water was there; it couldn't be helped.

Tuesday morning they ran out of milk. There was no putting it off: they had to go to the marina. The south wind was back again, blowing up the surface. Big boats, some three-storeys high and trailing personal watercraft, were nose to tail in the main channel.

"Now we're in for it," said Blair.

The Molly went up the side of one of the huge crests that fanned behind a cruiser, and then down the other side: for a moment, the blue-shingled roof of the marina, even the twisted top of the pine trees, vanished into the troubled sky. Bernie and Simplicity clung to the sides. Blair didn't know whether to slow down or try to outrun the huge waves. She let the Molly idle; after each trough, they rose on the blackened water. At last, soaked and bone-jarred, they rounded the large red buoy in front of the marina. Bernie sprang up off the sharp edge of the boat to the wooden, solid dock, rope in hand.

Summer people lined the ramp up to the store. They were tousled, sweatshirted, grudging in their inspection of the horizon, the shape of the waves, the direction of the wind. Inside the store the owner scowled down at her books from behind the desk.

"Alls you buy is ice-cream bars and Bloody Mary mix," she said to anyone in earshot. "But you want me to stock a full grocery store."

An enormous blond man with eyes set in a permanent boater's squint and a stupid, amiable grin faced her. "We went all the way up to the Magnetawan; there's a new hotel there," he said. "We're not cooking on board."

"My wife took one look at the new boat and said, I don't like this—it's got appliances," said another man.

"More housework," said the woman standing near.

They laughed. The owner's frown went deeper.

Blair prowled the rows of the Wonder Bread, packaged soups and Kraft Dinner. The apparent moral obligation to buy gave her difficulties. Only the fishing lures were tempting; they had names like circus performers: "Golden Dazzle,"

"Mighty Mite," "Double Spotted Angel." There was a rack of wooden signs with the usual slogans painted on them. "FISH EATERS MAKE BETTER LOVERS." "WANTED: A GOOD WOMAN WHO CAN CLEAN FISH, COOK, WITH HER OWN BOAT. PLEASE SEND PHOTO-GRAPH OF BOAT."

She felt the man come up behind her, rather than saw him. His voice when he spoke was tense, practised, as if he were acting on plans.

"This one here is very good. I caught a pickerel like this with it." He pointed to a lure, then held up his hands two feet apart. Blair looked from the hands to the face.

"Did you?" Instinctively, she looked around for Bernie and Simplicity. The man made her feel unsafe.

"Andy told me to look out for you," he said, defensively. "I'm Abe."

Max and Andy had prepared her for Abe. He had the old cottage on the point, half hidden by trees. It had once been the landmark for driving across the bay in fog: if you steered for Abe's you were going in the right direction. But its white paint had now flaked off to the point where the cottage itself could have been a lichen-covered rock. When Andy lost his sense of direction at night he held it against Abe.

Abe lived without electricity in his little shack, year-round, alone. He had come from Germany twenty years ago; his wife ran off somewhere; there were no children. A sense of des-peration, unarticulated, seemed to hold his body hostage.

"You're our neighbour," she said, attempting to smile.

Andy had said that Abe fixed things. He also dropped by the dock at dinnertime, hungry, with his dirty clothes, which he hoped Andy wouldn't mind putting through the wash. "Go get him if you need help. But don't get suckered into cooking for him," Andy said. "And watch out. He's a writer. If you're not careful you'll have to read all his manuscripts. I did."

"And what did you say to him about them?"

Andy shrugged. "What can you say?"

"That one? You recommend it?" said Blair to the wide, washed-out face. Abe's eyes were palest blue, bloodshot, narrowed against the light. The lure was a yellow fish made of hard plastic permanently curled as if to swallow its tail.

"You'll catch good fish with it," he said. He had colourless hair in a thin patch on top of his head, and an inch-long stubble on his face. His shoulders he held up high, as if to ward off pain.

"Has the weather been like this all summer?" They moved, side by side, toward the cash register.

"I like bad weather. Otherwise I just working outdoors all the time and have no time for writing. That is the problem with summers. Everybody wants so much work done. Winters are fine, the people are gone, I am alone," he said. His eye caught Bernie and Simplicity on the other side of the store.

"Your little girl is look exactly the same like you," he said. Then he stopped. "Who is that?"

Bernie was wearing a long, red T-shirt over a bathing suit, showing her smooth, brown legs. Her once-braided hair hung loose and waving down her back. For a moment, Blair saw her as Abe must. She looked twenty, not thirty-two, out here with the wind and the water—black-haired, earthy, proud.

"That's Berenice, my friend." She paused. "She also helps me with my daughter."

At the cash desk, as Blair turned her twenty-dollar bill over to the sulky storekeeper, Abe stuck close behind her. He was buying tins of beans and Wonder Bread.

"You must come and see us some time," said Blair.

Abe continued to look at Bernie.

"I am just about finishing my novel," he said. "This for the third time. But I have a good letter from magazine in

Colorado. They like very much to take an excerpt."

"That's wonderful. Abe is a writer," said Blair to Bernie.

"Hello." Bernie flashed a brief white smile and looked down to examine a tangle on top of Simplicity's head.

Abe's admiration for Bernie was palpable. It filled the space around the cash desk. He stood lost in it while the woman rang up the sale. Sissy held up a package of cheesies. "I think you have to ask your mummy about that," Bernie said. She did not lift her eyes. Blair watched as Bernie became humble. Her eyes dropped. Her air of competence vanished. She looked at Sissy, not at him.

She appeared to be giving Abe a message. "Make no mistake. I am not a woman. I am a babysitter. Direct your attentions elsewhere."

Blair made Sissy take the cheesies back and helped her choose some jujubes. "I know it's junk, but it's better junk," she explained to the storekeeper. The unhappy woman waited sourly for the seventy-five-cent sale, betraying no interest in Blair's maternal guilt.

"It's bad for her, but not as bad as the other," she prattled to the storekeeper. Not since her first days in Canada had she seen Bernie acting like a servant.

Sissy pulled at the plastic of her jujube package. By now, Abe had manoeuvred Bernie nearer to the door. Bernie kept her eyes on the floor.

"Mummy, what is that man saying to Bernie?"

"Shush, dear. He can say what he likes, can't he? She can have her own private conversations."

This Blair said with another smile at the woman behind the cash desk. Her second smile was also not returned. She gave up and bent down to tear open the jujube bag.

It was not true, of course: Bernie couldn't have her private conversations. She was not free. She would not be here on her own. She was attached, derivative. Coming to the marina had brought back city assumptions. They were in public, being watched. Bernie, perversely, seemed to play to expectations: spoiled, middle-class woman and her babysitter. What made her do it? Was it the great preponderance of WASP Canadians, here in their natural habitat, looking as pinched and honest and astounded by their prosperity as ever?

Or was it Abe? As he stood gazing at her, Bernie shrugged, listened passively. Her posture expressed some lack of freedom Blair had failed to perceive before. Was Bernie as nanny prevented from being a sexual creature? Or was she simply afraid of men? Or this man?

The conversation took only a minute. Then Abe walked out the door and down the gauntlet of thwarted holiday-makers. He climbed into a strange old wooden boat, which looked as if it had been made out of barrel staves, with "Prince Lucas" painted on its side. When he was gone, Bernie walked out alone, twirling a lock of hair over her shoulder.

Blair and Sissy took a different path. By the time they had untied the Molly and were turning around in the open space between the docks, the Prince Lucas was at the red buoy. Abe turned and waved, jauntily. Blair put Sissy's jujubes in her mouth to stop herself from asking Bernie questions.

"What did he say to you?" said Sissy.

"Sissy, don't ask her, I told you, it's a private conversation. Bernie's allowed."

"It's nothing," insisted Bernie.

Then nobody said anything more until they got to the dock.

Thursday afternoon they picnicked on a lichen-laced rock. They basked in the sun until it turned suddenly hot. Blair inched down the rough granite surface to the edge of the water and let herself sink into it, cool, green, silky. Bernie and Simplicity found a gentle slope and stood at the rim of the water, moving one foot at a time until they reached the depth of their knees. Blair called encouragement to them, thinking how alike they were, beset by fears, too proud to take help.

As they putted home in the Molly, hot, sleepy and sunburnt, a yellow cast came over the sky. Suddenly it was clotted with cloud. All during the late afternoon, while Sissy painted a picture and Blair read, there was the distant rumble of thunder. By evening, the wind had stopped, but grumbling to the north and west continued. Blair was cooking dinner when the storm hit, in a violent thud that puffed the screens and began to bang the doors in a series all through the cottage. Spatters of rain struck at intervals, and the sky was suddenly black.

"Please let me finish cooking this spaghetti before we lose our power," said Blair to the heavens.

Simplicity turned her yellow tape deck up loud, to drown out the noise. While the wind and rain assaulted the sides of the cottage, she flitted around the main room with a straw hat and a basket, singing, "The girl that I marry will have to be . . ." Her resolute, pale face was a mask, her dips and kicks blocked out the explosion of the elements.

Bernie and Blair ran down to the dock. The Molly was tugging and banging on its rope. They dragged it up on the sand. Across, on the point, they could see Abe's sailboat bobbing, and the Prince Lucas riding majestically beside the dock. Something that hung on the mast—a dinner bell?—clanged and clanged. The women were heading back up the dock again when they saw him untying the Prince Lucas.

"He's mad," said Blair.

Bernie looked at the boat for a few seconds. Then, with an unreadable expression on her face, she disappeared into the cottage. There seemed no doubt he was heading for their place. Perhaps he needed help. But no, when his boat crashed up against the dock and he sprang out, rope in hand, it was with offers of assistance for them.

"You must be having trouble," he shouted. "I saw you on

the dock."

"No trouble, none at all," Blair shouted back from higher up, on the cottage deck. "You shouldn't have come out in this."

He strode up the sloping wooden walk from the dock. "But now I'm here."

Abe set up the Coleman stove and lamp, and made sure they had candles and flashlights in case they did lose the power at some point. Then he finished off the spaghetti.

The storm must have hit several miles away. All they got was wind, rain, a show of lightning, which moved along the horizon from north to south, and distant thunder. By eight o'clock the sun was emerging from behind the cloud bank, an undraped, saffron orb about to set. Abe and Bernie sat in the rain-splashed screened porch with mint tea. Having danced and sung herself into exhaustion, Sissy came to sit on Blair's lap inside. Through the window, they watched the conversation between Abe and Bernie. Blair could hear a little.

"Everyone in Canada has two places to live," said Bernie. "They have cottage and they have house. At home we live maybe ten people in place like this cottage. And that is the only house. Where my friend lives in Scarborough, many Filipinos own their own house. Bungalow," she said.

"You will never catch up," said Abe. "Don't even think about it."

Bernie said nothing, but she was not dissuaded from thinking, clearly.

"I lived in Toronto when I was working," said Abe. "I spent all my money travelling to work and buying suits to wear and eating lunch. It costs too much to earn your money there. People should come up to the north, to the bush, to the lakes. It's much better. TV I don't have, and only an old car, and no telephone, but I don't need these things. I have my freedom. I can do with my life what I want."

"Yes," said Bernie.

"It's a new era," whispered Blair to Sissy.

Sissy did not look happy. "I don't like him."

"He helped us, didn't he?" said Blair.

"We don't need help, Mummy."

When Abe left, Bernie moved nervously around the cottage, snapping her fingers by her side and making her tuneless, breathy whistle. She had a shower and washed her hair and sat for a long time in the dark, looking out at the sky.

Not long after breakfast, a spruce-looking Abe glided up to the dock, standing on the deck of his sailboat. He wore a madras shirt and seersucker Bermuda shorts; his grizzled face was shaven, and his eyes had a fisherman's light.

"Bernie's never been out for a sail," Abe said to Blair, as if Blair had failed to provide the necessities.

Bernie demurred.

"It's all right, it's fine," said Blair. "Sissy and I are going on a picnic, anyway, aren't we, Sissy?"

Sissy scowled at Abe.

Blair and Simplicity sat on the cottage floor. Each had a plastic tray of portraits before them. Each face was different. Some had blond hair, some black, some red. Some were bald. There were women and men, a few with hats, a few with glasses, a few with big noses. Under each portrait was a name: Claire, Herman, Peter, David.

"Mummy," said Sissy importantly. "Does your person have a beard?"

"No," said Blair.

"Okay, then I can put down all the people who have beards!" She slapped four of the cards down on the tray. "You ask."

"Sissy," said Blair, "is your person a man or a woman?"

Sissy screamed. "You can't ask that! You have to say is it a man? You have to ask one question so I say no or yes."

"Oh, *sorry*," said Blair sarcastically. "You be polite to me or I won't play." Sissy howled and ran off to her room.

Blair was angry at Sissy for being six and for not liking to go outside and lie down in the sun and read books. She was angry at Max for being in the city, and at Bernie for leaving her. Bernie had been gone with Abe for four hours now. She told herself not to be angry. Bernie was entitled, after all. But it seemed like a long time. Abe knew his way around the lake, she supposed; there was no danger. He'd lived alone here for ten years.

"Do you suppose that *ever* in the past ten years he has asked a woman out for a Sunday afternoon sail?" she had asked Max on the phone.

"When I first used to come up here on my own, he asked me. Then he made me read his writing."

"What was it like?"

Max thought. "The writing? Bizarre, awkward, but fascinating in what it revealed. Long descriptions of sex."

"Oh no," said Blair. "Worse and worse."

"Mummy, does your person have blue eyes?"

Blair had forgotten who her person was. She looked down at the card in front of her. It was Herman. He did have blue eyes.

"Yes!"

When you got a yes you knew your opponent was closing in.

"Is your person Herman?"

"It is. You won, Sissy. I lost."

A smile of pure triumph overtook Sissy's face.

Finally, they had played enough. Sissy got a book and went out to lie in the hammock. Now Blair was liberated, but unable to turn away; she stood on the porch watching her daughter. In the white netting, the small body hung directly downward; the ends of the hammock stretched open to the ropes. She looked like a bat hung up by its toes. A moth emerging from a chrysalis. She needed to overtake someone, and the chosen person was her mother. It was what Blair was here for. To give power to this child, then to give her up. Sissy was growing. Bernie was finding herself. Max never veered from his self-determined course or so it seemed. Only Blair herself was stuck, stopped.

She walked restlessly out on the point, scanning the water in three directions. She was a housewife without a husband. She had always been bold, but now she was turning into a stay-at-home, an enabler. Was this the future? That she should give up working and just look after people? It looked as if work had given her up, in any case.

That would be easy. Or would it? Max wanted to live with her and Sissy. He asked and she could not answer. The winter had been long with waiting. Waiting for news of Ruby. Waiting for it to be over, waiting for tears, waiting for some unknown event that would break them all out of stasis.

But there had been no news. No more diaries, no new intelligence from Dick Nolan. And no new job for Blair, except for a few commercials her agent scoured up for her. Now summer had come down, rich and warming and rife with birdsong. The last season. When it was over, a year would have passed since Ruby had gone.

Blair went in the canoe to Loon Lagoon. It was so shallow and still she could see the bottom-feeders; two feet below her, a huge catfish skirted off in search of shelter from the shadow of her canoe. Locked in by rock and weeds, the water was motionless; water lilies, with their round, green palms and pointed, white fingers, coated the surface. When she dipped her paddle, she drew it through the elastic strings that attached them to the bottom.

Forty summers, and I can count the ones to come, thought Blair. I can look ahead and say, there might be forty more. Fifty more, if I'm lucky, but I won't be out canoeing. Life has become finite. When we are children, time moves so slowly, it is terribly painful to wait. Gradually, the speed accelerates, the stream begins to race. The end comes into sight.

She let the canoe fall motionless. Underneath the fish began to gather. If she stayed here she might stop everything. Stop Max from moving into her life. Stop Bernie from moving on, taking a next step. Stop Simplicity from being hurt, as she was bound to be, by whatever was to come. Stop—it all.

A wind twisted the tufted top of a pine tree. A heron, startled, rose out of its unseen rest, cranked its wings twice, tucked its long legs back and flew over the trees. She put her paddle down. Minnows darted out in all directions; the flowers, like eggs with their white petals and yellow centre, jiggled on green plates. She thrust herself forward, off her knees. The canoe teetered. The possibility of swimming in all these threads and weeds, with the turtles and the fish and snakes, did not appeal. She grasped the gunwales. When the canoe stopped rocking, she pulled the letter out of her pocket.

It was from her mystery man. Astonishingly, it had arrived at the marina post office. She had no idea how he knew where to find her. How could he have known? But there it was. A cheap white envelope with that spidery writing in a pen with ink and a proper nib, an old-fashioned pen. She had taken it home in her shorts pocket and left it there for a day, until now. Now she tore open the envelope.

My dearest B.

Where have you gone?

I still live in contemplation of your image, an image I have of you sprawled across my bed, your lovely legs bare, all the rest of you ready and waiting for that which must be yours—my love. But perhaps I will never see you here, perhaps you will never come. I wonder why you waste your life—you'll think this hard, but has the time not come to be blunt?—Why do you hide out? Why do you avoid your true vocation, which is obviously love? You are thinking of marriage. I know it, you can't lie to me. I can read it in your face. Can you not imagine how repulsive those dutiful, lethargic, heavy matings must be, those learned and practised ways to bring a kind of pleasure which is as like true sexual pleasure as pork and beans are to caviar?

She stopped reading. So he was divorced, was he? Or not . . . those matings "must be"—perhaps not. He was a watcher, not a participant. It all began to remind her of somebody, someone. But who?

Married sex, from what I surmise, is so deadening, so soul-destroying, that people have been known to crochet doorknob covers while it is underway. You've steered clear this long. Never let yourself, don't be trapped. Come away, come away, oh human child, from the shores of Lethe. Come to me and you shall see what life is really like, what love is really like, what passions, given a little plot in which to root, can produce. Come with me to live on the edge— risk everything to have something, instead of dull, dishwater life.

The literary pretensions struck her as more and more fantastic; possibly some author had seized upon this epistolary courtship as a way of practising his craft. Was she the wrong "B"? But no—he knew her. There was enough truth, just enough, for it to be terrifying. And the question. Who was he? Someone who knew how to get a letter to her at the cottage, someone who prided himself on living on the edge. Something tantalizing, scant memory, passed. She could almost, in the recesses of her mind, see him. But like the minnows, the name and face darted off.

If you don't, if you fall into this trap, with this "man," then you are not who I thought you were. You are not the wild girl, you have no more charm, you deserve what you get. And I promise you, I will hate you.

The canoe trembled on the water, radiating little waves. She sat in shock. The passion that never was had turned ugly, the billet-doux to threats. They were through. "For every ounce of joy you'll pay with a pound of pain." That was her mother, with one of those bone-chilling pragmatic western sayings. The affair that never was had come full circle. She had to pay for the pleasure of reading those first lust-laced notes. The water lapped minutely at the canoe.

The important thing to do was to destroy the letter, she thought. But how? She could tear it up into tiny pieces and drop it in the lake—but the water was so calm that the pieces would float, they would drift in to shore. With her luck, a piece with her name and some incredibly compromising phrase would attract Bernie's sharp eye, or stick to Max's toe as he clambered over the rocks. Sissy would cry pollution.

She could try to hide it somewhere on her person—inside her bra, for instance—but that risked her being distracted by some demand, and forgetting about it until she undressed for bed. Then it would fall out on the floor and Max would scoop it up, and say, "What on earth is this you've secreted next to your heart?"

Dear Max.

Could it be Max who'd written it? Of course not. The first one had come before she met him. She looked at it again. She felt it was someone she knew. But she could not think of who. She wanted only to get rid of it. It appeared to be written with a fountain pen. It was not the paper she need dispose of, but merely the writing on it.

She leaned over the side of the canoe and trailed the piece of paper in the water. Immediately, the peacock lines began to dissolve, to drift away into the deeper green water. She swished the paper around. The lines got all jumbled; the ink bled off the paper even faster. She lifted it out of the water to look. It was unreadable; all that remained were a few long, blurred, blue veins. She submerged the note again and swung it back and forth at the side of the canoe. Then she crumpled it and put it in the floor of the canoe. When she got home she'd drop it in the fireplace. If anyone asked, it was a bit of litter she picked up while canoeing.

The telephone rang, one long and one short.

"It's ours!" cried Simplicity. She jumped down from the table where she was drawing and ran for the telephone.

"Hello?" Simplicity's voice was high and piercing. "Hi Max. When are you coming?"

Blair tried not to think about Max during the week. She tried not to wait for him. She walked slowly to take the call.

"You won't believe what I've got for you," said Max.

"Won't I?" She picked up the crayfish claws that someone had left on top of the dresser and made them dance on the wood surface.

"No. Shall I tell you?"

"Will it upset me?"

Max thought for a minute. "Yes. But maybe in a good way."

"Ruby."

"I'll tell you when I get up."

"No, tell me now. I hate surprises."

"A package."

"Have you opened it?"

"Of course not. It's addressed to you. And it came by a courier wearing a pair of steel-toed boots and a bikini riding a pink mountain bike."

"When can you get here?" said Blair.

Blair and Sissy spent the day at the beach, fishing in the little boat. Threading worms on hooks, their little pink squishy insides squirting out the top as the hook went in the other end, Blair thought only, Ruby is alive. I know it. She has sent me one more instalment, after all this time. At five o'clock they stood hand in hand in the screened porch watching Abe's fishing boat draw away from the dock with Bernie in it, sitting up high in the bow looking at him, like a Cleopatra. As the sun went down, Blair sat on the porch in the wooden chair with the wide arms. The sun came around in the perfect angle to strike the table and the floor. The light was shattered by a pine tree, needles and rays becoming one. The sheer force of its brightness in the west bore through the trees on the far shore.

The hot, still days of summer had arrived. The sky was like painted china; the lake lay deep and calm, with a thin surface skin that moved continually eastward: sign of good weather to stay. The woods smelled of drying pine needles; scattered wildflowers had come to the rocky wastes at the back of the lot—the yellows and purple-pink of midsummer: mulleins, fireweed, wild roses clung to their bushes at the edge of the water.

It was nearly time to pick up Max. The wind began to rise. The bell on Abe's sailboat clanged across the water.

"It's going to be a long ride," said Blair to Simplicity, as she started the boat. "You sure you want to come?"

"Yes." Her yellow sweater with hood stood out against the angry blue water.

He was waiting on the dock with the usual pile of white plastic grocery bags and his sports duffle. Sissy jumped up and down and hugged his legs. As he leaned over and kissed Blair's cold cheek, she reached for the brown-paper package he had tucked under his arm. It was covered all over with shiny brown plastic tape and addressed to Ms. Blair Bowker. Blair recognized Ruby's round, upright handwriting.

"You drive back, okay?" she said.

"I'll help you," said Simplicity.

Max and Sissy sat together, holding the tiller, while Blair sat in the bow facing the water and wind, with the package on her lap.

It was a whole notebook this time, with hard orange covers. Most of the pages had been torn out; only a few remained. She scanned for dates. It began where the last one left off.

I kept this thing in my bag and it hasn't been easy to write 'cause there's never any privacy. That's what I miss most, more than bedsheets, respect. Even more than moisturizer. <u>Privacy</u>.

So where are we? Gotta get this down before it's lost forever. After the search got going, I slipped out of town to the east. A guy gave me a ride up to the Ottawa Valley. A family of spaced-out musicians was building a barn. One guy had a broken back and lived on tranqs; he thought the Mounties were in a conspiracy to overthrow the local government. I hit a little lost pocket of '60s madness: my luck. As long as I helped, they didn't care who I was, but after a couple of weeks the bucolic splendours and the bad plumbing wore on me and I got myself a ride back down to Toronto. Called Oswald and we met in some mall up on Finch. You wouldn't have caught me dead there a month ago even.

He had a sheaf of newspaper clippings but I said I had escaped myself and I didn't want to know about my business or Marvin or anyone. And he said well they all want to know about you and I said too bad. There's actually no me to know about right now, I'm in an embryonic state, I have left one self behind and the other one is developing. Tell them nothing. He gave me money and warned me to stay out of Toronto.

I hitched a ride on the 400 and got off somewhere north of Barrie where I saw a sign in the window of a truck stop, HELP WANTED. Turned out these people needed somebody to replace the university kids who worked there all summer. It was a split shift, hours none of the local women would take because they couldn't be home to make dinner or breakfast for their husbands. They even have a little cabin I can sleep in, meals in the restaurant. Perfect. I'm Jennie Wilson and I'm running away from my husband, who likes to bash me around when he's had a few. So they all love me and here I am, getting fat on bran muffins and chips with gravy all day long.

This is the kind of job I love. Now I find out! It's so simple and there are so few decisions to make. I can't get proud, I can't fuck up, at least not seriously. Maybe get the eggs wrong with the bacon, or be slow so the soup's cold. But if I do the guys tell me, and I say sure, you're right, and I take it back to the cook, and we gripe a bit, and it's over. No creative espionage. No waiting for judgment from some pundit. No just looking, thanks. People need food and they choose from what's there. I'm part of a dinner event, that's all. We talk— the menu, the road, the weather. My pay envelope comes, and my tips come, and I put it all in my purse and lock the little cabin. No bills, no bank, no nothing. Nobody notices that for Jennie Wilson, where a personal history ought to be, there's a yawning silence.

The truckers love to laugh and they all read the Sun. Today I leaned over the counter, having given this guy a refill of his coffee. I look down and I see this big picture of what I call "old me," half the size of the page, and it reads, in this huge, filthy, black type, "WHERE IS RUBY MASON?" The face is upside down and it barely even looks familiar, so I laugh and look back up at the truck driver and say, "Where do *you* think?" And he looks at me. He's a regular, comes in every second day on his runs to Sudbury and back, and he says, maybe she's right here. It's a joke but I nearly upchucked (old Alberta expression) right there.

I don't want to be caught. I don't want to go back. So I'm on the run. I have to keep reminding myself I'm not a criminal or anything. I just went away. It's a basic human right, or it ought to be. To cut ourselves loose and reinvent ourselves. I had nobody needing me.

So tonight I'm splitting. I figure if I don't they'll be on to me. If I let myself I'd feel sad. I liked it here, and I liked the owners and the people who came in. They were not elegant but they let me live. They'll freak in the morning when Jennie Wilson doesn't show up for her shift. They'll come out to check and find the place empty, figure my husband caught up to me, check the till to see if I've robbed it.

I would've had to go by winter anyway. It wasn't heated.

October 15

Toronto again. It's a magnet. I'm sucked to it. The <u>fix</u> of it all, car horns and litter and pink-mirror towers; people people people. But it was not wise. Not wise for me to come here. This time I didn't call Oswald 'cause I had some money saved and I knew he'd tell me to get out of there. That was about ten days ago. Cocky I guess 'cause I'd got the job up north, but I couldn't get one here. It was either wear a shell-pink uniform with a white cap or go in drag, black tie at some high-class joint. I can't go too clean; people might recognize me. And now I've got a big scab on the side of my nose where someone pushed me into a wall outside the mission.

I'm trying the streets. Thought I might see my bag lady fashion consultant again but no luck. I've got a bag of my own now, couple of sweatshirts and some socks I got up north, and my second great pair of track shoes. The jacket is fantastic. You can feel winter coming. The big bugaboo. "Winter," we street people mumble to each other under our breath. People die.

Worse than winter, a guy came on to me last night. He stank of cheap wine and his own encrusted sweat. He actually tried to strike up a conversation first, you know, like, how did I like the food, and where were the mattresses the best. Then he lunged and got my head in a hammer lock. He got a hand between my thighs. It felt kind of harmless so I cocobonked him and turned my back. But he knocked me down and got on top of me. Those wiry old guys are strong. He had one hand squashing my windpipe and his knee in my groin; he was trying to get my pants off when a couple of women came along and started kicking his ass and he moved off.

I've seen some places now, I've slept in some places, shared some meals, you wouldn't believe. I can't write most of it down, because I don't want my street friends to think I'm a tourist. I tell them I lost my business and had a bunch of debts and a bad man; that's pretty close to the truth. It's not so different from their stories. I know people now, living in the rubble by the railway bridge south of the Dome, a fair-sized camp. There's an abandoned roundhouse there, with broken windows, we sleep in. These folks are settled. They've got silverware. When they make a fire sometimes the cops come and harass them, but not always. They've got some seats from cars, and a concrete flat place where they sit around and share the newspapers.

I know people who sleep in doorways too and over grates by Simpsons, in the entrance to the George R. Gardiner Museum. Betty and Don, they're like grandparents, they can't have been out here long or they'd be dead by now. It's better than going to the missions. I guess the ladies' dorms are supposed to be safe but they freaked me right out; it doesn't suit my fancy to be tucked in with thirty others. Plus listen to the earbang, an hour of preaching before I can go to sleep. Just like at home with Mum. But the worst of it is how they all cry and rage in their sleep.

But taken all together, I can live. I can get food, find a place to sleep, and then it's the next day. What else is living, I ask. I feel like this is right, somehow. This is the future. People have been good to me, except for the crazies. They call me "new-timer" and they give me tips—how to spot social workers and the sex fiends. But I'm so dirty. I went to the Harrison Baths one day, rented a bathing suit. Did my stately breast stroke in there with the drunks and the beat-up Indians, the stroke I learned at Medicine Hat High School. Then I was clean. Came out by John Street. My hair stands on end: old haunts. Another Ruby Mason crossed this corner five thousand times. The corner shows no sign of it.

It's funny what I think about. Not time, that's for sure, not what day it is. Not rushing out to the next appointment, and if I can get a taxi. Once in a while I think about Arthur and Mary. They'll be slow to let go, you know, slow to say we can't find her so let's forget her. My mother, too, she'll never stop fighting. But that's her way of plugging in to the world. I stood at John and Queen tempting fate. No one noticed me in my scummy jeans and savaged hair. No one came to find me. And I felt a worm, deep in the core of me, starting to grow. A new Ruby Mason, inside the old rotten core.

Oct 29

Saw Blair today.

I couldn't believe it. She was striding along Front Street in front of the Convention Centre. I'd just come up from my rubble-ground home behind the Dome and was hugging the walls of a hoarding across the street. I shrank behind a post. But there was no need. She looked right through me. She was looking good, her cheeks were hollower than I remember, and her posture—forward, tense, determined, like a marathoner. I even thought for one crazy second she was looking for me. Had to restrain a reflex to throw myself across her path.

It got me wondering.

I'm taking too many risks! Is this lack of resolution? Don't tell me I'm weakening. I gotta get out of town. Harrison Baths again today and got myself fluffed and buffed, so to speak. Oswald freaked out when I called, telling me to get the hell out of here. He says the search is still on: Mensa wrote something. But I know how to throw my weight around. Fifteen years in business didn't teach me but a month on the street did. I said, in my new, tough voice, "Just meet me under the Bay at 10 tonight or I'll blow you away." He whimpered a bit but I knew he'd come.

No Park Plaza this time. Folks might not recognize me under the railway bridge but they might sipping cognac. O and I went to a Druxy's for coffee; I kept on my toque and dark glasses. Runaway battered wife look. He wanted to know, had I reached enlightenment yet, and I said very funny, but there is something in this, and I recommend it. He said no thanks, I'd be the one who got knifed. On to the next life, I said, 'cause I never believed he actually believed in that stuff, what's the difference. He had the grace to blush.

I put it to Oswald that I was getting ready for my new incarnation and I needed a sort of incubator, a quiet, warm place to spend the winter, so what did he think? He said he'd work on it, what did I want, and did I mind the wilderness, did I mind being alone? I said, no problem, it's people I've gone beyond. Wilderness would be a picnic compared to downtown streets, and he said if you say so.

The only company I need, I said, is the tracks. Wherever I go I've been near the tracks. I do like the whistles and I've got used to train rumble. If possible I'd like to go by train, but he has to get the ticket. He said he'd work on it.

Blair stopped reading. She had a pain in her chest. So she had passed Ruby. She could almost—almost remember that brilliant fall day she'd walked Front Street from Church to Bathurst. And hadn't recognized the embryonic person. This pain, too, she hadn't recognized. It was anger. Blair was angry at Ruby. To hell with tears and sorrow. Ruby had cut everyone out of her life, like an unscrupulous surgeon. All ties. And Oswald did know. He must know everything.

She lay in the hammock with her eyes closed, tears sitting on her lashes. She could hear Sissy and Max down by the water, throwing stones. Max was containing his curiosity until she finished reading. Max was a burden. One too many people to care about. She wished he would go away. She did not want to have to account to him.

But the loneliness.

There was one more entry in the diary. She turned the page to read it.

November—date?

Wild wind in stone grey skies; tree trunks stained black by rain. The fallen leaves have been wetted, frozen, peed on by dogs, infiltrated with thrown-away cups and silver gum wrappers; run over by car tires.

A wrinkled pumpkin remains on a doorstep, in-folded, an old man with his teeth out. The sidewalk is glazed with a layer of ice, invisible but deadly. Women in high heels balk, looking down before their toes, skitter sideways. While out on Yonge Street the kids in their open Roots jackets welcome the wind as it flattens their sweaters against their chests.

That wind flies straight out of the north and over the crest of the hill. St. Clair it is, named after Saint Clare, misspelled, the maiden who doted on Francis of Assisi. (So says Blair, anyway.) I'm in her territory. Oswald won't take my calls.

How I know that trick. But where shall I find my incubator? What can I do for winter? Down to my last fifty dollars.

Wind carries me down the stages of hill, to the lake, cold green-grey whipped and turbulent and slapping the concrete docks built to contain it. I walk for hours in my woollen toque and hockey jacket: no one knows me. Panhandler by Eaton Centre turns up his collar as the flying bits of sleet hit and says, "Winter's come."

"It always does," I say.

Comes for five, maybe six months of darkness at five o'clock, the bare exposure of life in a place all too graceless to be caught this way. Six months of heavy coats, leather boots with white salt lines waving around the insteps and over the heel; six months of "I'm not going, it's too hard to get there."

I watch the skating at City Hall. Children of immigrants pushing metal blades across pocked ice. Like all the others now but for soft brown eyes and brown skin, and nobody happier than the parents, teeth chattering, thin coat, standing alongside with the camera. And an old couple, arms crossed behind each other's waists, swaying in unison, one foot to the next, crossing over when they turn the corners, real skaters, waltzing, just like they used to do at the rink in Medicine Hat, those long-blade prairie experts.

Whistle blows. Off the ice. Zamboni's coming—

It broke off there. Blair sat unmoving, staring at the page. November. Her voice was near, but this was nine months ago. Surely, if she had died on the streets, she'd have been identified. Blair hoped she'd found her warm place. It was a long winter.

16

The Lighthouse Keeper's Cottage

Bernie bent low over the little green bushes with their load of dull, blue berries. It was Tuesday of the second week at the cottage. Simplicity picked berries alongside her. Her hands and face were stained blue. She had mosquito bites all over her arms and legs. When she found the berries she pulled them off the branches and ate them. When she didn't find any she picked them out of Bernie's yoghurt container and ate them.

"Are you going out tonight?" said Sissy.

"If it's okay with your mummy."

"Why do you have to ask her? You're big."

"Maybe she needs me to be here with you. Maybe she's going out herself."

"Uh-uh," said Simplicity. "My mother never goes out."

Bernie moved off to another cluster of bushes. They were under and around a nasty juniper bush. She squatted on her heels and reached in, avoiding the prickles.

"Here's some," said Sissy, putting out her hand to take the grey-blue juniper berries.

"Not those, you can't eat those. Those are poison."

"You die?"

"I think so," said Bernie.

Sissy sat down and contemplated the poison berries. She might die this afternoon, so that her mother could go out and Bernie could go out and no one would have to stay home to look after her.

"You don't like staying with me all the time," said Sissy. "You don't want to always be looking after a little kid."

Bernie sat down beside her. She offered the yoghurt container of berries.

"It's my job," she said. "Do you think I would do it if I didn't like to?"

"Yes. You have to. Because you want to stay here."

Bernie was quiet.

Sissy got up and began to walk down the path. "I'm going away because you don't want me," she said.

Bernie watched to be sure she went into the cottage. Then she continued picking berries.

Bernie sat on a rock at the end of the island. A green boat appeared out in the bay, travelling on its own reflection. Two lines spread out behind it like a bride's train. It circled, slowly, with a low gurgle from its motor; the driver stood up behind the wheel and looked down. It was as if he had lost something in the water. A tall-masted sailboat had drawn up to the cottage with the tennis court and hung there, suspended in the stillness.

A host of little black-masked, yellow-breasted birds had arrived this morning. They were leaping from branch to branch in the cedar stand. They flew in short bursts, their wings exploding and flapping all at once, then folding invisible into the round bodies as they soared. Bernie wondered what the name of the birds was. It was all very beautiful. If only it were hers, she would love it. For a long time Bernie had been loving other people's things. Other people's children. It was becoming difficult.

Simplicity was a sweet girl. She cried when you told her something sad, and she always cared how someone else was feeling. But then she could open her mouth and say something that was so unkind and so true, it took your breath away. She cut to the bone, in her gentle way. This was something about Canadians Bernie was still learning. She must never forget that Canadians were different than they let on. She would be a Canadian before long. Being up at the lake, Bernie had almost forgotten about files and interviews and assessments. But as long as she was here, she was waiting. She was waiting for permission, she was waiting for her status, she was waiting for her real life to begin.

Bernie was patient. She liked to work hard. She had done so for a long time. But now her long and terrible patience was cracking, shattering like a layer of thin ice rapped with a stick. She could not wait any more.

She could not wait because by the end of every day she was listless and bored, and a strange hum came out of her that she didn't even recognize. She could not wait because she spent two or three hours each night doing a jigsaw puzzle of Treasure Island, a puzzle that was too hard for Simplicity, that interested no one, not even Bernie herself. She could not wait because this was not her real life she was waiting in. She was attached, as a convenience, to other people's lives. And no matter how kind, how friendly those others were, they were on a different journey.

The letter was in a pile of mail that Max brought up from the city for Blair. It was among the bills, in a small envelope with no return address. It was typed on an old typewriter with dirty keys; the "p"s and "h"s were plugged black. Blair unfolded the single sheet of paper.

Dear Blair,

I am writing on behalf of Ruby Mason. She wishes you to be at Toronto Island airport on Tuesday August 23 at 6:00 p.m., at which time she will convey something to you. If you tell anyone about this letter there will be nobody there to meet you.

It was unsigned. Blair read the letter over three times. She could not make out whether Ruby would be there to meet her, provided she told no one, or whether it would merely be a messenger. It might be a trap. She thought of calling Oswald but Ruby would know, somebody would know, and Ruby would not come.

She folded the letter and put it in her pocket. This one she would hide in her bureau drawer. If it was a trap, she thought, and she didn't return from wherever she went on Tuesday, then Max would search and find the letter. She was filled with wild elation, which she disguised as pleasure at seeing him.

They went, with Bernie, to the fishing lodge for dinner. It was old and made of whitewashed logs. The usual relics were prominently displayed: stuffed and varnished animal heads, snapshots of men cradling enormous dead fish; the anchor from the wreck of a steamship that once travelled this way; a large photograph of the lodge minus its roof after the big storms of '34. In the screened porch old men sat reading. The sun inclined to below the roof ledge.

Dinner was lamb chops and mashed potatoes. The waitress was a young girl who couldn't decide if Bernie was an adult or a child. At first she didn't offer her wine, and then she changed her mind, came back and did. Bernie laughed and said no, at which point the girl decided perhaps she'd been wrong, perhaps she was still a child.

Bernie was jolly tonight, jolly and at the same time sad. Tonight was the end of an acting role she'd played for four years of her thirty-two years of life. Before that she was Dugale's woman; before that, her mother's child. Acting, acting. Her mother said God cursed Bernie with no children because she was wicked and lifted her skirts for Dugale before he asked her to marry. And that was why he never asked. Her mother screamed and threw hot water and pots around the house, saying this.

That terrible night, she had decided to go away, and this was where she landed. In Canada, in Toronto, on this little island; one particular place, for no particular reason. *There was no reason for it.* That was what Bernie thought as she sat at the fishing lodge and sipped her glass of grapefruit juice alongside Simplicity. In front of them were paper placemats with pictures of wildflowers on them and a map of Ontario. Bernie reached into her pocket and drew out two coloured markers. She always carried them in case Sissy got restless. Sissy began to practise her writing. She made her "s"s backwards, and her "n"s and her "h"s.

On another island, children were going hungry, getting fevers, missing school, running loose. Dugale was drinking and getting fat. While here, for the exquisite torture of loving strangers, Bernie was paid enough money to keep them alive. Bernie wondered if what she was going to do tonight was the same kind of mistake that she had made that night at home. Bernie did these things. She was a stayer and then a jumper. She stayed for too long and then jumped off a log into deep water. But the log was not stable, it was not going to hold her up; it was not even her log.

Blair and Max, their heads inclined toward each other, their eyes trained on the tabletop, spoke in low voices.

Blair had been kind to Bernie. Bernie was part of the family, she always said. Abe snorted. You are not part of their family, he said. That's what they say to exploit you. That's how they appeal to your emotions. Bernie had promised Abe she would tell Blair herself. She said it wasn't fair for him to make the announcement.

Abe was like Dugale had been; he was too proud. How

could she explain to him, who was so sure of himself, that it had been all right? Anything was all right when you knew you were only waiting. Blair was her friend. Together they laughed about the things Sissy said. Together they had discussed the world, and Canada, and how it worked, and Bernie was grateful. She could not explain this to Abe and she did not bother to try, because she knew he said what he did out of love for her. And that was good, to have someone on her side now.

She imagined what her mother would say. "He is filling your mind with his dangerous ideas."

"It is not my mind he is filling it is my body, filling it up where it has been vacant," Bernie would reply.

"What is this idea you have that loving a man is the way to settle your problems?"

"Because there is one thing in life you, Mother, never understood, and that is physical love." Which was not a sin, Bernie knew, it was not wrong, especially if you were in love and you planned to marry; it was probably never wrong unless you were forced, or it was someone else's man. "What have you got, Mother, with your little house in the village and your pride and your clean floors, and no man ever to love you?"

Abe walked in the door of the dining room. He was dressed in a clean, ironed shirt. His posture was as stiff as ever, but his face was broad, and lit with happiness. Max and Blair looked up. Blair understood at once. Bernie stood up at her chair.

"Go out," she said to him. "Go and wait in the porch. I am not ready."

Abe stopped, but he did not want to turn around; he did not want to go. "Do you need any help?" he said. He was afraid she could not do it.

"No," she said. "I've only been waiting."

Abe walked out of the room. Bernie looked at Blair. Blair's

eyes filled with tears. Bernie's did too. Sissy looked up from her colouring. She put her hand on Bernie's arm. She looked at her mother and at Bernie and saw that they were both crying. She began to wail.

"Blair, I am going to leave my job," said Bernie. "You are a nice woman but I am going to marry Abe."

"Well, why not?" said Blair to Max as they lay across their sheets, naked, in the stifling cottage bedroom. "It's as good a solution as she's going to find. Why shouldn't she?" She cried as she spoke. She was going to miss Bernie so much.

"Because you'll be left without a nanny," said Max. "That's why."

"She's got bigger problems to think about than that," said Blair.

"There's something called loyalty. Giving notice." Max looked grimly at the ceiling. A spider dangled from it. In his world, people did not treat jobs like that.

They had finished the dinner with Abe at the table and ordered a celebratory drink in the screened porch. They toasted the marriage as the last pink feathers of cloud darkened in the abandoned sky. Neither Bernie nor Abe drank. They left soon after, for his cottage.

"It doesn't matter," said Blair. "What does it matter now? She's gone. It's her right."

"Why do you always defend people who do you in? She's not giving you any *notice*, Blair. It's unfair."

"That's Abe. He can't stand to see his wife-to-be working as domestic help. Anyway, I don't think I'll get anyone else. I have an idea it's right for all of us," said Blair.

"What's she going to do all winter up here in the bush for God's sake? It's long, dark and cold."

"She'll love it. She'll make him a home. And he'll sponsor her family. They'll be pioneers, riding to school by snowmobile. I think it's a brilliant solution."

Max grunted. A breeze made its way through the screen at last. His eyes were heavy.

"Well, as long as you think you can manage."

"*I* think *I* can manage?" she said. He made it her problem. And he had almost convinced her they could live together. So, she said to herself, it will always be the same. Simplicity and me.

Simplicity lay in her bed but she did not go to sleep. After a long time, she got up in the darkness and silence and crept to Bernie's room. She opened the door and looked in. The bed was empty, the blanket stretched flat over the top of it. Bernie had gone away. She wasn't going to be Simplicity's babysitter any more. She was going to babysit that man Abe.

She saw her shadow, cast by the nightlight, stretch across the floor. It was huge. Simplicity felt stretched and empty. Something very large was happening to her; she would never forget. For the rest of her life, in some place inside her, she would be standing in the open door looking at Bernie's empty bed.

A pile of Bernie's clothes was left on the dresser. Simplicity went over and took down one of Bernie's T-shirts. It smelled like her, delicately, of something that came from trees, nuts maybe. She took it back to bed with her and spread it on her pillow. Then she pressed her face into it and cried herself to sleep.

Blair pushed her way through the office workers who cut across the lobby of Union Station en masse, like an army of corks afloat on a floodwater. She crossed Front Street in front of an idling taxi and darted behind a honking van. The bus to the Island airport was waiting, throbbing, the baggage hatch open. Surely no one would follow Blair Bowker today, or know her from the frazzled commuters edging down the bus aisle. But at the last minute she decided not to take the bus. She flagged a taxi.

Behind her sunglasses, she watched the rush-hour traffic jerk and crawl down Front Street. The taxi took an abrupt left turn and clanked to its sudden halt at the edge of land, an unceremonious lip of gravel. The sky was blue but the wind was fierce, whipping up little waves against the concrete slab banked with rubber tires that served as ferry dock. Blair ducked out of the blow into the shelter. A businessman in a perfectly tailored blue suit stood gazing blankly through the dirty glass. His white fingers were clenched around the handle of a leather briefcase.

Blair stood beside him and contemplated the narrow passageway of choppy water—two hundred metres across—that separated the island from the mainland. *Mainland.* Toronto did not feel like mainland: it was a moated city, connected to nothing; the water, the lake running to St. Lawrence and sea, the wilderness to the north, were all part of a world that Toronto held off.

On the island side of the channel, the flat-topped ferry blew its hoarse whistle and slowly pushed off. Blair came out of the shelter; wind whipped her hair around her face. But she was too soon, the ferry was making no perceptible progress across the narrow gap. She walked behind the shelter into Little Norway Park. A huge lion's head and paws of concrete for climbing, a maze made of green-metal screening and an orange plastic tube slide, the kind Simplicity liked, waited for children to come. To keep her rendezvous with Ruby, Blair had left Max at the cottage, telling him she had an audition. She dropped Simplicity with Rebecca, down the street from home. Simplicity had looked back at her with that tragic, nobody-wants-me face.

She turned from guilt to face the channel, with its half-dozen little sailboats tacking through, its seagulls patrolling overhead. The ferry was nearing the dock, its Canadian flag climbing higher over the gate as it approached. The ferry men, in luminous green suspenders, hoisted a giant, rusted hook and fit it into a hole on the concrete deck. Rapidly, the passengers descended the gangplank and disappeared into taxis and cars.

Blair boarded with men with briefcases, one very posh woman and a truckload of young workmen. In the narrow cabin old orange life-preservers were packed into the ceiling, each one stamped "Child Only." The workmen had followed her in. They wore orange or green monkey suits and crowded together reading a copy of the *Sun*. The story was about the execution of Bundy, the murderer of twenty women in the United States. Their faces were slack, passive, absorbing welcome horror from that other country across the water.

Now she stood dead centre in the dingy little airport and studied the schedule. A flight from Ottawa disgorged many grey-suited, grey-haired men and women with hundred-dollar haircuts. Briefcases fat with a change of shirt and toothbrush, they fled out through the lobby, down to the ferry dock. Blair stood on in the emptying waiting room. Planes were due in from Newark, Buffalo and Montreal. From which direction would she come? Would she come at all? Maybe it was a trap. Max would have thought so, if she had told him. But she couldn't. She would take any risk now to see Ruby. One thing was certain: if she were coming, Ruby would not take a seat in the middle of the Arrivals and Departures; she would not run up to Blair with open arms. She would set herself up somewhere, stage a presence, if not an entrance.

Behind Blair was the Lighthouse Keeper's cottage, a tiny old, blue-roofed house, which had lost its original function and now served as café. Wondering if she were being watched, Blair left the terminal, crossed the keyhole drive and climbed its wooden steps.

She could feel the old lighthouse keeper in the walls, the dark, warped floors; she could follow his lonely, long-distance gaze through windows that looked back to the city and the other way, out across the lake. The rooms where he had lived were small, square and wood-trimmed. Kitchen tables and chairs that might have been his were in use. The bar and a dirty grill for hamburgers occupied what would have been the hall. A sign hung over it: "THE COOK WENT HOME." The bartender had a long ponytail and a series of tattoos up his arm. There were only two people in the place, each in a different room, reading the *Sun*. Neither of them was Ruby.

Blair sat down beside a window. The warped old cottage window, the patched wall, framed a view of the city towers, which appeared to be floating on a wafer. The towers would sink if they weren't weightless, made of light—silver, gold, pink, metallic blue. The wood-painted window frame was earthy, grounded. Which was Toronto? Elaborate fantasy, or basic carpentry?

When Blair first came she saw only the heavy, red-brick houses and solid respectable housefronts—a vision of durability, so unlike wind-rattled prairie clapboard and false fronts. But now Toronto seemed more ephemeral even than those low-lying towns. Its grandeur rode so precariously atop this wafer-thin, floating kingdom. This comedy perhaps accounted for the tensions of the executives now boarding the ferry to go home, little put-up kings and queens, lords of lands that were owned elsewhere.

And suddenly Ruby was there, walking in the door with a canvas knapsack. Materializing like one of Oswald's spirits, from another dimension. Her gaze swept the room; it was the only way Blair knew her. She was covered up in white harem pants and a purple sweatshirt, a large black felt hat with cloth ties under her chin and sunglasses that curved around her head and reflected back the walls, with their travel posters of the Greek islands. Nothing showed but her cheeks and her bowed, uncoloured lips.

Blair stood. Her knees wobbled; she thought she would cry. She stretched out her arms. But Ruby's manner stopped her. Slammed her like a fist in the stomach. Ruby confronted her, met her head on, stubborn and separate.

"Returned from the dead," said Blair. She covered her tears by pressing the side of her face against Ruby's. The cheek was cool.

Without taking off her glasses or hat, Ruby dropped her knapsack on a chair. All the baggage tags had been removed, leaving little elastic bands dangling from the leather strap. Then, slowly, stiffly, she reached out with both arms and took Blair in her arms. They rocked, hugging and moaning. They had never embraced before. Though they had thrown arms around men they hardly knew, kissed boys for hours in the front seats of cars. They had discussed their bodies endlessly, the faults and attractions candidly. But sexual wariness meant they did not touch. To press her face against, her breasts against, to encircle with arms another woman had been taboo. Now it was necessary. A huge and gaping hole seemed to surround Ruby, and she reached out from it.

Blair felt Ruby's cold hands on her back. Again she was chilled. Instead of drawing her in, the embrace made her aware of how changed, how *other* Ruby was.

Ruby dropped onto a chair, still without removing her sunglasses.

"Sit down, you're attracting attention."

Blair sat down. Tears sat on her cheeks. She opened her mouth. Her voice shook.

"Where have you come from? Where did you go?"

Ruby gave Blair a withering look; of course she wouldn't say.

"I have to wait for the diary?" It was an attempt at a joke.

At last Ruby smiled. "I shouldn't have, but I had to tell someone. I had to tell *you*," she corrected. "You're my audience. You knew. The others thought I was dead."

Blair didn't tell Ruby how often she had dreamed the others were right. "Why should I know?"

Ruby shrugged. "You understand me."

A shaft of pure rage went through Blair. She said nothing.

"But of course I couldn't tell you everything. It's not easy to pull off," said Ruby. "You gotta keep reminding yourself, you tell one person, they tell two. Rule of thumb."

Why was she here now? Did that mean she was prepared to reappear? Blair didn't ask. Ruby might stand up again, throw the knapsack over her back and walk out.

"You look good," she said. "Better than I expected."

Ruby thrust her leg forward. "Feel my thigh. Is it perfect?"

Blair put out her fingers and squeezed Ruby's thigh. It was not as hard as before. "Almost."

"I'm doing yoga."

"Where?"

Ruby laughed. "If I told you, you'd know."

Again the anger flashed hot in her head. What was it? A lover from India? Or some ashram, some identity-washing cult? A late sunbeam caught the glass pane of the little window beside them and flashed once, twice, communication from some alien star.

"You just have to promise not to ask questions. Not to make demands. Or I'm *gone*," said Ruby fiercely.

Blair took her bottom lip between her teeth, to steady it. She felt Ruby was an unknown. Why was she here, why were they both here? Trying to find some meeting place in their past, or trying to prove they could cut it off, and start again?

"Everything you said in your diary—"

Ruby waved her hand. "Thinking on paper. No one to talk to. . . . Did you like it?"

Blair nodded slowly, then shook her head. "A bit disturbing. Especially when you thought you knew somebody."

Ruby smiled. "Might get a publisher," she said. "Change

the names and all."

"They'd know."

"You're right," said Ruby. "There's certain disadvantages to being disappeared."

"You can't be a celebrity."

"Oh, I don't know. I figure I got more attention from disappearing than I did from all the work I did for fifteen years."

"But you can't cash in on it."

Ruby smiled. "You're right. That's something I had to give up." They sat in silence. "You'll have to talk. Tell me everything. How's Simplicity? Where are you working?" said Ruby.

So those were her rules. Ruby could ask questions, Blair couldn't. "I'm out of work. Bernie's leaving. Simplicity's heartbroken. I might just stay home with her. But I'll be poor."

Ruby raised her eyebrows. "Maybe having a career doesn't do much for you. Look at me, I had one and gave it up! In fact, why don't you take mine? It's sitting there," said Ruby. "Ready-made."

The ferry whistle blew, rude, intrusive. Out the window they could see the ferry men throw the hooks off their concrete posts. The water churned; the boat began to move away from the shore. Blair was overcome by a wave of fatigue. All the time, the fears, the dreaming, and now she sat at a table with Ruby. A version of Ruby. Unable to say what she felt. All she wanted was to ask why. Why, aside from everything she already knew. *Really* why. "Why?" she whispered.

Ruby was looking back across the water at the city. It was nearly seven o'clock. The sun was slanting off to the west. Great waves of gold came off the glass into the air. She began to speak.

"It just came to me, suddenly. When I was going down Queen's Quay in a taxi that night, with the window down. I just thought, I can do this. I can pull it off. There I was. So alone. Depending on nobody. Nobody depending on me. There's got to be some advantages to being all that. What can I do that nobody else can? The answer was die. Or *like* dying, disappear. *And not be missed.*"

Blair sat silently.

"It's perfect. No victims. And I realized all the skills I'd developed all my life led up to this one act. My whole life was a costume parade. I knew how to create myself once. I could do it again."

"Two things," said Blair. "Not be missed is wrong. I, for one, missed you. And then second—what about *missing*? You missing people?"

Ruby shook her head. "At first I missed Marvin. But I knew I'd get over it. Marvin was just an obsession. When you learn to give up one thing, you can give up anything. Once you learn how to shake one, you can shake them all." Ruby smiled slowly. Her beautiful lips and teeth under the sunglasses made Blair long to see her eyes. Her skin looked rougher, she'd been out in the wind. No moisturizer, she remembered from the diaries.

"No victims," said Blair slowly.

"Well."

"Your mother."

Ruby flushed. "She's got her notions. Wouldn't take me as I was. Thinks I've gone to God probably—"

"—not by your own hand—"

"—give her someone to blame, makes her feel better . . ."

"Your family figures Oswald had something to do with it. Think he's a voodoo artist."

"Oh Oswald," said Ruby.

"He tells people he's communing with you from beyond the grave. Marvin too."

"Great," said Ruby, waving her arm. "Perfect. Gives them something to do."

"You must admit," said Blair, going back to the idea of

there being no victims, "people looked pretty hard. They still are, I figure. It's not as if we didn't care—"

"Don't try to pressure me! Don't *push*. I said listen, or I'm gone!" Her voice cut the air.

"You didn't. You said don't ask questions. I can say what I want."

"You can't," Ruby hissed. "Because you're not in control. I'm in control. Listen to me. Or I'll go."

Blair listened, eyes stinging. "You are so stubborn."

Ruby sighed, looked around once and took off her glasses. "One thing," said Ruby. "One." She opened her knapsack and pulled out an envelope. In the envelope was a photograph. She passed it to Blair. It was a colour snapshot of a shack in a grove of poplar and spruce. In the background were hills, rolling upward to blue foothills. It looked like Alberta.

"You went home?"

Ruby snatched it away. "Not really. Just so you know," she said. "I haven't been sleeping in doorways."

"Is it near the railway tracks?"

Ruby tucked the photograph back in her bag. "Say nothing," she admonished herself.

"So Oswald helped you get away, in November."

Ruby said nothing.

"And you found your incubator." She gestured to the photograph, tucked in the knapsack. "Is it his shack?"

Ruby looked a warning. Stop, or I'll be gone.

"Maybe I'll find out in the next instalment," said Blair. "You will send more diary?"

"After it's too late," said Ruby, through stiff lips. "Too late to trace me. Then I will." The lustrous frenzy of the fashion exec was gone, and in its place—a low fire in her brown eyes. Of the earlier Ruby something remained, or was exposed. Ruthlessness. She had unlearned how to hide it.

Blair watched Ruby's face. There was no point blaming her. There was no point enumerating the pain. She was alive, and she had chosen this; she had rendered Blair and everyone else insignificant. One, singular, unattached life. One reborn woman. Not just independent. *Un*dependent.

"So is it better? The new incarnation?"

Ruby considered. She cocked her head like a bird, listening. "Newer," she said finally.

"What did you get?" said Blair. "I know what you gave up. What did you get?"

"Freedom," said Ruby.

Blair laughed. It was just a word.

"People suffered," said Blair.

"People," said Ruby. "You know, I was glad to lose almost every one of them. I had time to think about why. Maybe I'm not like other people. Maybe there's something missing. Either that, or there's a giant fraud everyone is perpetrating, clinging to love and family. I don't *need* other people. I don't get what I need from them. I get it from me."

The lump rose in Blair's throat, the need to deny what Ruby said.

"But you came back to see me."

Ruby looked puzzled. Then she spoke, this time more gently. "I needed a touchstone maybe."

Blair lifted her beer glass to cover her face. She swallowed, put the glass down.

"Touchstone," she said. Touch. Stone. A cold feeling; a point to return to as a reminder. "But I'm not a stone. Maybe you are."

Ruby's hand caught Blair's; they squeezed, hard, so that the knuckles showed white. The love of two women was too much alike. Love like a mother's, so strong it can't afford to go wrong. Too much power to destroy.

Blair pulled away first.

Ruby leaned back and put the sunglasses on again. She said nothing for a while. But she waved for another beer. She wasn't ready to go, not yet.

"That's gonna be tough on you, Bernie leaving."

"My next-best friend," said Blair grimly. "It feels like."

"You'll get another."

"Yes," said Blair, not knowing if she meant another nanny or another friend. "Maybe."

"You could have such a nice life," said Ruby, suddenly, impatiently. "Why don't you just let it happen?"

"It's not that easy."

"Hey, I gave you Max," said Ruby. "Don't ever say I didn't do anything for you."

Blair stared at her quizzically. "You did, didn't you? How come?"

"I just had a feeling. I had a feeling it would work."

"I wonder what it feels like when it works? I wonder what that means," said Blair.

"You're the expert on relationships. Lived your whole life in terms of them."

"You said that. You said—"

"I said you live your life in terms of other people. You see yourself in relationship to them—"

"Friend—"

"Daughter—"

"I don't."

"Yes you do. And mother, or wife—face it, Blair."

Blair shook her head. "Mother is different. It takes you over. You can't help it. The others I deny."

"Why should you?"

"It's too dangerous. You lose yourself if you live that way."

"Being alone's dangerous. Look what happened to me—"

"Come back next year and you'll see what happened with Max and me," said Blair. "I'm not giving any hints. I honestly don't know."

Travellers came in and drank their beer. A man with a short black ponytail and a moss-green trench coat played the video machine. The sun went down over the Western Gap.

Blair drank in every angle of Ruby's face in the darkening room, the incurve of her cheek, the squared, thrust chin, the wide-apart, pitiless brown eyes. Blair told her about the search, about Dick Nolan, and Mary and Arthur. Ruby nodded and smiled, unmoved. Even Marvin's predicament only made her raise an eyebrow. She was like a ghost, a ghost who had made a random appearance in the clutter of daily life. Best only to watch, and mourn, and love, by leaving her unloosed, free to pass and not to be clung to.

"I must go," said Ruby, finally.

"Where?" blurted Blair inadvertently.

"I have someplace," she said. "You don't need to worry."

"Will you stay gone?"

"I will, and if you even *hint* to anyone you've seen me, you're dead meat."

"You mean they'll come after me? 'People I wouldn't touch with a ten-foot pole'?"

"You *bet*."

The joking died suddenly. Blair's mouth was dry. Her anger had dissipated.

"If it's easy for you," she said slowly, "arrange it so we find out you're dead. If you're serious about this. If you're not coming back. Because it's hard on people. The not knowing. Furthermore—"*Let's make this a joke*, she said to herself, *otherwise I'll never get through it.*"—take pity on Dick Nolan. Good public money is going to waste looking for you."

"Now that's a worry," said Ruby. And they both laughed. But Blair knew she had heard. "I'll consider it."

"These people—this person—whoever helps you, could they arrange something like that? The people I wouldn't touch with a ten-foot, etc.?"

"Habeas corpus? Hey, they can do anything. Provide a body?" Ruby was joking now too. "Dresses and drawers? Dental records? You name it. Only the energy never dies, right?"

"I sometimes wish I believed," said Blair.

"You do believe. You're the biggest believer I ever met. People and all their messy feelings—that's what hooks you. That's what holds you."

"It would be a kindness," said Blair firmly, "to provide a body." And then she thought, is this me being good old Blair, wanting to tidy things up? Taking responsibility for Ruby, even when it was not in my own interest? Because if Ruby didn't create her own death, she might be found. She might reappear some day, and Blair would have her back.

But Blair did want to tidy the record, ease the suffering of others, even people who had nothing to do with her. There was nothing she could do about it. Her persona, unlike some others, was fixed. She did not believe in life after cutting out. She did live on "people and all their messy feelings." That was why, unlike Ruby, she did not have the power to create, or uncreate, herself.

"If you promise to come back and see me, I'll even go along with news of your death," said Blair. It sounded too much like Peter Pan and Wendy. Peter was off to Never-Never Land. "And straight on 'til morning!"

"You'll believe it," said Ruby.

"I said I'd go along with it. I'll never believe it. Even if they come up with a perfect likeness. I'll know you've got a new life. So you see, you *can't* die, now."

On the windy concrete slab by the curled rubber tires that stopped the ferry, Blair and Ruby stood, embracing. Blair was like the child who would not leave the open coffin: as long as she could see Ruby, she was not lost to her. Saying goodbye now was worse, somehow, than burying her would have been. To accept this disappearance was to face, constantly and forever, the fact that Ruby had willed her old life away. She thought of Max, and his nightmares about the woman who jumped in front of the subway. He was more right than he knew; Ruby *had* decided to kill herself.

Yet here she was, or someone so like her—sturdy, cheerful, holding Blair's shoulders in a firm grip. The life that surged in her had no guilt, no remorse. Wherever she was, whoever she was, it must be good.

"And memories?" Blair had said in the Lighthouse Keeper's cottage. "Have you escaped them, too?"

"Very nearly," said Ruby. "Only occasionally a dream gets through, from the old life." She smiled, her lips splitting over large white teeth, her eyes so dark they seemed all pupil.

"I wouldn't want to. I don't think I could live without my past."

"Some people have to."

"But why you?"

"Because I *could*."

And they clasped hands quickly as Ruby turned and sprinted back to the terminal. "Goodbye." Blair hurled her voice into the wind. "Goodbye."

Blair's feet made hollow thumps down the gangplank.

Simplicity sat on the front porch steps at Rebecca's house. She scowled. The other kids were playing TV-tag. You ran around for a while and then froze and pretended to be some character from a TV show. Simplicity couldn't run fast and she didn't watch TV, so she couldn't think of anyone to be. Except the Polkaroo, from "Polka Dot Door," and she already did that once.

"Siss! Sissy!"

They were calling her from down on the sidewalk. She pretended she couldn't hear. She put her chin in her hand. The other hand undid her laces. She took off her shoes and sat on them. There. Now if they came and tried to drag her off she couldn't go.

When her mother came back from her meeting they were going to McDonald's. Then they would go home to sleep in their normal house. She could see her house from here. It was not far away, on the other side of the street. It seemed like a long time since she lived there. They had been at Andy's cottage forever. Tomorrow morning they were going out to buy new shoes for school. School started next week.

The house looked scary; it had no one in it. Simplicity didn't want to sleep there and she didn't want to come back next week and she didn't want to go to school. She didn't want to go back to the cottage, either. Bernie was gone. It was probably her mother's fault. She would give her mother one chance to be nice. If she didn't pass the test, then Simplicity would run away from home.

Rebecca's mother came out the door.

"Aren't you playing tag with the other kids?" she said.

Didn't she have eyes?

"No," said Simplicity.

"Do you want me to take you down there?"

"No," said Simplicity. "I haven't got my shoes on."

Rebecca's mother laughed.

"That's not an insurmountable problem," she said, and bent to look for Simplicity's shoes.

"Yes it is." Simplicity withdrew her feet quickly and sat on them, too.

"Do you want to come in and read a book?"

"No," said Simplicity. "I can see my house."

She's homesick, that's what it is, thought Rebecca's mother. "That's fine then, you just keep sitting there," she said pleasantly. Strange child, she thought. Not a bit of trouble though, unless you counted wondering what was going on in that head.

Blair and Sissy chose a table near the play area at McDonald's. Blair had been late to pick her up. Simplicity had that pale, set look her mother feared. The look she'd had before she bit Rachel.

On their table were two styrofoam hamburger cartons, two plastic drink lids, two cardboard fries envelopes, straws, wax-covered cups, a dozen crumpled paper napkins, and several small plastic bags, ripped open, which used to have ketchup and mustard in them. Simplicity's T-shirt looked as if a crime of violence had been committed nearby. It was decorated with red and yellow drips. Blair sipped a cup of coffee.

"Aren't you going to go in and play on the slide?"

"No."

Blair heaved a sigh of annoyance.

"That's why we came here. Do you think I brought you here for my health?"

Simplicity scrunched her face into an evil squint. "You must be tired, Mummy."

Blair resisted the urge to snap at her. All the kids, pushing and crying at the door of the play area. And no parents. A few grandparents, some obvious babysitters, mostly nannies. She could hear Tagalog, with its soft, popcorn sounds, from the corners. If you were a nanny from the Philippines this was a big social spot. Blair envied their happy camaraderie.

"That's why we came here, so you could go in and play," she repeated.

Simplicity watched a nanny and two children on the slide, sadly. "I don't want to."

"Yes you do."

"I do not."

"You do," said Blair, tiredly. They did this hopeless dance together. *I'm stuck with you, and you're stuck with me, and there's nothing we can do about it.*

Blair made a superhuman effort to change the steps.

"Tomorrow morning we get your new shoes for school."

"I'm not going back to school," said Sissy.

"You're not? Why? Don't you like school?" Blair knew that was the wrong question, that it was wrong to even ask a question. But she was too tired to be creative.

"No."

"Why not?"

Sissy didn't answer at first. Finally she looked up from her Coke. "Because it's boring. We just have to play all the time."

"You don't like to play?" But Blair already knew that.

"Not at school. The kids aren't my friends. And the teachers aren't my friends."

"Who is your friend?"

"Bernie is."

"Aha," said Blair. "But Bernie's gone away."

"Don't talk to me, Mummy, just don't talk to me about it!"

Blair and Sissy walked down St. Clair Avenue hand in hand. It was eight-thirty. To the west, peaked and uneven rooftops blocked the sunset. Only a little bit of light was left in the sky. Blair remembered how Ruby used to say in Toronto you could walk and walk and never see the horizon.

A surprising number of people were on the street, shouldering their way around a woman and a dawdling child. They had plastic bags of groceries in their hands, or rode past in neon bicycle shorts. They ran to catch a movie, as harried about their pleasures as they were about their jobs. Blair stepped aside to let them go. She had been away. She was not like those people.

"When did you decide that you weren't going back to school?" Blair had wakened up now, she was alert now, in charge of all her skills. This was an emergency, and she had to rise to it.

"Today."

"Oh dear, that's too bad."

"No it isn't. School is dumb. School is boring."

"Sometimes you think that. But other times you have fun."

"I never have fun. I hate school. I hate it."

"Do you hate Miss Boggs? And Miss Rushton?"

"I don't hate them, Mum," said Simplicity, with an air of great patience. "They're just stupid."

Blair laughed. She agreed, actually. And if she agreed, then why should she make Simplicity go?

"Are schools all the same do you think?"

Simplicity scowled. "You just want me to go to school so you don't have to look after me. You want to work."

Blair was stung.

"That might be partly true. But it's also true that I think school is good for you. I used to love school, Sissy."

"You see? You're doing it again," said Sissy. "You're talking about when you were a kid. And don't call me Sissy. My name is Siss."

"Okay, Siss," agreed Blair. It seemed the least she could do.

They had progressed across St. Clair Avenue to Avenue Road. The pavement felt hard underfoot after a month of woody paths, and the traffic drowned out Sissy's soft voice. There was a tiny park at the corner of Avenue Road and St. Clair, the one with the statue of Peter Pan in it. Ruby's face returned with a painful stab to Blair. *And straight on 'til morning!* If Sissy had wings she would fly away now. Blair sat on a bench and took the girl between her knees. Peter Pan watched.

"Mummy, did you tell Bernie to go away?"

"No. I did not tell Bernie to go away. It was her own idea."

"Did you want her to go away?"

Blair thought a few seconds. "No I didn't. But I can understand it. It's probably a good idea, for her. She's got to have her own life, you know, away from us. It had to happen some day."

Simplicity pushed Blair's hands away. She sobbed. "Who's going to look after me?"

"I will."

Simplicity let her mother hug her. "Are you mad at Bernie?" she said. Simplicity did not look up into her mum's eyes. If her mother was mad at Bernie, Simplicity said to herself, she would run away for sure.

Blair's eyes filled with tears. "No I'm not." But her voice was shaking. Why does everything happen at once? she thought. I can't handle this. Not now. Not after Ruby.

Simplicity's voice went high in alarm.

"Oh Mummy, what's wrong? Don't you cry."

"I'm just tired. Just very tired. It's been a very long day."

Blair sat on one of the swings and watched Sissy climb the slide. Slowly, deliberately, she did it, not like a child at play. *This is something I must learn how to do*, her posture on the ladder said. *This is how kids play*. What made her like that? So joyless and determined? Had her father been that way? Blair could hardly remember.

When Sissy got down the slide she came to sit on Blair's lap.

"I don't want to go to our house tonight," she said. "I want to run away."

"Somehow that doesn't surprise me."

Simplicity watched her mother's face. "I am *going* to run away," she said.

"Are you?" said Blair. "Well, if you are I'm coming too."

Simplicity's feet were in the dusty patch where there was no grass, under the swing. She slid them back and forth, getting dirty.

"Well?"

"I'm still running away."

"I guess I'll have to come too."

"Okay."

Blair and Simplicity walked down the hill to the car. It was parked by Rebecca's house, not far from their own. They had sweaters in the car, and long pants, a blanket even, that Blair kept there in case of breakdowns. The wind had dropped along with the sun. The sky was still half lit.

"Where are we going to go?"

"I don't know. Do you suppose we should camp out?"

"That's a good idea," said Simplicity, delightedly.

They put their long pants and sweaters on over their other clothes, so they were all bulky and shapeless. It felt better that way. Blair took forty dollars and tucked it into her pants pocket; she locked her purse in the car and carried the blanket.

They took Blair's favourite walk, alongside the triangular park to Clarendon and into the ravine. They walked across the side of the hill where Blair had sat nearly a year ago, where she had seen the reservoir as an ancient tomb. It was nearly dark now. A few people were out walking their dogs across the paths; they were silent and intent on their task, the dogs frisking at the ends of their leashes.

"I'm getting very tired," said Simplicity. "It's late, isn't it?"

"Nine-thirty."

"Where are we going to sleep?"

"I know a place." Blair took Sissy by the hand. They walked farther across the hill, cut under the Spadina overpass and downhill to the very bottom. There was a two-track path there. Sometimes the park vehicles drove on it. The grass was high between the tracks; no one had driven here for a while. Blair remembered the place she'd seen, at the end of this track, where it met with the side of the hill and a set of steps went up to St. Clair Avenue. There was a little camp there, where people slept.

It was getting too dark to see. "Here it is," said Blair finally. She whispered. She didn't think the tramps were there. Maybe they would come later. She hoped not, but it really didn't matter.

"Here," she said. She found a patch of flattened grass and spread the blanket. Sissy lay down on half of it. Blair sat on the other, and wrapped Sissy up, and held her in her lap. "You can go to sleep now."

Simplicity put her arms around her mother's legs. "Sing me a song," she said.

Blair sat in the darkness in the ravine. She could hear the traffic on St. Clair; it wasn't very far away but it was invisible. They were invisible too. She felt the heavy weight of Sissy in her lap. There were no bugs. That in itself was amazing. City air pollution. Toronto was death to mosquitoes. She sang. All the old songs, but softly, until she felt Sissy relax.

She was glad they were sleeping out. It was a good idea. She did not want to go back to the house either. The house meant too many things—it meant an occupation, an arrest. It meant the resumption of a life that Blair was deciding, even now, as she sat in the long, flattened grass, not to resume. Blair was not made for houses. She was made to be a mother perhaps, but not an employer of babysitters, or a radio host, or the person who knew where Max's trousers were. Freedom, she thought. That word I laughed at. I want it too. Despite—what was it Ruby said? People and all their messy feelings.

It wasn't worthwhile to ask why. (*Why* is the worst question, Oswald said.) Some women sought roles as keepers of men and children and houses. Many said they wanted such a position, but failed to find one. Blair avoided it, but it came to her anyway. Came to her because she sought it, and then tried to run away.

Perhaps it was Ruby, who wanted out of everything, who'd given her this germ. This virus: to escape. Ruby was action, her own story. Blair was waiting, reception. Blair was where all the other stories met. She could not have her own story; she was compelled to a kind of stasis, to aid and to understand other lives. "You always lived your life in reaction to everyone else. Just like a girl," said Ruby.

Her legs were getting stiff and cold. Blair rearranged herself, lying down with Sissy—"Siss"—on top of her. The child was so thin Blair could see her bones. They were growing, they were tilting, curving, revealing a precocious knowledge of their adult shape. The bones had wisdom. But the skin was different, unutterably soft, the malleable sweet skin of a child, bewildered as it is stretched to cover the growing.

The ground was damp. There were plastic bags around she could tear up and use, but if she moved she'd wake up Siss. Siss—a big girl. Someone who would gather speed now, become an adult. Meanwhile, Blair's life seemed suspended. She ought to make peace with that. "You could have such a wonderful life." She ought to be grateful. There was no need to rush. The gift is slowness. If she, Blair, does not take that gift, then who will watch Simplicity's agonizing, exhilarating metamorphosis from child into young woman?

Back and forth, she argued with herself. To be free of everyone else, their limiting needs; to wait, and be the centre, and hold. As the darkness became complete, Blair was aware that sleeping out here was mad. Mad from the outside. Exactly right from within. It occurred to her that she ought to have called Max and made some kind of excuse. He would have called the house by now. He'd be wondering where they went. But with any luck, he'd go out drinking with a bunch of men after the Laser race and forget all about them.

Later, the tramps came back to their little home. It was dark and they had drink. They stumbled around and made a lot of noise. Blair woke up. She was not afraid. She knew they wouldn't hurt her. She remained very still, her arms around Sissy. She didn't want to talk to anyone. Soon, they all went to sleep, all but one, who raged and mumbled and thrashed about alone, in some private agony. Finally he was silent.

17

Tract

Max tied up the Molly and loaded his Laser onto the dock. He'd tried too hard and dumped halfway through the course.

After being whipped up all morning with a tricky northeast wind, the lake had gone still. Max poured his usual gin and tonic and went to sit on the screened porch. From here he could see only Abe's cottage and the back of an uninhabited island. He could see the heron as it flew from one of its marshy spots to another, the osprey on its platform, and the sun sliding into the ragged tops of the pines.

He wondered how Blair's errands in town had gone. If she had bought Simplicity's new shoes yet. Done whatever else she had to do. He watched the sunset. He could have kept Sissy today. A couple of other kids watched the race. It would have been fun. Why did he refuse? There was a certain still, resigned look on Blair's face when she made it clear she wasn't going to fight him over this, she was just going to cope on her own. He was beginning to understand that look.

The loons were kicking up a real fuss out there. It sounded as if something had got one of their babies. He got up from the chair and went to the telephone. Probably Blair would be home now and he could find out how it went.

He let the phone ring ten times. Maybe they went to McDonald's for dinner, in which case they'd be back at eight at the latest. Sissy would be exhausted. She got up at six. Staying with Rebecca would have worn her out, having to play like other kids. The little grown-up. Maybe when she got to be thirty she'd loosen up. Like he did.

At eight o'clock and eight-ten and eight-twenty he phoned: no answer. It was nothing serious, but he was bugged. He might as well have gone with then, for all the relaxing he did.

He tried to remember the last name of the neighbours where Sissy spent the afternoon. Rebecca—Rebecca who? He drew a total blank, didn't know if he'd ever been told anyway. Finally, at nine, he called Mr. Boswell across the street, the old guy in the hat. *His* name Max remembered, at least. He was always hanging out in front of the house keeping an eye on things.

"Jim!" he said. "Max Ostriker here. Blair Bowker's friend, across the street. Sorry to bother you. I'm up at the cottage. . . . Beautiful weather, beautiful. But tell me, I sent Blair down to the city today with Simplicity, and I'm just trying to track them down. The phone may be out of order. Tell me, is the car in the driveway?"

The old man didn't hesitate.

"Nobody in the house, Max. Though I thought I saw the car earlier, little up the street."

"Yeah, that would be near Rebecca's house. Sissy spent the afternoon there. Drove off afterward, did they?"

"No they didn't. Came back, pulled some things out of the car. I remember noticing. But they went off on foot. I can tell you there's no one in the house. No car, no lights. I woulda noticed if they'd come in."

Now Max was suspicious. She must have had a plan. Perhaps a plan to spend the night elsewhere? That's why she hadn't wanted Sissy with her. A wild, jealous tattoo started up in his heart. Secrecy in Blair he hated. And she *was* secretive. "Never love an independent woman," his father used to say. "That's trouble." Blair had ample opportunity to cheat. She could do just about anything she wanted all day in the house. Only Bernie would know, and Bernie was as loyal as any secretary.

It was a beautiful evening. If they were here they'd go out in the boat for a deep swim in the orange-streaked, still water. From the east a breeze stirred, faintly, carrying with it the clang from Abe's moored sailboat. Even that had a forlorn sound. Bernie and Abe had gone down to the city too. She was going to live with her sister until the wedding; Abe was now being introduced to the vast network of uncles, cousins and in-laws that Max and even Blair had never seen.

He could not even enjoy sitting on the porch swing, which normally Simplicity claimed. Here it was, free and empty, the sunset begging attention, and Max was wandering around the cottage, not even knowing what he was looking for. He thought for a while it was a telephone number; he opened all the drawers in the kitchen where the telephone sat. Then he went through the books, the games, pulling out loose pieces of paper, without thinking. He found half-played games of Xs and Os; Simplicity's practice writing, with all her reversed letters carefully corrected by Blair; a torn shopping list. In the main room, next to the dining-room table, was a chest; in the top of it were all the guarantees and the bills of sale from Andy's gadgets and appliances: electric screwdriver, halogen light, vacuum cleaner (circa 1955).

He passed the tape deck, snapping his fingers and hitting the sides of his thighs: music was perhaps what he needed. Yet as soon as he put on the Cowboy Junkies, their smooth, unassuming presence began to irritate him. It was music made to be background. And background to what? He had no foreground, he was just a restless, marauding male.

He found himself in the bedroom, sorting the supermarket receipts and hair barrettes on top of Blair's bureau. Then he was going through the top drawer. Underwear in neat little rolls, the way Bernie always delivered it after a wash. Plastic rain-hat from some previous guest. And in the bottom, an envelope. Open, with a note tucked inside.

He lifted the letter from its nest with a sense, not of surprise, but of inevitability. The utter predictability of this moment. Some assumption had crept into his affair with Blair, riding on their insisted-upon autonomy. Not precisely dishonesty, but an assumed lack of disclosure. He knew for certain Blair hid things from him. Letters, at least. He hid things from Blair, too—for instance, telling Mensa about the diary. He didn't want to explain himself, to be circumscribed by his own accounting. He wanted to impress Blair, to surprise her with a solution. He opened the envelope.

I am writing on behalf of Ruby Mason. She wishes you to be at Toronto Island airport on Tuesday August 23 at 6:00 p.m. at which time she will convey something to you. If you tell anyone about this letter there will be nobody there to meet you.

A jolt went up and down his spine. His feet seemed to press into the floor, his head to jut into the ceiling. Not a lover. Worse, much worse. It was Ruby. Damned Ruby again. Was Blair, too, having seances with her departed friend? Did her secrecy go that far? Or was she innocent, lured to a rendezvous, only to be kidnapped herself? Who had written the note? "People I wouldn't touch with a ten-foot pole," said Dick Nolan.

The last squares of fluorescent orange from the sun were floating on the water, like loose life-jackets. Max grabbed his sweatshirt and his wallet. If he left now, he could make it to the highway just before dark; he'd be in the city be eleven.

Driving down the 400, Max beat his fist on the steering wheel to his oldie-goldie collection. That song he loved,

"Desperado, come down from your fences." He could chart his emotional life in the past twenty years through song lyrics. He could see the eyes on all those old pop singers, the Band, the Grateful Dead. Men with lots of facial hair and a gentle, straight-on, dilated stare. It all had to do with the Vietnam war; they were making it clear they weren't killers.

Hearts of Flame had been like that—soft, direct, unaggressive. While he, Max, had been a guy in a suit, trying to borrow their stance, to inhale their air. He supposed Blair had despised him then. He never forgot her, standing on the stoop of that little dormitory in the twilight—defiant, enraged, innocent. And the others: Philip, gentle, but with some huge, held-back power; Ruby, radiating sex and drive; Oswald, contained, calculating. They had everything, the dark and the light, they were complementary, complete. They were a family. And, like a family, reserved their powers for decades, striking now to take Blair away from him.

His gaze took in the speedometer: 130 kilometres. With difficulty, he lifted his foot from the pedal and slowed to 110. He had to make a plan. A plan for what to do when he got home and discovered, as he knew he would discover, that Blair and Sissy were gone. He would get Marvin on the phone, threaten him with arrest on his drug offences. He would call Andy. Cops, detectives. Mensa. Oswald. He put his foot back down on the gas.

In Toronto, the darkness, and a brisk wind, had erased the foul haze that normally hung over the city in August. The sky was black; the lights on the flat ground lay in seductive patterns, the stars faint and persistent in deep space. Blair's house was dark. It felt abandoned, dusty, lifeless. Blair had been away for over a month, and Sissy, too. He came in during the week only to dump the mail onto the front hall rug, taking the interesting bits up north, and to water the plants. Or he was supposed to. Even that he'd forgotten. The spider plant was brown and limp.

He went upstairs. The bedroom was neat, and told no tales. The clothes were in the closet, her shoes on racks; the drawers were shut, and inside them, sweaters and tights lived in tidy piles. Max's things were overlaying hers; his slithery stack of magazines beside the bed; a couple of bags with CDs inside, or paint cans, some project he had in mind for the house, left in the hall. He was a visitor, and an absent-minded one at that.

Maybe she had gone to his place. He was briefly elated with this idea. She had a key, just as he had a key to hers. Maybe she had been depressed going into her house on MacPherson, as he was. He got in the car and flew down Charles Street, parked in the cool underground and came up the elevator, security mirrors aimed down at him from above.

But his place was even worse. Dry-cleaning dropped over the back of the sofa, a new framed print leaned against the wall, not hung up. A mass of tools from his tool kit spread around the floor, from last Thursday when he hadn't been able to find the screwdriver head he needed.

Max was struck, looking at his place the way a detective would, by his relations with *things*. The man who lived here bought things and then abandoned them—in the back seat of the car, on the living-room sofa.

In the bedroom beside his pillow was a pile of news magazines wrapped in dust. The contents of his pockets for the past many months—restaurant receipts, plane tickets, plastic wrap off his new shirt. Things rotted in Max's keeping. He could not take care of things. His bicycle had been out in the rain. The folding chair on the front porch—same thing. One tennis shoe was lost.

Now, as he could not search for Blair, he searched for the other shoe. He opened the door to the closet. He got down on his hands and knees and dug, throwing the shoes that littered the bottom out into a pile behind him, shooting them between his legs as a dog would so much dirt. The tennis shoe was not in the pile. He left the rest of the things in the centre of the floor. He crawled over to the bed and lifted the edge of the bedspread: not under there, either, but he did find his racket.

He knew he was wasting valuable time, but he could not stop looking. He wandered the house swinging his tennis racket. He would have liked to hit things. But suppose some neighbour should come in and find him doing violence. Violence was something Max forbade himself. He only violated things, and even that indirectly, by misuse and neglect. But things were not people, things could not have feelings, or even be the cause of feelings.

This idea surprised Max. It seemed to him his whole life had been acted out as if they were. Money was love: his father taught him that. His father bought him a new racket, a new toy, instead of going out to play a game with him. Max had to act happy. But the objects, the toys, were a continual disappointment to him. Even if they were the best, they had a habit of developing problems. If they didn't develop problems, then they made him feel inadequate. He remembered himself one day on the tennis court, a lonely fourteen-year-old, picking up a game with an older boy.

"You don't deserve this racket. You're not good enough."

And it was true. He wasn't. The tennis racket became a talisman. He had it, which put him above the ordinary. It was a sign that he was loved, valued. But he couldn't play with it, which made him angry. No one ever taught him. No one ever took the time to watch him make mistakes.

Max began to feel very sorry for himself. He lay down on his bed. Unfamiliar, hot, stopped-up tears came onto his cheeks. Too late he realized that if Blair were in trouble somewhere and tried to call him, she would call the cottage, and not be able to reach him.

At three o'clock in the morning Max woke up. He debated whether he should wait until dawn. Somewhere in this big city, right now, his girlfriend—why wasn't there a better word?—and her child were in danger. The Island airport, said the note. Had they gone on a plane, last night, crossed a border? They might be far away by now. At dawn, perhaps, it would not seem so bad. At dawn he could go out on a ferry and ask for them. He could talk to Rebecca's mother. But dawn might be too late.

He wanted to call somebody now. He wanted to call Andy and ask him what to do. But what if Blair was all right? What if the letter was just some kind of code? What if she was spending the night with a lover and was planning to arrive in the morning, fresh and innocent? Then he would look a fool. Sweat poured from his back. He twisted the bedsheets. He couldn't let pride stop him, if he had a chance to rescue them.

At six o'clock in the morning he left the house and went to his office. From there he called Andy.

The phone rang six times, but Andy's voice, when it came, was crisp and ready.

"I don't know how you pull yourself to attention like that," Max started. "Presumably from a dead sleep."

"Long practice. What's going on?"

"I can't find Blair. There's a note. She *thought* she was going to meet Ruby." Later he was to reflect how a crisis brought out the star-quality in his friend. "And Sissy," he said, nearly choking on his guilt. "Sissy was with her." He didn't recall all that Andy said, or even how he soothed Max, at the same time making him feel as if the problem was dead serious, and help was at hand.

By seven o'clock, Andy was in the office too. By nine they had checked with Rebecca's mother, the airport, the borders and Philip, all of whom knew nothing. The car with Blair's purse in it was found out on the street. They alerted the police. They had a search on for Marvin, who was nowhere to be found, and a Missing Persons alert on the radio. Dick Nolan had a man on every person he'd investigated when

Ruby disappeared. They were keeping it quiet. No media, Dick Nolan said. "It'll scare them off."

"I guess this is how it's done," said Max, sitting behind his desk, tugging at his unwashed, tangled hair. He had sat there and listened, mainly, while Andy called his friends.

"It's Andy Mugwell here. Listen, my partner's wife and child . . . common-law," Max heard him say about thirty times. "I'd appreciate it." And, "What's the news on Marvin Arbat? Can you run a check? Any signs of action? . . . We are in a situation here. It's difficult. . . . In the circumstances, sounds like the best—"

"It doesn't look great," he said. "When there's a clear plan like this to draw her somewhere, chances are whatever was intended to happen has already happened." Their best hope, he said, was a ransom call.

This was how it was done, apparently. Max felt very sad, and very silly.

The announcement on the police wire was simple.

"A Toronto woman and her child are missing after being lured to the Island airport for a supposed rendezvous with fashion designer Ruby Mason, who disappeared last year in mysterious circumstances."

Max drummed his fingers on the desk. A bad omen, he thought, to have Ruby come back into his life like this.

Blair woke up to see the first rays of light sneak over the hill. Her legs were twisted uncomfortably under her. She had dozed with Simplicity lying across her stomach. The unmistakable, nose-twitching odour of piss-soaked, sweat-aged clothing came over her shoulder. Turning her head, she could just see the mounds of ragged clothing and blanket that were their companions in the grassy nest. She remembered they had been drunk in the middle of the night, which meant they probably wouldn't wake up.

She sat up, pulled the grass out of her hair and woke up Simplicity.

"Let's go get breakfast," she said. She felt in her pocket for the forty dollars. Still there.

Simplicity buried her face in Blair's lap.

"This was your idea, kid," said Blair. "You're the one who wanted to run away."

"So did you," grumbled Sissy. "You said you'd come with me."

"Right, well I did," said Blair.

They climbed up the embankment and emerged onto St. Clair Avenue. It was six-twenty. The street was empty, except for two black women standing on the streetcar island. There was a Donut Shop on Bathurst that was open twenty-four hours. Blair felt in her pocket again for the money. She liked being without her purse. Not having to carry it, protect it from being stolen. A purse was a kind of predestination. Without it, things would take shape as they ought.

Blair noticed that the attitude of their running away had changed overnight. It had hardened, become purposeful. She really did not wish to be found. Not until they were ready.

Blair examined herself in the mirror of the Donut Shop Ladies' room, and found her face the same, only slightly puffed and sleep-marked. A little cold water and a paper towel helped. She tried to comb Sissy's hair with her fingers but it was tangled and Sissy howled.

They emerged into the sugary warmth of the restaurant, with its wall-sized murals of doughnuts and croissants and muffins, its orange, moulded chairs and arborite tables. Sissy ordered a Hawaiian and a chocolate milk. Blair ordered a large black coffee and a carrot muffin. The waitress was long-faced, introverted; she took their money without looking at them.

At a table in the back corner a pimply black kid with a

hairdo like Grace Jones moved his lips and nodded. His walk-man leaked a static beat across the room. Two women in zip-pered jackets and jogging pants, their hair held back with sweatbands, chatted with happy vigour; they had power-walked their two miles before breakfast. An easy-listening radio station pumped out watery strains. The door opened and closed steadily as people came in for take-out.

"This is fun," said Simplicity. She had sprinkles on her cheeks.

"Did you like running away from home?"

"Yes I like it. It's not over."

"Well, we should phone Max, anyway." Blair earnestly hoped he was unaware and sleeping at the cottage.

"I'm not going home," said Sissy. "I'm not going to school."

The seven o'clock newscast came on. Something about Iraq, something about an earthquake, something about Gorbachev being booed. The local items were the last.

"Police are investigating the disappearance of a local woman and her six-year-old daughter. The two were lured away from their home at the promise of a meeting with Ruby Mason, the Toronto fashion designer who has been missing since last September—"

Blair heard her name, a public announcement. She slid a hand to the side of her head. Heat radiated from it. It was a strange kind of panic, a violation of context. People on the news, people in trouble, were *out there*, part of the noise; Blair went on in padded silence, in her head. In that moment, the wall between her and the world broke down. She was out there, her act an item of news.

So Max had gone into the drawer and found the note. Of course he would. She had left it there for him. Max was only doing what she had expected him to do. Still, she was furious. Now there was Ruby to think about. If people searched they might catch her now.

Blair stood, feeling her pockets for change. "We've got to go," she said. She tucked her chin down, hoping her red face didn't attract the attention of the power-walkers.

Sissy began to sing, "The answer, my friend, is blowin' in the wind, the answer . . ."

"Siss?" said Blair, her hand still cupping her face, "a little softer, please."

"When will they e—ver learn?" warbled Sissy, louder.

"Siss, would you like to go and visit Philip?"

"We're running away."

"Not so loud. People are having their nice, quiet morning coffee."

"We are running away. No visits!"

"You know *Philip*," said Blair. "It's just Philip. He won't tell on us."

"He made my Humpty Dumpty costume."

"That's right."

"Okay," said Simplicity.

Walking out of the restaurant, Blair fixed her gaze on Sissy; she moved in her daughter's wake, her posture asking onlookers to ignore her. Out on the street, they moved a few stores west and then waved down a taxi.

Bernie walked around her sister's bachelor apartment—It only took fifteen steps—snapping her fingers. She stopped at the door and checked the locks. There were three of them. The one set into the door, which came with the apartment, which they didn't trust because the superintendent had a key and who knows who else. Above that was the deadbolt her sister had put in, and below it the chain, which they got for any robber who might come by to break. The insurance didn't pay on break-ins unless there was damage.

The tiny apartment contained several pieces of enormous furniture, a sofa, a dining table and a china cabinet, loaded with photos of smiling, dark-haired people. In the corners were a rice dispenser, the microwave, the television and rolled-up bedrolls. The balcony was full of aluminum chairs, which they brought in when they had company. And Bernie's suitcases.

She had a restless, worried feeling, from her dream about Simplicity and Blair. In her dream they were sick, or in danger. She couldn't see exactly where they were walking—maybe it was at the cottage, maybe those were the paths to the dock and to the beach. Not on a street. The grass was long and dry, there were some red leaves in it, some small bushes with red leaves.

That was it—just Sissy and Blair walking in dry grass. The dream stayed with her after her shower and after she had blown her hair dry. It threatened to ruin her day. Bernie had a great deal to do today. She had to go to her bank and see how much money she had saved. She would give up all her cleaning jobs, and return all her heavy keys. She had agreed with Abe that, if she helped him with his building company, half the money they earned would be hers. That much she had learned from her time in Canada. You had to tell people what you were worth, because they weren't going to tell you themselves.

After the bank, she would meet Abe and help him to buy a pair of city pants and a jacket. Later, she would meet Conchita to shop for her wedding dress. Later still, she would pack all her clothes from Blair's house and give back the key. The key to that big house that had been her home, but not her home.

Now she dressed carefully, in a pair of black pants and a clean, ironed, white blouse and her flat tie-up shoes in fake patent, which Blair's friend Ruby—*bad* Ruby, thought Bernie—has so admired. She crimped her hair so it stood out all around her head in a black cloud. Maybe before she went to the bank she would drop around at Blair's to check the mail. That way she could make sure Blair and Sissy were all right.

Max's car was in the driveway, which was odd, because he was supposed to be at the cottage. Bernie supposed he had found some urgent work to being him down. She looked in the mailbox: nothing there. She pulled out her huge clump of keys, expertly sorted them and put the Schlag in the lock. She opened the door on Max. He was in his cottage shorts and an old, ripped T-shirt; his eyes were red and wild, and he started toward the door with an unmasked look of hope. It stopped her dead.

"Excuse me!" she said.

"Oh, it's you," he said at the same time. His face went slack. "I thought you were Blair."

"I just came to get my mail." Bernie was frightened by his face. He looked like a crazy man. She saw the large, untidy pile of envelopes at the foot of the stairs.

"Where is she? Are they at the cottage?"

"I thought maybe you knew," mumbled Max. "I wanted to phone you at your sister's but I didn't have the number."

Something was wrong. Bernie knew. Her dream had warned her.

"They came back to the city?"

"They came back yesterday."

She looked through the pile of mail. There were two air-mail envelopes from home. One from her aunt, another from a sister-in-law. She tucked them in her purse. The house felt odd. It was more than just the oddness of it being the place she used to live and the place she used to clean and the place where she spent the hours and days and nights of her waiting. It was an abandoned house.

"I have to go to the bank," said Bernie. "But I can do something for you. If you need me. For a few hours."

Max sat down heavily on the living-room couch. "I hardly slept last night. I've been at the office. I just came to get dressed."

"Where are they?" Bernie stood holding her airmail letters in her neat, not-a-housekeeper clothing, on her way out the door. She demanded to know, with the power she had earned.

Max gave a half-laugh. "That's what I don't know."

"They're lost?"

"They went off to meet Ruby."

"Oh no," said Bernie. "I had a dream."

Max was looking at her, at first, but when she began to talk about her dream he looked off; he seemed to be listening for the telephone, the doorbell.

"I had a dream that they were walking through tall, dry grass. And there was a black dog," she remembered.

"Thanks, Bernie, I know you're worried too," said Max. "I gotta get showered and get back to the office."

Bernie was offended. Max paid no heed to people like her. Only Blair knew that her dreams could find lost things. She watched him, running his fingers through his hair. He was like a prisoner in his own body. He could not reach out. She could not reach in. Was it because he was a man? Because he was a Canadian man? But Abe was a man. Abe was not so stiff and distant, though. She could reach Abe. One day she might even love him the way she once loved Dugale. Whereas Max always had his wallet full of money; he wore his shirts ironed crisp and his suits with the square shoulders and the tight tie, and big heavy shoes.

But he was helpless. She examined her letters. She examined her heart. She felt sorry for him.

"I can find things that are lost," she said. "One time at home my mother lost a ring that was very valuable for her. And I dreamed—" Her voice began to fade away. He was going out the door.

"Thanks, Bernie," he said. "If you hear anything call me, okay?"

At Philip's garage, Blair and Sissy knocked on the aluminum door. Its tin roar provoked no response. "He's probably asleep in the van with his headphones on," said Blair. She bent down and lifted the door. It rolled upward on noisy ball-bearings, to the height of her waist, where it stuck.

"Come on," she said, catching Simplicity's hand.

They crouched down and walked under.

They brought daylight under the door and across the floor; it lit the heaps of fabric and bales of wire, the pots of paint and crumpled balls of paper. The upper reaches were in darkness. Blair did not peer into them, you never knew what might be hanging up to dry.

"Remember," she whispered, "nothing in here is real. Not the monsters or the dead bodies or anything like that. Philip makes these things for his work."

The van was there, with the side door open. Philip was on the mattress on the floor, sound asleep.

"I don't think we need to wake him," she said, slightly louder now.

Simplicity hadn't moved from where she stood. Blair could see now, in the gloom, the light-switch over by the staircase. She went over and turned it on; then she rolled the garage door down. She could see the telephone on its little table under the stairs. She could see his horrible guns lined up on the wall.

"Let's go upstairs. You can watch cartoons."

She tried the earphones on Sissy's head; they were huge but they stayed on. She crept downstairs again, picked up the telephone and retreated to the farthest point the cord could reach, behind the staircase, against the wall. She dialled the cottage number.

She let it ring six times. No one was there. She called her house. It rang four times. The machine came on, its canned excuses. "Hi! It's Blair, and I'm sorry, I'm not available . . ." She was getting annoyed. What if they really were kidnapped?

How could anyone get in touch?

She called Max's office. He answered on the first ring.

"Oh, hello," she said.

"*Blair*," he said. His voice was hollow. She imagined him gesturing to some cop in the background. Trace this call.

"I won't stay on long," she said, "I just wanted to tell you I'm okay. You shouldn't have done that with the radio. You know perfectly well this isn't a kidnapping."

"Do I?"

"Of course you do."

"I didn't do it," he said. "Mensa did."

"Mensa? What's Mensa going to do?"

"Leak it," said Max, shakily. "I gather he already did."

"You told *Mensa*?"

"I've been worried about you."

"No you haven't. You're not really worried about me."

Max let out an explosive breath. "Why do you say such ridiculous things?"

"Because I believe it," she said. She looked into the gloom of Philip's workspace. A female form was swinging from a hook. Blair worried about other people. No one worried about her.

"Because it's true. What gives you the right to investigate Ruby? Or me for that matter," she said hotly.

"Blair, you asked me to. You were desperate to find her."

Blair was silent. From being wounded by Ruby's decision, she had come to sympathize with her, to participate in her escape. It seemed to Blair now that Ruby was right, to escape herself and everyone else. Why should it be only time that passes? Blair said to herself. Why should we not choose, ourselves, to move away from what it has made of us?

"Where are you? Where's Sissy?"

"Right here with me. It was her idea, actually," said Blair. "This has nothing to do with Ruby."

"Then why did you leave the note?"

Blair said nothing. He pressed on.

"You don't know who you're dealing with."

"And you do?"

"Yes I do. Blair, I found the *note*."

"You search my drawers now, do you? That's private. And it's none of your business who I meet. Ruby's my friend."

"She is? Did she show up then?"

Blair thought, I'm terrible at deception. But now's the time to learn. "*No*."

"You see, you were lured. You're being duped. I tell you, major drug interests are involved in this. *Major*," said Max, with conviction.

"Oh Max, don't be absurd. This is just between Siss and me. I won't fight. I called to tell you to call off your dogs! You don't *know*."

"I do know, and you're lucky to have got away from these people. I can't tell you how I know. Just take my word for it."

"What people? There are no *people*, it's only me."

The thought that Max had been spying on her made Blair even angrier. The arrogance of men! If anything, he'd got her in danger. He called the cops. He called Mensa, the mouth. Thinking there was some giant conspiracy. Anything seemed more believable to him than two women friends wanting to see each other.

"I won't take your word. Why should I?"

"Because I love you?"

"Love is no excuse. That's what men always use to get the better of women. You're the lawyer. You ought to know that."

"You're so *bitter*," sighed Max. "I wish I knew why."

Blair looked over at the van with the open door. It jiggled. Then it was still again. She held herself defiantly silent, as if she were making sense, as if she had made an unmootable point. *Why is the worst question*, she thought, but didn't tell him.

"Yes, I am a lawyer, and I might as well tell you, your

friend Ruby was hanging out with some pretty dangerous people."

"You know what happened to Ruby. You've read the diaries. She went off on her own."

"We don't know what happened after that," said Max ominously. "This is our biggest fight. Why do we have to have it on the phone? I'll come and we can have it in person if you tell me where you are."

"Not until you call off this *woman*hunt you started." Blair knew a sure way to goad Max was to use gender-adjusted words. "How could you do it to me? Put it on the radio."

"I didn't put it on the radio. *I* don't decide what's news." He felt guilty about Mensa. Maybe it was a mistake.

"If it wasn't for you, no one would have known! You could have just waited. I'd have called."

"You didn't call. You ran away. Everything else followed. What happens turns into news. That's the natural process. Anyway, why shouldn't it? People have a right to know." This was Max's way, to turn their differences into an intellectual debate. Blair fell for it.

"What happens does not turn into news, not without help. News is just somebody's agenda, that's all. You want to find me, you get Mensa going and make it a news story. Suddenly I'm a runaway. I'm just leading my *life*," protested Blair.

"Oh come on, Blair, you're just blaming the messenger. You *chose* to run off. You can't stop it from becoming known."

The van shuddered again. Philip was about to arise.

"Apart from anything else, if I really *was* in danger it would have made it worse. You make a big deal about your clients' confidences. What about personal confidentiality? If you really cared about me you wouldn't have done this. You just wanted to make a case out of it. Maybe you just wanted to get your picture in the newspaper. Like Andy," she added. "Your picture, holding hands with the defendant?"

Max swallowed his retort. Blair knew she'd got him. He had to give in. Like Ruby, she was in control. If she hung up, she was gone again. He gave in.

"I don't see what else I could do. You were gone. *Are* gone."

"Wait. Trust me."

"That's another conversation," Max said. "Trust. Don't you think I know about you and your letters?"

"Letters?" Blair bit her lip. It was her turn to swallow. How could he know about the letters?

"Where the hell are you?" he said. "Just tell me where the hell you are."

"I'm, I'm—I don't know, Max," she said tearfully. "Are they really searching? The airport and everything?" Did Ruby get away all right, is what she meant. "Did they find out anything about Ruby?"

"I doubt it. They never find out anything," he said. "Not the smartest cops in the world."

"Good."

They were united, briefly, in their scorn of cops.

"But Andy's called in all his pals. 'My partner's wife,' and all that."

"Oh, so I can't even run away as myself? I've got to be somebody's *wife*?"

The van jiggled again, definitely this time, and Philip's legs, from the knee down, came out and hung over the edge.

"Shit!" she whispered into the phone. "I can't talk."

"Where are you? Tell me."

"I'm all right."

Philip's torso and head appeared in the open van door. He looked dazed and not at all pleased. Blair raised her hand in his direction. She mouthed, "Hi!"

"So can we meet?"

"Tell them to stop looking for me."

Max said nothing.

Philip sat there, his legs dangling, his hands folded in his lap, listening, like a man on a window-ledge, waiting to jump.

"I don't know what good it is being involved with you," said Blair, in her final parry. "You're supposed to be this big powerful lawyer. If you're so smart you'd have found Ruby ages ago. When I want help, you don't give it. Now I want you to lay off and I can't get you off the case! If anyone is, *you're* putting me in danger."

Philip raised his shoulders and his hands in a shrug. He mouthed words of simulated anger as riposte.

"Sorry, Philip," she mouthed at him.

"Look Blair, let's at least get together and talk. Okay? Just talk?"

"I'll phone you later," she said, and hung up.

"So I'm to be flattered, it that it?" A shaky Philip had been sent out, and now returned with café au lait and grape juice. "That you choose me?"

"I had nowhere else."

"No house on MacPherson?"

"I can't go there."

Philip shrugged. He did not wish to delve into this too far. It was his goal in life to maintain an orientation toward the unreal. He hated having his space invaded. Somebody else's kid watching cartoons on his TV. Somebody else's love affair coming apart on his telephone. Especially Blair's.

"Of course there's a certain morbid interest," he admitted, thinking aloud. "For a bachelor like me."

"Pretty standard stuff, I expect," said Blair airily. "I dunno."

"I guess it was a good idea for me not to get married, eh Blair?" Philip looked at her across the telephone table, his magnified, pale-blue eyes both guileful and frightened. "You know, I do wonder how Max survives the turmoil. Maybe going back to his desk full of papers, his phone calls from the petulant rich, will help him forget it all."

There was an echo in his words; it reminded Blair of something. His defensive passion, his bitterness. Of course. The letters. Her secret lover.

"For five cents I'd phone the cops and turn you in," said Philip. He wanted his privacy, the square emptiness of this place, his dummies and his masks with their frozen, exaggerated features. Real people walking around, with their real life dramas, scared him. Blair showing up like this, at last.

"We're not fugitives. We're just running away from home. Didn't you ever run away from home?" said Blair gently. She watched his face. Philip was her secret lover. She felt only tenderness.

"Always," said Philip. "That's why I live like this. Not so I can take in strays." He let that sink in for a moment. Blair understood: they had spoken of the letters, and now it was over.

"What about this Max?" he said. "Can't we just call him and tell him where you are?" He brought out some plaster of Paris and began to mix it.

"Boys on the same side, is that it? I thought you hated him."

Philip had been wakened up too early. This thing unrolling in his shop was like a video he'd picked up in the wrong section. Drama instead of horror. He wanted to take it back to the store. He always avoided people in emotional extremes, yelling and clutching each other. Give him good clean blood and guts and monsters from the deep any day.

"I'm making masks," said Philip. "I've got work to do."

"I'll help. We'll help," said Blair, as Sissy came down the stairs. "It's good to be here. I just want to be here with you."

"I guess you can fool around with some of the plaster," he said grudgingly.

They all sat at the counter and began massaging the cool, chalky substance. Sissy sang. Blair had taught her all their old songs. Now she was doing "The Night They Drove Ol' Dixie Down." Philip's blue eyes watered, as if emotion was welling up. But his face was hidden behind the beard, the glasses, the extra weight in the cheeks. He made a mask of fear from a photo of a pizza store man who was held up. He made a mask of joy from the photo of the woman who won the lottery. he put the two of them out to dry. You could hardly tell them apart.

"Blair—" he said, "—I've gotta go out and try out some prosthetic legs." He felt exhausted. He felt as if he'd already fallen in love, been disillusioned, and given it all up, lived a passionate year and survived to tell the tale, all in one morning.

Max sat at his desk waiting for the telephone to ring. He had told Maureen not to answer it; if Blair called again and got his secretary, she'd probably hang up. The only thing was that the phone kept ringing and it was other people. But Max had a simple solution, He hung up on them. He had hung up on thirteen different voices so far. He was keeping a tally. Nine of them were male, and four were female. He thought he recognized some of his important clients among them.

He remembered, sitting at this desk and hanging up on people, that day Blair came in with the dead bird and made him hang up on Mr. McNaughton. He laughed out loud. It was a lot easier, now, to hang up on people. He wished Blair could see him. He would like her to know that he'd learned to do this; he hoped she came back some day so that he could tell her.

Maureen was locked out of his office, in the hall. That was another trick Blair would appreciate. "Those people *run* you. Your secretary, your clients," she said to him. "You don't own your own life."

Be odd on your own time. But it was all his time. He had

begun to understand. Time was like water, it had no divisions, it flowed on, taking his life with him, whether it was billable hours or not. Firm time and his time, it was all the same. He had to be odd all the time, if he wanted to be any of the time. And he could be. He only had to be desperate enough. It was important to be desperate. From time to time.

The phone rang.

"Hello?" he said.

A dubious voice, uncertain. "Is this Ostriker, Mugwell?"

"Who's that?"

"Is this the law firm Ostriker, Mugwell?"

"Who do you want?"

"I'm calling from Host, Anthony, Yellin? For Mr. Ostriker? It's Mr. Anthony who would like to speak to him?"

"Not now! Get off the line!" Max dropped the receiver.

He walked over to look out his window. The SkyDome was there, like a white half-grapefruit, face down. But the true dome of Toronto was the sky, the white-cut horizon along the lake like a cut into flesh, under the smog cloud. To the west of him were the red-brick warehouses, Ruby's territory, and to the south and east a bad mix of spit and trestle. Directly below, a few wedding-cake grey edifices and more glass and steel.

There was a city down there, of which he was the central point. Streets reached out in points to a wide, flat belt of suburbs, and beyond that to farmers' lands. A city down there, thought Max, and I fly over it, without being in it. I seem to be young, I seem to be lofty, I seem to be looking down and seeing the pattern, powerful. But it's only because I'm twenty-nine storeys up. The truth is I'm getting old, and heavy, and I may never get what I want.

The streets down there are full of kind people. People I went to school with. People who know me. Even the strangers, as they say, are only people I haven't met yet. I could walk up the driveway to any house in any suburb, knock and ask for a glass of water. Can I come in? And they would open a door to me.

Despite everything I read and hear, I still believe this to be true. Why do I believe it? Is it because I'm Canadian—a lately joined member of this small nation with notions of gentleness and delusions of grandeur? Is it because (as Blair thinks) I'm spoiled and naive, a born elitist? Is it because I have never tried, so I can't prove myself wrong?

Is it because I'm right?

This morning, watching Andy in action, calling his friends, Max understood something more about How Things Work. Andy called his cop friends, his lawyer friends. "Well, hello Joe, how are you? Wasn't that a stunning piece of Dominion Securities? Thor will be roasted over there today, roasted!" A wide-open, good-hearted laugh. Joe and Andy had gone to school together. "Listen Joe, you know I never do this, but I've got a tidbit for you. You remember Ruby Mason? Hear me out—"

And Joe must have said something like, didn't that woman have drug connections, wasn't it her boyfriend who did her in, was it only a domestic thing? Because Andy sparked a little, and in his careful, pointed way said, "Hey, a woman's disappearance, unsolved? If her friends did her in, that doesn't make it any less of a murder. I'm a *little* surprised, Joe, that you haven't—"

And on they went, until Joe said he'd have somebody look into it, and that as to Andy's partner's wife or girlfriend or whatever being involved, they'd keep it quiet. Max watched the expression of satisfaction on Andy's face as his mouth moved firmly around the words "That's right, and that's how it ought to be done," and "Thanks, Joe, I knew you'd want to do this right," and "Will you be at the golf tournament this year?" and "See you there."

Ruby's story showed up Toronto for what it was. You never find a nice girl in a trunk. Most people believed it. Errant behaviour deserved punishment. Punishment was titillating. Guilt followed. Andy knew the attitudes and played on them. He managed to use the city's littleness, its meanness, its clubbiness, against its opposite impulses. He found the pulse of a would-be raciness and dash. He used Toronto against itself. He, Max, could never do that.

His was the ascent—from hellbent outsider to diffident inheritor of privilege in one generation. Here he was, up in his tower: the new-world syndrome. It led to a peculiar myopia. What he saw and how he was seen. Blair considered Max Establishment, but he could remember having his face rubbed in snow for being a Yid. Money had stopped it, he supposed. Stopped it from being said out loud, at least. Max felt sorry for himself. But money had robbed him of many pleasures. Once he wanted to be a photographer. His Dad gave him an eight-hundred-dollar camera. Max was in heaven until he discovered his pictures were shit. What a loser he must be, if he couldn't make the best camera you could buy work. The Pentax went to live in some bottom drawer, and Max, to cheer himself up, bought a Yamaha guitar. Tried to be a musician. Thus, barely used goods piled up in the basement. Eventually, he had to escape from under the pile.

Maybe that was why he lived so high up. High up on a pile of consumer goods, which were rapidly decomposing under him. Whereas Blair lived low down and was self-sufficient. Her roots went sideways, not down—sideways to friends and neighbours, to her nanny, for Christ's sake. He wanted to throw out the things of his past and save people. She wanted to save her past and—so it seemed—throw out him.

Well, Max thought, perhaps I have been spoilt from childhood by prosperity. If so, my madness is the madness of our time. Blair's madness was something else: nostalgia for a place and time that could not be retrieved.

Bernie got off the train at Bathurst and walked along St. Clair toward Avenue Road. On the train, her dream had come back to her—Blair and Sissy walking through the long, dry grass. The black dog. She squinted, to help see the picture better. She knew the place, or at least she could find it.

The sidewalk passed alongside the playground on top of the reservoir. She used to bring Sissy here, before she went to school. Sissy would cry and say she couldn't climb. The only thing she liked was the baby swing. Bernie taught her to climb, how to put one foot after the other. Sissy had needed help. She was not going to be there to help Sissy any more. But Sissy had Blair. Only sometimes Blair needed help, too.

Bernie cut across that playground and down the hill to where the path split off to Poplar Plains. The dream seemed very close now; she was walking into its landscape. She walked over the edge of the big bald hill that Blair said looked like somebody's tomb. She followed one of the little footworn paths downward to the valley, under the concrete pillars that held up the bridge. Two men stood around the pillars, smoking. One of them had a black dog on a leash. But it was not the black dog of her dream. This one was small and curly-haired.

Bernie was in a place she would never go alone, or with Sissy, but her courage carried her. The path wound under the bridge, growing narrower, the grass on either side of it taller. It was exactly the same brown, dry colour as in her dream. There were some bushes with fuzzy red torches standing up from their leaves. They were the same bushes she'd seen at the cottage. Abe told her you could make tea out of them, whether from the leaves or the flame part she did not know. She thought how she would find out all the plants you could grow and eat at their cottage. She thought how much lighter her purse would be when she gave back all the keys she carried.

The path turned and rose a little. It got even more narrow.

It was just a trail; it would not go on much longer. She saw, at the end of the path, a nest, a flattened area in the grass. Some broken concrete steps led back up to the street. Somebody lived here. Somebody slept here. Bernie went up to look at the place where the grass lay down. There were some old newspapers and some dirty, torn clothes, sheets of plastic. The people who lived here were coming back. She looked a little way away.

Here the grass had been flattened too, but not so much, and for not so long a time. A blanket lay on top. Without surprise, Bernie saw that it was Blair's blanket, the one she kept in her car. Hidden under it were sweatshirts and sweatpants, theirs. In the grass something glittered. Bernie reached down for it. It was Sissy's pink plastic bracelet, woven the way Bernie taught her.

Bernie stood beside the flattened grass. The silken rush of cars going by on St. Clair was not much louder than the nearby rattle of small insects in the grass. She felt easy, light. She was certain that Sissy and Blair were not hurt. She sat down to wait. The insects droned around her. A grasshopper sat still on a leaf. She looked closer; it had a damaged leg. She sat. The grasshopper sat. No one came to the camp. Bernie looked at her watch. It was two o'clock in the afternoon. The two men who had been smoking under the bridge slowly approached on the narrow trail, following the black dog.

Blair sat on a bench in Turtle Park with a take-out capuccino in her hand, watching Sissy climb the green metal turtle. She wondered if people were looking for them, or if Max had called the search off.

To Blair, Toronto had always been full of unwatched spaces—ravines, stretches of sidewalk between apartment blocks, alleys, parks. That was why she liked it. She came here to be eccentric, she supposed, if it was eccentric to raise her kid alone, to be free of the curious neighbours in Medicine Hat. For that, and to be famous, to make a name, to follow her vocation, to act, sing, talk or otherwise call attention to herself. In short, to disappear from people close up, and to be seen by people far away.

It was the same reason they'd all come here—Philip and Ruby and Oswald. Each in their way had found a way to be seen, and not seen. Blair wondered now if she really wanted all that. One conundrum: in a small place it's easy to believe you're important, but you can't find a platform to get up on. In a large place, the platform is there, but, with all those people, all those millions of people, it's hard to remember what it was you wanted to say.

Today, Toronto felt closed and small. There was a search on for a woman and child. Their descriptions had gone on a police wire, and on the radio. At this very minute, people could be looking out the window of that house on Brunswick and thinking they ought to call the police.

One mother darted off the bench and let out a shriek. Her child stood at the top of the slide, about to go down backwards. "Don't!" she said, standing at the foot of the slide. "Turn around. Sit down."

"I can't!"

"Then climb back down the stairs. Here, like this, put your hands back on the rails. Step. Step."

The mother climbed up the ladder, scolding with every step. No one commented when, roughly, she grabbed him around the waist and carried him down, screaming. No one noticed Blair, either. Why should they? These are the people whose news broadcast is interrupted five times by demands for more juice, to get the prize out of the bottom of the cereal box. News was consumed by others, not by mothers of young children. Regimes could rise and fall, financial empires crash, and these women and their children would continue in the necessary round of sandbox and lunch, nap-time and walks.

Blair observed herself to be swinging on a long pendulum. One minute she felt exposed, *obvious*, an object of speculation. The next she swung back, on a wide arc: invisible. Other mothers' gazes were reserved for the children; their demeanour suggested that they were of a lesser order of reality than their charges. "I'm only here because the child wants to play, I don't belong in this picture." Some unseen force had dulled their passions; for the time, they were only watchers of children.

"Let the other little girl go down the slide, don't block it!"

"The shovel belongs to this boy. What's his name? Matthew. There, look, Matthew wants to share it with you!"

Exposed/invisible: significant/nonentity. Which was it? If she were a man, sitting here, watching the children, she would be taking time out from a pressing agenda. But as she was a woman, she was only doing the expected. There was an "until" look about the mothers. "Until she's in school . . ." "Until he's out of diapers . . ." Blair had foreseen this, dreaded this. She had fought it off, in advance. She had hired babysitters; she had continued to work. But people she hired were free to go. And the jobs, though necessary, were no longer what she cared about. She only really cared about Simplicity. Even the will to resist has been arrested, thought Blair. I have accepted the conditions.

Perhaps she had done it all wrong. There were women who could make it work, who had their own trajectory, as well as their children's, simultaneously in mind. Those women she read about in magazines, who manage a fast-track career in government and three small children at the same time? Whose husbands get up and do breakfast while they go down to the club and work out? Who go back to their desk after the children's stories have been read and teeth brushed at nine o'clock? Perhaps the problem was Blair's, some over-indulgence in the maternal passions.

Being Sissy's mother was as debilitating as having a love affair.

She'd avoided love affairs for the same reason. She didn't want to need someone else, to serve someone else, to want someone else. She could manage one—a lover or a child. Not both. She thought the child was safer. But Siss came on her unawares. She took her from within. "Don't let the little bastard get the better of you"—that was what the childbirth instructor said, when the legs stretched and kicked her ribs from the inside, knocking her breath out of her lungs. But she had. Blair had not been on guard against her, that pale, narrow being who now clung to the gate and examined the ground because a bigger kid had pushed her off the slide.

Perhaps it was not Ruby who disappeared, but Blair. Ruby vanished, but in fact went on, to her reformed destiny. And Blair, who had begun to disappear from the inside six years ago, remained visible, although vacant. Like in *Invasion of the Body Snatchers*. Who was she now? As far as she could tell, she was a vagrant, sitting on a park bench, ruled by a despot of six.

"How's your coffee, Mum?"

Blair remembered to take a sip. "Cold."

"You forgot to drink it."

"That's true, I did." Blair put her arm around Siss. The day was sunny, but she felt cold. It was something to do with not being able to go home.

"Why did you have that sad look on your face?"

"Did I have a sad look?"

Simplicity jumped off the bench. "I think you're tired. I think you need a nap."

Blair laughed. "Well, we can't go back to Philip's."

"We could go to our place in the park."

"We could," said Blair. Maybe if we go there and lie down that will be enough, she thought. Maybe that will count as sleeping out. Then I can get her to go home. She was thinking of home herself now.

"Are you tired of running away?" she said to Sissy.

"A little."

"I was going to buy you new shoes for school."

"No!" cried Simplicity. She made two fists and worked them up and down in front of her chest. "I'm not going to school!"

"Grade two!" exclaimed Blair, bargaining desperately. "You can read more books."

"I hate school!"

Blair went carefully now. It was like stalking an animal. "Why don't you like school?"

"I don't like school because school doesn't like me."

"Aha!" said Blair. "School isn't a person. School can't like you or not like you. School is a place."

"If it was," said Simplicity, "I could change to another one. Just like now. We could move to another park."

Blair stood up with her cup in her hand. She took Simplicity by the other hand. "I think I understand something now," she said. "Let's put this in the garbage and then we'll go to our place for a nap."

She thinks she has no power. She knows she can run away from home but not from school. She is trying to show me that, thought Blair, as she was standing on the platform at the Spadina subway to go north to St. Clair. She's trying to bargain with no power. That's hard to do. I know all about that.

They took the long walk to their spot, across the top of the Churchill Reservoir, down the toboggan hill (running, rolling) and then, looking behind, so as not to be seen, holding hands and walking down the path. Two men and a black dog were standing under the overpass, smoking.

"What if I teach you at home for a while? Teach you how to read and do arithmetic?"

"I can stay with you and be a free worker?"

"Freelance worker, you mean? Sure."

"Can I have a desk?"

"We should be able to manage that."

They walked around the corner. In the long grass, a large, black dog loped free. "Shhh!" said Blair. But there was no noise. Still, she could sense; people had been here. The grass looked walked on. Then she saw him. A man with black, curly hair sitting on the flattened grass, where the tramps slept.

She took Sissy by the hand.

"He found us." Sissy dropped Blair's hand. Max stood up. Sissy began to run. She caught his hand and jumped up. "We were running away from home," she said happily.

He lifted her into his arms.

Max put Sissy down. Blair wanted to run to him herself, but she couldn't lift her feet, suddenly.

"How did you find this place?"

"Bernie dreamed it," said Max. "She came here and found this."

He held out the pink bracelet.

Blair remembered the men under the bridge. Of course. "Those are police," she said.

"I told them it was all a misunderstanding. I told them it had nothing to do with Ruby." He smiled. He knew. She had not told him, but he knew. Blair smiled at him then.

"I thought maybe you were going with her," he said.

"It's too late. She's gone. Anyway," she added with difficulty, "I didn't really want to." The effort of putting any more into words was too great, the distance too great. She reached out to him.

Blair was at Andy's cottage with Max, recuperating. They said she'd had a nervous collapse. She got her own diary and began to write in it. And she thought, when it's far enough in the past so they can't trace me, I'll send it to Ruby.

To Ruby, who went beyond the limits of freedom. She can do anything, except die, thought Blair. Because I'll know any account of her death to be a hoax.

———————

I can't let the story down, into defeat in this way. To accept the intractability of words, and language, the intractability of people. Intractible. Tractible. Tract. (Where is Bernie? We could look it up in the dictionary together.) Tract: a polemical statement. A piece of land.

It's over now. In my mind I can see Ruby's shack. In the foothills somewhere, she's by herself, or with some new acolytes making her own fabric, that's what she wanted. One day I'll go and find her. It must be Oswald's shack. He said he had one. Probably we could have found her if we looked.

But for now, we'll stay here. Max will busy himself outside, moving stones around. There are so many stones, cast here and there. Stones adamant in their weight, their jaggedness, their <u>non-meaning</u>. He wishes to rearrange these stones into some order that can give pleasure, give meaning to him, to express his views of how stones should be. Or perhaps he does it simply to rearrange. He is ingenious, lifting these huge stones alone. He balances them against his thigh, or chest. There are more ways than one, says Max.

And I am inside, moving words around. Each one as heavy as the largest stone, as obdurate, as full of itself, its own mystery. Why should it be willing to express my ideas, formed elsewhere, in some fluid, curved place, away from these jagged points and cruel angles? No reason. But I persist in seeking to make words into some shape that pleases, some shape that explains, that speaks to memory.

That'll be me, inside. And Max, out there.

It was one year to the day since Ruby had gone away. Hugh Mensa was suffering. He was in agony. He sat with his head drooping, his long, freckled hands wrapped over his bald pate. His abdomen was racked with pain. His heart was palpitating. He was looking at the most amazing story of his life, and knowing that he was going to pass on it.

In front of him were Ruby's diaries, copies of the pages she had sent to Blair. Blair had duly given them to Max, and Max, before he handed them to Dick Nolan as he was meant to do, had xeroxed them for Mensa. Exactly why Max had decided to do this Mensa did not fully understand. Perhaps he, too, simply needed an audience. Or perhaps he did believe that Mensa could help, that he, a journalist, could act altruistically. Max was naive.

And yet, here he was, Hugh Mensa, the nose, deciding not to publish them. He felt sick. Something he never believed would happen had happened. His better instincts, his human instincts, were ruling him. It came down to the fact that Ruby was his friend. It came down to the fact that the diaries were private. It came down to artistic freedom, if you like. Hers, not his. If this was the statement she had to make, then he would not stand in the way of her making it. If the diaries were made public they'd track her down for sure.

Mensa, too, was writing. He'd put aside his plans for a book, however. His problem was still plot. He thought now that as it was about life, he needed a plot more than ever. And he was still waiting. He wrote a small piece for the newspaper, on the anniversary.

Metropolis, *September 6 1990*

MOTHER AWAITS WORD

An icy hand grips the heart late at night when a loved one fails to arrive.

Martha Mason has had a year of those nights. And there is no let-up in sight.

One year after her daughter Ruby, the well-known Toronto fashion designer, went missing, Martha sits up with a start at 11:30, Toronto time, every night, in her home in Medicine Hat, Alberta. 11:30 is the hour she last spoke to Ruby.

"I can hear her voice, it's like she's talking in my ear. I look at her pictures, the old ones when she was a little girl. I hold some of her dresses. And I pray. Prayer brings her closer."

Ruby was last seen one year ago today by a cabbie who dropped her off at the Royal York Hotel. She had been going to a wake for a friend, but changed her mind at the last minute.

Her mother, a large, powerful woman, lets the tears flow. Her voice soars, showing her many years' experience with a church choir.

"She was my baby. My darling. She was so beautiful. She was headed for success and she was taking everyone with her. But she got in wrong with somebody. Somebody wanted her out of the way."

Martha Mason holds firm to her conviction that her daughter was kidnapped, and possibly murdered. However, no trace of foul play has been discovered.

In Toronto, Ruby's house sits untouched, her brother Arthur paying the mortgage. He believes she'll come back one day. Her design business is managed by associates, and carries on in her name.

Ruby had no history of depression, or memory-loss. She took none of her clothes, only what she wore, and never used the bank account or credit cards she carried.

About fifty friends combed the downtown area for days after her disappearance. Police used tracking dogs, helicopters and psychics to no avail.

Hopes were raised two weeks ago when a friend received a note from Ruby, but it was a hoax. A bizarre false alarm about her reappearance led to a tramp's hideout in a Toronto ravine as friends sought the trail, which had long been cold.

Friends tell Martha she'd better give Ruby up for dead. But she can't do that.

"No Mason would give up until they put their loved one in the ground," she says. Martha prays that a clue will come to light.

Ruby Mason is five feet, six inches, weighs 130 pounds, and has curly brown or red hair, and brown eyes.

Anyone having any information can contact the police or Hugh Mensa, at this newspaper.